WILD NIGHTS
of
ARKANSAS STRIPPERS

BASED ON A TRUE STORY

STEFAN DIAMANTE

Wild Nights of Arkansas Strippers

Based on a True Story

Written, Photographed, Designed, and Published by Stefan Diamante

First Edition, 2020

Paperback ISBN: 978-1-7340268-3-2

stefandiamante.com

Dedicated to the amazing female strippers who made Hardbodies Entertainment of Arkansas a legitimate entertainment agency along with me. While I always knew they gave me more credit than I afforded myself, this became fully apparent upon my retirement from all aspects of the industry during the writing of this book. I'll never forget our wild nights.

Special thanks to Tori for sharing her firsthand insight into girls who like girls

Contents

I need you to bend over and assume the position.

June

"Oh my God," Sarah sighs, "You smell delicious."

The birthday girl's face buried in Magnum's neck while he grinds and thrusts on her lap. His chest tight against her tits. Cock dangerously close to her pussy. Her arms wrapped around him as they simulate fucking before a live audience. Rocking it poolside. Cheers fill the warm, early June night air along with "Salt Shaker" by Ying Yang Twins. She's in a leopard print bathing suit. A multicolored beach towel around her waist like a makeshift skirt. Perfectly anticipating summer's arrival days from now. The bright patio light casting long shadows across them. Twenty people gathered around. Watching in awe. Including Candi, his newest talent acquisition and stripping partner in crime tonight, as he shows everyone how it's fucking done.

Candi came aboard two weeks prior and he was instantly taken with her. Beautiful and charming. Selling him on her dependability and passion for entertaining audiences. Sweet and innocent yet sexually adventurous with a taste for both men and women. An ideal female stripper for his young exotic entertainment agency. Receiving its share of bachelor party bookings but just as many for events with coed audiences. As well as for female audiences wanting a girl. Either solo or in tandem with a male stripper. Candi is tailor-made for those latter parties. The client for tonight's party, a woman named Pamela, booking her alongside him with the male guests in mind.

There's been sexual tension between Magnum and Candi from the start. A mutual attraction sparked during their initial phone conversation. Growing steadily after meeting in person. As he took glamour shots of her for prospective clients. Even as he helped her dress before the shoot. His hand brushing against her silky thighs while attaching garter belt straps to sheer black stockings. Inherently naughty as he may be, he'd sworn to himself upon launching his agency that he'd never fool around with the girls. Worried about coming across like some casting couch goon. Refusing to create unnecessary drama when there would inevitably be more than enough already.

Like any good entrepreneur, he started his business for the sole objective of making money. Not for fucking female strippers and applicants. Nor to avoid working. On the contrary, this venture is a way to ensure his talents and self-discipline are better rewarded compared to every "real" job he's had. Driving from Little Rock to Sherwood tonight was a surreal experience for him. Something he did every day until a few months ago after quitting his job and going into business. And here he was. Back in the town where it sort of all began. This time navigating the streets of Sherwood at night. And for an entirely different objective. Having a beautiful woman by his side truly confirmed to him that his life has already changed forever in ways he hasn't had time to consider. Until tonight.

Candi is experiencing a similar moment of clarity. This night marks her private party debut. Not just for Magnum's agency. This is her first private party performance ever. All her prior experience acquired working in upscale gentlemen's clubs on the East Coast. Upon moving back to Arkansas and discovering the drug-infested mess that is every strip club in the state, she went looking for something different. And here she is. Her anticipation sky-high for the audience, Magnum, and herself. Excited and nervous all at once for this new chapter in her stripping career. And feeling more comfortable by the minute in his company.

These two sexy cops greeted with raucous shock and enthusiasm upon entering this suburban backyard party. Candi watching and learning as Magnum declared the event over. Demanding to speak with Sarah. After failing to satisfactorily explain herself, he made her stand, bend over, and assume the position. Frisking her. Running his hands up between her legs before revealing to everyone she's been in this position before while humping her butt. Laughter ensued as he made her take a seat, placed her in handcuffs, and informed her that she's in violation of penal code 6969. Candi started the music on his cue. "Bad Boys" by Inner Circle blasted from his audio system. At which point he straddled his shy yet excited birthday girl.

Magnum continues dancing on Sarah, who gleefully accepts this hot stranger all over her. He tears off his shirt. Placing her hands on his rock-hard pecs before guiding them down his abs. When the belt comes off, he has her stand and assume the position once more for a birthday spanking. Having her grab the waistband of his tear-away pants. Stepping backward out of them to everyone's delight. Down to a black g-string and cowboy boots. Falling forward and catching the edge of her chair. Placing his face between her thighs. Moving up her legs. Along her torso. Rubbing his face in her ample breasts before they're face to face.

He turns around and straddles her. Falling forward once again. Landing on his hands. Simultaneously kicking his legs backward.

Squeezing her thighs. Positioned crotch to crotch. She spanks his bare ass after much audience encouragement. He turns to face her again. Running his fingers through her hair. Stroking her cheek while lowering himself face to face with her. His chest again pressed against her tits. Losing himself in her eyes. She can't stop giggling with her eyes lost in his too. He places her hands on his butt. She holds on as they bump and grind against each other. His cock grows bigger and harder. Feeling the warmth coming from her pussy. She's embarrassed as hell but still losing herself in the moment. Totally going for it.

"Don't worry. She's single," Pamela announces, "You can do anything you want to her."

"Stop it!" Sarah giggles with embarrassment while everyone else laughingly concurs.

Magnum gestures Candi to retrieve the can of Reddi-wip from his stripping bag. She removes the plastic cap and tosses it to him. He shakes it before applying a line of whipped cream to Sarah's cleavage. Putting his head down. Running his tongue between her breasts. Licking it all up. Her heart racing as more cheers fill the air around them. He takes two dollars of her tip money. Placing one bill between her tits. The other between her thighs. Against her pussy. Dropping to his knees. Placing his face in her lap. Grabbing the first dollar with his teeth. Tossing it aside and moving up. Removing the second one from her girls the same way to more cheers.

"Okay, rookie," he motions Candi to join him for her moment of truth while dollar bills are shoved in his g-string, "It's your turn."

Magnum straddles one of Sarah's legs. Candi positions herself over the other. "Get Low" by Lil Jon plays as Candi removes her sexy female cop costume. Down to a black bikini top, g-string, and platforms. She turns around, bends over, and wiggles her butt at the birthday girl, who gives in after a few seconds and spanks it. Sliding dollar bills in her g-string. He reaches over and unties Candi's bikini top. She lets it fall off. Standing and shaking her liberated titties to her approving audience. He sprays more Reddi-wip on Sarah's chest.

"It's your turn," Magnum instructs Candi.

"Oh Lord," Sarah squeaks nervously yet curiously.

Candi turns and drops low. Licking whipped cream from the birthday girl's cleavage as they giggle together. Candi's stripper self-confidence full throttle. Taking the Reddi-wip from him and applying some to his nipples.

"We'll do it together," she orders the birthday girl.

The audience wracked with giddiness as Candi and Sarah each take a nipple. Giggling while licking and sucking them free of whipped cream. Their mouths and tongues are magic. Making him tremble slightly. Candi notices and smiles sassily at him. Never one to hesitate when it comes to upping the ante, he snatches his Reddi-wip from Candi and decorates her nipples. Inviting Sarah to join him in sharing a naughty snack. Her self-confidence also now in full effect. Instantly latching onto Candi's left breast as he takes the right. Candi grabs their heads. Smothering them with her titties while they swirl their tongues over her nipples. The audience now truly beside themselves in shock and awe at witnessing this naughty spectacle.

"What happens at my birthday party stays at my birthday party," Sarah lectures her friends.

They laugh in agreement as Magnum and Candi begin devoting attention to them. He takes his turn with every woman. She does the same with each man. And a few of the more curious girls. Their g-strings filled with cash over and over. Passing the Reddi-wip back and forth until nearly gone. He can't believe how amazing a team they make. Owning their audience. Dominating them. Keeping them overstimulated while raking in a growing pile of hard-earned money.

"So, this is the first time you two have worked together?" Sarah asks her strippers and they nod in agreement, "Does that mean you've never given each other a lap dance?"

"Nope," Magnum answers while Candi shakes her head.

"You totally should right now," Sarah excitedly handles the last of her tip money.

It's a valid point. He's already exchanged lap dances with the other girls he represents as a matter of professional familiarity if you will. Representing nothing beyond demonstrating a shared skill for one another. At most satisfying each side's curiosity as to how the other does it.

So, it's no big deal when Magnum has Candi take the hot seat to "Hot in Herre" by Nelly. He's in no mood for a buildup. Straddling his new stripping partner. Sliding his torso down hers. She grabs his ass. Spreading her legs. His cock once again growing bigger and harder. Thrusting it against her pussy. Grinding against it. Feeling her become hotter and wetter. Dropping to his knees. Placing her feet on his shoulders and rising. Holding her legs up against her. Humping her pussy with his cock. Staring aggressively into her eyes. Oh God, he wants to fuck her. But he promised himself he wouldn't. Lowering her legs as he drops again to his knees.

He adds more Reddi-wip to her nipples. Licking and sucking them long after the whipped cream is gone. She holds his head. Shaking her tits on his face as he moves between them. Back and forth. They can't hear the audiences howling and shrieking in approval, but they feel it. And he feels Sarah shoving dollar bills in his g-string. He pulls back. Spraying Reddi-wip on Candi's inner thighs and around her pussy. Licking each one from the knee up, then circling her pussy. Making her tremble. Unable to stop himself. Pulling her g-string aside. Touching her clit with his tongue. She immediately grabs his head with both hands. Forcing his tongue inside her. Moaning as he licks her soaking wet pussy back and forth. Her girl juices so sweet and delicious. He feels more cash going into his g-string.

The instant he removes his face from Candi's pussy she stands and guides him to take her place. Immediately sitting on his lap. Gyrating her hips. Rubbing her throbbing pussy against his raging cock. Rising slightly to smother his face with her titties. Shaking them back and forth. Letting her nipples slide across his tongue. He spanks and squeezes her bare ass. She drops to her knees. Removing his now-massive cock from its g-string prison. Placing it between her tits. Stroking every inch as they titty-fuck. People lining up to shove dollars in her g-string. He can see on their faces how much they enjoy this spectacle. He rationalizes his breaking of an arbitrary rule to giving his audience what it wants. This is simply he and Candi being consummate professional entertainers.

She empties the Reddi-wip can on the length of his cock. Licking slowly from balls to head. Consuming every bit of whipped cream. Looking into his eyes seductively. Swirling her tongue around his head. Taking his entire shaft down her throat. Sucking him to perfection. Their audience cheering and screaming louder than ever now. His juices flowing like crazy into her mouth. Sarah sliding her last dollar into Candi's g-string. His partner in crime lifts her head. Raising her arms in the air to demand applause for this improvised pièce de résistance. Applause received in deafening spades as their birthday girl hugs them both.

Magnum grabs a white bath towel from his bag. Wrapping it around his waist before he and Candi lead their audience through one big dance party to end the show. Both strippers in the center with Sarah. The others surrounding them as "Yeah" by Usher cuts through the night. An apropos conclusion to an exotic entertainment performance for the ages.

Things wind down and audience members begin drifting from the circle to jump back into the pool, grab more refreshments, or sit down and recuperate from the previous action-packed hour. Pamela leads Magnum and Candi to a bedroom where they can change. They return to find a freshly grilled burger and cold beer waiting for each of them. They thank her for the hospitality as they're now starving after all that physical exertion. Eating while chatting with her, Sarah, and a few surrounding guests. Answering their questions about stripping and his agency. Continually praising the show and thanking them for coming. Wishing them the best when they finish their meal and head out. But not before posing for one last photo with their birthday girl. The three of them embracing a final time before the two strippers say their goodnights and depart.

"Thanks for getting me this party," Candi expresses her gratitude as she and Magnum exit the back gate and leave the sounds of birthday celebration behind them.

"Thank you for doing it," he comes back without hesitation, "They totally loved us. This should definitely help word of mouth."

"I hope I was okay," she muses with sincerity.

"You were excellent," he assures her.

"I'm glad," she breathes a sigh of relief, "So were you.

"Thank you," he replies.

They stash their gear in the trunk of his car. Leaving them standing there. Looking at each other. Until an unexplained force has them gripping each other tightly. Their lips locked together. Tongues dancing. Underneath a streetlight bathing them in its soft illumination. Now he's crossing even further the line he drew for himself. It's one thing for him and a female stripping partner to be somewhat intimate for performance sake with the right audience. That's to be expected. But there is no audience right now. Other than the night. Bearing witness to their giving into carnal desires building since she first contacted him. It's now official. They're going to fuck. Self-imposed rules upon himself be damned.

And they can't get to fucking fast enough. Racing down U.S. 67/U.S. 167 from Sherwood to North Little Rock, I-30 to Little Rock, and then I-630 across town back to his place. Weaving through traffic in this concrete jungle of industry and mass consumerism. Alternating his right hand between the gearshift and her knee. Her thigh. Her pussy. Massaging it through her increasingly damp yoga pants. She reaches over and rubs his denim-imprisoned cock. Growing bigger and harder with each passing moment. He imagines what it would be like if she leaned over and sucked him on the highway. She'd probably do it at his suggestion, but he's still getting over his moral dilemma. "What would Billy Idol do?" he asks himself as the platinum one serenades them in the midnight hour. He'd make Candi cry more, more, more with a rebel yell. And that's exactly what Magnum is going to do.

Barely through his front door when they begin kissing insatiably. Reaching his hand down her yoga pants. Her pussy drenched. He has no problem sliding his middle finger inside. Massaging her g-spot while she unbuttons his 501s. Mercifully freeing his cock. Gripping it tightly. Stroking it back and forth. Their knees getting weak. Buckling as they fight to stay standing. Moving his other hand down the rear of her pants. Squeezing her bare ass for added arousal and stability.

"You really do smell delicious," she kisses and licks his neck.

"So do you," he does the same to her and honestly can't remember the last time he wanted to fuck someone this badly, "I need a shower."

"Ooh… Me too," she responds.

Magnum takes Candi by the hand. Leading her to the master bedroom. Turning on the nightstand lamp. She slips off her flip flops as he removes her t-shirt. Freeing her girls once again. She pulls down her yoga pants. Facing away, she bends over and removes them. He lingers on her sexy butt. Making his juices flow even more. She turns around and removes his t-shirt. He takes off his cowboy boots and socks before pulling down his jeans and stepping out of them. Taking a few seconds to bask in the thrill of them being totally naked together. Putting on some music before leading her to the bathroom. Embracing and kissing while awaiting hot water. He steps into the shower and guides her by the hand to join him.

He wastes no time pulling her tight against him. Kissing her passionately as hot water covers their smooth skin. "Can U Deliver" by Armored Saint joins them from the bedroom. He's in a headbanging mood. Grabbing the soap. Lathering it up. Rubbing it all over her tits.

"You were a very dirty girl tonight, Candi," he taunts her playfully.

"Well…" she giggles, "Someone was a very dirty boy tonight."

"Who me?" he asks with faux shock.

"Yeah you," she sasses.

They resume kissing as he slides his hand down her stomach. Rubbing soap on her pussy. Massaging her clit and lips. Fingering her. Teasing her g-spot. She closes her eyes and moans. Her pussy getting tighter and wetter. Both trembling while she orgasms. Him too.

"I just had an orgasm," she confesses with an endearing wide-eyed innocence.

"Me too," he reveals.

"Really?" she asks, "I thought guys couldn't do that."

"They can if they embrace sensuality," he explains, "It's totally possible for a man to orgasm without ejaculating," he smacks her ass, "And it leads to a whole new level of male sexual dominance."

"Ooh..." she bends over, "Dominate me, Magnum," wiggling her sexy round butt at him as he squeezes and massages her cheeks before spanking them, "Oh yeah! Spank my ass!"

She faces him and takes the soap. Lathering up his chest. Rubbing her titties on him. Then rubbing soap on his cock and balls. Stroking his shaft. He leans back against the wall. Closing his eyes. Her adorable giggling and magic touch making his juices flow like crazy. Moaning and sighing. She leans forward and gently bites his bottom lip as they orgasm again. He opens his eyes to the sexiest facial expression he's ever seen. It's like she can't believe what's overcome her right now, yet she's loving every second of it. His face telling her the same. It's all too much as he spins them around. Pressing her back against the wall. Kissing her deeply. She reaches around and smacks his ass.

"I can dominate you too," she laughs.

"We'll just see about that, missy," he playfully points his finger in her face.

"I guess we will, mister," she smiles devilishly.

They laugh as he kisses his way down to her tits. Taking her right breast in his mouth. Swirling his tongue around her nipple. Sucking while rapidly flicking. Repeating with her left breast. Looking in her eyes the entire time. She holds his head to her chest with both hands. Kissing down her stomach and dropping to his knees. Grabbing her leg and guiding her foot onto the edge of the tub. She braces herself in the corner. Now shaking with anticipation while he licks each inner thigh before lapping her pussy in a long slow stroke from back to front. Burying his face between her legs. Tasting her sweet juices as they stream forth. Fingering her again while licking and sucking her clit. Hot water streaming down his cheeks while devouring her throbbing pussy. His cock achingly hard as she moans and screams. Feeling her cum on his face.

"Oh my God, Magnum," she catches her breath, "I just came."

"Yes, you did, naughty girl," he stands, "You came all over my face."

"Mmm…" she coos while tasting her own sweetness on his lips as they kiss.

"Your turn," Candi announces.

He presses his back in the corner. Holding onto her waist. She licks and sucks his nipples. Looking up at him with a smile that is simultaneously evil and sweet. So fucking sexy. So soft and gentle with her mouth and tongue. Bringing chills to his body despite being continuously sprayed with hot water. He strokes her increasingly wet hair. Keeping her face free of rogue strands.

"Aww…" she's genuinely touched by the gesture.

She kisses her way down his stomach. Dropping to her knees. He pushes his butt tighter against the wall. Placing his hands on her shoulders for stability as she grabs his cock. Stroking it while licking and sucking his balls. Taking each in her mouth. Gently circling her tongue around them. Kissing them. His precum gushing forth. He shakes and moans. Struggling to stay upright while she teases him.

"Fuck it. I can't wait any longer," she takes his cock down her throat in one fell swoop.

He's beyond impressed. And orgasmic as fuck. Feeling every muscle fiber in his body growing tighter and tighter. Until the pressure releases all at once. The sensation of her tongue swirling around his head and shaft. Teasing his frenulum. Probing his cock hole as he releases a tidal wave of juices into her mouth. He orgasms again. Pressing his arms against the walls. Fighting to stay upright in his corner.

"Do you ever cum from head?" she looks up at him.

"No. That's not to say I'm not loving every second of this. You're fucking amazing," he assures her, "But I'd rather cum in your pussy anyway."

"I want that so badly," she reaches over and shuts off the water.

They help each other out of the shower. Drying off before he pushes her back into the bedroom. Literally pushing her in there. A primal instinct overtaking him. Smacking her ass repeatedly towards the bed. "Lay it Down" by Ratt tears from the speakers.

"Get your sexy fucking ass on that bed," he commands with another slap on her butt.

She giggles while following orders. He joins her. Without warning, she forces him on his back. Holding down his wrists. Getting on top of him.

"You're not the only one who can play rough," she laughs.

"I can't wait a second longer," he confesses, "I have to know."

"Me too," she nods in agreement.

Candi straddles Magnum. Sliding her pussy onto his massive cock. She's unbelievably tight yet so drenched that she has no problem taking in every inch of him without hesitation. It hits them both. They've crossed that imaginary line. He's now fucking one of his female strippers. And she's fucking her agent. But they'll lament the issue later. Right now, they're living in the moment. He grabs her waist. Lifting her up and down. She tosses her head back and sighs. Falling forward onto him. Lips locking. Tongues dancing. Squeezing her ass, he thrusts his cock relentlessly inside her pussy. Her juices gushing while thrusting back on his cock. Her face buried in his neck. He spreads her cheeks. Running his middle finger from the top of her crack to the bottom. Brushing lightly across her asshole. She kisses and licks his neck more aggressively. Curiosity gets the best of him. Placing his finger in his mouth. Getting it wet before returning to her butthole. Gently penetrating her backdoor with his fingertip. Heart racing while awaiting her response.

"Ooh… That's nice," she breathes in his ear.

"You like that?" he asks softly with a hint of nervousness.

"Mmm-hmm…" she confirms, "I love having my ass played with."

Breathing a sigh of relief, he fingers her butt while pumping her throbbing pussy with his aching cock. They resume kissing while he double penetrates her. Both moaning louder and louder. She lifts her head. He leans in and sucks her tits. She rubs them on his face. They laugh. It's too many moving parts. Both his cock and finger slide out of her slippery holes. They laugh even harder as he flips her on her back. Getting on top. Reinserting his hard cock into her tight pussy. Wrapping his arms around her. Pressed against each other. She wraps her legs around his back. Thrusting violently against each other. Moving closer to cumming.

"Oh God, I want to fuck you so bad!" he fiercely states matter of factly.

"Fuck me, baby!" she demands in a raspy bedroom growl that's possibly the sexiest thing he's ever heard and quite the contrast from her sweet country drawl.

"I am, Candi!" he shouts for the world to hear, "I'm fucking you so fucking deep and hard!"

"Yes you are, Magnum!" she moans loudly, "You are fucking my pussy so deep and so fucking hard!"

He gazes at her in the dim amber glow of the nightstand lamp. The breeze of the ceiling fan above providing a welcome chill to his skin. She tilts her head back. Grabbing the pillow underneath. Fighting to keep from shattering into a million tiny pieces. He feels her heart about to pound out of her chest. The escalating sexual tension of the past two weeks finally reaching its breaking point. At the risk of rationalizing to himself, he thinks about how they needed to explore this. There was something between them demanding that they know each other intimately. The same thoughts fill her mind too as they reach their shared climax. Neither knows what effect this will have upon their working relationship but can't worry about that right now.

Candi screams like a banshee. Her pussy ejaculating warm girl juices all over Magnum. He can no longer hold back. His cock exploding deep inside her pussy. Filling her sugar walls with scalding hot cum. Burning him the entire way out. Holding back since the party. Since they played with each other before an enthusiastic audience. Now they're cumming together. Wave and wave. They embrace for dear life. Shaking profusely. Screaming their way through agonizing bliss. Gladly suffering the glorious pain of sweet release in each other's arms. Comforting themselves with wet kisses. Surviving this together. Screams become heavy breathing when the anguish of white-knuckle pleasure subsides. And then uncontrollable laughter as he rolls over next to her.

"So…" she giggles half-jokingly, "Is every night like this for you?"

"I wish," he shakes his head, "My life is more boring than most people assume."

"I know what you mean," she nods, "Mine too."

"You want a beer?" he gets up.

"That sounds great," she watches him head for the kitchen, "Thank God for that ass!"

"Right back at you!" he laughs while tossing a bag of popcorn in the microwave.

He's laughing not only at that compliment but at the entire night. Starting to feel that he might have fucked up. Yet marveling at how seamlessly and naturally everything between them is progressing.

Grabbing two beers from the fridge. Collecting everything in his arms and rejoining Candi on the bed.

"It's like a sexy picnic," she giggles.

"That's right," he agrees, "Like a nudist resort, but without the ugly people."

"Oh my God," she nearly chokes, "You're so right," pausing to look at him, "You just make me laugh."

"Because I'm funny looking," he responds with the goofiest expression he can conjure.

"No, it's because you make me feel so good," she clarifies, "And you are so fucking hot."

"Thank you," he's consumed by flattery because, no matter how many times he hears that, it always gets to him, "And so are you. Candi."

"Aww… You have no idea how much that means to me coming from you," she coos before pausing to take a sip, "Honestly, that was one of the reasons I contacted you. Aside from not wanting to dance in the clubs here, I was very interested in working with you. Not only do you instantly come across as focused and professional, but I was curious to know you better."

He's at a loss for words. Choked up. Grabbing her knee while thinking of a verbal response.

"I'm so happy you did," he finally musters, "I was instantly taken with your photos and background along with how charming and professional you came across. I wanted to know you better too. Although I hadn't planned on this. I hope I didn't take things too far tonight."

"Not at all," Candi shakes her head and smiles, "We made an excellent team tonight. And now I like to think we're good friends too. Why can't friends make each other feel good sometimes?"

"I like the way you think," he concedes, "Right now, I'm married to this agency. Doing everything to ensure we all make lots of money. As for my personal life… I have no fucking clue what I want," he pauses, "Maybe this is what I need right now."

"I feel the same way," she agrees, "I just uprooted and came home to Arkansas. It's all still sinking in. And I'm not sure what I want either."

They take turns tossing popcorn into each other's mouth with "Hysteria" by Def Leppard filling the air. Laughing and joking as the conversation turns naughty.

"I was really taking a chance earlier when I fingered your ass," he confides, "It was an urge that overcame me. And I just went with it."

"Oh, I'm so glad you did," she admits, "I'm all about getting fucked in the ass."

Now it's his turn to nearly choke. And nearly fall off the bed as she grabs onto him.

"I'm sorry," he laughs, "I just wasn't prepared for that."

"Am I saying too much?" she asks with concern.

"No, not at all," he assures her, "It makes me feel good that we can talk about our sexual interests."

"Me too," she agrees, "You make it so easy for me."

"You make it easy for me too," he responds before taking another sip, "So, tell me about getting fucked in the ass."

"Well, I've only ever done it with my ex-boyfriend, who's like the only actual boyfriend I've ever had," she explains, "I didn't think I'd like it. I always thought it sounded painful. But we got bored one night and decided to try it. We took our time and a lot of lube as he slowly worked his cock inside my ass. I couldn't believe how incredible it felt once I loosened up and he was all the way in. Like one orgasm after another with every stroke. My pussy got so fucking wet. I came so hard that I squirted all over him. It was unbelievable."

"Wow," he catches his breath after enduring the intensity of her storytelling.

"What about you?" she inquires, "Surely you've buttfucked a few girls."

"Only one," he confesses while flattered by her assumption, "An ex-girlfriend. I never liked her."

"Why did you date a girl you didn't like?" she asks, "I'm sorry. That's probably too personal a question."

"Not at all," he shakes his head, "Being a pretty girl, you know what it's like for people to tell you to beware of guys wanting to take advantage of you."

"Oh yeah," she agrees, "It's the story of my life."

"It's a different story for pretty boys," he explains, "You're supposed to give in to a girl if she likes you whether or not you like her. And the same older women who tell you to be picky when it comes to men? They'd trick me into bed the first chance they got."

"You know…" she briefly ponders this revelation before nodding her head, "I can totally see that."

"Anyway," he gets the conversation back on track, "I dated this girl for several months. She was into anal, so I'd fuck her in the ass here and there. It was alright. It felt good, and she made me cum. I just wish it'd been with someone I like."

"I totally get that," she muses, "Like, I wouldn't let just any cock in my ass. Or in my pussy for that matter."

"I can tell," he smiles at her before continuing, "One thing I'm into is eating ass. Well, I would be if I could find a girl to do it with. And if I didn't feel embarrassed about it."

"You shouldn't be embarrassed," she strokes his arm, "I've never done it, but I've fantasized about it too. Both giving and receiving. With guys and girls."

"Ooh… With girls?" he gets intrigued, "Actually, it was seeing it in girl on girl porn that piqued my interest."

"Then what are we waiting for?" she sets her beer on the nightstand and lies on her stomach, "Do what you want to me."

Magnum feels no need to argue. He lies upon Candi. Kissing her neck and shoulders. Grinding his reinvigorated cock against her ass.

Pressing it between her cheeks. She sighs. He sits up. Massaging her shoulders and back. Humping her butt. He drops forward. Kissing and licking down her spine until reaching her magnificent booty. Caressing her round cheeks with his mouth as she trembles. Massaging them. Then giving each one a firm slap.

"Have I been a naughty girl?" she asks sassily.

"You've been very naughty," he playfully scolds her, "It's time for you to take your licks, missy."

She giggles and sighs while he squeezes her ass. Slowly dragging his tongue along the length of her crack from bottom to top. Then back. Deeper this time. Both strippers shaking with anticipation when he spreads her cheeks wide open. Revealing her asshole. So pretty and pink. Like a forbidden pearl within a soft, bouncy shell. It's so fucking sexy like the rest of her. In the course of a few hours, he's gone from refusing to fuck any of his female entertainers to being seconds away from eating one's ass.

He leans down. Licking inside her crack and around her butthole. Teasing the same way as when he eats pussy. She coos softly. Chills cover their bodies. It's time for the moment of truth. Allowing a little saliva to drip from his mouth to her tight little booty hole. Touching it with the tip of his tongue. She moans and stretches as he circles her delicate ridges. She's so sweet. Like candy. Feeling an orgasm build within him. He's finally fucking doing it. Finally licking a girl's asshole for the first time. And it's better than he ever imagined. Of all the girls he's experienced sexual firsts with, Candi is easily the best. His newfound confidence in eating ass kicks into overdrive. Licking more vigorously. She encourages him with her reactions. He spreads her cheeks even wider. Opening her butthole and pressing his warm wet tongue deep inside. Face buried in her ass. Sliding his tongue in and out while she humps his face with her butt.

"Oh my God. Your tongue feels incredible in my ass," she sighs, "You're a fucking natural."

"Thank you," he replies coyly.

Magnum continues licking Candi's yummy butthole like there's no tomorrow. Holding her cheeks open with his face and left hand. Moving the right to her pussy. Running his middle finger along it before penetrating her soaking wet hole. Massaging her g-spot while eating her ass. She moans louder. He's making her tighter and wetter. Fingering her pussy and tonguing her asshole simultaneously. Rubbing his hard, throbbing cock on the comforter. Juices flowing relentlessly. His entire body tingling. Trying not to shake. Every muscle fiber in his body contracting tighter and tighter. He feels her experiencing the same thing. Until it's all too much and they release together. He moves back on top of her. His cock firmly between her cheeks. Coating her crack with precum. He kisses her neck and shoulders. She turns her head to face him. Eagerly taking his tongue in her mouth to his twisted delight.

"Mmm…" she giggles, "My ass tastes yummy."

"Yes, it does," he barely manages past his lips as embarrassment overcomes him.

"Okay," she gives him a reassuring smile, "My turn to eat some sexy ass."

He slides off and she gets on her knees. Straddling him, Sitting on his ass. Grinding her wet pussy on his cheeks. Massaging his back and shoulders. Making his body limp as he enters a rare state of total relaxation. Normally living in a state of tenseness. Constantly feeling he must prove himself. Not yet having earned the right to take it easy on occasion. He'd probably make an excellent Calvinist if not for the whole stripping thing. He assumes they also frown upon eating ass. But she has no such reservations. Bending down. Kissing down his back. Caressing and licking every inch of his cheeks before spanking them.

"Now I get to spank you, naughty boy," she states proudly.

"Who me?" he asks coyly.

"Yes, you," she continues spanking him lightly, "You have been a very naughty boy tonight. It's time for you to take your licks, mister," spreading his cheeks wide open as they laugh, "Oh my God," she whispers breathlessly.

Not wasting any time, she dives right in. Circling his butthole with her tongue. Pushing it inside him. Just as thrilled as he was to be eating ass for the first time. Nearly overcome with disbelief that she's sharing this experience for the first time with such a hot and sexy guy. It's just everything about him that gets her motor running. Not only his looks but kind nature and playfulness as well. Even his serious side. His naked ambition with running his business and performing for audiences is undeniably charming. Even if it results in some degree of a proverbial wall between him and the rest of the world.

"Mmm…" she moans, "Guess what?"

"What?" he asks.

"I'm totally kissing your ass right now," she giggles.

"You make me laugh," he informs her superfluously while laughing.

"That's because I'm funny looking," she makes a goofy face when he glances back.

"Whatever," he scoffs, "You're fucking gorgeous."

"Aww…" her heart melts, "That makes me want to French kiss your ass," she slides her tongue deep inside his asshole.

She buries her face between his cheeks. He sighs and stretches from head to toe. Grabbing the pillow underneath his head. Squeezing it tightly. Like he wants to do with her when they go to sleep after this. That is if she wants to spend the night. And even then, that's if she wants to sleep in his bed and not in the guestroom. Realizing he's probably getting way ahead of himself. Although not sure why he's worried about being too forward now that each of them has tasted the other's butthole. He feels his new favorite stripper grinding her pussy on the comforter as she continues eating his ass. Licking and tonguing it with unbridled enthusiasm. Cooing and giggling nonstop to both the act and his reactions. He shakes and moans while she squeezes his cheeks. Swirling her magical tongue around his asshole. Bringing them both to another orgasm.

"Mmm…" she sighs "You taste so sweet."

She crawls upon him. Her warm titties feel amazing on his cold back. She rubs them all over him. Kissing his neck and shoulders. He glances at her to be greeted by her lips.

"Oh my God, that was so much fun," she gushes, "I'm so glad you suggested it."

"I think you suggested it," he counters.

"No," she shakes her head, "It was you. I simply went into stripper mode and made you feel comfortable about your fantasy. Because you totally should. And it was better than I ever imagined. So sexy and intimate. I loved it."

"I feel the same way," he admits while she rolls off him.

The night becomes surreal. Magnum and Candi enter a dreamlike trance. Neither speaking a word yet conversing nonstop in body language. His physiology overtaking him. Reaching into the nightstand and removing a bottle of strawberry Astroglide. Candi slides her legs off the bed. Bent over. Grabbing a pillow. Embracing it tightly against her chest. He's intoxicated by her willfully compromised position. Warming lubricant between his fingers. Dropping to his knees. Pulling one cheek open with his free hand. She reaches back and holds the other. His tongue revisits her delicious asshole. It's even sweeter this time. Growing completely relaxed with his new kink. Licking in and around her butthole while she moans softly.

He circles her sexy pink hole with his middle finger. Coating it with Astroglide. Gently pressing the tip inside. Patiently allowing her to relax more and more. Pushing his finger inside. One knuckle at a time. Until it's all the way in. Rubbing the velvety walls of her forbidden love tunnel. She moans and trembles. He's trembling too. Butterflies fill his stomach. His mouth getting dry. Wracked with nerves and excitement all at once. She's now loose enough to take his index finger too. Rocking her butt against his hand while he slides his fingers in and out. She breathes heavily. Hugging her pillow even tighter. He can barely breathe as the inevitable arrives. This won't be the first time he's fucked a girl in the ass. Yet it's already guaranteed to be the best anal experience he's ever had. Although he's still not sure his cock will fit. But he's about to find out.

Magnum slowly removes his fingers and fills his hand with more Astroglide. Generously lubricating his achingly hard cock while tasting Candi again along with the flavor of strawberry. His tongue slides effortlessly insider her butthole. She squeezes her pillow even tighter in ecstatic anticipation. He spreads her cheeks wide open. Pressing the head of his cock against her asshole. Hands shaking. His stomach packed with butterflies. He gently pushes his pelvis forward. She takes a deep breath before he penetrates her bubble butt with patience. First his head. Then his shaft. Inch by inch as she loosens up entirely. Taking his entire cock deep inside her ass. He grabs her cheeks tightly. They thrust against each other slowly and gently. Taking their time. Getting to know each other even more intimately. The whole room spinning around them. "Get it Right" by Raven amps the tempo to eleven. They break their silence with moans and screams of agonized delight. He fucks her ass deep and hard. She fucks his cock right back. Equally hard with every stroke.

"Do it, Magnum," she sighs aggressively, "Fuck me in the ass."

"Oh, I'm doing it, Candi," he breathes heavily, "I'm fucking your ass deep and hard."

"Fuck it, baby!" she cries, "Fuck my asshole deep and hard!"

Candi's pussy gushing all over Magnum's thighs. He's balls deep in her ass. Squeezing and spanking her cheeks. Making them bounce. Her butthole clamping tighter around his cock while he grows bigger and harder insider her. Throbbing and gushing in her booty. She grabs the comforter with one hand. Vigorously rubbing her clit with the other. Shaking uncontrollably as they fuck. Faster and harder to the relentlessly driving outro of the heavy metal song filling their ears. Along with screaming and shouting likely waking his neighbors in the dead of night. Pumping her asshole with reckless abandon. Her pussy gushing and squirting all over him. Their entire bodies a tingling mass of nerve endings. Anticipating their shared climax closing in. Holding their breath. Holding back release. Until they can hold back no longer.

"Oh fuck, I'm cumming!" he yells, "I'm going to cum in your ass!"

"Do it, baby! Cum in my ass!" she demands, "I'm cumming too! I can't hold back…"

Candi's words interrupted by her own screams of carnal anguish. Her pussy exploding hot girl juices all over Magnum. She's shaking so much that he can barely stay inside her slippery butthole. Digging his fingertips into her firm cheeks. His cock unleashes a stream of hot sticky cum deep inside her ass. Filling her so full it oozes back onto him. He fights to remain standing while they throw the earth off its axis together. Screaming in the night himself. His climax seemingly refuses to end. Her pussy won't stop squirting either. He falls on top of her. Wrapping his arms around her shuddering body. Keeping his cock pressed deep and hard in her ass. Getting each other through this together. Her ever-tightening hole locking his cock in place. Until finally it's over, and laughter overtakes them.

"Oh my God," he shakes his head in disbelief, "What the fuck was that?"

"Um, it was you fucking me in the ass," she giggles.

"Okay, smartass," he slaps her ass.

"You mean tight ass," she wiggles her butt and causes his cock to fall out, "Oops."

"It's okay," he assures her, "I'm a little sore now."

"I'm sorry, baby," she apologizes while sitting up to face him.

"Don't be sorry," he laughs in lingering awe, "You were fucking amazing."

"So were you," she leans forwards and kisses him.

Leading to a sweet moment of silence. Lost in each other's eyes.

"I need another shower," he breaks the spell.

"Me too," she replies.

It's their second shower of the night. Not as exhilarating as the first but still fun. Lots of talking and laughter. More mutual washing. A little kissing too. Embracing each other while hot water caresses their skin. Once again drying off before returning to the bedroom. He doesn't have to worry about asking her to stay the night as she immediately drops her towel and slips into bed. Pulling up the covers. Smiling and waiting on him to turn off the music and lights. He joins her under the covers. She instantly curls around him. They share a long goodnight kiss. She lies on her side. Staring at him. Even though it's dark, her face glows so brightly that he can make out every feature.

"So," she inquires with sincerity, "How do you feel now about us working and playing together?"

"It's all good," he ponders seriously.

"Gee, thanks," she laughs.

"Hey," he protests, "This is new for me. All of it."

"I'm just kidding," she assures him, "I know that. It's all-new for me too."

"No, I'm totally psyched about having you on board," he admits, "You're flying solo next weekend. I can't wait to hear about how it goes."

"I'll have them eating out of my hand," she boasts, "I know you'll be doing the same with your audience."

"That's right," he agrees.

They gaze silently into each other's eyes. Drifting into another dreamworld…

It's Sunday morning. The sun's rays creeping through Venetian blinds. Creating an entirely different ambiance in the bedroom compared to hours earlier. As consciousness sets in, Magnum looks around and finds himself alone. Candi is gone. A note in her place rests on the pillow next to him. Once his eyes focus, he reads it.

Good morning, Magnum,

I hate to skip out, but I have a lot on my schedule today. Thank you for an incredible party last night. Not to mention our after party. It was out of this world, and so are you. Talk to you later.

French kisses,

Candi

He closes his eyes and it hits him. His agency is truly in business now. Nothing will ever be the same from here on out.

September

Magnum exits I-30 in Benton on his way from Little Rock to El Dorado for a bachelorette party. Making excellent time cruising down AR 35. It's a warm September evening. Summer going not so gently into that goodnight a few days away. The Guns N' Roses version of "Live and Let Die" blasting from his car speakers and into the night air. Lush green trees line the highway. He passes communities with names like Kentucky, Crows, and Owensville. Towns he doesn't recall seeing on the map before departing.

Upon reaching Hot Springs Village, it hits him. He drove twenty minutes in the wrong direction. And he's not even on AR 35. Nope. He's on AR 5. Heading in the opposite direction of his destination. Seventeen months since arriving in Arkansas and he's still learning his way around the state. Frantic as he immediately turns around and calls his client to tell her he's now running forty minutes behind. Akin to an admission of defeat given his being a stickler for punctuality. Fighting to get the words out without choking on them.

"Oh, that's okay," Heather cheerfully assures him, "We're not on any schedule. Just be safe getting here."

Nevertheless, Magnum guns it right down the line. Feeling awful about his error. No time now to soak in the gorgeous drive ahead of him. Well, maybe a little. Arkansas is, if nothing else, a beautiful place. Romantic in its own way. Especially at night. That's what strikes him while driving south on U.S. 167 from Sheridan to El Dorado. A never-ending sea of rich earth tones illuminated by moonlight. Air so fresh and clean. Windows down. Volume up. Impatient to get his bachelorette and her girlfriends in the position. Bottoms up. He's a cowboy tonight. Complete with bullwhip. And you'd better believe some butts are about to get spanked.

It's 10:30pm when Magnum parks on Washington Avenue in downtown El Dorado. Across the street from a nightclub in which his party girls have reserved the upstairs loft. He calls Heather and waits for her to come outside and meet him while getting his gear together. Speaking of butts. And boobs… She appears in a short and lowcut blue satin cocktail dress that leaves little to the imagination. Her luscious titties daring to explode forth. And that delicious ass just begging to be squeezed. He takes a deep breath. Reminding himself that his chance will come soon enough.

"I'm so sorry," he apologizes, "I took a wrong turn out of Benton and…"

"Don't worry about it. I get lost on these highways all the time," she laughs, "We're just excited you made it. We tried this two years ago for another girl's bachelorette party, and he never showed. Or even called."

He knows how true that is. Few male strippers ever show up to parties. He's never understood it. Private parties are the best. And why do guys agree to parties only to cancel or no-show? That's a rhetorical question. It's because they're cowards. Unable to fly solo. Still afraid of girls no matter how well built they may be. Also dependent on the beta male peer approval that comes with performing in male revues. Something he observed quickly in this business that's become shockingly more apparent in these early days of his agency. Five months in and already having nearly worked his way through all the experienced male strippers kicking around the state. Without Candi and the other girls, there would be no agency.

"That's awful," he sympathizes, "If only I'd been in Arkansas then."

"Oh, I know," she smiles, "We were reluctant to try again, but the bachelorette really wanted a male stripper. And you really sold me on yourself."

"Then I'd better not keep her waiting any longer," he grabs his stripping bag.

Magnum's sin of taking a wrong turn is absolved by Heather's giddiness and bouncy bubble butt as he follows her inside. This old building has an aesthetic and feel that is equal parts rustic and industrial. A warm amber glow engulfs red brick walls and exposed wooden beams. People mostly sitting, drinking, and conversing while a DJ spins tunes. Magnum normally insists on providing his own music, but this hip-hop set containing many of the songs he normally uses will suffice. Heather is requesting "Cowboy" by Kid Rock for Magnum's intro upstairs when the club's owner approaches him.

"Feel free to get as wild and crazy as you want with those girls," he assures Magnum with a figurative wink and a nudge, "I'll make sure no one disturbs y'all."

"Okay," Magnum nods, "Thanks."

Magnum is super excited right now. How can he not be with Heather, so friendly and full of life, running around in that dress? He can't wait to meet the rest of his bachelorette party crew. Standing at the foot of the staircase to the loft. Nearly breathless with anticipation to take that first step towards the circle of pre-wedding debauchery awaiting him. She lets him know with a sassy smile that all is good to go while passing him on her way upstairs. He waits a moment before climbing his personal stairway to heaven on the opening notes of "Cowboy" to discover a dozen young women beside themselves with excitement for his presence. Screams of female hysteria fill the air along with a song celebrating good, old fashioned, American decadence.

No one is more excited to see Magnum than Mandy. His vivacious bachelorette who, upon seeing the whip in his hand, stands up and bends over her chair. The bottom of each ass cheek peeking out from underneath the short skirt of her tight black cocktail dress. Giggling as she wiggles her butt and receives several light lashes from his coiled leather whip. He unrolls it and produces a thunderous crack that echoes throughout the cavernous venue.

"Sit your sexy ass down," he strips away his costume while dancing on her.

"Oh my god, you smell amazing," she buries her face in his neck as he grinds on her lap.

"You smell amazing yourself," he whispers in her ear.

And she feels amazing to him as well. The sensation of her silky-smooth legs rubbing against his is bliss. His g-string can barely contain his cock as he applies Reddi-wip to her cleavage. Burying his face between her perky tits, he consumes every bit. Repeating the process on her inner thighs. Licking his way towards her pussy. Oh so close to tasting her. Feeling her warmth on his face. So excited to know he's making her wet.

Magnum gives Mandy a chance to catch her breath and moves onto her friends. They're all great, but Heather is the standout. Teasing him from the start with her generous cleavage and short skirt that begs for exploration underneath. He enjoys whipped cream served off her titties and gives her the leg treatment. Making his way underneath her skirt. Licking up her right thigh to discover she's not rocking any panties. She shudders when he gives her clit a quick tongue lashing before consuming the remaining whipped cream from her left thigh. His tongue runs along chills of anticipation upon her soft skin. This time he lingers on her pussy a little longer while sampling her sweet juices.

But he can't stay more than a few seconds lest the other girls begin wondering what's going on down there. With Heather blushing and giggly, he returns to Mandy for a second round with his bachelorette.

Unbelievably, the other girls head downstairs. Leaving Magnum and Mandy alone. An unprecedented act in his three years of stripping to this point. Are they unconcerned that something may happen? Or facilitating a little something extra between them? Proving to be the latter as, now seated on a sofa while he straddles her on his knees, she removes his rock-hard cock from its g-string prison. Stroking him with both hands. "Freek-a-Leek" by Petey Pablo thumps around them as he processes what's happening. His bachelorette is clearly having the time of her life. Smiling. Breathing heavily. Getting herself off. Is he crossing a line here? Maybe. Yet he doesn't tell her to stop. Not because he doesn't want to hurt her feelings. But because he finds her attractive and her touch amazing. The firm grip of her delicate hands upon his long throbbing shaft makes his body shake.

"Ooh… Someone's juices are flowing," she wipes precum from the tip of his cock and tastes it, "Mmm… Yummy."

"It would feel even better deep inside you," he suggests without thinking in the heat of the moment.

"I know it would," she coos, "Maybe we can make that happen later."

"What the fuck?!" he wonders to himself, "Is she for real?"

"I don't love him," she shakes her head as if reading his thoughts, "I truly don't. And I don't want his cock to be the only one that's ever been inside me."

Part of him wants to press for details but knows better than to break the spell of the moment. Maybe she's using him, but he's kind of using her too. Romance is hard for a career male stripper. Especially for one in the early stages of building his own agency of male and female entertainers. Candi is oodles of fun, but they have a barrier of sorts between them. Strictly friends with benefits, so the field is his to play. Mandy has proven to be such a sweet girl in the mere minutes he's known her. That he knows she would stop stroking his manhood without complaint if he asked makes him want her even more.

The sound of her friends laughing and stomping up the stairs ends this round of foreplay. He attempts to cover himself and begins dressing. Waiting for his cock to shrink enough to fit inside his jeans. Until finally able to slide it down his right leg and button up his tight faded 501s. Still rocking his black cowboy boots along with a black t-shirt now. He puts his black cowboy hat back on. Looking like some sort of sexy as all fuck outlaw of society. Because that's totally what he is. Night after night. And this night is still young. He's still filled with electricity yet now lacks an outlet. But that problem quickly rectifies itself.

"You're coming with us," Heather announces.

"Coming where?" Magnum looks up while kneeling before his stripping bag.

"Come on, stripper man," Mandy takes his hand.

He grabs his bag and follows her downstairs with friends in tow. The temperature now borderline jacket weather when he steps outside with the bachelorette party. Stashing his gear in the trunk and walking with his party girls around the block to another nightspot. Past one charming old building after another. Underneath streetlamps. Down the sidewalk. Trees spaced incrementally. They enter this new venue and pass a blues-rock band on stage before heading up a new flight of stairs. Reaching the second floor to be greeted by strobes and multicolored disco lights flashing in dizzying arrays across a small black space punctuated with bare metal trusses. Bodies packed on the dance floor. Crunk beats thudding relentlessly. Who would expect such an ultra-hot dance club to be hidden in this small Arkansas town? He sure as fuck didn't. But color him pleasantly surprised.

Magnum dances with his party girls. Giving special attention to Mandy. Bumping and grinding on each other to "Yeah" by Usher. He's off the clock. But it's not about money now. It's about finding out how serious she was moments ago. How badly does she want his cock deep inside her pussy? If so, how badly does he want to oblige? In spades as she shakes her booty against his crotch. Bringing him to full attention once again within his denim prison. Yeah, he wants to fuck her tonight. Heather looks at him with a figurative wink and a nudge. Confirming that the feeling is mutual for Mandy. Still, a twinge of uncertainty lingers. He's more used to women cockblocking his sexual advances towards their girlfriends. Not encouraging them. He spent mere seconds playing with Heather's pussy. Was enough to convince her that he's what the bachelorette sorely needs days before she walks down the aisle. He knows all too well that anything is possible. Last call is announced as they keep on dancing to "Back That Azz Up" by Juvenile. Purple and blue lights illuminate Mandy as she throws her arms around his neck.

"Are you coming home with me?" she whispers in his ear.

"It would be my pleasure," he licks her ear.

"Ooh…" she coos, "Mine too."

The group heads out of the club and back onto the street. It's 1:30am as they walk back to their vehicles. The night air even cooler now. After exchanging goodnights with his party girls, Magnum watches Mandy mouth the words "follow me" to him before getting in her car alone. He jumps into his. Ready to roll. They wait for the other girls to leave first. Once the coast is clear, he follows her down Washington Avenue. Then through a maze of residential streets lined with charming older houses. "In My Dreams' by Dokken pumps from his speakers. Feeling both excited and nervous all at once. Is he really going to fuck a bachelorette? That's certainly a first. Thinking maybe he shouldn't get mixed up in her drama. Then realizing he's been in the middle of it ever since Heather booked him.

Mandy pulls into the driveway of a small, white home. Magnum parks across the street. Shrouded in calm so dead. In only a few minutes, he's gone from being surrounded by dancing people to feeling like he and this girl are the only two people on earth. And, in a way, they are. Looking all around while crossing the street. As if someone may be watching them. Under cover of trees. Protected by the darkness high above. Save for the dim amber glow of a lone streetlamp. She smiles and motions him to enter through her backdoor. Finding himself in her kitchen. She opts to leave the light out. The outside illumination filtering through the windows perfectly complimenting the current mood. Culinary objects cast long, dark shadows upon them. He and his bachelorette gaze at each other in silence. Tears build in her eyes. Is she having second thoughts? Is he?

"I love this house," she glances around the kitchen and opines in a voice so wracked with vulnerability it sends chills down his spine.

"It's nice," he replies, "It packs a certain charm and cuteness befitting a single young woman."

"My parents own it," she explains, "They're the ones in love with my fiancée. Not me. But… whether I marry him or not, I can't live here anymore."

Magnum has no wisdom to offer and doesn't insult her by attempting otherwise.

"Don't get me wrong," she continues, "He's a good guy. And I like him. But… I guess I have to keep reminding myself that he's good people," she concedes while fighting back tears, "You know?"

Good people. A phrase Magnum is sick and tired of hearing. So many opportunities he's earned through talent and ambition ripped away and handed to "good people" instead. Because why? They had mouths to feed? Maybe those "good people" shouldn't have had kids they couldn't afford. Or perhaps they should put forth the same devotion to excellence as he does night after night. Despite – or because of – his honesty to a fault, he'll never qualify as good people. It's a good thing he loves what he does because it's his sole option for any semblance of financial stability right now.

He replies to his bachelorette by taking her in his arms. Holding her trembling body tight against his. Their lips meet. Melancholy gives way to the mischief of earlier. It's time to finish what they started at her party. She picks up where she left off by unbuttoning his jeans and removing his aching cock. Aching to explore her pussy as she resumes her hand job from earlier. Slowly stroking the entire length of his shaft with her tight grip. Making his manhood tingle. Throbbing like a racing heart. Juices flowing onto her soft, delicate hands. Their lips still locked tight. Tongues dancing in ecstasy.

She drops to her knees. Taking him deep in her warm wet mouth. He grabs the edge of the kitchen table behind him. Fighting to stay on his feet while she makes him weak in his knees. Looking up into his eyes. Her tongue caressing his head and shaft. The tears in her eyes replaced with bad girl sassiness. Licking and sucking his cock. Teasing every nerve ending. Making his sweetness flow uncontrollably. He removes one hand from the edge of the table. Stroking her face and hair. She continues teasing his head and frenulum with the tip of her tongue. His body tensing more and more until an orgasmic wave sweeps over him. Lifting her up. Kissing insatiably. Stripping each other totally naked.

"Park your sexy ass on that table, missy," he demands with authority.

"Ooh…" she giggles while following orders, "Whatever you say, mister."

He buries his face in her neck. Kissing and caressing her soft skin. Moving downward. Slowly. She trembles. Breathing heavily. Heart racing when he reaches her tits. She grabs his head. He swirls his tongue over her nipples. Flicking them rapidly while sucking. Her soft moans deafening to his ears in the perfectly dead quiet of darkness surrounding them. Embracing them as she embraces his head. Holding his mouth tight against her breasts. Upon her nipples. Feeding each one's burning desire for the other. He kisses down her stomach. The sound of a passing car briefly joins the avant-garde score to their lovemaking.

Magnum doesn't feel like taking his time. Diving tongue first into Mandy's soaking wet pussy. She doesn't feel like waiting either. It's her turn to grip the table's edge for dear life. He twirls his tongue upon her clit. Wave after wave of warm sweetness on his face. Trying in vain to consume every drop. She shakes uncontrollably as he licks her from back to front. Bringing her closer to orgasm. Her moans growing ever louder in the night. Every muscle fiber in their bodies contracting tighter and tighter.

"Oh God," she moans breathlessly, "I'm cumming."

"Cum for me, baby," he encourages her, "Cum on my face.

He thrusts his tongue inside her. Lashing her velvety sugar walls. Her sweetness gushing forth. Grinding her pussy on his face. Humping it relentlessly.

"Oh fuck!" she cries while orgasming all over his face.

She stands and tastes her girl juices on his lips. Turning around and bending over the table. Her pussy unbelievably tight when he inserts his middle finger and massages her g-spot. Making her pussy even wetter. Making her moans grow louder. He knows he can top this as he spreads open her cheeks with his other hand. Leaning forward and teasing her delicate butthole with his tongue. Licking and probing her. Surprised by his confidence and absence of hesitation in eating her ass.

"Ooh… I like that," she giggles, "You really are a naughty boy."

"The naughtiest," he assures her with total swagger.

Fun as this may be, Magnum can't wait a second longer in giving his cock what it has wanted all night. Giving Mandy what her pussy has hungered for since meeting him. He stands and intimately enters his bachelorette's world. Sliding his throbbing manhood deep inside her. Both shuddering in orgasmic release. Their burning lust for each other finally consummated following hours of foreplay. It's all too much. No time to waste. He grabs her hips. Viciously pumping her with his massive cock. Over and over. Deeper and deeper inside her velvety love tunnel with each thrust. Her pussy becoming even more drenched. Gushing incessantly while he spanks her naughty ass. Their rhythmic chorus of moaning and grunting joined by the sounds of a passing train. They are a fucking machine. Pounding harder and harder into late-night sexual oblivion.

"Fuck me, Magnum!" she aggressively insists, "Fuck my pussy hard!"

"Oh…" he throws back with equal attitude, "I'll fuck your pussy hard, Mandy."

He's fucking her as hard as he can. Feeling the table move slightly forward with each unbridled thrust. She's bent over one end and grabbing onto the opposite edge. The feel of her ass smacking against his pelvis with each stroke makes his body tingle. Hers too. His knees weaker than ever. She grabs an orange from the bowl of fruit next to her. Crying in sexual anguish into the night while squeezes it. Harder and harder until it explodes. Sending fresh orange juice everywhere. She throws the rest against the wall. Safe and secure in her vulnerability. Letting this sexy stranger whom she just met fuck her over her own kitchen table. Tonight is the most alive she's ever felt.

"Take me!" she screams, "Take what you want!"

"I'm taking it!" he shouts, "I'm taking it all!"

It's all too much. His throbbing cock explodes deep inside her swollen pussy. He shakes profusely. Filling her with an endless wave of steaming cum. Squeezing her butt as the tension release makes him lightheaded. Her pussy squirting hot girl juices all over him. Hanging onto the table with a white-knuckle grip from each hand. Their combined screams drowning out the nearby train still thundering past. Finally leaving them behind. Moving on through the night. All is quiet once again.

The only sounds left now are those of the stripper and his bachelorette struggling to catch their breath. He holds onto her luscious ass out of fear he'll collapse. After what feels like an eternity, his cock falls out of her pussy. He steps to the side and leans on the table while she struggles to stand. Once on her feet, she wets a tea towel for him before running off to the bathroom. Leaving him naked and alone in a strange kitchen. Cleaning himself. Processing the events of tonight. Everything that led him to this moment and place in time. Is he dreaming? If so, he'll gladly take it. She reenters the kitchen, rocking a red silk robe as he finishes dressing.

"Are you sure you're good to drive? You can stay if you want," she offers nervously, "I mean… You know…"

"Thank you, but I'm fine to drive home," he quickly saves her.

There's no need to complicate things. Not for her. Not for him. He likes her. And that's why he can't allow himself to do something stupid like fall in love with her. She sees him to the door where they share one last kiss forever.

"Be safe driving back to Little Rock, sexy stripper man," she instructs him.

Her final impression upon him being one of sweetness and sass. Watching him walk alone not so gently into that goodnight before closing the door behind her. On her way to an empty bed while he gets into his car for a long drive home by himself. The two of them relegated to curling up and keeping each other warm in spirit only. And just like that, she is out of his life forever. A difficult reality for him to process since the spontaneous events of tonight haven't had a chance to completely set in.

On the plus side, he finally has a chance to truly soak in the gorgeous Arkansas scenery. Albeit at 3:00am. Regardless, he enjoys cruising up US 167. Just he and his thoughts. And that's always a special occasion for him. Despite the late hour, he's wide awake. "Don't Close Your Eyes" by Kix serenades his contemplations. How did Candi's party tonight go? How lame is Mandy's fiancé really? Should he have tried to get Heather back at Mandy's as well for a threesome? Will his bachelorette party tomorrow night even hold a candle to the excitement of this one? This night is certainly like a dream. Then again, that's true of most nights one way or another. And tomorrow always brings another wild night.

May

"Oh wow!" Rob exclaims.

The young bachelor is simultaneously sheepish and enthusiastic as Candi lap dances him into submission. Seated in a dining room chair in the center of the living room before a captivated audience. She straddles him with authority in nothing but a g-string and platforms. Gyrating her hips to the rock and roll thrust of "Girls Girls Girls' by Mötley Crüe. She may be one girl but oozes the unapologetic sexuality of at least three. Smothering his face with her bare titties. Grabbing his head with both hands. Pressing her girls against his chest. Sitting on his lap. Burying her face in his neck. Blowing softly. Making him eat from her hand. Like she's done with her entire audience on this warm Friday night in late May.

Candi isn't big on bachelor parties and doesn't do many. More partial to entertaining coed audiences at birthday parties. Either solo or in tandem with a male stripper. She's even down with performing for lesbian audiences. It's not that she hates men by any means. Nor does she worry about her safety in a room full of men. On the contrary, bachelor party guests are often too shy and reserved for her tastes. Sometimes to the point of being so aloof, they come across as rude towards her. She's also aware that, unlike some female strippers who absolutely thrive in any roomful of men, her skillset typically plays better to a different audience.

That said, the client for tonight's bash was dead set on booking Candi from the start. A young man named Michael, who just got home from a tour in Afghanistan. Barely in time to organize a bachelor party in style for his best friend before returning overseas for another round. Even sending his parents out of town for the weekend. Utilizing their spacious farmhouse for tonight's festivities. It was this dedication to his friend that sold Candi on accepting the booking, along with his cool confidence and overall sweetness on the phone. Coming across as an honest to God nice guy who addressed her with the utmost respect. Winning her over not only with his guarantee of financial generosity but also by virtue of his sheer likeability.

"Oh my God. He's hot," Candi thought to herself upon seeing Michael for the first time. Greeted by his handsome face and athletic physique after making the two-plus hour drive from Little Rock to a rice farm north of Alma, Arkansas. Not far from Fort Smith. A town mostly famous for being one of the settings in *True Grit*. Well, Michael can spank her anytime as far as she's concerned. He, the bachelor, and their dozen friends are a fun and friendly group of early twentysomething men. A little intimidated by her perhaps, but still polite. Instantly accepting her as one of the guys in a way. Albeit one with hips and tits. And she's ecstatic about it. Rewarding them for their hospitality. Making sure each gets his chance to be up close and personal with her. Guiding nervous hands to her soft silky thighs. Relishing her aggressive methods in owning them.

Candi returns to Rob with a can of Reddi-wip. Def Leppard's "Pour Some Sugar on Me" tears from her audio system. The south side of the living room all windows. Facing a vast rice field extending into the dark void of nighttime in rural Arkansas. She drops to her knees before him. Reaching forward and grabbing his thighs. Pulling herself closer. Facedown along his thighs. Tossing her hair over her face and his crotch as she mimics sucking his cock. Impressionable young men gasp in astonished delight. Encouraging her every step of the way. She pushes herself upward. Meeting her bachelor face to face. Sitting on his lap and applying whipped cream to her nipples. Motioning Michael over to join them. He and the bachelor quickly lick her nipples clean.

"Not so fast, boys," Candi grabs their heads and hold them tight against her chest, "My tits aren't done with you yet."

"But I'm getting married next weekend," Rob breaks his mouth free of her breast after lingering on it long enough to contradict his protest.

"That's right. You are," she shakes her head with mock disapproval, "You need to be punished for your naughty behavior, mister. Stand up, turn around, and bend over."

Rob obeys Candi's orders while she retrieves a studded black leather paddle from her stripping bag. An unsynchronized chorus of, "Oh shit!" fills the room as she returns to the bachelor in his compromised position. Smacking her free hand every swaggering step of the way. Her pussy getting wet by the thought of what she's about to do.

"I'm not scared," the bachelor drops his pants and underwear before wiggling his bare ass at her, "Come and get it, baby!"

"Aww, dude!" his friends collectively groan and instinctively flinch in disgust.

Everyone watches her raise the paddle above her head. She has no intention of hurting him, but the gauntlet has officially been thrown down. Delivering a loud whack to her bachelor's taunting butt that echoes throughout the house.

"Damn!" he overreacts in semi-pain, "How am I going to explain this to my girl?"

"Don't worry," she assures him, "You'll be healed before your wedding night."

She continues paddling him. More gently now. His friends cheer them on until both are laughing too hard to continue.

"I guess you've learned your lesson, young man," she announces.

The audience gives her a round of applause while Rob pulls up his pants. Catching Candi off guard with a hard smack to her bare ass when she turns away. She jumps and looks back at him.

"I owed you that one," he states proudly.

She laughs it off while returning the paddle to her bag. Michael approaches her for a private conversation as the bachelor gets more alcohol poured down his throat.

"You mentioned something on the phone about other goodies you have in that bag," Michael inquires with two hundred dollars in his hand, "I can't imagine you being any more amazing than you've been so far, but is such a thing possible?"

"Absolutely," she takes his cash with one hand and places the other on his face.

She gently strokes him before sneaking a quick peck on his cheek while no one is looking. Smiling at him being pleasantly taken aback before he returns to his guests. She grabs her bag and takes it to the middle of the living room. Setting the hot seat aside and laying a blanket on the floor. Everyone watching in excited curiosity. She can hear them thinking, "What the fuck is going on?" as she sets a bottle of Astroglide on the blanket along with a vibrator. Turning away from her party boys and pulling down her g-string. Bending over. Flashing her pussy. Pulling her unmentionable over each platform and tossing it to the side.

"Well, what are you boys waiting for?" she asks with a sassy tone after turning to face her now slack-jawed audience, "Gather around and watch what I do when I'm home alone."

They obediently pile on the large leather sofa. She sits on the blanket, facing them. Spreading her legs wide open. Cherry Pie" by Warrant comes on. Her cherry pie quickly becoming soaked just from having all these young men under her thumb. Completely at her mercy.

Hanging on her every move. Even something as simple as brushing a stray hair from her face is met with extreme anticipation. She could ask them to kill someone on her behalf and they'd do it without hesitation. Sitting naked and giving her audience a front-row view of her pussy has her on the verge of orgasm. She may be the only one naked, but they are the vulnerable ones. This is totally her show.

"I like to start simply by licking my fingers and rubbing my clit," she informs her audience in a voice that is equal parts schoolteacher and phone sex operator. Looking in their eyes while licking the fingers of her right hand. Placing them on her pussy. Rubbing her clit slowly in small circles. Subtly biting her lip. Watching their every nervous move. Her audience is silent, but their shared enthusiasm fills the room. Enveloping Candi's naked body as she masturbates for their viewing pleasure. It's a lot for them to handle. And her as well.

"Oh my God," she moans while experiencing a small orgasm, "Whew!" she giggles as every man's jaw drops further. "Then I like to finger my pussy a little."

Slowly she pushes her middle finger inside her pussy. Holding herself up with her left hand. Fingering herself with the right. Thrusting in and out of her love tunnel faster and faster. Her pussy growing wetter and wetter. The sound of Candi finger fucking herself matched only by the music and racing hearts of her captive audience. Softly moaning. Bringing herself to another orgasm. Closing her eyes momentarily to fantasize that it's Michael's finger in her pussy. Opening them to look straight into his eyes when she orgasms again.

"Now I need a volunteer," she says, "Is there a bachelor in the house?"

"I'm sorry," Rob shakes his head when everyone else looks at him, "As much as I'd like to, I just can't."

She nods approvingly. Not at all offended by his devotion to his future bride.

"What about Michael?" he suggests, "He's the only single guy here, and I know it's been a while for him."

"Shut the fuck up," Michael slugs the bachelor in the shoulder as their friends cheer this idea, "So… Um… What do you need from me, Candi?"

"I need you to get down here and sit next to me," She instructs him suggestively.

Michael joins her on the blanket. His friends exclaim, "Woo!" like a roomful of Ric Flairs. She grabs her vibrator. One designed for g-spot stimulation and featuring vibrating rabbit ears. Holding it up for everyone to get a better look.

"The rabbit ears are what makes this toy a must for me," she explains, "Because even if I'm too exhausted to do anything else, massaging my clit with this is enough to get me off and help me fall asleep quickly. But right now," she turns on the rabbit ears and hands the toy to her assistant while licking her lips, "Michael will do the honors."

Michael takes a deep breath. Trying not to shake too much. Slowly lowering the toy to her pussy. Ever so slightly touching the rabbit ears to her clit. She immediately throws her head back and moans.

"Oh yeah! That's the spot," she sighs, "Just keep it there."

She's trembling more than ever now. And so is her audience. Barely sitting still as she isn't the only one experiencing sensory overload right now. Michael is shaking so much that she isn't sure whether it's the toy vibrating her clit or him. Really, it's a combination of both. This sweet and sexy man bringing her to another orgasm while his friends watch and learn. Her pussy is drenched. She can feel the blanket getting wet underneath her ass. "At least the living room has tile and not carpet," she rationalizes in her mind. Another orgasm building inside her. Every muscle fiber contracting tighter and tighter.

"Fuck yes, Mikey!" she shouts as all bodily tension releases in one fell swoop before catching her breath and looking at Michael, "I'm sorry. You probably don't want me calling you that."

"You can call me anything you want right now," he responds with a combination of shock and amusement.

Everyone else cheers as she takes the vibrator from Michael and lubricates the shaft with Astroglide. Turning on the g-spot stimulator and handing it back to him. Lying on her back.

"Put it inside me, Michael," she rubs her pussy.

The entire room holds its collective breath. Michael struggles to keep his hand steady. Pressing the vibrator against her pussy. She uses both hands to spread herself wide open. Allowing her audience to see inside her before Michael slides the vibrating shaft within her sugar walls.

"Deeper, baby," she sighs.

He pushed it further inside Candi's pussy. Hitting her g-spot.

"Oh, fuck yes!" Candi exclaims, "That's my g-spot!"

"I can tell," he responds with a dry chuckle while shaking as badly as she is.

Everyone else is shaking too. Sweating bullets of anticipation despite the air conditioner chilling the room. She's on fire. So is Michael as he holds the vibrator in position. She's loving every second of it. The physical stimulation. The enthusiastic eyes all over her naked body. Michael getting her off. Closing her eyes and imagining it's his cock deep inside her pussy. Rubbing against her g-spot. Making her girl juices flow more and more. Badly wanting him insider her. Arching her back and gripping the blanket with both hands. Her moans now turning into screams of ecstasy. She may still be dominating everyone else, but she's now submissive to Michael. Embracing being under his thumb. Her impending climax builds and builds. Fighting to hold back. From pressure to aching to pain. Her pussy hurting for Michael's cock to fuck it deep and hard. It's all too much now.

"Oh my God, Michael!" her banshee-like scream tears through the house.

It frightens her audience. Making them flinch backward. She cums hard. Her pussy exploding. Squirting a stream of hot juices. Soaking the entire blanket along with Michael's hand and arm. Shaking uncontrollably. Her body goes limp. Taking a moment to catch her breath along with everyone else.

"Candi," Rob finally breaks the silence, "That was fucking awesome! All I can say is… My girl and I are totally reenacting this on our wedding night!"

The audience gives her a standing ovation. Michael removes the vibrator from her pussy. She sits up and grabs a towel from her bag. Drying Michael's arm before cleaning herself. The other guys dig whatever cash they have remaining from their pockets and drop it into her bag.

"You guys are the best," she coos, "And I mean that. I don't do that many bachelor parties. But Michael told me what an amazing group you are. And he wasn't lying. Thank you all so much."

"Well, I gotta go see my girl right now," Rob abruptly announces, "I can't wait until our wedding night to try this out. We have to do it now."

Candi is flattered. Giving him a naked hug and kiss on the cheek. The other guests echo the same sentiment. Saying their goodnights. Rushing out the door to their wives and girlfriends for some explosive sex action. Gone so quickly that no one notices they left her alone with Michael. Still naked, she stands in the center of the living room. Watching as he starts cleaning up. Even watching him conduct a mundane task gets her motor running again. It's everything about him. His good looks, of course, but also his kindness. As well as the aura of dedication and focus that exudes from him. A sense of personal pride. Doing for himself while doing for others. The sort of man who is unobtainable beyond one night due to their respective life circumstances and whom she only could encounter through stripping.

"So, what's Afghanistan like?" she inquires in an awkward attempt to make small talk, "Forgive me if I'm getting too personal."

"Not at all." he looks over and smiles before turning to pick up empty beer bottles off the floor, "Mostly, I have people telling me what it's like for me to serve overseas than asking me what it's like. At the end of the day, it suits me at this point in my life."

"You have to do what's best for you," she opines, "And what makes you happy at any given point in your life."

"That's right," he agrees, "You certainly seem happy with what you do."

"I am," she laughs before turning seductive, "I know exactly what I want to do right now."

"Sweet Child o' Mine" by Guns N' Roses plays while Candi walks over to Michael. Taking him by the hand. Leading him to the sofa. Pushing him back onto it. Straddling him on her knees. Gyrating her naked body over him. Taking his hands. Placing them on her ass. He squeezes her round cheeks. She puts her hands on his chest. Rubbing him gently. Looking deep into his eyes. Grabbing his thighs. Stroking them. Starting just above his knees. Moving slowly upward until reaching his cock. Massaging it through his jeans. Feeling him grow larger. Aching to feel him inside her.

Aggression overcomes her. Grasping his head. Pulling his face to hers. Planting her lips on his. Forcing her tongue inside his mouth. Moving her hands to his cheeks. He kisses her back with equal passion. Squeezing her ass tighter while she sits on his lap. Getting even wetter from the sensation of his warm cock throbbing against her tightening pussy. Unlocking her lips from his. Pushing his head to her breasts. Holding him against her girls. He licks and sucks her right nipple. Taking it in his warm wet mouth. Swirling his tongue around it. Repeating with the left breast and bringing her to another orgasm.

"That's right," she sighs in carnal anguish, "Suck my tits, Michael."

Candi's pussy gushes on Michael's jeans. She pushes him back and removes his t-shirt. Sliding her body down his to lick and suck his nipples. Squeezing his firm pecs. Pleasuring them orally. Looking into his eyes. Circling and flicking each nipple with her tongue before sucking them between her soft lips. Giggling sassily at his facial expression. She pulls back. Dropping to her knees on the floor. Removing his boots. Unbuttoning his jeans and pulling them off. Then his underwear. Licking her way slowly up his inner right thigh. From his knee to his pelvis. Then again with the left. Teasing him. Watching his massive erection throb. Precum flowing from the tip. She can't wait to taste it but not before giving attention to his balls. Kissing and licking his most sensitive area. Taking each in her mouth. He trembles both from the pleasure he's receiving now and in anticipation of what's about to come.

She looks into his eyes and touches the tip of his cock with her tongue. Getting her first taste of his juices. Making them flow even more. Licking up and down every inch of his shaft. Swirling her tongue around his head. Taking him deep in her throat. Sucking his manhood while he strokes her face and hair. She can't get over how sweet he is in every way. From his caring and affectionate nature to his big delicious cock. It's all making her pussy even tighter and wetter along with his moans and sighs. Bringing him to orgasm. Hell-bent on giving him as many as he's given her tonight.

Michael stands, grabs Candi by the arm, and drags her down a dark hallway. Into his moonlit bedroom. She's an enthusiastic captive as he throws her onto his bed. This manhandling has her tingling all over. Her girl juices flowing even more. Already feeling the bed getting wet underneath her. He pounces his naked body upon hers. Kissing her passionately. Tongues writhing. Lips getting wetter and wetter. He sucks her titties again. She grinds her girls on his face. He kisses and licks down her stomach. Giving the same treatment he received from her. Licking up each inner thigh. Circling her pussy with his tongue. Flicking her clit. Sending an electrical shock through her body.

She arches her back in pure decadence as he eats her hot throbbing pussy. Sucking her swollen lips. Sliding his tongue deep inside her sugar walls. Licking up her endless tidal wave of sweet juices. Savoring every drop while licking her pussy back and forth. Rubbing her breasts and nipples at the same time. She grasps the bedsheet with both hands. Then the pillow underneath her head. After wanting all night to have his beautiful face between her legs, she looks down to see her fantasy is now a reality. Grabbing his head with both hands. Grinding her pussy on his face.

"Oh God, that's it. Eat my pussy," she whispers in the darkness, "Eat my soaking wet pussy, Michael."

He slides a finger inside her. Then another. And then another. Licking and sucking her throbbing clit. Expertly massaging her g-spot in a way that no fancy toy could ever match. Hitting it oh so right. She's moaning and screaming. Her pussy getting even tighter and wetter. Clamping down on his fingers. Gushing all over them. It's heaven, but still not enough. The anticipation of soon feeling his giant cock inside her leads to another orgasm. Squirting warm juices on his face and in his mouth as he continues licking and fingering her pussy.

A near-superhuman strength overcomes Candi. Grabbing Michael and yanking him forward. On his knees over her face. Lifting her head to suck his cock. His juices flowing as uncontrollably as hers. Gladly drinking up every drop she can. Prepping him for the main course. The thing she's wanted all night. For him to fuck the living hell out of her.

She shoves him on his back. Getting on her knees. Straddling his cock. Taking a deep breath before lowering her soaking wet pussy onto his raging manhood. Exhaling with the sensation of his cock sliding deep insider her. Grabbing his chest and taking him all the way inside. Hearts racing. Wasting no time riding him like a cowgirl. He grabs her ass. Lifting her up and down. Thrusting his cock hard inside her velvety love tunnel. Her juices gushing all over him. Fucking the living hell out of each other like there's no tomorrow. Each experiencing one orgasm after another.

Michael rolls Candi over on her back and gets on top. Sliding his throbbing cock inside her aching wet pussy. Wrapping his arms around her body. Pressing his chest against her tits. Fucking her deep and hard. She wraps her legs around his back. They thrust against each other in unison. Their affections manifesting as volatile penetration. He can't fuck her deep enough. She can't take him deep enough. His cock somehow growing even larger. Her pussy getting even tighter.

Screaming and shouting together. Fucking each other with more and more reckless abandon. Each building closer and closer to an earth-shattering climax. Holding back for as long as they can. No matter how much it hurts. Letting the pressure build as much as they can stand. Until their bodies won't allow for another second of delayed gratification.

"Oh God, Michael!" she screams loud enough for the entire time zone to hear this time while exploding all over him.

"Oh fuck, Candi!" he shouts as his cock erupts deep inside her wanting pussy.

He fills her full of searing hot cum. They scream together. Suffering gladly through the agony of a shared orgasm that feels like it shall never end. And, in that moment, neither wants it to. Gripping each other for dear life. Shaking uncontrollably. Wholly consumed by the sensory overload coming from all directions. Everywhere at once. They maintain this position for what feels like an eternity. Long after the climax has passed. Recovering in silence. Staring into each other's eyes. Part of her wants to stay, but she knows that would only end in heartbreak for both. Their relationship has run its course. Each having to resume their respective life's course in two different directions. That's just the way it is.

"Don't get up," she stands and leans over to kiss him one last time, "Be safe, Mikey."

"I will," he laughs and touches her face, "You be safe too, Candi."

She nods in agreement. He smacks her butt as she turns away. She giggles and walks out of Michael's bedroom. Out of his life forever. The living room is empty now. Its silence deafening while she dresses and packs her things. Turning out the lights and locking the front door behind her. Departing into the darkness on the long drive home. Towards another party and another wild night.

October

Magnum calls it Adult Halloween. The Saturday night before Halloween. When grownups have grownup fun. If they're not being childish. He stands in a nondescript McMansion kitchen on the west side of Little Rock. The home of Janice's sister. Janice being the annoying and pretentious sort of girlfriend he acquired some months back. He's not sure how that happened. It's as if he woke up one morning and there she was. Having attached herself to him in true *Alien* facehugger fashion. She doesn't have a problem with the whole stripping thing. But that alone doesn't justify the relationship.

He's at this Halloween party uncharacteristically early. Unlike the strict punctuality he adheres to with his performances, this is a stark contrast to his trademark fashionable lateness as a party guest. Something he's perfected over the years. Ensuring that his entrance immediately makes him the center of attention. But not tonight as he chills alone in the kitchen. Drinking a beer. Watching Janice run around like a chicken with its head cut off. She and her sister overreacting with unnecessary melodrama to the impending wave of guests. All they'll want to do is drink, converse, and dance. It's not like they'll be moving in or anything.

Magnum is more excited about his bachelorette party in downtown Little Rock in two hours. This night is shaping up to be spooktacularly sexy, Janice notwithstanding. He's currently rocking his Halloween costume. Not so much a costume as it is him getting back to his glam rock roots. Black leather pants, pyramid studs, snakeskin cowboy boots, and a Union Jack t-shirt a la Def Leppard. Rocking mascara and liquid eyeliner. He's always found liquid easier to apply than pencil. Even lines in thirds in the blink of an eye, no pun intended. Totally in his element right now. He's not sure what exactly Janice is supposed to be. Her black dress looks sort of witchy, but she's also wearing some Mardi Gras mask thing. Fuck if he knows. Or cares. He just hopes she doesn't dance tonight. She can't even get that right.

"Ooh… Looks like someone's world is getting rocked tonight," laughs a sexy female voice to his right, "Oh my God. You smell incredible."

As if on cue, Susan makes her entrance with "Don't Cha" by The Pussycat Dolls cranking from the living room. A friend of Janice's sister, this is his first time meeting her. He's seen photos on Myspace. He knows she's hot. But nothing could've prepared him for the real thing. She's minus her husband tonight. Strutting with the newfound freedom of a woman who has mentally and emotionally checked out of her dying marriage. A marriage clearly with a do not resuscitate order. She's not even wearing her ring. The French maid costume leaves nothing to the imagination where her rockin' tits and ass are concerned. And though plenty of guys find Janice attractive, he truly wishes his girlfriend was hot like Susan.

"You have no idea," he flirts right back, "And you can clean up afterward."

"I can, huh?" she sasses, "We'll just see about that."

The mutual attraction is instantaneous. There's no proper introduction. They jump right into conversing about everything and anything. She already knows what he does for a living. Asking him all about it. Intrigued by his profession and all it entails. He gives her the CliffNotes version of performing at bachelorette and birthday parties. She's loving every minute of it. Not only is she showing genuine interest in his work, but she's asking all these questions in a raspy voice that is sexy as all fuck. All smiles and cleavage. Her luscious breasts threatening to pop out at any time. So soft and inviting. He wants her more with every passing second.

"What costume are you wearing to your other party?" she inquires.

"I'm a cop tonight," he nods in a cocksure fashion, "I think I'll be encountering some very naughty girls."

"Oh, and I'm sure you'll have nothing to do with that," she taunts.

"Of course not," he laughs, "I'm innocent and pure."

"I seriously doubt that," she shakes her head, "And I hope you're not."

"Why?" he interrogates with growing curiosity, "Are you a naughty girl?"

"What if I am?" she pushes back, "What would you do to me, officer?"

"I'd make you bend over…" he ups the ante without hesitation, "…and spread 'em, missy"

"Oh, you think so?" she challenges.

"I know so," he doubles down as both are intoxicated with the thrill of the chase.

"Is the seven-layer dip still in the kitchen?" Janice squawks from the dining room.

Her whiny voice drenching Magnum like a bucket of ice water. Breaking the spell as Susan tries not to laugh.

"Why are you wasting your time with her?" Susan asks without opening her mouth. Her eyes say it all. And they tell no lies. He has no logical response to this question. And he knows others are thinking the same thing. Including Candi, who tries her best to be supportive of the whole Janice thing. But always feels his partner in crime shaking her head at him. And despite Janice, he and Candi still have playtime here and there. Janice either being oblivious or looking the other way. He doesn't know which it is. Nor does he care. Besides, it's not like Candi is volunteering for the girlfriend position. Clearly enjoying her freedom. Just as he still does for the most part, even with Janice in tow. Whether it's Candi or someone else. Like say, Susan. Potentially. But she'll have to wait since it's now time for him to get ready for his other party.

"If you'll please excuse me," he explains, "It's time for me to get ready."

"Do you need any help?" she asks impulsively before laughing nervously, "I'm sorry. I…"

"Oh my God!" Janice's shrill voice once again cuts through the air from the dining room, "Where's the chicken spaghetti?"

"Yeah," he whispers, "Follow me."

Magnum and Susan glance towards the dining room to make sure Janice isn't watching before they race upstairs. Quickly. Stealthily. Into the eerie void of the darkness above. Feeling his way down the hallway. Leading his sexy maid by the hand. Into the guestroom where his stripping gear is stashed. He flips on the nightstand lamp. A dim amber glow fills the room. Not giving a second thought while stripping naked before his new friend. She's delightedly caught off guard. Jaw dropped while watching him retrieve a bottle of baby oil from his bag.

"Here," he holds out the bottle towards her, "You can oil my body."

"Ooh… Wait," she begins undressing, "I don't want to get any on my costume."

"Good idea," he's astonished and impressed with her forwardness.

He wonders if she'd be interested in stripping. Momentarily fantasizing about her joining him and Candi for playtime. A man can dream. But in the now, naked Susan takes the bottle from him. She applies a light coat of baby oil to his nude body. Touching him all over with soft and gentle hands. Up one leg. Then the other. Rubbing oil into his arms, shoulders, and back. Taking her time on his ass. Giggling while massaging and squeezing his cheeks.

"Someone's having fun back there," he playfully remarks.

"Just like those girls you're about to go entertain," she sassily retorts, "I'm just getting you warmed up for them."

"Is that what you call it?" he laughs.

"Mmm-hmm…" she coos before moving to face him.

She gazes into his eyes while oiling his chest and abs. Biting her lip. He feels her hands grip his hard cock. Stroking his shaft back and forth with lubricated hands. Smiling from the sensation of feeling him grow larger. He places his hands on her ass. Squeezing her bare cheeks. Slightly cold to the touch.

"Someone's ass needs warming," he informs her

"Then I guess you'd better warm it for me," she smiles seductively while continuing to stroke his manhood.

They continue this way for a few more seconds. But it feels like an eternity. One that neither wants to see end. They're on the verge of fucking. If not for his impending professional commitment. Finally breaking free from each other. She watches intently as he dresses in his cop costume. More curious than ever now about all things Magnum. Watching as he checks himself in the mirror. Packing his things. Getting ready to head out.

"Good luck," she throws her hands around his neck and kisses him, "Hurry back."

"Thank you," he fights to stay focused on the task at hand, "I will."

Still naked as she watches him exit the room. He moves quickly down the stairs and out the front door to avoid Janice. Encouraging as she may be, there's no way in hell she can top the send-off that Susan gave him. One that is perfect for getting into character on the drive downtown. The cool October air provides him with a much-needed smack in the face. Getting him focused on the task at hand. Making his bachelorette's last night of freedom one she'll never forget. And for all the right reasons.

"I wanna taste you but your lips are venomous poison," Alice Cooper snarls as Magnum races across Little Rock on I-630 towards downtown. Its illuminated skyline beckoning him. Surrounded by the ugly brutality of concrete barriers. The night oozes devious energy. He can feel it. Growing ever closer with the shadow of each overpass under which he crosses. Taking the Broadway exit. Past closed banks and open fast-food restaurants. Towards the hotel just before the river. His party girls awaiting his arrival from their presidential suite.

The underground parking garage is empty. Consistent traffic above assuring he hasn't stepped into an eighties Italian post-apocalyptic film. Much to his partial disappointment. His steps echo as he struts through another concrete jungle. Towards the elevator. Waiting in anticipation. Reflecting in his own reflection. Riding it to the top where his party girls are cocked, locked, and ready to rock. Him too upon reaching their floor. Using his lust for Susan for additional motivation. His client, Nicole, giddy as all fuck while meeting him in the hallway. She's motivated by his authoritative sexiness and her tipsiness.

"We're ready," she giggles through excitement and embarrassment, "Kirsten's a little tipsy."

"Sounds good," he nods, "I'll be on your tail."

"Ooh… I can't wait." she hurries back to the suite as he touches up his cologne and gets his music ready.

"Police!" he pounds on the door, "Open up!"

Nicole opens the door. Magnum is barely inside when Kirsten runs and jumps into his arms.

"Oh my God!" his bachelorette exclaims, "Mmm… You smell incredible!"

And before he knows it, Magnum is tearing up the presidential suite under cover of disco lights. "Na NaNa Na" by Nelly thumping forth.

Straddling his handcuffed and delightfully hysterical bachelorette. Dry humping the fuck out of her. Exclamations of shock and awe filling his ears. Alcohol and Reddi-wip flows. Doing shots with his party girls. Off their bodies and his. Licking whipped cream from cleavage and thighs. The feel of their soft, smooth skin electric on his tongue. They return the favor off his ass and nipples. Moving from one girl to the next.

Until it's down to him and Diana. A little older yet aging like a fine wine. Her fake titties ready to burst from a half-unbuttoned white blouse. Begging to be kissed, licked, and sucked. Totally money well spent as she has every reason to be proud of them. Along with the obvious aesthetic value provided, this confidence-building physical enhancement brings out her other amazing qualities in full force. Charisma, charm, sassiness, and undeniable warmth. He drops to his knees before her chair. Applying an ample amount of Reddi-wip deep within the valley between her saline peaks. Steadying himself with one hand on each of her breasts. Burying his face between them. Taking his sweet ass time while looking into her eyes. She responds by shoving a twenty deep inside the right cup of her bra. He attempts to retrieve it with his mouth but to no avail. Although he does manage to lick her nipple. Gently swirling his tongue around it. Pretending this show of affection is unintentional. Kirsten's excited and intrigued face up close to the action.

"Did you get it?" Diana asks.

"I only succeeded in licking your nipple," he admits in defeat.

"Exactly," she sasses.

"You should totally bust out the girls and let him suck them," Kirsten's inner voyeur now out in full force.

"Oh, I don't know…" Diana mocks hesitation.

"Stop it," Kirsten interrupts, "You show them to us all the time. We've all touched them. Might as well let Magnum have fun with them too."

The other girls voice concurrence in varying states of intoxication. It's all the motivation Diana needs. Unbuttoning and removing her blouse. Magnum wastes no time reaching behind her. Unclasping her bra one-handed. Her girls magnificent in their newfound freedom. He sprays whipped cream on her nipples. Licking it off. Flicking his tongue over each one. Sucking her expensive titties. His cock rock hard. Throbbing in glorious agony. Her hands on his head. Holding his face tight against her breasts. He's in heaven. Nearly oblivious to her moaning and the girlish shrieks all around him.

Magnum stands and Diana frees his raging cock from its g-string prison. Her spectacular titties demanding to be fucked. He slides his aching manhood between them. Coating her girls with an endless wave of precum. She takes him in her mouth. Savoring his warm juices. The other girls gathered around in unbridled enthusiasm. Kirsten's face as close to the action as she can get without joining in. All eyes upon them. The air filled with screams and relentless crunk beats. His eyes on Diana while she moves her tongue around the head of his cock. So soft and wet. He squeezes her tits. Massaging her nipples with his thumbs. "Get Low" fills his ears. She stands, spins him around, and pushes him into the chair. Lil Jon and the Eastside Boys with him saying, "And we all like to see ass and titties."

Diana now delivers on the former. Slowing removing her skintight jeans. Dancing for Magnum. Commando tonight. Going for broke. Grinding her bare ass on his cock. Working it between her firm, round cheeks. Teasing him with her asshole. "But we just met," he can't help but think. Fuck it. He'll just go with it. Spanking and squeezing her bouncy cheeks. Kirsten joins him in spanking her friend.

"You are being very naughty, Diana," Kirsten laughs.

"You know you like it," Diana scoffs playfully.

"I do," Kirsten concedes, "So does Magnum."

"Fuck yeah!" he slaps Diana's butt again.

"Oh, whatever," Diana laughs, "I'm sure this is every night for him."

"Not even close," he assures her, "There's no one like you."

"Aww…" Diana turns around. Straddling him. Lowering her soaking wet pussy onto his massive cock until he's deep inside her. Riding him like a cowgirl whose heart is a rodeo of pure decadence. He bucks and thrusts hard within her tight sugar walls. Gripping her waist. Lifting her up and down. Her hands on his shoulders. His expression surely matching the fierce animalistic one she rocks. Wrapping her arms around his neck. Pressing her tits against his face. Smothering him with her breasts. Fucking each other deep and hard. Her pussy gushing and squirting more and more.

"Oh God!" Diana shouts, "I'm cumming."

"Do it!" he commands, "Cum with me."

"Yeah!" Kirsten slaps her ass, "Cum with Magnum!"

Hysterical laughter at the bachelorette's adorable antics compliments the moaning and screaming. His cock growing even larger. Her pussy even tighter. He pumps her ever harder. Ever Deeper. His body consumed with shaking and tingling. Hers too. Both truly living in the moment with their spontaneous lovemaking. Losing themselves within its embrace. Drunk upon the wild party atmosphere all around them. Taking it all in. Fucking faster and faster. Keeping it going for as long as they can. Until they can hold back no longer. He fills her pussy with wave after wave of hot cum. Making her scream loud enough to wake the entire hotel.

"Holy fuck!" Kirsten exclaims, "This is the best bachelorette party ever!"

The other girls give Magnum and Diana a standing ovation. They hold each other momentarily while catching their breath. Breathing turns to laughter at what they've just done in a roomful of girls. She stands and takes his hand. Leading him to the bathroom. He breaks protocol and removes his cowboy boots at a party. Multicolored disco lights trickling from the living room. The other girls crowd inside. Watching intently as Magnum and Diana step into the shower.

"We've got to get you all squeaky clean before sending you back to your Halloween party," Diana proclaims.

She lathers up her big, wet titties. Rubbing them all over his naked body. Repeating the process with her butt. Grinding her soapy ass on his cock. He lathers up her pussy. Teasing her clit. Sliding his middle finger inside. Massaging her g-spot. Kissing her. The other girls cheering them on. He leans down. Sucking her tits while fingering her pussy. Making her tremble and moan. Bringing her to another orgasm. Laughing together at their antics. Their audience shrieking with pleasant disbelief over the entire series of events.

The other girls dry off Magnum and Diana. Everyone returns to the living room. He dresses and packs his things. Watching with a tinge of melancholy as Diana gets dressed. He'll never see her naked again. Or clothed for that matter. That's the business. He and his party girls chatting away as if nothing out of the ordinary has happened. Just like any other party. And what happens at the bachelorette party stays at the bachelorette party. He's elated enough on the surface about enjoying another successful performance. But even more so over getting laid on Halloween night. As well as over not having to fuck Janice to make that happen.

"Thank you so much for coming," Nicole hugs him, "That was… Amazing!"

"Thank you for having me," he laughs, "You are all amazing."

"Yes, we are," Kirsten embraces him, "And so are you," kissing him on the cheek.

"Yeah," he playfully taunts, "You're okay yourself."

"Oh, whatever," Kirsten laughs.

"He knows better than that," Diana presses her tits against his chest one last time.

"I do," he squeezes her girls one last time, "Have a good night, everyone. Be safe."

Magnum's party girls wish him the same. Watching him exit the suite. Out of their lives forever. He's now but a memory for them. One that will grow ever distant over time. He ponders this on the elevator ride down to the garage. Walking back to his car. Getting back on the road. Shifting gears as his thoughts shift back to Susan. That amazing Diana action aside, he's raring to go. Racing back to West Little Rock and the Halloween party. Back to Susan. Hoping his new friend is still there. Even though he just got some, he's enamored with the idea of making that naughty French maid his main course for tonight. Wanting her so badly he can taste her. But how far is she willing to go? He'll find out soon enough.

Vehicles line either side of the street upon his return to the Halloween party. Requiring him to park several houses away. He walks with anticipation. Past one cookie-cutter house after another. The sounds of people on the back deck growing louder with every step he takes closer to his destination. Closer to the party. Closer to Susan. Wondering if she's still there. If she still wants to converse with him. And more, perhaps? Despite his general success with women, he never gets too cocky about pursuing any girl. Knowing it takes two to tango. That he must prove himself to her equally as she must to him. Not allowing confidence to slip into hubris. Each chase feeling like his first.

And he's intoxicated by the thrill of this chase upon reentering via the garage. Through the kitchen to grab a cup of punch. Past multiple conversations occurring simultaneously and into the living room. Illuminated with the sort of multicolored disco lighting he just left behind. Not excusing or explaining why Panic! at the Disco is playing. Fuck it. He'll blame Janice for that. Her annoying voice drifting in from outside. Blabbing about paper mache or something. Meanwhile, no one in the living room is dancing, because of course they aren't. He cuts through the crowd to find Susan on the sofa. Back in her French maid costume. Instantly breaking from her current conversation upon seeing him approach. Excitement and curiosity splashed across her face.

"So, how did it go?" she inquires.

"Another smashing success," he crashes next to her.

"Did you give them lap dances?" she asks with curiosity and intrigue.

"Of course," he nods matter of factly, "So, did I miss anything?"

"Not really. Just a lot of eating, drinking, and talking," she laughs and plays with her hair, "I'm sure you had a more exciting time."

"Yeah, you should've been there," he teases, "We could've put on one hell of a show together. The cop and the naughty French maid."

"Oh my God," her face lights up even more, "That would've been amazing."

"Well… Maybe I could've sold them on that," he playfully lectures, "But no. You had to wait until tonight to introduce yourself to me."

"I know," she sasses, "I just fucked up everything."

"That's right, missy," his primal instinct takes over, "Maybe I just need to fuck you up."

"Ooh…" she giggles through shock and awe, "Maybe you should, mister."

They sit in silence. Lost in each other's bedroom eyes. Adrenaline pumping through their bodies. Awash with excitement and nerves. He feels his hand instinctively reaching for hers. Sliding along her bare leg. Silky smooth. Ready to lead her back upstairs. Back to their guestroom hideaway. To finish what they started earlier. Eager to fully explore their mutual lust. To know each other intimately. Seeking comfort together from the storms of dysfunctional relationships. Both deserving better. Both finally realizing it.

"Oh my God!" Janice drunkenly breaks the spell, "You're back already? So… how was the… um… you know… the thing?"

"You mean the party?" he sighs in frustration as Susan tries not to laugh, "It went well."

"I'm so glad," Janice slurs obnoxiously, "You… um… I should give you a lap dance later."

"Yeah, I'll keep that in mind," he pretends to hear something, "I think your sister is calling for you."

"Really?" she turns and stumbles away, "Hey, sis!"

"Fuck me," he sinks back into the sofa and slams the rest of his punch before looking at Susan barely containing her laughter.

"I'm so sorry," she apologizes, "I know I'm being impolite."

"Not at all," he assures her, "I know what everyone's thinking about us."

"Believe me," she touches his hand, "I'm in the same boat right now."

"Oh God," he shakes his head, "I just hope she forgets about wanting to give me a lap dance tonight."

"Is it that bad?" she asks, "I'm sorry. That's none of my business."

"Don't be," he laughs, "It's one of the most disturbing things you'll ever see."

"So, how did you do it? What are your lap dances like?" she pushes coyly, "Maybe you can show me sometime."

Always one to up the ante, he heads for the kitchen. Returning with a chair from the breakfast table. Setting it in the center of the living room. Curiosity takes hold of the other guests. Instinctively gathering around. Gripped with anticipation. Wondering to what debauchery they're about to bear witness. Susan too, as Magnum takes her by the hand. Leading her to the nearly anointed hot seat. Making her sit. Searching through the mix CD on the stereo until locating a suitable track. "Pussy Control" by Prince cuts through the night along with a chorus of cheers and gasps while he straddles his sexy new friend.

Magnum grinds on Susan's lap with undisputed authority. Owning his audience and object of affection like any paid gig. Her face glowing with elation. He slides down her body. Rubbing his face in her titties while they threaten to explode from her costume. Standing and stepping back. Falling forward. Face between her thighs. Feeling the heat of her pussy. Pulling himself up until they're face to face. Nose to nose. Her arms around his neck. Laughing together at their antics. Consumed with the thrill of being showered with oohs and ahhs. She learns and embraces the adulation he experiences night after night. Letting herself go as he leads the way.

"Oh my God! You're so amazing!" Janice spews forth loudly and obnoxiously, "That's my boyfriend, everyone!"

Magnum tries not to cringe while once again dropping to his knees. Between Susan's legs. Rising slowly. Her calves on his shoulders. Rubbing his leather-clad cock against her wet silk panties. Making him harder. Making her tighter. An array of colors splashing across their faces. Glaring at each other intently. Overcome by animalism of the wildest variety. Provoking displays of shock and amazement beyond everyone's wildest imagination. He's just that fucking good. And so is she. Figuratively fucking before a live audience. They can't help themselves. They won't. It's now or ever once the song reaches its abrupt and fateful conclusion. The moment of carnal truth upon them.

The party immediately resumes its regularly scheduled programming. People eating, drinking, and chatting up a storm about every topic imaginable. From Jesus to black metal. There's nothing left for Magnum and Susan to do at this point but sneak upstairs. Looking at each other knowingly. Everything tonight building to this moment in time. Taking her hand in his. Looking around before leading her into the darkness above. Beginning their escape upstairs when someone yells his name. He looks back to see a douchebag friend of Janice's brother-in-law named Rusty, because of course his name is Rusty, having planted himself in the hot seat.

"Hey, where's my lap dance?" he drunkenly asks while looking directly at Magnum, who's ready to kill this motherfucker for both thwarting his getaway with Susan and being a creep.

Everyone now stares at Magnum and Susan standing at the foot of the staircase. But an unexpected savior emerges. Janice rushes over to Rusty. Giving him the low-end gentlemen's club treatment with the most God-awful lap dance imaginable. Looking like she's struggling to remain seated upon a galloping horse. A fucking disturbing spectacle if there ever was. Set to some Third Eye Blind song totally inappropriate for a party. Much less a lap dance. The audience so enthusiastic for glam rocker and French maid seconds earlier now groans and chuckles uncomfortably at this travesty of sexual expression. Serving Rusty right. Once again proving that one must be careful what one asks for lest he gets it.

All eyes now off Magnum and Susan making their clandestine journey upstairs. Hand in hand. Hearts racing in anticipation. The world around them growing darker until they reach the blackened hallway. Taking solace within the guestroom he commandeered earlier in the night. Locking the door behind them. Where it all began with her oiling his naked body. Once again embraced by the dim amber glow of the nightstand lamp. "Smack That" by Akon blasting downstairs. She giggles when he smacks her bubble butt. Grabbing her hips. Dancing with her arms around his neck. Slowly. Sensually. Once again lost in each other's eyes.

"What about Janice?" she asks.

"I'm as concerned with her right now as you are with your husband," he responds.

Susan gives Magnum a look that says touché before he pulls her tight against him. Pressing his lips against hers. Opening their mouths simultaneously. Tongues dancing. He could devour her right now. It's exactly what he needs. Even after the excitement at the bachelorette party. And despite everything he gave earlier to Diana, he's totally hot to go with Susan. She's gunning to rock his world right back. Embracing her newfound liberation. Making him finally realize he doesn't need to keep someone around who's not up to par. Both wanting and needing each other like nothing else in this moment.

They continue kissing and dancing. He unzips her French maid costume from the back. Pulling it over her shoulders. Letting it fall to the floor. She steps out. Clad only in black pumps and white silk panties. Her luscious titties pressed against his chest. So warm and comforting against his skin. Squeezing her body tighter against his. She responds in kind and they laugh. Moving his face to her neck. Kissing and caressing her skin. So soft and sweet. And smelling incredible. She does the same to him. Her lips and tongue sending chills all over his body. Holding onto her. Allowing her heat to radiate through him. She does the same with him. Trembling and breathing heavily together. Totally consumed by the thrill of their cheating ways.

"Oh God, Magnum," she sighs, "Are we really doing this?"

"Mmm-hmm, Susan," he whispers in her ear before licking it, "Are you scared?"

"Kind of," she admits breathlessly, "And I love it," she pauses, "Are you?"

"Not at all," he slides his hands down the rear of her panties and squeezes her bare ass, "I want you."

"Ooh…" she giggles, "Then take me."

"Oh, you're getting taken," he slides his right middle finger inside her pussy, "Whether you like it or not."

"I want it," she shudders in ecstasy, "More than you can imagine."

He takes her right breast in his mouth. Tongue swirling on her nipple. Flicking rapidly. Sucking hard as she wraps her arms around his head. Holding him tightly. Breathing even heavier now. Moaning softly. He moves to her left breast. Still fingering her pussy. Massaging her g-spot. Making her wetter. Making her tighter. Bringing her shaking body to orgasm.

"Oh God!" she pushes him and yanks off his shirt, "Your turn."

She moves back and forth between his muscular pectorals. Her warm wet tongue magic on his skin. She opens his black leather pants. Unleashing his raging cock. Gripping it tightly. Stroking it vigorously while licking and sucking his nipples. His juices gushing onto her hand. Making his entire body tingle. Tasting her sweetness upon his finger. Now he must savor it firsthand.

"My turn again," he drops to his knees and pulls down her panties.

She's now totally naked except for the pumps. Wasting no time as he draws circles upon her clit with his tongue. Slowly. Gently. She can barely stand. Putting her hands on his shoulders.

"Fuck yes," she whispers through anguished breaths, "Eat my pussy, baby."

"Mmm-hmm…" he pushes her back onto the bed. Spreading her legs. Devouring her sweet pussy. Licking and sucking her clit. Pulling on her sweet lips. She lies back. Placing her hands on the back of his head. His tongue penetrating her. Exploring deep inside her velvety sugar walls. Consuming her warm sweet girl juices. Gushing forth into his wanting mouth. She grabs a pillow and bites it. Fighting to stay quiet. Her moans grow louder. Turning into screams of agonizing delight. Grinding her pussy on his face. Shaking uncontrollably as he brings her to another orgasm.

"Oh, fuck me!" she gasps between clenched teeth. "I have to taste your cock."

She has his pants off before he knows what's happening. Ready to go down on him. But he's not done eating her pussy. Compromising as he lies down. She crawls on top. Her mouth like velvet. So warm, wet, and soft. Taking his cock all the way down her throat. She has him so fucking big and hard. Throbbing like crazy. His juices flowing relentlessly into her eager mouth. And hers into his as he continues licking her pussy. His tongue effortlessly sliding deep inside her from this angle. Lifting his head slightly to tease her tight butthole. Pressing his tongue inside. So sweet like the rest of her. She's pleasantly shocked. Moaning on his cock. Her tongue swirling around his head and shaft. Making him buck his hips. Fucking her face. She grips his manhood tightly. Stroking him once again while licking and sucking his balls. Giggling in ecstasy from the sensation of his finger sliding in and out of her asshole while he sucks her delicate lips.

Magnum can't wait a second longer. Rolling Susan on her back. Pouncing on top as she spreads her legs. Sliding his massive cock deep inside her swollen pussy. Wrapping his arms around her hot, naked body. His chest pressed tight against her titties. Thrusting deeply and powerfully. Kissing like there's no tomorrow. Fighting back the moans and screams building within them. Fucking harder and faster. Growing closer to mutual climax. All he can feel is her soft skin against his naked body. Caressing each other from head to toe. Enveloping each other. Her legs wrapped around his back. Hanging on for dear life. Her pussy can't take his cock any deeper, yet he can't fuck her deep enough.

"Oh my God!" she exclaims in a hushed cry, "Your cock feels amazing in my pussy."

"Baby," he shouts between clenched teeth, "Your pussy is out of this fucking world."

"You're out of this world," she coos.

"So are you," he kisses her insatiably.

"Hey… Magnum!" Janice screeches from the hallway, "Are you up here?"

Magnum and Susan look at each other. Struggling to hold back their laughter. Instead of stopping, he places his hand over her mouth. Fucking her even harder now. His frustrations with Janice boiling over. Taking them out on Susan in the sexiest way imaginable. And she's not complaining. Pulling him inside deeper with her legs.

"Magnum! Are you in here?" Janice whines as she tries opening the door, "Who's in here?"

Magnum and Susan cover each other's mouth while fucking even more viciously. Thrusting hard with reckless abandon. She thinks of her own situation. Taking out her frustrations on him in turn. Pounding her pussy against his pelvis. Determined to milk his cock empty insider her. The sensation of her gushing and squirting pushing him over the edge. It's all too fucking much and they explode together. Her pussy unleashing a tidal wave of hot juices all over him. His cock filling her with an endless flood of hot, sticky cum. Biting their tongues. Fighting in vain to keep this between them. Holding each other for what feels like an eternity. Recovering from their sexplosion in silence until they hear Janice retreat downstairs.

"Oh wow!" Susan exclaims.

"That's right," he nods, "You are so oh wow."

"Nope, it's you," she sasses.

"It's you too," he assures her.

"I probably got you in trouble," she second-guesses herself.

"Not at all," he stops her, "I have to make some drastic changes in my life."

"Me too," she concedes.

They dress in silence. Not because of shame or regret. Rather because it feels right in the moment. And that's exactly what they have done tonight. Gone with what feels right in the moment. Nothing more. Nothing less. Taking solace together. Each helping the other realize they're too good for the person with whom each is currently wasting time. And life is too short for that, they now both realize. The party downstairs is still hopping. But the night is over for these two crazy kids. He takes her in his arms one last time. Kissing her goodnight. And goodbye. Forever. Their whirlwind romance lasting only a few hours, yet setting each on a new course headed towards a point of welcomed no return.

"Goodnight, Susan," he looks deep into her eyes, "Watch out for g-g-ghosts."

"I will," she flashes that playful and seductive smile he'll never forget, "Goodnight, Magnum."

With Susan heading downstairs five minutes before Magnum, he has time to think. That's to be expected following two amazing sexual encounters with two wonderful girls on the same night. Each special in her own way. And then it hits him during this moment of post-sex clarity. He doesn't need to waste another second with Janice. Starting now. He can just sneak downstairs and outside. Never speaking to her again. And that's what he does. Rushing past heavily intoxicated partygoers before they know what's happening. Turning off his phone and getting into his car for the drive home. Janice's free ride with Magnum stops here. Her moment in the sun now officially over. And he has no reason to feel guilty about it.

The Interstate is emptier now but alive as ever. Alice Cooper's "He's Back (The Man Behind the Mask)" serenades the drive home. And just like Alice and Jason Voorhees, Magnum really is back. It was always business as usual. But a major distraction was present. A miscalculation in judgment on his part. As much shit as he gives Janice, the fact remains that he allowed it to happen. But then he never would've met Susan. Her sweetness still fresh on his lips. Signaling that it's time for him to not merely sell hedonism to his audiences. But to embrace his own inner hedonist. To spread his wings of debauchery and soar majestically. All that he wants to experience and explore will be his one of these nights.

February

Candi waits. Surrounded by fresco paintings of windows simulating the feel of being in a Tuscan village square. Tawny marble columns rise from the floor as sure as Kilimanjaro rises like Olympus above the Serengeti. Blonde ceiling arches support chandeliers striking the right balance between clarity and ambiance. The dining room a sea of white tablecloths adorned with Italian cuisine along with glasses of red and white wine. Complimented by a symphony of clinking, chatter, and more in the spirit of John Cage's "4'33". A balcony overlooks it all. But not tonight. Screened off from the world below. A private refuge for the sapphic audience whose world Candi is about to rock. Unbeknownst to the diners all around her on this Friday night in February.

A brisk and clear night while she made the hour drive from Little Rock to Hot Springs, Arkansas. The gorgeous natural aesthetics of U.S. 70 apparent even in darkness. Winding upward through an ocean of majestic trees into Hot Springs National Park. The eastern gateway to Ouachita National Forest. Electricity was already in the air as she cruised Central Ave for a parking spot. As she strutted down the sidewalk towards her destination. Past the neon glow of restaurants, bars, and hotels bristling with life. It's the day after Valentine's Day, but many have opted to celebrate tonight instead. She found her client waiting underneath a burgundy awning sheltering a stone veneered entrance. Candi was asked to give her audience five minutes before making her grand entrance upstairs. That was three minutes ago. And so, she waits.

Candi is excited about tonight. Excited about being in Hot Springs and making some money at the same time. It's a fun place. Wishing she had someone to hit the town with after the party. And excited about the party itself. Patty, the client, having booked Candi for her wife's fiftieth birthday party. An intimate affair comprising two other middle-aged lesbian couples and one twentysomething straight girl. To hear the client say it, this should be a lively and generous audience. And this allows Candi to explore her own sapphic tendencies. Having played with fellow female strippers at bachelor parties before as well as curious women at other events. Not that she's expecting anything too wild but ready to rock with an all-girl audience.

Showtime arrives, and Candi climbs a dark and narrow staircase. Stripping bag in one hand. Audio system in the other. The world around her growing strangely quieter with each step. "Are they up here?" she wonders upon reaching the balcony. Removing her jogging suit to reveal a zebra print g-string and bikini top. Replacing her athletic shoes with clear acrylic platforms. Covering herself with a sheer black babydoll lingerie dress. Stepping quietly towards the screened-off portion. The people below oblivious to the scantily clad beauty above them while she rounds the corner and catches her audience by welcome surprise.

"Oh my God!" a cute and perky woman, who's clearly the straight girl being the only one around Candi's age, gushes with unbridled enthusiasm.

"Happy birthday, baby," Patty kisses Marcie.

"What have you done?" Marcie laughs while looking at Candi with embarrassment.

Patty introduces the other women. Including April, the lone straight girl. Nervous anticipation fills the air when Candi hits play. "Girls Girls Girls" permeates the immediate area. Just loud enough to not attract the curiosity of diners below. She approaches her birthday girl. Slowly. Seductively. Straddling her. Hips gyrating. Rubbing her tits on Marcie. Gazing into her eyes.

"Can I touch you?" Marcie asks meekly.

"Of course you can touch her," April states matter of factly as laughter ensues.

"I just want to be polite," Marcie explains.

Candi smiles while taking her birthday girl's hands and placing them on her bare thighs.

"You are so sweet to do this," Marcie informs her with sincerity.

"It's fun," Candi confides, "And I like girls too."

"See?" April points out, "There you go."

Everyone laughs again. Candi smiles at April. Appreciating her smartass rhetoric that's helping Marcie and the other guests to relax. Plus, she's hot. Making Candi enamored with her. Curious about her. Wanting to see how far she's willing to go. This gets Candi's motor running. Amping up her performance by removing her babydoll dress. Holding it up with one hand before letting it fall to the floor. Standing and dropping forward. Her face landing in Marcie's lap. Tossing her hair around as she mimics eating her birthday girl's pussy. Rising slowly until they're face to face. Both giggling when she stands, turns, and shakes her g-string clad booty in Marcie's face.

"Oh lord," Marcie laments.

"Spank her ass," April demands to more laughs.

Candi bends over and touches her toes. Wiggling her bubble butt. Asking to be spanked. Marcie overcomes her shyness and gives Candi a light smack while everyone cheers.

"No, no, no," April stands and rushes towards them, "You have to do it like this," giving Candi a firm spanking on both cheeks before squeezing them as the others watch in shocked amusement.

"I swear," Marcie shakes her head, "You straight girls are far quicker to feel up one another than we are."

"Hey," April retorts, "Hot is hot."

Candi removes her bikini top and drapes it around April's neck.

"Woo hoo!" April returns to her seat, "Got me a trophy!"

Everyone laughs harder while Candi turns to shake her girls in her birthday girl's face.

"Ooh…" Marcie compliments with a hint of sass as she comes out of her shell, "Very pretty."

"Thank you," Candi smiles, "Here, get a closer look."

She smothers Marcie's face with her pretty titties. Shaking them while moving her hips. Reaching into her bag for a can of Reddi-wip. Everyone watching in anticipation as Candi applies whipped cream to her nipples. Inviting Marcie and Patty to suck them clean together. They look at each other. Summoning the nerve to indulge Candi. Each overcoming her embarrassment long enough to give into decadence. Quickly licking the Reddi-wip from her nipples with reserved yet sincere encouragement from the other two couples. And highly enthusiastic support from April. These two may not be Candi's type. Regardless, she embraces the thrill of having two women sucking her breasts at once.

"Hells yeah!" April shouts, "Suck those titties!"

"I'm about to smack you, April," Marcie nearly chokes on Reddi-wip, "Behave yourself."

"Do not get us thrown out of here," Patty laughingly scolds.

Candi makes her lap dance rounds. Beginning with the client before moving onto the other couples. Each woman being shy to some degree, albeit friendly and receptive. Complimenting Candi on her looks, moves, and entertaining prowess. Quickly filling her g-string with cash. Then again after she empties it. And again. She's happy. They may not be the wildest audience she's ever entertained, but she appreciates their kindness and generosity. There have been worse audiences for sure. Both male and female. She's happy to have made the acquaintance of this fun group of women. Especially April.

"Oh yeah! Bring it over here, sweet cheeks," April orders while holding up the Reddi-wip, "I'm ready for you. Get it?"

The other women groan as Candi straddles April. "Same Ol' Situation" by Mötley Crüe plays. Candi's pussy begins tingling. Growing tight and wet. She's fond of all her party girls, but April is special. Now deciding she would totally fuck her if afforded the opportunity. This may be the closest that comes to happening. Every second counts. Demanding to be savored. Her own anticipation kicking in. Watching April decorate her tits with ample amounts of whipped cream. Ecstatic about feeling this sexy and silly girl's warm mouth on her breasts.

"See?" April announces, "This is how it's done.".

She takes Candi's right breast in her mouth. Licking and sucking her nipple long after the Reddi-wip is gone. Repeating with the left breasts. Squeezing Candi's ass with both hands all the while and purring exaggerated, "Mmm…" sounds. The other women laughing and cheering out of both amusement and shock. Candi's pussy getting wetter with each passing second. Imagining that April's is too. The thought of tasting this girl's juices makes her own flow even more. Hoping she doesn't notice her g-string is soaked. Or maybe hoping she does notice. It all feels so dangerous. And she can't get enough of this wicked sensation.

"Come here, baby," April pulls Candi's head down and kisses her. Pushing her tongue past Candi's lips along with the whipped cream still in her mouth. Candi swallows it while sliding her tongue inside April's mouth as they kiss aggressively. Mutual giggling overcomes them. They break their oral embrace. April shoves dollars into Candi's g-string. Working her way around before sticking a twenty down the front.

"Oh my God, her pussy is so wet," April looks at everyone else, "You all got her ready for me."

Now it's Candi's turn to be embarrassed. The other women already at a loss for words as April rubs Candi's pussy through her wet g-string. Then slowly licking her fingers for all to see.

"Mmm, she's so sweet," April coos and makes Candi's pussy even wetter while every other woman's jaw drop.

"April!" Marcie scolds, "Behave yourself!"

"I can't help it," April motions for Candi to turn around, "Look at this sexy ass."

April applies a line of Reddi-wip to each cheek. Squeezing them tight. Licking up each one before delivering a firm slap. Candi's pussy gushing even more. Her g-string now totally drenched.

"Okay, let's hear it for Candi," Patty leads everyone in applauding her performance.

"Thank you so much," Candi takes a bow, "You were all incredible."

"Thank you," Marcie hugs Candi and kisses her on the cheek, "You're amazing."

"Thank you for doing this," Patty adds, "You totally made her night. And everyone else's."

"Don't mention it," Candi hugs her, "I'm so glad you booked me. You're all lots of fun."

"That's right," April sasses as she hugs April before kissing her on the mouth, "We're all sorts of fun."

"Okay, April. Give the woman some space," Patty orders before turning back to Candi, "It's been a long day for us. Driving here all the way from Memphis. So, we're heading out now. We'll let the staff know you're still up here. That'll give you some privacy to get dressed."

"I really appreciate that," Candi says, "Have a great night."

"You too," Patty replies, "Be safe driving back to Little Rock."

"I will," Candi assures her.

Candi exchanges goodnights with the other women before they head around the corner and downstairs. This small alcove of debauchery now almost eerie without her party girls. Without April and her sexy antics. The things Candi would've done with her given the chance. She removes her platforms and soaked g-string. Going commando as she puts on jeans, a black lowcut t-shirt, and black cowgirl boots. Collecting her things and tips. Throwing on her black leather jacket and heading downstairs. Walking briskly outside and into the night. Turning to the left and heading for her car.

"Hey, Candi," April's voice cuts through the cool late-winter air.

"What's up?" Candi turns to face her next to the restaurant entrance, "I thought you all split."

"The old ones did," April laughs, "The night is young, and so am I," she pauses, "Can I buy you a drink? I mean, unless you need to go. I understand if you do…"

"I'd like that," Candi interrupts, "Let's find a place."

"Okay," April lights up, "Um… Great."

April follows Candi back to her car, where she stashes her gear in the trunk before they walk further up the block. Arriving at a small bar with pool tables and perhaps the world's tiniest dance floor. They sit at a table in the middle of the club against a red brick veneer and order drinks.

"Hey, um…" April stammers, "I want to apologize if I went too far before. You know… um… I may have had some bad wine, I think…"

"Not at all," Candi laughs, "It was my show. You did all those things because I allowed and encouraged you too. And I enjoyed it."

"Oh, I'm glad," Aprils sighs in relief, "I just got caught up in the moment. I'd never done anything like that before. You know, with a girl."

"It's okay," Candi pats her hand, "You don't have to explain it to me. I've been there."

They pause as the waitress serves their drinks.

"I think you shocked the hell out of your friends," Candi laughs.

"Not at all," April explains, "They loved it. They're my friends, and I love them. They've been so good to me. It was fun to put on a show for them. They know how outlandish I can be. You know? It probably would've been strange to them if I hadn't done something like that. I don't know if that makes any sense," she pauses to take a sip of her drink, "And I enjoyed the chance to play a little with another girl. It's something I've wanted to do for a long time, but it's hard to know who to approach."

"Oh, I know," Candi assures her, "It's hard enough to find a girl you're attracted to. Then you worry about whether they'll be offended if you approach them. Or think you're a lesbian."

"Exactly," April nods, "It's like, I love cock and wouldn't give it up for anything, but sometimes I just want to be sensual with someone pretty. You know?"

"Believe me, I do," Candi agrees.

"You know what?" April opines, "I just need to find a pretty boy who's sensual and has a huge cock."

"Absolutely," Candi concurs as they giggle and clink their glasses, "Actually, I know someone like that."

"Really?" April asks intently, "Don't hold out on me."

"It's the owner of my stripping agency," Candi pauses to take a long sip, "He's so incredibly hot. And a tremendous entertainer. We perform together sometimes."

"Ooh, I'll bet that's wild," April suggests.

"It really is," Candi continues.

"So, are you two like a couple?" April inquires, "Forgive me if I'm prying."

"I wouldn't call it that," Candi pauses for another long sip, "He's already married to this business. Which is a good thing for all of us financially. You know, for someone as attractive, intelligent, and confident as he is, I think he sells himself short in many ways. Especially in his personal life. Or what little personal life he allows himself to have."

"I've known men like him," April confides, "Everything a girl might want yet unavailable to us," she pauses and looks around the bar, "But there's no shortage of losers. I hate to sound mean. But look around us."

"Oh, I know exactly what you're saying," Candi monitors the patrons, "There isn't a single guy in here right now who gets my motor running," she places her hand on April's knee and whispers in her ear, "But you totally get my motor running," before licking it.

"Ooh…" April trembles and sighs, "I can't believe you're doing this right here."

"So what?" Candi shrugs, "Let these clowns think we're a couple of lipstick lesbians they can never have. It'll serve them right for being so fucking lame. Letting two hot girls in their midst go unsatisfied," she slides her hand up April's leg, "Did you like the taste of my pussy on your fingers?"

"Mmm-hmm…" April barely manages past her lips as Candi rubs her pussy through her jeans, "Will you teach me?"

"I'll teach you by showing you," Candi kisses her lips.

She takes April by the hand and they stand to leave. Walking past the sorriest excuse for a dance floor ever when "Pussy Control" comes blasting through the PA system.

"Oh my God!" Candi exclaims, "We have to dance to this song first."

April shrugs her shoulders in bemused agreement and they overtake the dancefloor. Bumping and grinding to the purple one's slamming beats and naughty lyrics. Candi wraps her arm around April's waist and rides her leg. April throwing her hands in the air. Leaning all the way back while people hanging at the bar, too uptight and insecure to ever let loose, look on with disapproval. Men because they'd never have a chance with these two. Women because they're worried about losing their men to them. Pathetic bullshit while Candi and April tear up the tacky, linoleum dancefloor. Each girl ecstatic that she's minutes away from fucking the other. They reach the exit before their song has crossfaded into the next. The rest of the bar watching Candi smack April's ass out the door. Then squeezing it as they walk back to Candi's car past other pedestrians under the glow of neon lights and streetlamps.

"There are people around," April protests.

"It's okay," Candi reminds her, "We're lipstick lesbians right now."

They giggle incessantly until getting inside Candi's car. At which point she grabs April, pulls her close, and kisses her deeply. April returns the passion. Tongues twirling in each other's mouth. Lips getting wetter and wetter. Pussies too. Candi slips her hand down the rear of April's jeans to find nothing but bare ass.

"Someone isn't wearing any underwear," Candi squeezes her bare cheeks.

"You know what?" April performs the same inspection on Candi, "Someone else isn't wearing any underwear either."

"Where are you staying?" Candi looks deep into April's eyes.

"That one hotel on the lake. With the sports bar," April informs her, "Do you know the way?"

"Yeah," Candi answers.

"Good, because I don't remember," April laughs.

"Smartass," Candi retorts while pulling into traffic. Racing down Central Avenue and across Hot Springs with a beautiful girl by her side. Alternating her hand between the gearshift and April's thigh. She can't reach their destination fast enough. Speed limits be damned. And if they do get pulled over by a cop, maybe they'll just invite him along for extra fun. Tonight, nothing is off the table for Candi or her delicious companion. Out to raise hell in the midnight hour as Billy Idol serenades them to the edge of Lake Hamilton where fog rolls in from the water. She wants more, more, more indeed. Her pussy throbbing at the thought of making her new girlfriend rebel yell all night long.

Candi and April sprint through the parking lot and hotel lobby. Hearts racing with anticipation while waiting on the elevator. Once inside, Candi pushes April against the rear of the cab. Looking out the corner of her eye. Watching herself make out with this sexy girl in the reflection of polished metal interior. Holding her brand new lover tight. Kissing her with reckless abandon. Putting on a show for anyone who may be watching them through a surveillance camera. All the way to the top floor. Giggling and running down the hallway to April's room. Trying not to shake as she inserts her keycard into the lock.

"It's shower time," Candi wastes no time getting undressed.

"I'll be waiting," April turns on a bedside lamp.

"Waiting for what?" Candi laughs, "You're taking one with me. Get those clothes off, missy. Chop chop."

April complies as Candi watches. Her pussy getting wetter with each item of clothing her new friend strips off. Finally getting to see her naked.

"Girl, you are so hot!" Candi takes April's hand.

She leads her to the bathroom. Turning on the shower. Running their eyes and hands over each other's naked body while waiting for hot water.

"You have been a dirty girl tonight, April," Candi jokes, "I think you need a good scrubbing."

"Oh, I'm not the only dirty girl here," April laughs.

Once in the shower, Candi wastes no time pulling April to her. Kissing passionately as hot water flows down their soft, smooth skin. Candi takes the soap. Lathering it up in her hands. Rubbing it all over April's tits while they kiss. Candi reaches down and soaps up April's pussy. Massaging her clit and lips. Inserting her middle finger inside. April closes her eyes and moans.

"Here's your first lesson, baby," Candi whispers.

She fingers April. Teasing her g-spot. Making her moan and sigh. Making her pussy tight as they kiss. Trembling together. Bringing them both to orgasm.

"Show me what you've learned," Candi demands.

April takes the soap and lathers up Candi's tits. Caressing and squeezing them before rubbing her own titties against them.

"I'm improvising," April giggles.

She soaps up Candi's pussy. Stroking it back and forth before sliding her middle finger inside. Massaging her g-spot.

"Oh, I've taught you well," Candi sighs.

"Mmm-hmm," April enthusiastically fingers Candi and they achieve another orgasm together.

"Whew! You're a very naughty girl, April," Candi mock scolds, "I think you need a spanking."

"Spank me, Candi," April turns around, bends over, and wiggles her butt, "I've been a very naughty girl. Very cheeky."

"Oh my God!" Candi laughs.

She spanks April's cheeks and squeezes them. Rubbing soap all over her new lover's soaking wet ass as they giggle uncontrollably.

"Your turn," April turns to face Candi, "Bend over and show me that sexy ass, young lady."

Candi laughs and complies. April soaps up her butt while spanking and squeezing it.

"I like you in this position," Aprils humps her pussy against Candi's ass. They nearly fall over from laughing so hard. Grabbing tightly onto each other and catching their balance. Candi pushes April against the shower wall and kisses her. Grabbing her tits. Licking and sucking her nipples while looking in her eyes. Smiling at each other as April moans softly.

"Oh my God," April whispers, "You're so incredible at that."

"Thank you," Candi responds sassily.

She kisses down April's stomach. Dropping to her knees. Grabbing April's leg. Guiding her foot onto the tub's edge. April bracing herself in the corner. Trembling as Candi licks her pussy in a long slow stroke from back to front. Burying her face in April's hot throbbing pussy. Tasting her sweet juices flowing like crazy into her mouth. Fingering her again while licking and sucking her clit. Hot water streaming down her face. Devouring her new friend's pussy. Making April shake. Bringing her to orgasm. Candi's pussy getting tighter and wetter.

"Oh my God, Candi," April breathes heavily, "I just came."

"Yes, you did. You naughty girl," Candi nods proudly, "You came all over my face."

She stands. April immediately and aggressively grabs her face and kisses her. Tasting her juices on Candi's lips as they giggle and sigh. April pulls back and stares into Candi's eyes with pure carnal instinct.

"Your turn," April orders, "I want you to cum on my face, baby. I want to taste you badly."

"I want that so badly," Candi sighs, "Show me what you've learned."

They change positions. Candi holds herself up. Her foot on the edge of the tub while April dives tongue first into her pussy. Proving to be a quick learner. Candi overcome with chills underneath the hot water. April expertly eating her pussy. Gently yet authoritatively. Tongue lashing her back and forth. Fingering her and sucking her clit. Candi feels her juices gushing into April's thirsty mouth. Moving closer and closer to cumming on her face.

"Oh God, I'm cumming," Candi moans.

"Oh yeah, cum for me," April encourages her, "Cum all over my face."

Candi presses her arms and back tight against the shower wall as she cums. Grabbing April and lifting her up for a kiss. Tasting her juices on April's lips and tongue while shutting off the water. Leading her by hand out of the tub. Grabbing a towel and drying her off before April returns the favor.

"Oh my God!" April exclaims, "That was fucking amazing!"

"You were amazing," Candi smiles.

"Aww…" April coos, "So were you."

"We just know how to have fun," Candi explains, "And the fun isn't over yet."

Candi leads April to the queen size bed and pulls back the covers. Dropping her towel and getting underneath. April follows suit. Facing each other. Embracing. Pressing their naked bodies together for warmth. Gazing into each other's eyes. Kissing softly. Tongues slow dancing in silence underneath a dim amber glow. Candi pulls back. Lost in April's eyes. Stroking her face and wet hair.

"So, how was your first time with a girl?" Candi inquires.

"It was out of this world," April confesses enthusiastically, "I'm so glad we met."

"Me too," Candi smiles as flattery overcomes her.

"But," April whispers softly, "I thought you said the fun wasn't over yet."

"It's not," Candi announces while shoving April on her back without warning. Getting on top. Holding her wrists to the bed. Kissing her aggressively as they giggle.

"That's what I'm talking about!" April exclaims.

"Oh yeah, baby!" Candi shouts before returning her lips to April's before they kiss and lick each other's neck simultaneously.

"Hold on," April pauses the action, "Let me put on some music."

She rolls over to the alarm clock radio. Surfing the dial until she finds an eighties station. Returning to her position underneath Candi as "Let's Go All the Way" by Sly Fox fills the room. Candi resumes going all the way with April. Kissing and caressing her breasts. Licking and sucking her nipples. Flicking them with her tongue while April holds her head.

"Oh yeah. Suck my titties!" April grinds them in Candi's face while they laugh.

"You are such a naughty girl!" Candi exudes, "What am I going to do with you?"

"Anything you want, Candi," April dares her, "Let's be really naughty girls tonight. The naughtiest girls ever!"

"That's right," Candi agrees, "We are a couple of naughty ass bitches!"

"Hells yeah we are!" April exudes.

Candi resumes sucking April's tits before kissing and licking down her stomach. Spreading her legs. Licking each silky inner thigh from her knee upward. Teasing around her pussy. Both girls trembling in anticipation.

"Any day now," April muses in a smartass tone.

"Who's the teacher here?" Candi gently pats April's pussy, "Know your place, missy."

"Are you getting tough with me, baby?" April sasses, "Feel free to get as tough with me as you want."

"Oh my God, you are so adorable," Candi laughs, "That just makes me want you even more."

She proves the sentiment by eagerly licking April's pussy back and forth. Consuming her delicious girl juices flowing uncontrollably. Sucking her delicate lips. Sliding her tongue deep inside. Exploring her soft velvety sugar walls. April arches her back. Grabbing Candi's head. Pulling her tongue in deeper. Smothering Candi's face with her pussy as it gets tighter and wetter.

"Don't stop," April sighs breathlessly, "Don't stop eating my pussy, Candi."

Candi indulges April. Loving every second of licking and sucking her pussy. Caught up in the heat of the moment. The heat of the night. One that began with a successful party. Now ending with her fucking a beautiful woman. Her sapphic desires being explored and fulfilled far beyond what she imagined upon accepting this booking. She's having a total fucking blast. Feeling extremely hedonistic and decadent while eating another girl's pussy. Overcome with a sense of relaxation. Consumed by a warm sensation inside and out. It's the girl on girl encounter she's always fantasized about and then some.

April moans incessantly. Moving her hands from Candi's head to the sheet underneath them. Grasping it between her fingers. A massive climax building deep within her. Candi feels an orgasm of her own coming on. Licking and sucking April's clit while fingering her. Flicking and circling her party girl's tiny pleasure button. Massaging her g-spot with one finger. Then two. Then three. Taking April's clit between her lips and sucking it. Her lover's warm sweetness covering her face. Candi feels her own juices flowing as she rubs her pussy against the comforter.

"Oh God, I'm cumming!" April shouts between anguished moans.

"Do it, baby" Candi encourages her, "Cum for me. Cum on my face.

"Fuck!" April's swollen pussy ejaculates all over Candi's face and into her mouth.

"Oh yeah, baby!" Candi massages April's g-spot more vigorously, "Make that pussy squirt!"

Her pussy again fires juices into Candi's wanting mouth. Holding them as she pulls herself up to April and kisses her. Releasing them into her mouth. Savoring her sweetness together.

"Mmm… I taste yummy," April giggles.

"Yes, you do," Candi agrees.

They giggle and kiss. Wrapping their arms around each other. Without warning, April rolls Candi onto her back. Making them laugh hysterically. April slides down and sucks Candi's tits.

"You were amazing sucking my titties at the party," Candi confides, "Are you sure you haven't done that before?"

"Never," April shakes her head, "Your titties just make me highly motivated."

April continues licking and sucking Candi's nipples before kissing down her stomach. Licking up each inner thigh as Candi did to her.

"You're an excellent student," Candi informs her.

"Oh, you haven't seen anything yet," April states with total confidence before licking Candi's pussy deep between her lips.

"Holy fuck," Candi moans, "You weren't kidding."

"Let me tell you something," April stops to look at Candi matter of factly, "I don't kid when it comes to making love."

"Then make love to me, April," Candi coos.

She grabs April's head. Pulling her lovemaking cohort's face tight against her pussy. The sensation of April's warm wet tongue deep inside her sends electrical shocks through her body. Arching her back. Tossing her hair around. It's more pleasure than she can take, but she never wants it to end. Her juices flowing faster and faster. Covering her enthusiastic lover's face.

"Ooh… Your pussy is so wet. I just want to rub my face all over it," Aprils admits before rubbing her entire face all over Candi's soaking wet pussy as they laugh.

"You are so naughty," Candi smiles, "I love it."

"So are you," April replies sweetly.

She continues eating Candi's hot throbbing pussy. Sucking her swollen lips. Sliding her tongue deep inside. Then her finger as her tongue dances on Candi's clit. Kissing, licking, and sucking her clit while massaging her g-spot. Working from one finger to three. Candi's pussy growing tighter and wetter. On the verge of a massive climax.

Grabbing the pillow beneath her head. Squeezing it for dear life. Tilting her head all the way back. Enduring the sensation of her pussy aching to explode. Now hurting to explode. Looking back down towards April. Her lover's body squirming and writhing. Rubbing her own pussy on the comforter just as she did minutes earlier. She can't hold back a second longer.

'Oh God, I'm cumming!" Candi unleashes hot girl juices all over April's face and into her mouth.

"Fuck yeah! Squirt in my mouth, Candi!" April demands.

Candi complies. Ejaculating in her new friend's mouth. April pulls herself up to Candi. Her face drenched with sweetness. Savoring it together while kissing insatiably. Leading to more giggling as April rolls off and lies next to Candi. They catch their breath together.

"Oh wow! That was unbelievable," Candi breaks the silence after a moment as she and April look at each other.

"You were unbelievable," Aprils glows, "And the best teacher ever."

"Whatever," Candi replies, "You're a natural."

They laugh as Candi touches April's hand, who responds by squeezing it.

"Ooh… We're holding hands," April sasses, "Now we're really being naughty."

"That's right," Candi agrees, "Not to change the subject, but all this naughty playtime has me starving."

"Oh my God, I'm so sorry. It's probably has been a while since you ate," April sits up, "I have some food in the fridge."

Candi watches April get up and walk to the small fridge across the room. Lingering on her sexy ass bouncing with every step. Watching her titties jiggle as she returns with refreshments. Sitting up on the bed. April rejoins her with a carton of strawberries, a small tub of chocolate dip, and a bottle of Korbel.

"I'm sorry I don't have more," April apologizes while opening the packages.

"No, this is great," Candi assures her, "Thank you for feeding me."

"Don't mention it. I should've offered to feed you earlier," April responds, "I'm not being a good sorority sister. As soon as anyone came over, we were shoving food and drink in their faces."

"You're so sweet," Candi laughs softly.

"Thank you. So are you," April dips a strawberry in chocolate and offers it to Candi, "Here you go."

"Why don't you feed it to me?" Candi opens her mouth.

"My pleasure," April holds the strawberry by the stem and place it in Candi's mouth.

"Mmm… That's good," Candi bites and consumes her strawberry, "Thank you."

"You're welcome," April smiles.

"Now it's your turn," Candi informs her.

She takes a strawberry, dips it in chocolate, and holds it to April's mouth. April bites it off at the stem. Chewing as she turns her attention to the Korbel. Removing the foil and muselet. Placing the bedsheet over the bottle. Popping the cork.

"Oh, I need to get some plastic cups from the bathroom," Aprils starts to get up.

"Don't worry about it," Candi stops her, "We can just drink from the bottle."

"Are you sure?" April asks with genuine concern.

"April," Candi looks at her with amusement, "We just came on each other's face twice. I think we're close enough now to drink after each other."

"Good point," April laughs.

She hands the bottle to Candi, who takes a drink and hands it back to April. She takes a sip before preparing another chocolate-covered strawberry for Candi.

"Open wide," April jokes as she feeds Candi again.

"Your turn," Candi prepares one.

April eats her strawberry from Candi's hand. Leaving chocolate on the corner of her mouth.

"You have a little chocolate on your mouth," Candi informs April as she instinctively looks for something to wipe with, "Don't worry. I got it."

Candi leans into April. Face to face as she licks the chocolate from April's mouth and swallows it.

"Oh my God," April expresses with surprise and arousal, "That was so fucking hot."

"I was thinking about earlier at the restaurant," Candi confesses, "About when you kissed me with the whipped cream and passed it into my mouth."

"I know. I kind of jumped the gun there," April apologizes, "I felt bad about that."

"I didn't," Candi continues, "I couldn't believe how much it turned me on."

"Really?" April is stunned.

"Yeah," Candi assures her, "Here, let me show you."

Candi takes a strawberry, dips it in chocolate, and puts it in her mouth. Chewing it a few times before pulling April close and kissing her. Chewing and passing the strawberry between their mouths repeatedly as they consume it together.

"Oh wow," April giggles, "That made me lightheaded. Let me try it."

She prepares one and puts it in her mouth. Planting her lips on Candi's as they once again eat a chocolate strawberry together. Kissing until it's all gone.

"Have you ever heard of that before?" April asks.

"Nope," Candi shakes her head, "I mean, I'm sure we're not the first two people to do that, but I've never heard of anyone doing that. Or even seen it in a porno."

"Me neither," April ponders, "And I watch lots of porn."

"You are so crazy," Candi laughs.

"You like it," April sasses.

"I do," Candi admits.

She takes the Korbel from April. Filling her mouth with champagne. Locking lips with April. Tongues dancing while passing the bubbly between their mouths. Until every drop is consumed.

"Now that's how you drink champagne," Candi boasts sassily.

"Agreed," Aprils concurs before they share a sexually charged moment of silence.

"Ooh, you know what I want for dessert?" Candi breaks the spell.

"Well, this kind of is dessert that we're having when you think about it," April muses.

"Smartass," Candi retorts, "Just work with me here."

"Okay," April agrees, "What do you want for dessert?"

"Wait for it," Candi builds the suspense, "Chocolate titties."

"Fuck yes!" April's face lights up, "Do it!"

Candi scoops chocolate dip into her hand. Smearing it on April's nipples. She shakes her chocolate-coated breasts enthusiastically.

"Get you some chocolate cupcakes!" April orders as Candi takes a sip of Korbel.

"Oh my God!" Candi nearly chokes on champagne with laughter.

"Hey, I've got sugar in me," April giggles, "Now come get you some sugar, sugar."

Candi can't stop laughing as she hands the bottle to April. Taking April's right breast in her mouth. It tastes better than any strawberry. Kissing and licking it clean. Sucking the chocolate from her nipple. Swirling her tongue around it while April drinks from the bottle.

"Get yourself a second helping," April turns slightly and places her left breast in Candi's face.

"You are so wrong," Candi shakes her head and giggles before licking and sucking April's left breast. Savoring it for what she knows is likely the final time she will get to suck the crazy and wonderful girl's tits. Making the most of this last call. Vigorously flicking her tongue on April's nipple until her mouth starts getting sore.

"You have some chocolate on your mouth," April leans in and circles Candi's mouth with her tongue before kissing her, "Okay, your turn," she scoops a large handful of chocolate dip and smears a thick layer across Candi's chest.

"Fuck, April," Candi laughs, "You know you have to lick that all off, right?"

"Don't worry about me," April scoffs, "I'm all over this."

April leans down and plays with Candi's right breast. Licking off some chocolate while spreading around the rest. Giggling incessantly.

"You're kind of making a mess down there," Candi observes before taking a sip of champagne.

"Not at all," April explains between sucking and giggling, "This night isn't going to last forever, so I've got to milk this for all it's worth. Get it? Milk this Titties."

"Oh, April," Candi groans. Which she follows with a moan. Not only is this crazy wonderful girl sucking her tits like a pro, but she's feeling the same way Candi is in that moment. Trembling from April's warm, soft mouth as she fantasizes about them running away together. A bad girl duo traveling from town to town. Seeking only the sexiest of men to fuck the hell out of when not playing with each other. Or perhaps joining forces with Magnum and forming the ultimate sexual power trio. Something she's begun fantasizing about recently. The combination of these ideas and Candi's mad suckling skills brings her to another orgasm.

"I think I have chocolate on my face," April giggles.

Candi opens her eyes to see April's face covered with chocolate and a charmingly innocent expression.

"Here," Candi laughs while reaching over the side of the bed for a bath towel from earlier. Wiping April's face clean before taking her in her arms. Thanking her for an unforgettable night with a passionate kiss. April takes the towel and wipes the remaining chocolate from Candi's chest and her own. She gets up, drops the towel to the floor, and returns the food dip to the fridge. Candi eyeing her naked body the entire time while taking another sip of Korbel.

"There's one last sip for you," Candi hands the bottle to April as she returns to the bed.

"Bottoms up," April finishes off the bottle and sets it on the nightstand.

"Speaking of bottoms up, it's time for your final lesson," Candi lies on her back, "Sixty-nine with me, baby."

"Hells yeah!" April hops on Candi as "Lick it Up" by Kiss comes on the radio. Burying her face in Candi's pussy while sitting on her face. Candi barely has to do anything but enjoy her lover's sweet, warm juices. Her tongue sliding effortlessly inside April's pussy grinding on her face. Her own floodgates opening once again while April's tongue strokes her throbbing pussy. Growing ever tighter and wetter. April sucks her clit and licks deep insider her. Candi kisses her clit. Sucking it while spanking and squeezing her wiggling butt.

"Spank me, Candi," April coos between licks, "I've been an extremely naughty girl tonight."

"Yes, you have, April," Candi holds onto her ass. Licking back and forth deep inside her pussy. Girl juices covering Candi's face as she moans louder and louder.

"Oh God, you're making me so fucking wet," April moans.

Her trembling escalates. Grinding her pussy harder on Candi's face. She can barely breathe but doesn't care. It's her last time eating April's pussy. Maybe even the last time she has an experience like this with another girl. Sure, there will be two girl shows at parties. As well as playing with bi-curious birthday girls and other guests. But none of that will be as extensive as what she's experienced with April. The playfulness, bonding, and sexual exploration all reached unprecedented new heights tonight. Heights that will be difficult to match going forward. Just like her soon to be former lover, she must milk the encounter for all it's worth in this moment.

"Oh fuck! You're making me cum!" Candi screams from a place of sexual and emotional anguish. Her body overcome with chills. Her trembling escalates to uncontrollable shaking. Her aching pussy gushing wave after wave of juices all over her playmate's face. April experiencing the same sensations. Her swollen pussy flowing relentlessly on Candi's face. Into her mouth as she drinks up every drop she can. Wanting to remember April's sweetness for the rest of her life.

"Cum with me, Candi!" April's moans turn to screams, "I'm cumming too!"

"Do it, April," Candi shouts, "Let's cum together."

They devour each other's pussy with reckless abandon. Holding back through the pain for as long as they can. Until they can deny the gratification of sweet release no longer. Squirting hot juices into each other's mouth. Candi wrapping her arms around April's back. Hanging onto her for dear life while riding out an explosive and seemingly endless climax into carnal eternity. As if they'll never stop shaking, moaning, and gushing. Consuming each other's sweetness one last time. Making one final, earth-shattering memory together before going their separate ways. Bonded forever only by the shared decadence of a cool February night long ago. A night about which only they will ever know. After seemingly an eternity, their shared climax ends. April shivers. Slowly rolling off Candi. Pulling the covers over her. Candi spins around and joins her. Taking April in her arms as they warm each other's shaking body.

"Well, you certainly melted my butter tonight," April smiles.

"Oh my God," Candi rolls her eyes and laughs.

"It's true," April coos.

"And you melted my butter too," Candi admits before they share a deep kiss and gaze into each other's eyes.

"Only one thing was missing," April breaks the silence, "A hot guy with a huge cock."

"That's right," Candi laughs.

"Candi," April inquires, "Where do you think stripping will take you?"

"I don't know," Candi ponders while looking at the ceiling, "It's decent money. Usually fun. Occasionally really fun. Like tonight," she pauses to laugh, "I enjoy doing it for the most part. It gives me something to do while I figure out what I want in life. In a career. In a man. I'm still figuring out those things."

April doesn't respond. Candi looks over to find that she's fallen asleep. She gently strokes her lover's hair while looking at her. Closing her eyes momentarily. Waking two hours later to April's loud snoring. She stealthily gets out of bed and turns off the radio. Quietly dressing and checking to make sure she has all her things. Turning out the light. Leaning over April. Kissing her softly on the cheek. She sighs in contentment while Candi takes one last look at her one-night girlfriend before exiting the room. The entire hotel is dead. Riding the elevator with zero excitement this time. Even the night clerk is nowhere in sight as she walks out the door. Through the fog sweeping across the parking lot to her car. An hour's drive ahead to reflect upon tonight. Will she think this was all a dream in the morning? It's definitely real. But forever a dream.

April

Magnum has reached that crucial point. The one at which U.S. 67 and U.S. 167 cease running concurrently and split at Bald Knob. Yes, Bald Knob. Perhaps the most infamous of countless Arkansas towns with funny names. He's only booked a gig here once. And it relocated to another town before showtime. But he later made up for this by scoring a party in the town of Weiner. Recalling that cold winter night while heading to Batesville on this warm Saturday in April. Taking U.S. 167 north into the Ozarks as its sister highway cuts northeast into the Delta. There's not much to say about Batesville on his end. Occasionally traveling there for parties. Most have been decent. The only standout being, for all the wrong reasons, a bachelorette party crashed by the groom-to-be. Upset over Magnum's presence and responding to it by sitting in the backyard and crying. For shame indeed.

Magnum's ascent into the Ozarks is where his drive becomes magical. Trees in the throes of spring bloom extend into infinity. Elevation increasing. Terrain growing rockier. Passing through communities with names like Velvet Ridge, Pleasant Plains, Huff, and Southside. Windows down as "Lonely at the Top" by Tygers of Pan Tang screams into the rural Arkansas night. Signs beckoning to mysterious Arkansas highways such as 14, 157, and 230. He'd love to explore each one if he had the time. Even in darkness. Alone too. Single and ready to mingle. Embracing his sexual freedom more than ever before. Although still overly hard on himself.

He's awash in thought while crossing the White River into Batesville. Pondering the spring resurgence of his agency following a long cold winter. November was slow as always, but things never picked up in December. Or January. Or February. Then March roared in like a lion with parties for him and all his girls on the very first day. And business hasn't relented since. He's thrown himself booty shake first into making up for lost time and money. Feeling great right now. Yet hesitant to celebrate. Knowing all too well that everything can go south in a hurry. But he's totally in the mood for fun regardless. Cautious optimism notwithstanding.

U.S. 167 guides Magnum down a steep and curvy decline before turning into the main drag through Batesville. Upon him are all the usual fast food and convenience store chains. Along with banks, office buildings, and used car lots. Not particularly romantic. Blah is more like it. There's nothing to do in this town. No wonder he's never had an exceptional party here. And yet it's something of a wonder his agency doesn't get more calls about parties here. The scenery becomes more inspiring after turning onto Main Street. Greeted by old buildings and unique businesses. An old Coca Cola ad decorates the entire side of one brick building. Faded by time but still legible.

He crosses the hopelessly Arkansas named Poke Bayou and arrives at his destination. A small older home in a quiet neighborhood. Ten minutes to nine. All is quiet along this narrow street. Houselights competing against the long shadows of old trees. Even the party house is inconspicuous considering what is about to go down inside. There's no sidewalk. Just an aged concrete curb dividing street and grass. Cracks adorn where bright yellow paint is now reduced to faint splotches. He dons the remainder of his firefighter costume. Preparing to put out some fires tonight. Knowing he'll start more than he extinguishes.

"Hey there!" Sabrina approaches him as he pulls up his red suspenders with Christie in tow.

"Hey, you two," he looks up to see his clients, "Are you ready?"

"Hells yeah we're ready!" Christie laughs.

"I have to warn you though," Sabrina cautions, "Olivia and the other girls got an early start on drinking. They're a little tipsy right now."

"What exactly do you mean by 'a little tipsy?'" he ponders to himself. His head filling with visions of drunk girls running for the bathroom and passing out. Visions based on past experiences. This could end the party before it begins. Regardless of his concerns, all he can do is nod and smile.

"Don't worry," Christie assures him as if reading his thoughts, "We'll take good care of you."

"You'd better," he nods authoritatively, "I'll make my entrance in five."

The girls giggle their way back inside. He once again stands alone on that dark and quiet street. He can't help but think about Sabrina and Christie. So innocent and wide-eyed. How he wouldn't mind getting in between them. But there's an excellent chance he won't be here long if the other girls are already drunk. He's been cockblocked every other possible way at least once. Why not by excessive inebriation this time? He'll find out soon enough. Strutting confidently towards the front door. Head held high. Not even the devil can stop him tonight. As if the devil would bother with such a conservative town like Batesville, where the sale of alcohol is prohibited, but whatever.

"Oh my God!!!" Olivia exclaims in a slurred scream upon seeing Magnum walk through the door like he owns the fucking place. Because he totally does for the next hour. Save for all the girly Christian knickknacks displayed on a bookcase in the corner. His new living room is cozy. And not only because it's small. The sofa is begging for someone to fall asleep on it. That has him a little worried. Along with Sabrina, Christie, and Olivia, there are two other girls. Each as intoxicated as the guest of honor. The good news is that his bachelorette isn't shy in the slightest.

"Oh yeah! Give it to me, baby!" she screams to the hysterical female delight surrounding them.

Magnum can't help but laugh at this. He's been stripping long enough to know that it comes from a good place. A place of honesty and warmth. So excited to have him at her party. And he's excited to be here. Her arms and legs wrapped around his body. Thrusting her pelvis against him with reckless abandon. His chest tight against her tits as they simulate fucking to "You Can Do It" by Ice Cube. She struggles to wear her condom veil. Finally giving up and tossing it aside. Continually shoving dollar bills in her cleavage so he can remove them with his teeth. Then between her legs.

The electricity of Olivia's silky-smooth legs on Magnum's cheeks prompts him to up the ante. Grabbing a can of Reddi-wip from his stripping bag. Tracing each thigh from her knees to her tantalizingly short Daisy Dukes. His tongue glides effortlessly along her soft skin. The warmth of her pussy caressing his face with each pass. Moving up to her breasts. Repeating the process. His face buried between her girls. The other girls shrieking with excitement. He revels in her Opium fragrance. A sensation that is mutual.

"Oh my God, you smell incredible!" Olivia announces to everyone.

"Thank you," he laughs, "So do you."

"He really does," Sabrina concurs, "That was the first thing I noticed about him."

"Me too," Christie adds.

Magnum gives attention to the other two highly inebriated girls individually. Each attempting to stay upright on the sofa through incessant giggling. Lavishing them with much the same attention he showed Olivia. Resulting in much the same reaction from both. Thrusting his way through them in rapid fashion. Sucking whipped cream from their cleavage. Bombarded with squeals of embarrassed delight. Alcohol overruling the ring on each girl's finger. His bachelorette and clients cheering them on. Feeling himself becoming intoxicated despite not having yet consumed a drop of booze tonight. Rocking the collective world of his drunken duo until they suddenly begin succumbing to fatigue.

"Oh, come on," Olivia scolds them, "You lightweights."

"I think I wore them out," he jokes cockily.

"I think you did," Sabrina laughs, "Can I fix you a drink?"

"Sure," he glances her way, "What do you have?"

"Whatever you want," she sasses, "Smirnoff, Bacardi, Jack…"

"Jack and Coke?" he interjects.

"Absolutely," she heads for the kitchen.

"Check this out!" Olivia bends over before Magnum and rubs her ass on his crotch as "In Da Club" by 50 Cent plays, "It's just like I'm in da club!"

"If we had a club in this town," Christie laughs, "We ain't got shit here."

"What do you do for fun here?" he inquires, "I mean… I've done parties here before. The town is always dead at night."

"You know what we do?" she shakes her head, "We stock up on booze from the next county and throw wild parties."

"It's true," Olivia slurs, "We have all sorts of crazy fun in the basement," she points towards a door near the kitchen before placing her finger on her lips, "But don't tell anyone I told you. It's a secret. Shh…"

"Jesus Christ, Olivia," Christie laughs, "You just told him in front of everyone."

"Told him what?" Sabrina returns with Magnum's drink.

"Thank you," he takes a sip, "About your wild basement parties."

"Oh that," she laughs, "You don't know the half of it."

"Maybe we'll just have to show him," Christie giggles.

"I guess you will," he stands before them, "After I show you two something first."

The sofa girls now passed out as Magnum hovers above Sabrina and Christie. Olivia stands behind them. Watching with anticipation in voyeuristic fashion. Seated side by side in dining room chairs. They squeeze together. Running their fingers along his silky-smooth skin. Sliding dollars in his g-string. He thrusts against their legs. Face to face with them. The air filled with laughter and intrigue by this lap dance threesome. Naughty thoughts race through his mind. He and his clients. So much naughtiness they could achieve together. Now he really wants to go down to the basement.

"Oh, they're both single!" Olivia reveals with inebriated clairvoyance that is both adorable and helpful, "You can do whatever you want to them!"

"Olivia!" Sabrina laughs.

"It's true," Olivia continues, "Have them take you down to the basement."

"Maybe we'll take you down to the basement," Christie points at the bachelorette.

"Sounds good to me," Olivia retorts, "I'm feeling devilish right now."

"I'll show you devilish," he grabs his Reddi-wip. Applying a line to each of Sabrina's thighs and her cleavage. Licking up ever so slowly. From knee to crotch. Grabbing her titties and devouring the remaining whipped cream from her chest. She trembles and sighs from his caressing of her girls. Christie's thighs receive the same treatment before he moves to her breasts.

"Here," Sabrina pulls down Christie's tube top in the front, "Let me make it easier for you."

"What the fuck?" Christie giggles.

"Hells yeah!" Olivia shouts, "Get those titties out!"

Magnum wastes no time covering Christie's nipples with Reddi-wip before licking and sucking them. Her arms wrapped around his head. Moaning from the wicked sensation of his swirling tongue while Sabrina and Olivia watch and cheer.

"Your turn!" Olivia lifts Sabrina's top from behind and yanks down her bra.

"Oh my God!" Sabrina tries to cover her breasts, but Olivia and Christie hold her arms back. Laughingly submitting as he explores her nipples with his can of Reddi-wip. Starting with her right breast. Taking her in his mouth. Sucking hard while flicking his tongue rapidly. Sabrina's giggles now turning to moans.

"Let me help," Olivia leans over and plants her mouth on Sabrina's left breast.

"Olivia!" Sabrina exclaims in faux shock.

"This is just like partying in the basement!" Olivia exclaims.

"Well, that settles it," he declares, "I have to see this basement for myself."

"In due time," Christie teases.

She and Sabrina tag team and return the favor to Magnum. Licking and sucking whipped cream from his nipples. Olivia encouraging them. He turns around. Pulling down his g-string in the rear. Booty shaking in their faces. They've been so kind and generous that he's more than happy to let them spank and squeeze his firm, round ass. Yet catching him by surprise when they spread his cheeks apart. Simultaneously expressing a seductive, "Mmm…" Not the first time such a thing has happened, but it is rare. Perhaps they're satisfying a curiosity. Or maybe they have something more in mind. Something for down in the basement, perhaps.

A dance party erupts with him and his party girls still standing. The other two fast asleep on the sofa. No matter. The four of them bumping and grinding on one another to "Yeah" by Usher. Overall, his audience has held up well. And Olivia has proven to be no lightweight when it comes to holding her liquor. He really can't complain. And just like that, his bachelorette makes a mad dash for the bathroom. Sabrina and Christie rush after to ensure she's okay. The sofa girls oblivious to it all. And now the party is over. He turns down the volume and finishes his Jack and Coke in silence.

A feeling of awkwardness overcomes him. That happens on these rare occasions when he's left alone at a party. Standing there in nothing but a g-string and cowboy boots. Not knowing what to do with himself. Although the show had ended, he finds it rude to dress and leave without marking the conclusion official with his client. Maybe he's a little too nice for my own good. But it serves to endear him even further to his audiences. In this instance, he knows these girls will appreciate the gesture. So, he's content to sip his drink. Imagining getting to know Sabrina and Christie even more intimately. Experience tells him that anything is possible.

"We're sorry about that," Sabrina returns with another Jack and Coke for Magnum.

"Thank you," he takes a sip, "How is she?"

"She's done for the night," Christie informs him, "I think you wore her out."

"I guess I tend to do that," he laughs.

"I'm sure you do," Sabrina smiles, "You don't have to leave right away, do you?"

"No," he shakes his head, "And you have nothing to apologize for. You all were amazing."

"Aww… Thank you," she gushes, "So were you."

"Did we tip you enough?" Christie inquires.

"I'm happy," he glances at the pile of cash next to his stripping bag.

"Wanna see the basement?" Sabrina gives Christie a devilish smile that's returned.

"Ahh… The infamous basement," he nods, "I have to see it now."

"That's right," Christie giggles, "Follow us."

Magnum follows Sabrina and Christie through the mysterious door. Closing it behind him. Still nearly naked as he walks carefully downstairs in pitch blackness. Wondering why no one has turned on a light. Wondering if he'll ever leave this basement alive. All is quiet. Save for hushed giggling several feet before him. The dark void overwhelms his senses. Bright and deafening in its own macabre fashion. His body tingling from head to toe. Embraced from all directions by a malevolent force. It's evil nature oddly comforting. Instilling within him feelings of confidence and security in its presence. Inviting him to partake in acts of debauchery so bad they're good.

Suddenly, the entire basement is bathed in red. He can see it all now. The bare sheetrock. The exposed steel I-beams. The concrete floor painted black. In the center a giant pentagram. Inverted from the viewpoint of entering its domain. Painted in white, but red for all intents and purposes. Everything is red. The Ouija board set up in the corner. The large mirror adorning one wall. Presumably for summoning forth Bloody Mary. Sabrina and Christie are also cloaked in red. Standing naked within the pentagram. Each holding a sheathed dagger in both hands. "Under the Blade" by Twisted Sister comes at him from all directions.

"A glint of steel

A flash of light

You know you're not going home tonight"

He's attempting to deduce how they turned on the power despite not being anywhere near a switch when they motion him to join them.

Each taking one of his legs. Rubbing her pussy along it like a flesh stripper pole. Grabbing him by either arm. Dipping backward. They grow wetter. Making him bigger and harder. The girls stand before him. Laughing as they gaze into each other's eyes. Deviously. Lustily. Each simultaneously tracing the other's torso with her sheathed dagger.

"You wanted to know what we do for fun in Batesville?" Christie smirks at him, "Well, we're about to show you."

"Ever see a human sacrifice?" Sabrina asks him.

"You mean like the alligator scene in *Brutes and Savages*?" he responds sarcastically.

"Fuck no!" she scoffs while Christie sucks her tits, "Ooh yeah… Suck 'em, baby."

"Well, okay. We're not talking about a real human sacrifice," Christie explains as Sabrina returns the favor to her girls, "Oh God. They've been missing your mouth."

"Really?" he laughs, "Color me shocked."

"Whatever," she shakes her head at him, "It's more like a sexual sacrifice."

"We just need to go ahead and show him," Sabrina chimes in before looking at Magnum, "Pick which one of us you want to see sacrificed first."

"Um… How about you?" he nods at Christie.

"Ooh…" she giggles at Sabrina, "Sacrifice me, baby."

"You just wait," Sabrina retrieves a weight bench from against the wall and sets it within the pentagram.

"A weight bench, huh?" he laughs, "That's so Satanic."

"Well, we're all about to get a serious workout," Sabrina chides him.

Magnum observes with great expectations as Christie lies on her stomach. Arms wrapped around the bench. Dagger still in hand. Legs wide open. Pussy just beyond the edge. Sabrina stands over her. Holding up a bottle of Astroglide. Letting it stream down onto

Christie's back. Sabrina unsheathes her dagger. Revealing its "blade" to be a silicon dildo. She rolls it across Christie's back. Covering it with lubrication. Moving behind her friend. Penetrating Christie's pussy with her synthetic manhood dagger. Christie embraces her makeshift rack even tighter. Moaning from Sabrina rapidly sliding the dildo in and out of her.

"What do you think, Magnum?" Sabrina asks while staring intently at Christie's asshole.

"Sabrina, don't just stare at it," he grows ever more brazen in the moment, "Eat it."

"I was getting to that," she giggles, "You know? I think Christie's face needs sacrificing too."

"Mmm-hmm…" Christie enthusiastically sighs.

Magnum grabs a chair and sets it before Christie's face. Removing his g-string. Sitting with his butt on the edge. "L.O.V.E. Machine" by W.A.S.P. stomps forth. She grips his cock tightly. Stroking it vigorously. Twirling her tongue all around his head. Making him throb. Body tingling. Juices flowing. She takes him deep in her throat. Licking every inch of his shaft. Bobbing her head up and down. He watches Sabrina. On her knees. Eating her friend's ass. Teasing and caressing Christie's tight butthole. Thrusting her tongue in and out. She's no stranger to rimming. Now beside himself with excitement over meeting a kindred spirit in both heavy metal and eating ass.

"I think you two should switch," Christie removes herself from Magnum, "It's time to feel the real thing."

Sabrina's ass takes the place of Magnum's on the chair's edge. She holds onto Christie's head as her friend wastes no time eating her out. Sucking her clit and lips. Tongue thrusting deep insider her sugar walls. Sabrina's sweetness unleashing all over Christie's face. Magnum drops to his knees behind Christie. Giving her pussy the same treatment. Devouring her juices. So warm and delicious. His inner devil in full effect. Inserting his middle finger inside her. Massaging her g-spot. Circling the delicate ridges of her butthole with his tongue. Pushing it inside. She rocks her ass gently against his face. Inviting him to enjoy her forbidden candy. Demanding it.

Christie trembles from his fingers and tongue, and he's now ready to make her shake. Leaning over her body. Pressing the head of his cock against her pussy. She's so wet that he has no problem sliding every inch of his manhood inside her. His pelvis smacking against her ass with each thrust. Faster. Harder. Fucking Christie while watching her consume her friend. Sabrina grinding her pussy on Christie's face. Gazing devilishly at him. Their eyes speaking volumes to each other. Sharing a girl. Each getting off even more by watching the other have their way with her. Magnum can't get enough of watching Christie eat Sabrina's pussy. Sabrina can't get enough of watching Magnum fuck Christie from behind. And Christie is about to explode from it all.

"Oh God!" she exclaims, "I'm going to fucking cum!"

"Do it, baby!" Sabrina orders, "Cum all over Magnum's big hard cock!"

"Cum on my face, baby!" Christie instructs her.

"I am!" Sabrina cries, "While Magnum cums in your pussy!"

"Oh, fuck! I'm cumming hard!" he yells, "Let's do it!"

He unleashes a tidal wave of white-hot cum inside Christie's tight swollen pussy as her warm sweetness washes over his cock and pelvis. Streaming down his legs. Sabrina does the same on Christie's face. Smothering her friend with her pussy. All three crying out in agonizing ecstasy. Then overcome with laughter. Shocked and elated about what they've just done. Giving in to temptation so easily and extravagantly. Not even the devil himself can hold a candle to their insatiable decadence right now. The trio basking in the afterglow of an act so incredibly immoral by conventional standards yet feeling so unbelievably right. Their shared carnal excesses truly a light of salvation cutting through the darkness.

"Now that's what I call a human sacrifice," he removes himself from Christie and stands before helping her do the same.

"Hells yeah it is," Christie holds onto him, and Sabrina joins them for a three-way embrace as they kiss one another with reckless abandon.

"More drinks," Sabrina announces while grabbing Christie by the hand and leading her upstairs.

Magnum stands alone within his new demonic red heaven. Boots still inside the pentagram. He's never been much for religion or a believer in spooky kabuki stuff. Even if the latter does make for terrific arts and entertainment fare. But there's real-life magic about this spot. About this entire space in general. An escape from the judgmentalism and false morality of the immediate world outside. A world in which adults can't even legally purchase alcohol. How does that make any sense? And no matter what anyone would think if they knew what happens in this basement, he's all too aware that truly evil things are happening in the homes of so-called "good people" at this very moment.

"We're back!" Sabrina walks downstairs with Christie in tow, "Sorry, we were having girl talk."

"Girl talk," Christie hands him another Jack and Coke, "About your amazing cock."

"Thank you," he laughs, "For the drink and the compliment."

"You're welcome," she smiles, "It's true."

"So…" Sabrina bats her eyelashes at him, "Will I get to find out for myself how awesome it is?"

"Give me a minute," he sighs, "Someone just took a lot out of me."

"Of course. I didn't mean right this second," she laughs, "The night is still young."

"I'll drink to that," he raises his glass as Sabrina and Christie concur.

"You know," Sabrina opines, "We're not actually Satanists."

"I know that," he laughs, "I've known a few actual Satanists."

"Really?" she inquires, "What were they like?"

"Kind of boring, to be honest," he explains, "They spent more time rambling about their philosophies than living them. If you claim to be a hedonist, maybe you should do something hedonistic once in a while."

"Interesting," she ponders, "It makes me feel not so boring for being just a regular old Christian."

"You're clearly not a regular old Christian," he shakes his head.

"I guess you're right." she laughs.

"We just like to have fun," Christie puts her arm around Sabrina, "And we're really good friends," then kisses her.

"I can tell," he agrees, "That's great."

"This is where fantasies are made," she continues, "What's a fantasy you'd like to experience? Although I'm sure you've already done everything you've wanted."

"That reminds me," he stares at them, "What was the deal with you two checking out my ass earlier?"

"Oh that," Sabrina giggles along with Christie, "We were discussing eating your ass while watching you dance on Olivia."

"I'm sure you've had plenty of girls do that to you," Christie assumes.

"Not really," he admits.

"Really?" Sabrina is surprised, "I was picturing you having a hot girl eat your ass while another hot girl sucks your cock."

"That has never happened," he confesses.

"Well," Christie runs her finger down his torso, "Let's change that."

Magnum grips the steel I-beam above him. Struggling to stay on his feet within the pentagram. Still naked. But his cowboy boots remain. As they always do. He can't see himself not literally dying with his boots on someday. And if he were to die right now, he couldn't complain in the slightest. "Sucking My Love" by Diamond Head struts provocatively all around him. Sabrina on her knees behind him. Licking deep inside his asshole. Tasting him. Gently massaging every nerve ending with her wet and delicate tongue. She moans and whimpers with every lashing. As orgasmic as he is right now, he thinks she's somehow even more turned on than him.

"Oh my God," she sighs, "You taste so fucking good."

Christie on her knees before him. His hard, throbbing cock deep in her throat once again. So warm and wet. Soft like velvet. Her tongue swirling around his head and shaft. His juices flowing like crazy. Pressing the tip of her tongue gently into his cock hole. Another orgasm overtakes him. Filling her wanting mouth with even more precum.

"Mmm…" she hums on his massive cock, "Your juices are yummy."

"Ooh…" Sabrina removes her face from between his cheeks, "I need to taste them for myself."

"Then give me a turn on his sexy ass," Christie responds as they switch places.

Cold steel growing warm between clenched fists. Knuckles turning whiter as he grips for his life. Head tossed back in ecstasy. Pure decadence. The unadulterated hedonism others merely claim to embody. He's living it. Eyes shut. Seeing all. Naked in every way imaginable. In the company of two naked girls he's known for an hour or so. One sucking his cock. The other eating his ass. His manhood so ridiculously hard that it hurts now. Hurting wonderfully. He can't remember the last time he felt so fucking alive.

"I love it," Christie coos.

She alternates between circling his butthole with her magic tongue and sliding it inside him. He loves having his ass eaten, but not by just any girl. It's so erotic and naughty, but also extremely personal. To encounter two girls at once he feels comfortable with letting pleasure his booty is rare indeed. As Christie pushes her tongue deep in his asshole, it pushes more of his juices into Sabrina's mouth.

"Mmm… You taste delicious," she moans breathlessly, "I can't wait to feel you inside me."

"I can't either," he pushes from his lips while digging his fingers into steel from another intense orgasm, "You know what?"

"What?" she looks with curiosity into his eyes.

"It's time…" he lets go of the I-beam, "It's time for another human sacrifice."

"Fuck yeah it is!" Christie rushes around and slaps Sabrina's ass, "Get on that bench, bitch!"

"Who are you calling a bitch?" Sabrina lies down on her stomach and embraces the bench.

"You, you nasty bitch," Christie spanks Sabrina's butt repeatedly.

"Oh really?" Sabrina laughs, "I think you're the nasty bitch here."

"Oh, I'll show you a nasty bitch," Christie grabs her dagger off the floor, "Spread those legs wide open."

Sabrina obliges as Christie unsheathes her dildo dagger. Stroking it with a handful of Astroglide. Magnum returns to the chair. Sabrina resumes sucking his cock. Her tongue dancing seductively around his head. Along his shaft. Making his juices flow more rapidly than ever. She gasps and shudders from the sensation of Christie sliding the dildo inside her pussy. Gripping the handle tightly. Fucking her friend fast and hard. Christie spanks Sabrina's ass with her other hand. Making her cheeks bounce before squeezing them. Then kissing and licking them. Until finally burying her face between them and eating her friend's asshole.

"Oh my God, Magnum," Sabrina sighs, "Christie is licking my butthole."

"I see her," he laughs, "You're both a couple of nasty bitches."

"Hells yeah we are!" Christie confirms, "You know you like it."

"Of course I do," he admits, "Who wouldn't?"

"Oh my God, you're making me wet," Sabrina exudes breathlessly, "Both of you."

"You're both making me wet," Christie concurs.

"Really?" Sabrina glances back, "Let me see."

Christie switches places with Magnum. Tossing back her head. Eyes closed. Legs spread wide open. Sighing in pure decadence as Sabrina licks the length of her pussy from back to front. Deep inside her sugar walls. Losing herself in her friend's sweetness. Every wave. Every drop. Teasing her clit. Then her lips. Sucking them with authority. Both girls trembling from behavior that is taboo yet comforting. Dangerous yet safe. Consumed with the unexpected purity of submitting to their sexual deviance. Contrary to everything they've been taught. Feeling so healthy and right that it'd be immoral not for them to indulge their carnal desires. To allow their friendship the opportunity to break down arbitrary barriers of mutual pleasure.

All concepts he has pondered endlessly as time goes on. Here he is again. Exploring the real-world legitimacy of these philosophies. "Thunder and Lightning" by Thin Lizzy setting the appropriate rhythm and pace. His tongue dancing on Sabrina's clit. Deep within her soft velvety love tunnel. Making her even wetter from his oral lashing. Slipping his fingers inside her. Gliding his tongue around her pretty butthole. Trembling while pushing inside. Giving into anything and everything he wants to do with her. No fear. Giving himself entirely to his sexually dominant nature. Thrusting his tongue deep inside her ass. Because that's exactly what he wants to do right now.

"Magnum's tongue is deep in my asshole," she looks up at Christie.

"Yes. it is," Christie coos, "Watching him is making me even wetter."

It's all too much for Magnum. Rising and leaning over Sabrina. Gripping her ass with tingling hands. Plunging his massive throbbing cock all the way inside her pussy. So tight. So wet. His size forcing her to make room for him while clamping down at once. Yet her endless stream of girl juices keeps him on the brink of slipping out. But he's determined to stay inside her. Thrusting deep and hard. Over and over. Pounding her pussy with reckless abandon. Fucking the absolute fucking fuck out of her. Shoving her face-first into her Christie's pussy as she continues eating out her friend. He is truly living in the moment. Embracing his own devilish nature. Loving every minute of it.

"Oh God, Magnum!" Sabrina cries, "Don't stop fucking me!"

"Magnum has his cock deep inside your pussy, baby," Christie moans as Sabrina continues devouring her pussy.

"I've wanted his cock deep inside me ever since I first saw him online," Sabrina confesses.

"Ooh… Me too," Christie seconds.

He is overwhelmed with emotion by this. Responding by continuing to make Sabrina's fantasy a reality. Fucking her viciously. She gushes forth a tidal wave of sweetness. Gripping his steel rod tightly. Rocking her ass and fucking him back. Making his juices flow nonstop. She begins squirting from the sensation of his head rubbing her g-spot relentlessly. All three moaning and screaming insatiably from the pleasure they each give and receive. A rigorous exercise in carnal gratification. The devil himself smiling upon them to the beat of eighties speed metal.

"Oh God, I'm cumming!" Christie squirts hot juices into Sabrina's mouth and drenches her face.

"Me too! Fuck!" Sabrina unleashes burning juices all over him that makes his skin tingle even more.

"Oh fuck!" he can hold back no longer.

His cock erupts inside Sabrina's pussy. Ejaculating so much cum that she can't hold it all. Their combined love potion racing down their legs. He falls forward on her back. Christie leans in and holds him. They now feel a slight underground chill in the late April night air during their naked embrace. Comforting one another while coming down from their animalistic high. Shaking profusely from their mutual climax more than anything, however. Bonding in spirit as well as body tonight in multiple fashions. This moment representing the latest chapter in their one-night three-way romance.

They converse for a while. Until it becomes obvious that Sabrina and Christie, like their friends before them, have reached the end of the road for tonight. And now it's time for Magnum to leave. Quietly making his way upstairs. Still clad in only cowboy boots. The girls upstairs still asleep. He dresses and packs his things. Sabrina and Christie watch in silence. Still naked. He senses melancholy in both. While he'd be down for staying the night, that would require some explaining in the morning. He embraces his new friends, soon to be old friends, one last time. Each kissing him goodbye. Batesville itself has passed out. All is silent as he drives through town and back to U.S. 167.

Magnum is starved following his action-packed night. Stopping in Searcy after rejoining U.S. 67 for a late-night supper at IHOP. The place is hopping with college kids from the nearby private college. One noted for its religion-fueled puritanism. He wants to instinctively assume not one of them had anywhere near the night he has. It's a prudent assumption. They're just kids. Innocent and wide-eyed. Seemingly ignorant to anything near the level of sexual debauchery from which he has carved a career. And that's most likely the case. But he remembers how Sabrina and Christie came across initially to him. Innocent and wide-eyed.

He sits alone in his booth. Drinking coffee. Eating his omelet. Hopelessly reflecting upon his experience tonight within the general context of omnipresent Arkansas social conservatism. Privy to the façade that it is in many instances. An exercise in superficial morality. In maintaining appearances at all costs. A lie. And a dangerous one at that. Fascinated to no end by his extensive knowledge of what occurs beneath that surface. Wondering how far the depravity, both good and evil, extends beyond what he has witnessed firsthand. All bets are off after darkness falls. When the devil himself is watching.

August

For Magnum, there's something about the westbound drive on I-30 between Little Rock and Texarkana. Particularly on an early hot August evening such as this. A saturated green wall of lush and majestic trees lining either side of the freeway. Dividing it for numerous stretches. Everything about this trek exudes a special energy. Mile after mile. Moment by moment. There's no denying the excitement within him every time he drives to a party, no matter the route. But this one is different. A certain magic always filling the air. Like none he's felt anywhere else in Arkansas. Permeating through his memories of performing all along this corridor. This modern-day stretch of the Southwest Trail.

Memories he's currently sharing with Candi and Roxy on their way to a booking just outside Hope, Arkansas. Thirty minutes shy of Texarkana and the Arkansas-Texas border. "Motorvatin'" by Hanoi Rocks carries them along the blacktop. He ponders the oddity that, despite performing in Texarkana on multiple occasions, it's always been on the Texas side. As for Roxy... She's his newest talent acquisition. Albeit a temporary one. Having rolled in from Florida to assist her newly divorced sister with the kids for a year. Coming with both gentlemen's club and private party experience in South Florida and Manhattan.

"I've always heard that Hot Springs is fun," she muses as they pass the U.S. 70 turnoff.

"Yeah, I've had some fun nights there," he confirms.

"Me too," Candi adds.

Roxy is into bondage and incorporates it into her performances. She's also into girls. Instantly expressing an attraction to Candi after seeing her on the website. Candi returned the sentiment after he texted her photos of his latest applicant. Getting her expert opinion before bringing the new girl on board. And so, tonight is Roxy's first show through his agency. Performing with him and Candi at a joint bachelor/bachelorette party. All things considered, he can't wait to see his new entertainer in action.

"What about Magnet Cove?" Roxy inquiries near Malvern and the U.S. 270 turnoff.

"Just a small community on the way to Hot Springs," he answers before adding, "But... George Featherstonhaugh stopped there on his journey along the Southwest Trail in 1834."

He feels Candi and Roxy staring at him blankly while passing another trucker on their way to what promises to be an insane party. The bachelorette herself, an expressive young woman named Erin, booked the trio for her, her fiancée, and their closest friends. Informing Magnum that she wants to "go for broke" tonight with both a male and female stripper. It took little effort on his part to get Roxy on the bill too. The client loving the idea of two girls and one guy. She was also generous enough to offer them use of a guest house on her property. Meaning the strippers can drink all they want and not worry about driving back to Little Rock late tonight.

Although Magnum wasted no time breaking the rule about not fucking his girls when Candi came aboard, she remains the only one he's fucked. Numerous attractive women have passed through his agency since, but none ever got his motor running as she does. Until now. Roxy turns him on. She's been flirting with him. And not in the "please get me work" sort of fashion he's had thrown his way countless times. He confided in Candi about this, who laughed it off. Saying he was still being unnecessarily hard on himself. Admitting that she's also having impure thoughts about the new girl. Becoming even more enthusiastic about tonight when informed that Roxy would be joining them. Thinking the same thing he was. It wouldn't be the first time they've shared a girl. And anything is possible on a night like this.

"What about Social Hill?" Roxy ponders.

"What about it?" he laughs.

"I wonder what's on the other side of all those trees," she gazes to the south between Malvern and Arkadelphia.

"Right here?" he shakes his head, "The Ouachita River. And a tiny community named Brown Springs."

"Eww…" she giggles, "Really?"

"Believe it or not…" he informs her, "I did a bachelorette party there once."

"Are you fucking serious?" she asks.

"He did," Candi interjects, "And he likes bringing it up. You were bound to hear about it sooner or later."

"So," Roxy leans forward from the backseat, "How was it?"

"It was okay. Nothing special," he fills her in, "I mostly remember the home's interior being stuck in the seventies. Shag carpet and dark wood paneling."

"Did you put your dick up any girls' brown springs?" she asks as if desperately wanting the answer to be yes.

"What?!" Candi nearly spits water all over the dashboard while overcome with laughter.

"Did you just make an anal sex joke?" he glances at her with shocked amusement.

"Yeah," she nods sheepishly, "But it's a legit question. Besides, anal is hot."

"Oh yeah," Candi shoots him a sassy look, "With the right person."

"It's alright," he coyly agrees.

"It's alright," Roxy smacks him playfully on the shoulder, "Whatever, bad boy."

"He really is," Candi piles on, "I could tell you some stories."

"Well, I can't wait to see him be one tonight," Roxy enthuses.

"I'm not the one on the spot tonight," he reminds his newbie stripper.

"I know," she replies, "And I promise not to disappoint."

"Believe me," he half-jokes, "I'll be up your ass if you do."

"Magnum," she coos, "You can get up my ass anytime."

"There you go," Candi laughs.

"You too, Candi," Roxy doubles down.

"Ooh… Baby," Candi flirts as they giggle.

The conversation of Arkansas geography and various sex acts continues as they follow the sun into its western descent. Past exits for places like Caddo Valley and Gum Springs.

"You know," Roxy muses, "Gum Springs just doesn't have the same ring to it as Brown Springs."

Darkness quickly setting upon reaching Hope. Magnum turns north on U.S. 278. Switching off the air conditioner. Rolling down the windows as the humidity of a just-passed rainstorm fogs his vision. Taking in the fresh Arkansas Timberlands summer night air. "Animal" by Def Leppard carries them along the home stretch. No words spoken. The sheer beauty of the world around them all the conversation they need. A perfect calm before the storm of pure debauchery awaiting them down the road. He watches for a decommissioned cattle ranch along the highway just before Historic Washington State Park.

"Well, tie me up and spank me," Roxy basks in the natural beauty surrounding her, "This is fucking gorgeous."

"It truly is," he concurs, "I've been out here once before, but not for a party."

"It's exciting, isn't it?" Candi asks rhetorically as she knows him all too well.

"Yeah," he answers with a preemptive sentimentality uncharacteristic of him.

It's a feeling Magnum can't shake. Nor does he want to, he decides while coming upon a large white two-story home on the east side of the highway. Set fifty yards back against a wall of trees to the north. Another cluster along the west side. Its front faces south towards a gravel road. Buffered by a vast lawn. Ten or so vehicles parked on the grass. And the client in a midsize SUV parked at the end of a long dirt driveway. Awaiting their arrival right on time as night completes its descent upon the world.

"Hey!" Erin greets them with the signature mix of excitement and intimidation Magnum has heard countless times from clients, "Y'all made it!"

"Of course we made it," he laughs, "We couldn't get here fast enough."

"Oh my God, this is so exciting!" she gushes before composing herself slightly, "Um… So, follow me to the guest house. It's just down this road a way."

Erin pulls onto the gravel road. It's nice by gravel road standards. Well packed. And the rain from moments earlier holds down the dust. The warmth and stickiness of the air are apparent now that they're off the highway. But it still feels good. The absence of mosquitoes certainly helps. Magnum leaves the music off as he and his partners in crime enjoy the sounds of insects and frogs. Absorbing the country life all around them. Driving past large dilapidated cattle pens and overgrown grazing fields. Charmingly rustic reminders of a once-bustling ranch now slowly being reclaimed by nature.

The road winds around a short yet wide hill. Now half a mile from the road as they wrap around the other side. A pond rests at the base. Freshly stocked with rainwater. Filling the air with that distinctive aroma of purity and cleanliness. On the opposite side of the road sits an old cottage. Surprisingly well maintained given its location. Hidden from the outside world. The road ends a little further on at the entrance to a large barn that isn't so well preserved. An ominous specter giving the vast forest beyond this country oasis a haunted quality. Looking like the sort of place Jason Voorhees roams in the night.

"Oh wow!" Candi gets out, "This is amazing!"

"Totally," Roxy agrees.

"Yeah, I think it's kind of special," Erin confides, "Sometimes I like to spend the night here. Clear my mind, you know?"

"This would be the place to do that," he stretches his legs.

"Come on," Erin motions, "I'll show you inside."

She flips on a light and reveals a studio floorplan that keeps the interior from feeling cramped. Exposed wooden ceiling beams offer a nice contrast to the semigloss white walls. Sparingly adorned with stark black and white photographic prints of what appears to be the surrounding area. There's a kitchenette with an electric range and old refrigerator. An open door reveals a bathroom. The remainder of the floor space contains a king-size bed, dining table and chairs, sofa, and wood stove. There's also a pair of large box fans.

"I'm sorry there's no air conditioning," she turns them on.

"Don't apologize," he shakes his head, "This is great. We really appreciate it."

"Oh, you're most welcome," she smiles, "It's a long drive back to Little Rock. Plus, I'm hoping you'll have a few drinks with us too."

"We'd love to," Roxy instinctively responds before catching herself and looking at Magnum, "That's cool, right?"

"Of course it is," he laughs in appreciation of her enthusiasm.

"Oh, and here you go," Erin hands him the booking fee.

"Thank you," he counts it in front of everyone to ensure they're all on the same page regarding the money, "We'll get ready and be up there in forty-five minutes."

"Perfect," she smiles, "I'll get out of your hair. Text me if you need anything."

"I will," he nods, "Thanks."

"Thank you," she turns and leaves.

Magnum opens all the windows while Candi and Roxy retrieve their stripping bags from the car. After strategically positioning the fans to what he thinks will be a suitable arrangement, he walks outside to grab his gear. Not needing as much prep as the girls he takes his time. Standing alone outside. Soaking it in. The undeniable magic of it all. A gorgeous setting. The intoxicating scent of trees and rain filling his mind. Warm summer night air embracing him. Two hot girls chattering and giggling away inside. The trio hidden away in their own private fantasyland. And oodles of money about to be made. He'd kill like Jason Voorhees for every night to be like tonight.

A naked Candi is standing over the bed when he goes back inside. Bent over just enough to get his imagination running wild. Waiting on him to help her decide on an outfit and accessories for tonight. This has become a tradition for their joint performances. She's not indecisive. Rather she values his eye for aesthetics and respects his opinion. Not unlike how he consults with her before bringing new entertainers aboard. His respect for her opinion on various matters just as immense. Out of all the entertainers he's represented, she's the only one who's never done him wrong. Save for Roxy, but there's still time for her. Not tonight, though. He's confident that Candi will assist him in ensuring the new girl makes a smashing debut.

"What do you have going on here?" he asks her bare ass before circling to the other side of the bed.

"Well, since you're doing cowboy tonight," she holds up a skimpy white boho dress, "I was thinking this dress and this hat," pointing to a black cowgirl hat with turquoise band.

"Love it," he says to her tits before looking at all her clothes sprawled across the bed and wonders how she always manages to fit so much shit into a standard size gym bag, "This would go perfect with it," he holds up a turquoise g-string.

"I thought about that," she shakes her head, "But I don't have a matching bikini top."

"You don't need one," he embraces the inspiration striking him, "Just the g-string and dress will be perfect. Trust me on this. I can see it now."

"Are you sure?" she questions.

"We're in the country now, Candi," he remarks facetiously, "It's time to let your girls run free."

"Oh my God," Candi falls upon the bed in a fit of laughter.

"What am I missing?" Roxy enters from the bathroom with lipstick in hand.

"I'm just helping Candi get dressed," he replies.

"Oh good," Roxy grabs her bag and dumps its entire contents on the sofa, "You can help me pick out what to wear."

"Jesus Christ," he sifts through her sexy outfits and unmentionables along with handcuffs, ropes, restraints, a blindfold, paddle, and cat o nine tails, "You weren't joking about incorporating BDSM into your performances."

"Nope," she declares proudly, "Hey, this is very light stuff. I'm not into serious pain. Just a little discipline and restraint."

"Ooh, I have a paddle just like this," Candi joins them to see what all the fuss is about, "I use it on guys at parties."

"Ever use it on Magnum," Roxy inquires.

"No," Candi sighs, "He always has to be in control."

"That's right," he lectures, "The alpha must distinguish himself from the betas."

"Whatever," Roxy scoffs, "Now, tell me what me to wear."

"Exactly," he looks through her wardrobe.

Candi takes her turn at the bathroom mirror while Magnum sets up Roxy with her short buckskin dress and red g-string.

"What about a bikini top," Roxy asks.

"Nope," he shakes his head, "You and Candi are going titty commando tonight."

"Ooh… I like it," Roxy starts undressing.

Magnum sets his stripping bag on the table like a civilized person. Removing its organized contents one at a time. Tear-away jeans, denim jacket, black cowboy hat, and bullwhip.

"Oh my God! You have a bullwhip?" Roxy is completely naked and in his face without warning.

"Yeah," he responds matter of factly.

"You have to spank me with it," she demands.

"Don't worry," he assures her, "I will shortly."

"No. You have to spank me now," she bends over the sofa and wiggles her butt at him, "I've been a very naughty girl."

"Fine," he relents in an odd combination of curiosity and wanting to get her back on track for the task at hand. Standing behind her. Spanking her eager rear with his coiled whip. Not hard. Just enough to give her ass a slight sting.

"Ooh… fuck yes," she moans, "Spank me, boss man."

He keeps going.

"Oh my God, Magnum," she sighs, "You are making my pussy so wet for you."

"What the fuck are you two doing?" Candi walks in while he tries to fathom a response to Roxy's dirty talk.

"Magnum's getting me ready to perform," Roxy stands and faces them, "And now I'm ready to bring down the house."

She gets dressed while Candi shakes her head and laughs at him. It's one of those moments when he's not sure if she's annoyed with him. It's a weird situation with her. He knows she has feelings for him but also enjoys her sexual freedom. It's confusing for her too. Feeling a twinge of jealousy seeing him interact with other women. Then catching herself before coming across as hypocritical. Remembering that she likes playing with girls too. It's not so much jealousy as it is Candi not wanting him to forget about her. Loving every minute of their fun together. It's how their relationship has always been. So close yet so far apart all at once. They try not to think about it for the most part. It's now his turn to get naked. He strips down and grabs his bottle of baby oil. Preparing to get his shine on.

"Can you reach your own back with that?" Roxy asks.

"Pretty well," he answers, "I've had lots of practice."

"I've always wondered how guys get themselves all oiled up," she ponders.

"At the last male revue I did several years ago… The other guys were oiling up one another's back," he laments, "One even had the nerve to ask me if I would oil his."

"Eww… That's fucking gross," she cringes, "I hope you told him to go to hell."

"I told him to do what I always did at male reviews," he explains, "I'd grab a girl from the audience, take her to a private place, and charged her twenty bucks for the privilege of oiling up my entire body."

"That's what I'm talking about!" she enthuses, "Ever have two girls oil you up at once?"

"A time or two," he responds coyly.

"Make that a time or three," she looks towards the bathroom, "Hey, Candi!"

"What's up?" Candi approaches them.

"Magnum wants us to oil up his hot naked body," Roxy informs her.

"Why didn't you say so?" Candi looks at him sassily as she and Roxy help themselves to covering his skin with baby oil.

"Hey, not too much," he instructs them.

"We have to get you all shiny for that nice bachelorette who's letting us stay here tonight," Roxy explains while she and Candi each take a leg, followed by an arm.

"Get his back," Candi orders Roxy while oiling his chest and looking at him seductively.

"Male strippers oiling each another's back," Roxy mutters, "That's fucking bullshit."

"I know," he nods

"Ooh, that's nice," she coos before moving around and working his pecs with Candi.

"You should feel his ass," Candi leads her behind him to massage and squeeze his butt with oily hands.

"You know you like it," Roxy smacks his ass.

"Let's get his cock too," Candi giggles.

"What?" he questions, "I don't need my cock all oily."

"Yes, you do," Roxy argues, "You can titty-fuck us during the show."

"Let's not get too far ahead of ourselves…" he protests.

"Or," she cuts him off, "You can titty-fuck the bachelorette. She's totally down for it. Believe me."

"We'll see…" he trails off as Roxy gently strokes his ever-growing cock.

"You can go harder than that," Candi informs her while gripping his shaft and stroking vigorously, "He loves it."

"Oh fuck," he feels his knees instantly weaken.

"Like this?" Roxy replicates Candi's technique and nearly brings him to orgasm.

"Okay," he stops them, "It's nearly showtime."

The girls giggle and pack what they'll need before putting the finishing touches on their hair and makeup. He throws on his costume, gathers his necessities, and turns off the fans. Then the lights as they head out the door.

"What about the windows?" Roxy asks.

"We're in the middle of fucking nowhere," he reminds her.

"Oh yeah," she laughs as they pile into the car.

Windows still down as they head back towards the highway. To what is sure to be the wildest party in Arkansas tonight. Blasting music this time. "Welcome to the Jungle" by Guns N' Roses crashing into the night. Getting them into the mood for hedonistic fun with a crazy young couple and their friends. Magnum knows the gig itself is guaranteed to be epic. But what about the after-party? Skinny dipping? Spanking? Nude oil wrestling? Anything is possible on a night like tonight. He can fucking feel it. So does Candi. Already tingling with anticipation for the show and after-party with him and Roxy. Wanting to show off all that she's learned since that first night with him.

Pandemonium breaks out as the sexy trio enters the house. Cheers and laughter fill the air. Drenched in excitement and nervousness amped to eleven. Having one or even two strippers invade a party is crazy enough. But three? And the combination of one guy and two girls? Magnum guarantees in his mind this is the only place in the world right now where that's a thing. Their audience having every reason for being beside themselves with unbridled delight. Erin having every reason to beam proudly from ear to ear from what she's accomplished tonight. In that sense, this entrance alone is more than worth the booking fee just for its sheer impact upon this group of close friends.

As the strippers instinctively take in their new surroundings, it's obvious that all the stops have been rolled out for them. The cavernous living room devoid of furniture save for chairs. Lined up in a ninety-degree angle along two edges of a massive Navajo rug covering a hardwood floor. The vaulted ceiling reaching two stories, with the upstairs hallway functioning as a balcony on one side. The entire space illuminated by the ever-changing colors of disco lights. Everything here feels larger than it really is. Larger than life. Magnum feels the energy of Candi and Roxy standing on either side of him. The energy of their audience. His own energy. All of it about to converge and result in a sum greater than its parts.

Magnum sets up the music while Candi and Roxy walk the audience line. All in their places with bright smiling faces. Kid Rock's "Cowboy" puts things in motion as he struts to the center of the room. Unrolling his bullwhip. Unleashing a crack so deafening that everyone jumps despite knowing it was coming. He and his girls move Erin and her husband, named Aaron, to the center of the rug. Facing each other. Magnum goes to work on his bachelorette with Candi and Erin tag-teaming their bachelor.

"So, you both have the same name?" Candi makes small talk.

"That's right," Aaron laughs nervously.

"But they're spelled differently," Erin explains in all seriousness.

"I hope so," Magnum laughs.

"That was stupid," Erin sighs, "I know."

"No, it was adorable," he assures her.

Magnum straddles her lap. Wrapping his bullwhip around her. Pulling himself tight against her as she giggles. He drops the whip and takes off his denim jacket to the approval of all women present. Erin's girlfriends encouraging her while she squeezes his pecs. Slowly running her hands down his torso. He grinds on her lap. The guys in the audience hooting at Aaron as he finds double trouble in the form of Candi and Roxy. And at his bride-to-be's insistence. He's one lucky bastard.

"Mmm…" Erin whispers in Magnum's ear, "You smell incredible."

"Y'all better make the most of this!" shouts a woman, "It's the last night of freedom for both of you!"

"Whatever," Erin retorts, "We're getting married, not buried!"

The entire room erupts in shocked laughter at this possible revelation. Is it true? It's certainly possible. Magnum has learned over the years that monogamy isn't quite as widespread as many would believe. Avowed swingers aside, he's encountered many couples who share some degree of openness. Playing with girls together. Getting extra touchy-feely with other couples. Maybe not sexual intercourse. And maybe not often. But when the right playmate comes along and all the pieces fall into place, such a couple may feel free to temporarily broaden their horizons. However, this is no time for Magnum to wax philosophical on relationships. He stands and removes his belt. Smacking Erin's booty as she leans to the side.

"Get her good for this," Aaron calls out.

Magnum glances back to see Candi and Roxy holding up their skirts. Double booty shaking in Aaron's face while he fills their g-strings with cash. Prompting Magnum to get on with it. Having Erin grab the waistband of his jeans. He steps backward out of them. The female entertainers seizing the opportunity to grab his ass.

"Hey!" Erin scolds them, "You can grab his ass all you want at the pond later. It's my turn right now."

"Oh, you want some of this?" he spins around and rubs his butt on her tits, "Then get it!"

"That's what I'm talking about!" she fills his g-string with a mix of denominations while spanking and squeezing his cheeks before motorboating them.

"Erin!" a woman shouts.

"Hey!" she retorts, "I told you already."

He kicks his legs back and falls forward onto his hands. Thrusting his cock against his bachelorette's pussy while she continues massaging his ass. Candi and Roxy turn around and face their bachelor. Looking at each other knowingly before removing their dresses in perfect synchronicity. Everyone cheers as Magnum's girls shake their girls in Aaron's face.

"Four titties and one mouth, Aaron," Erin observes, "How on earth will you manage?"

"I may need your help," he taunts her.

"Hey, I'm down," she giggles.

"Not before me, though," Magnum corrects her.

He heads to his bag and retrieves a can of Reddi-wip. Shaking it as he walks back to his bachelorette. Her face lighting up. He kneels between her legs. Drawing a line of whipped cream along her cleavage. Squeezing her tits. Leaning forward. Licking it slowly. Until they're face to face.

"Ooh… That's nice." she sighs, "My turn."

He hands her the can. She applies whipped cream to his nipples. Grabbing his butt and leaning in. Taking her time licking and sucking his nipples clean. Making every attempt to please and arouse him. And it's working. She goes and sits on Aaron's lap. Magnum sprays Reddi-wip on his girls' nipples. Candi leans into the bachelor and bachelorette. They each take a breast. Gazing into each other's eyes while sucking a girl's tits together. Roxy takes Candi's place and the act is repeated. The audience in shock and awe at this display of pure decadence. Loving every minute of it.

"Alright, turn around," Erin order Candi and Roxy.

She applies Reddi-wip to their butts as they bend over. The bachelor and bachelorette lean in. Licking each wiggling cheek clean and slapping it.

"What about Magnum?" Candi suggests.

"You're right," Roxy returns Erin to her hot seat.

The girls kneeling on either side of her as he pulls down his g-string in the rear. Shaking his ass in their faces before Erin draws a line of whipped cream on each cheek.

"One for each of you," she informs Candi and Roxy before applying a third line along his crack, "And one for me."

Before Magnum can comprehend what's happening, his ass is treated to the soft, warm pleasure of three female tongues. Candi and Roxy kissing and licking his cheeks. But the real kicker is Erin's tongue sliding along his crack from bottom to top. Then back down. But deeper this time. All the way between his cheeks. The tip of her tongue grazing his butthole. Making him shudder in awkward delight.

"Oh, Magnum loves having his ass eaten," Candi announces to everyone much to his embarrassment.

She then ups the ante by spreading his cheeks open and circling his asshole with her tongue. Pushing it inside him as everyone cheers in shock and awe.

"My turn," Roxy takes Candi's place between Magnum's cheeks.

She explores his butthole inside and out with her tongue. He can't see Candi's face, but he can feel her surprised expression at this display from the new girl. Both caught off guard by her lack of shyness with them. Much to their mutual satisfaction.

"Oh my God, y'all are fucking out of control," Erin tells them as Roxy removes her face from Magnum's ass and he pulls up his g-string, "Aren't they the fucking best?"

Aaron and the audience agree enthusiastically. "Back That Azz Up" by Juvenile thumps across the floor while Magnum makes his lap dance rounds with the other women. Candi and Roxy take turns with the men and a few couples desiring a shared dance. Licking more whipped cream from tits and thighs. Girl by girl. Passing the Reddi-wip can to his female entertainers as a few guys and girls engage them in whipped cream titty play. Right down the line in their rural Arkansas den of iniquity. There's nowhere for this naughty trio to go tonight except for broke. And for all the right reasons.

"Oh my God, I'm so sorry." Erin breaks the spell, "I haven't asked y'all what you want to drink yet."

"Don't be sorry," he assures her, "What do you have?"

"Anything you want," she answers flirtatiously in good fun.

"Jack and Coke?" he inquires.

"Absolutely," she replies before looking at the girls.

"I'll take a Smirnoff Ice," Candi points to one held by the woman seated before her.

"Me too," Roxy says as Erin nods and heads for the kitchen with Aaron.

The strippers resume working over their audience. Rocking their world as they've never imagined in their wildest dreams. Milking them for every dollar in the process. Accumulating a mountain of cash next to their stripping bags. And every dollar is one well spent. Magnum, Candi, and Roxy turning the whipped cream on themselves. Two on one. Licking and sucking it from one another's nipples. A dozen faces pressed together for an up-close and personal view. The strippers daring their audience to join in the fun. But that's one line too many- after all the ones they've crossed tonight. It's all good. Everyone is giving their all. Entertainers and audience.

"Okay, kids," Erin returns with drinks in hands while Aaron carries a bottle of Patron Silver and several plastic shot glasses.

"That was fast," Magnum remarks offhandedly.

"It didn't take long since y'all got us worked up," Erin smiles mischievously.

"But first," Aaron announces while passing out shot glasses to everyone, "Let's do a shot together."

Everyone stands and gathers close.

"To wild nights of Arkansas strippers," he toasts as entertainers and audience raise their tiny plastic cups.

"To the hard partiers who make it all possible," Magnum adds before everyone downs their tequila at once.

He chases his shot of tequila with a long sip of Jack and Coke. Neither has ever tasted better than they do tonight. Watching his beautiful partners in crime drink their alcopops. Conversing and laughing with the audience. He should probably get involved, but he's too busy enjoying this moment of observation. Basking in the glow of all he's made possible tonight. It's everything and more he envisioned upon launching his agency years ago. The ups and downs. The trials and tribulations. The successes and failures. All of it made worthwhile as he stands here right now.

"Time to get serious," Roxy walks to her bag and returns with rope and a blindfold, "Tie me up, bad boy," she instructs Aaron.

She sits backward on a chair. He complies like a pro.

"You've done this before," she remarks.

"Oh, he's had plenty of practice on me," Erin discloses.

The audience laughs and gasps as Aaron ties Roxy's wrists and ankles to the chair before placing the blindfold on her.

"Okay, Magnum," Roxy says, "Where's that bullwhip of yours?"

"You mean this bullwhip?" he grabs it and gives her ass a light smack.

"Oh yeah. That's it," she sighs, "Let Aaron get in some licks."

"Which one?" Magnum laughs.

"Both of them," she replies.

He hands his whip to Erin, who proceeds to lightly spank Roxy. Trading off with Aaron back and forth. Roxy encouraging them nonstop along with "Party Like a Rockstar" by Shop Boyz. The audience screaming with excitement as Magnum and Candi look on with stunned expressions. Neither having witnessed something like this before in their combined years of experience. Proving there really is a first time for everything. Even for these seasoned entertainers. But they go along with zero hesitation. Partying like the rock stars they most definitely are night after wild night.

"Come on. You can spank my ass a little harder than that," Roxy chides the bachelor and bachelorette, "Magnum. Come put your cock in my mouth."

All eyes are on Magnum now. He glances at Candi, who gives him a look that says, "Might as well at this point." So, he goes for broke. Standing before Roxy. Removing his growing cock from his g-string. Pressing it against her lips. Grabbing her chair. Leaning forward as she opens her mouth. Taking him deep in her throat. Swirling her tongue around his head and shaft. Moaning and sucking his cock while getting spanked by Aaron and Erin. Magnum's precum flowing more and more into her wanting mouth. "Mmm…" she hums on his manhood. Rocking her head slightly. Stroking him with her mouth and tongue. Candi hands him his drink. Booze and head at once. He is truly living the dream right now.

"Your turn, Candi," Roxy removes her mouth from Magnum's cock.

He motions for a stunned Candi to take his place. She holds Roxy's head in her hands. Guiding her mouth to her pussy. Shuddering as Roxy licks and sucks her clit. Stroking Roxy's hair.

"Someone pull my hair," Roxy demands, "Not too hard, though."

"Don't worry, Aaron's had a lot of practice with that, too," Erin confides as Aaron gently tugs on Roxy's hair while she eats Candi's pussy.

"Mmm… Someone's getting wet," Roxy giggles.

"Someone's making me wet," Candi sighs.

She starts giggling. Then laughing as she falls backward. Magnum catches her before she lands on her ass.

"Hey," Roxy protests, "I'm not done with you yet."

Erin puts her finger on her lips while tiptoeing around the chair. Bending over and removing her thong. Lifting her skirt and leaning her pussy into Roxy's tongue.

"Hmm…" Roxy ponders while eating Erin's pussy.

The audiences' jaws dropped in stunned silence.

"Erin!" shouts the same loudmouth woman from earlier.

Roxy and Erin burst out laughing.

"Hey!" Erin snaps, "What happens at this party stays at this party!"

"I knew something was different," Roxy admits, "But you're too sweet for me to complain."

"Aww, thank you," Erin gushes.

"I need a break," Roxy says, "My limbs are starting to fall asleep."

"Oh, let's get you untied," Erin removes Roxy's blindfold before she and Aaron untie her.

The three entertainers take a bow and receive a standing ovation.

"More shots!" Aaron grabs the Patron.

Magnum, Candi, and Roxy get dressed before spending another hour with their party people. Drinking. Conversing. Dancing the night away. The strippers hit the food table. Starving after the drive and performance. Loading up on mini quiches and tiny chicken salad sandwiches.

"Take as much as you want when you leave," Aaron offers, "We got way more than we'll eat."

"Thank you," they nod towards him and Erin.

The guests begin leaving. Couple by couple. Wishing the strippers a good night and safe trip back to Little Rock in the morning. When it's down to them and the star couple, they begin packing up their things. Erin fixes a plate of food piled high, followed by Aaron presenting them with a cooler full of Smirnoff Ice.

"We picked up way too many of these too," he explains, "I figure y'all can have an after-party at the pond."

"Thank you so much," Candi and Roxy kiss him on the cheek.

"We'd love to join you," Erin laughs, "But you wore us out."

"Yeah," Magnum tells her coyly, "We tend to do that."

"Thank you for totally making our night," she hugs him while slipping an extra hundred for each of them into his hand.

"No, thank you for everything," he responds, "We truly appreciate it."

"Absolutely," Candi and Roxy agree in unison.

The strippers head out into the night. Loading their gear and hard-earned refreshments in the trunk before heading back to the pond. "Easy Come Easy Go" by Winger fills their space and carries out the windows while Magnum crawls down the gravel road. The insects sing along from all directions. He's a little buzzed, so he's taking it easy. Assisted by the presence of a full moon tonight. Candi and Roxy are buzzed too. Making out in the backseat. He can see them in the rearview mirror. Exchanging sloppy kisses and groping each other's tits.

"Let's take off our dresses," Candi suggests.

"Fuck yeah," Roxy agrees.

After a moment of struggling in what is barely a backseat in Magnum's sports car, they managed to get back down to g-strings. Roxy returns the cowgirl hat to Candi's head.

"Girl," Roxy laughs, "You look like a sexy Faith Hill."

"What the fuck ever," Candi rolls her eyes, "I can't even sing."

"Neither can she," he remarks.

"Good point," she places her hat on Roxy while leaning in to suck her tits.

"Ooh yeah…" Roxy sighs, "Suck my titties."

"I can't wait to taste this," Candi slides her hand inside Roxy's g-string to rub and finger her pussy.

"I can't wait for you too," Roxy moans, "I loved tasting yours. Girl, you are so sweet."

"Mmm… Thank you," Candi continues licking and sucking her nipples.

Roxy pushes Candi back and returns her hat along with the favor. Sucking Candi's tits while fingering her pussy.

"Girl, you are so fucking wet," Roxy giggles.

"You make my pussy wet," Candi moans.

"Ooh, you make my pussy wet too," Roxy smiles, "And so does Magnum. He makes it so tight and wet."

"Oh my God, I know what you mean," Candi agrees, "Magnum gets my pussy so fucking tight and wet."

Magnum doesn't know how to respond. He's always been one to embrace his vanity. Self-aware of how unbelievably fucking good he is. And yet humbled beyond belief right now. Maybe even a little embarrassed. And a touch shy. Because not only do these compliments courtesy of two rockin' hot girls give his ego a massive stroke, they touch his heart. Candi, on the other hand, thinks his self-awareness is lacking. Always in awe of his presence and performances every time she witnesses one. Wishing he'd cut himself some slack. Determined to ensure he does tonight.

"Hurry up and get us back," Roxy sticks her finger in his mouth and fills it with the unmistakable taste of Candi's pussy, "We're both ready for you."

"Hold your horses, cowgirl," he responds, "There's something we're going to do together first when we get back."

"What's that?" Candi expresses genuine intrigue.

"It's a surprise," he taunts her.

"Ooh, I love surprises," Roxy giggles, "Especially sexy ones."

"This one is especially sexy," he assures her as they come around the hill and upon their naughty oasis.

He backs up towards the front door. Headlights illuminating the pond's rippling surface. They unload the trunk and pack everything inside. Leaving the windows open was an excellent choice. The cottage now filled with a relaxing aroma of the natural world all around them. He turns on the fans. Candi and Roxy stare at him.

"Well?" Candi demands to know.

"Lose the g-strings," he orders them while undressing, "We're going skinny dipping."

"Hells yeah!" Roxy kicks off her platforms and removes her g-string.

"Oh, I'm totally down," Candi follows suit.

The stripping trio race outside butt-ass naked. He starts the car. Turning on the headlights. Opening both doors. Cranking the stereo. Joining Candi and Roxy at the edge of the pond. "Pour Some Sugar on Me" making itself the theme song of what's to come. Each girl takes his arm and they step into the water.

"It's a little colder than I expected," Candi shivers slightly.

"Don't worry," he embraces her from behind and grinds his cock on her ass, "I'll keep you warm."

"Me too," Roxy presses her titties against Candi's and kisses her, "Should we be keeping an eye out for cottonmouths?"

"That's partly why I'm shining the headlights on the water's surface," he examines the water's surface, "The music should also scare away any that might be around."

"Okay," Roxy trusts him as he leads them to the center, "It's not very deep," she observes the water level being just above knee level.

"There's only one snake you need to worry about," he embraces her from behind and presses his throbbing manhood against her butt.

"Oh, I'm not worried about that snake," Roxy giggles, "I'm quite curious about it."

"I remember being there," Candi reminisces while looking towards the barn, "What do you think's in there?"

"Ki-ki-ki, ma-ma-ma," he jokes.

"I hope not," Candi laughs with a twinge of nervousness, "We've been very naughty all night."

"Then we may as well go for broke," Roxy decides before kissing Candi, then Magnum.

She presses her tits against his chest. He squeezes her ass. Butterflies fill his stomach upon realizing that he's going to fuck Roxy tonight. And knowing Candi is going to fuck her too doesn't help. And yet he's still apprehensive about breaking his arbitrary rule a second time. Despite things having worked out well between him and Candi. Fucking party girls and cheating on annoying girlfriends is one thing.

But banging the help is still a taboo for him. And maybe that's part of the thrill. His body trembling with arousal and nervousness. Candi sees it. She gently rubs his shoulders. Reassuring him that all of this is perfectly okay. And reassuring herself as well. That it's okay for them to completely let go sometimes. For them to fully embrace the hedonism they sell to others on a nightly basis.

"I'm going to find some towels," Candi heads back towards the cottage as an excuse to give him a few minutes alone with the new girl.

Magnum and Roxy continue kissing. Tongues dancing. She strokes his throbbing cock as he slides his middle finger inside her soaking wet pussy. Masturbating each other underneath a full moon. Caught in the headlights. "Hot Cherie" by Hardline drifts their way. The scent of short-leaf pines filling his nose. The taste of Smirnoff Ice from her lips to his. Bringing themselves to mutual orgasm. Stopping and gazing into each other's eyes.

"Thank you for tonight," she coos, "I definitely needed the money. And I'm having so much fun."

"Thank you for doing this," he replies, "They loved the show. And you are oodles of fun."

"Aww..." she giggles, "You know, I'm not always like this. I mean..."

"You don't have to explain," he strokes her face, "Neither are we. If anything, I hope I'm not giving you the impression that this is how I do business..."

"Oh my God, you are so adorable," Roxy interrupts, "I never thought that for a second. You just make me feel comfortable being myself. Candi too. And we all have needs."

"I'm so glad," he laughs before pulling her tight against him and whispering in her ear, "And I'd love to fulfill some mutual needs with you."

"Ooh... Me too, baby," she sighs as he licks her ear and squeezes her ass, "Anything you want. Candi too."

"I know she'll like that," he assures her before they resume kissing.

He's aching to fuck Roxy right here in the pond when he hears Candi returning. Not that she'd mind at all if he bent their new friend over and fucked her right here. If anything, she'd demand her turn as well. But instead, he looks over to see her approaching with a Smirnoff Ice.

"Towels are on the hood," she informs them, "Let's have a toast to our night while we're out here."

Magnum and Roxy watch Candi take a sip. He waits for her to pass the bottle to him or Roxy. Instead, Candi grabs the back of his head. Pulling him in for a kiss. Unleashing the malt beverage contents of her mouth into his. He's shocked and turned on at once. All he can do is let go as they shift alcopop between their mouths until every crop is consumed. Leaving him speechless as she turns to Roxy.

"Your turn," she announces sweetly.

Candi takes another sip and pulls a shocked Roxy towards her. Repeating the process as they consume Smirnoff Ice together in the sexiest way possible.

"Oh wow," Roxy stammers, "That made me lightheaded."

"Me too," Candi giggles.

"Hold up," he interjects, "Where in the world did you learn that?"

"Remember that lesbian birthday party I did in Hot Springs a few years back?" she asks.

"Vaguely," he attempts to recall, "Was it the one at an Italian restaurant?"

"That's right," she nods.

"Wait," he attempts to piece this together, "You did this with the lesbians?"

"No, of course not." she laughs, "I did it with the straight girl who was there."

"You did this with her right in front of everyone?" his imagination going crazy right now.

"Well, we sort of did it accidentally with whipped cream during the party," she giggles with a twinge of embarrassment, "But we explored it with champagne back at her hotel room."

"When was this?" he inquires with intrigued disbelief.

"Right after we ate the fuck out of each other's pussy," she declares proudly.

"Fuck," he glances at Roxy, who is wide-eyed before looking back at Candi, "And you've been holding out on me all this time?"

"Oh, like you tell me everything," Candi laughs, "I know something happened with you and those girls in Batesville a few months back."

"Ooh… Tell us," Roxy presses her naked body against Candi's, "Then we can reenact it."

"That's right," Candi agrees before she and Roxy share another Smirnoff Ice kiss.

"Wait. I haven't done this with Magnum yet," Roxy grabs the bottle, takes a sip, and wraps her arms around his neck.

She presses her lips against his. Letting the alcohol flow between their mouths. He feels lightheaded himself as they drink it all. Candi embracing them from the side. Pressing her body tight against theirs. He and Roxy turn their heads to share a three-way kiss with her. Basking in the moonlight and headlights. Def Leppard's "Hysteria" enveloping them. Holding each for warmth with the temperature dropping slightly. Even with all the outrageous fucking they're about to go inside and do at hand, there's a small part of him that could die happy in this moment. If Jason Voorhees is going to kill them, now is the time.

Magnum leads each girl by the hand from the pond. Stopping at the car to dry off one another with the bath towels Candi found. The headlights casting nude silhouettes across the water. Three sexy rock stars in the Arkansas wilderness tonight. He shuts off the engine and headlights while the girls head inside. Enjoying one last moment in the darkness, alone and naked, before joining the ultimate after-party. Roxy is on her back. Centered upon the bed. Candi ties her wrists and ankles to the bedposts with black scarves. She's also fired up his party audio system. Joan Jett's version of "Do You Wanna Touch Me (Oh Yeah)" setting a perfect tone.

"Tight, but not too tight," Roxy instructs her.

"Hey, I'm getting a crash course in bondage," Candi looks up at him.

"Now put the blindfold on me," Roxy orders her.

"Okay," he surveys the situation, "Now what?"

"Now," Roxy sasses, "The two of you do anything you want to me."

"Um, I'm new to this," Candi stammers, "But, do you have like a safe word or something?"

"Baby, my safe word is more," Roxy laughs, "Seriously, I trust you two so much that it makes my pussy ache. There's a few toys on the sofa. Let your imaginations run wild."

"So…" he starts.

"So what? Roxy interrupts, "You can drink a milkshake out of my ass if you want. Quit stalling and get to it already."

Magnum and Candi look at each other, shrug their shoulders, and smile. She climbs on top of Roxy while he checks out what's on the sofa. Grabbing the feather since it looks the least painful. Candi plays with Roxy's pussy as they make out. Rubbing her new girlfriend's clit. Sliding her middle finger inside. Massaging her g-spot.

"Ooh, that's nice," Roxy coos between sloppy kisses.

"You're so fucking wet," Candi gushes.

"Give me a taste," Roxy demands.

Candi puts her finger in Roxy's mouth.

"Mmm… I taste yummy," Roxy giggles while sucking Candi's finger, "What do you think?"

"Girl, you are so yummy," Candi tastes Roxy on her finger.

Candi watches Magnum approach Roxy with the large pink feather and lightly trace along the new girl's inner thigh.

"Ooh…" Roxy giggles with delight, "Is that Magnum teasing me with the feather? Keep going, baby."

He repeats with her other thigh. Then along her stomach while Candi sucks her tits.

"Oh yeah, suck my titties. Your mouth is magic," Roxy moans, "Keep going with that feather."

He runs it down her stomach to her pussy. Circling and flicking her clit with the tip. Mimicking his cunnilingus technique. It does the trick. She arches her back. Releasing a long sigh.

"Fuck yeah, baby," she trembles in ecstasy.

Inspiration strikes him. Rushing to the cooler and grabbing two ice cubes. Handing one to Candi. Placing them in their mouths. He leans down and joins Candi in sucking Roxy's tits. Candi on her right breast. Magnum on her left. Cold water flowing from their warm mouths onto her nipples.

"Oh wow! Just fucking wow!" Roxy shakes profusely, "Now you two are getting creative. That's what I'm talking about, you sexy motherfuckers!"

Candi runs for more ice. He moves to Roxy's right breast. Sucking hard on her nipple. Vigorously flicking his tongue over it. She moans softly.

"Your mouth is magic too, baby," she coos, "So fucking magic."

Candi returns and inserts an ice cube into Roxy's mouth. He slides up and places his right nipple against her lips. It's unbelievable. The mixed sensation of warm and cold all at once. She expertly licks and sucks his nipples. Circling them with her soft tongue. Pushing melted ice past her lips onto his skin. Making him tremble.

"Oh my God!" she moans as he glances back to see Candi's face buried between her legs, "She's got ice on my pussy."

"Do you like it?" Candi raises her head.

"I fucking love it," Roxy approves.

Candi resumes eating Roxy's pussy. Pleasuring her with ice and long deep licks from back to front. Sucking on her clit and lips before sliding her tongue inside. Combining the ice water in her mouth with the new stripper's flood of warm girl juices to make things wet and wild. He moves his left nipple to Roxy's mouth. She swirls her tongue all over it. He feels a slight orgasm overcome him before going back for more ice while Candi continues devouring the new girl. Returning and placing another cube in the new girl's mouth. Candi moves up and smothers Roxy with her tits.

"Oh my God," Candi exudes with surprise from Roxy sucking her nipples with ice water, "That feels really good."

"Fuck yeah it does," Roxy moves her mouth back and forth between each breast as Candi pushes them together.

Magnum's butterflies are back as he pops an ice cube in his mouth. Positioning himself between Roxy's legs. Holding the ice between his lips. Tracing one inner thigh. Making her shake with anticipation. He's shaking too while teasing her other thigh. Putting his head down. Gently kissing her clit. The cool water flowing from between his lips. Trickling down her hot throbbing pussy. She arches her back. Candi's bare ass wiggling in his face. He gives it a firm smack. She giggles. He returns his attention to Roxy. The combination of warm saliva and girl juices with ice water creating a wet and delicious mess. Exposing her clit with his thumbs. She moans and shakes while he circles it with the ice and tip of his tongue. Sucking each of her swollen lips. Sliding his tongue deep inside her. Licking her back to front. Consuming her sweetness.

"Oh fuck, Magnum," Roxy moans, "You are making my juices flow."

"Let 'em flow, baby," he instructs her. Inserting one finger inside her. A second. A third. Her pussy gripping them tightly as he massages her g-spot. Licking and sucking her clit. Bringing her closer to orgasm. She struggles against her restraints. Unable to lie still from the stimulation of sucking Candi's tits while he eats her pussy. He can't stay still either. His cock so achingly hard. Juices flowing down his legs. Roxy's juices covering his entire face. Candi's sexy butt bouncing in his face. Relentlessly grinding her wet pussy on the new girl's stomach.

"I… I'm sucking your tits," Roxy whispers in anguish to no one in particular, "You're… You're… Eating my pussy," she pauses to catch her breath as best she can, "I… I… I can't… Oh fuck!"

She unleashed a tidal wave of juices. Cumming all over Magnum's face. Screaming while instinctively trying to hold onto something. But she's forced to endure her climax with zero distracting comforts. He instantly understands why she likes being tied up. Not sure that's something he could ever do. But he totally gets it now for her perspective. His heart pounding like a jackhammer. Rubbing his face all over her soaking wet pussy. Grabbing Candi's ass and squeezing it tight. Every muscle fiber in his body as tight as it can contract. Then releasing all at once. He can't stop shaking.

"I think he liked that," Candi looks back at him and giggles.

This makes her booty bounce even more. Taunting him even more. Her smile quickly turns to confusion. He can feel it happening. The sheer aggression rushing through his veins. An animal instinct taking over. Ready to attack. But there's also emotion overcoming him. A strange feeling of comfort in the company of his longtime stripping partner. It's all so confusing yet he can't get enough of it. And all of this is manifesting on his face. Striking fear, intimidation, arousal, curiosity, and intrigue within her. All of it manifesting in her face as she nervously yet excitedly awaits his move. Whatever that move may be.

And Magnum makes that move, physically and emotionally, in one swift motion. Lunging forward. Spreading her cheeks wide open. Sliding his tongue deep inside her tight butthole. Thrusting it back and forth. Sweet as candy like always. She instantly orgasms from his sex attack. Heart racing from his display of feelings towards her. Long having hidden those feelings of her own. Not only from him, but from herself too. But now, she allows her imagination to run wild in the moment. Interpreting this ass play as the kinkiest "I love you" ever. Yet stopping herself just short of thinking the same for him.

"Oh fuck!" she buries her tits in Roxy's face, "I think he loved it," she laughs and moans.

"What's he doing to you?" Roxy demands to know.

"He's eating my ass," Candi sighs, "Oh fuck, is he ever eating it. His tongue is all the way in my butthole right now."

"Do it, Magnum," Roxy encourages him, "Lick Candi's butthole. Lick it deep, baby."

He doesn't need Roxy to tell him that. His tongue can't get enough of Candi's delicious booty. Licking and teasing her asshole. Giving her a friendly embrace as only he can. So fucking happy to be with her right now. Playing together with the new girl. He wouldn't want it any other way. Candi leans forward and makes out with Roxy. Moaning into her mouth. It's all so much to the point of being scary for Candi. More terrifying than any hockey-masked killer possibly lurking around outside. And it gets her motor running like never before in her life.

"You two are so adorable," Roxy giggles, "And so incredibly naughty. I love it."

"He's never done it like this before," Candi catches her breath, "I don't know what's gotten into him."

"It's just Batesville," he mentions matter of factly.

"Are you fucking serious?" she asks with shock, followed by laughter, "Have you been doing this with other girls?"

"A time or two," he answers coyly, "Haven't you?"

"No," she laughs.

"Not even with that girl in Hot Springs?" he presses.

"Okay. I seriously considered licking her ass while we sixty-nined," she confesses, "But I punked out."

"Excuse me, Candi?" Roxy interjects, "Why aren't you and I in a sixty-nine right now? Magnum can still eat your ass while we eat each other's pussy."

"Good point," he extracts himself from between Candi's cheeks.

She spins around. Sitting on Roxy's face. Burying her face in the new girl's pussy. They waste no time pleasing and teasing each other. He positions himself above Candi's ass. Spreading her cheeks open again. Resuming his exploration of her tight pink goodness.

"Can you remove my blindfold?" Roxy asks, "I want to watch you lick her ass."

He removes it, and she returns her tongue to Candi's soaking wet pussy. Licking deep inside her. Watching intently as he licks Candi's butthole. Sliding his tongue in and out.

"That is so fucking sexy," Roxy enthuses, "Hey, Candi? Has another girl ever eaten your ass?"

"Nope," Candi murmurs into Roxy's pussy.

"Me neither," Roxy admits, "Have you ever eaten another girl's ass?"

"Nuh-uh," Candi responds between licks, "You?"

"Not until now," Roxy smiles, "Lean back, sexy."

Magnum raises his head and Candi rises slightly. Bringing her asshole down to Roxy's waiting tongue. The new girl wastes no time. Swirling her tongue around Candi's tight hole. Pressing it deep inside. Enthusiastically tasting another woman's ass for the first time. Thrusting in and out as Candi moans.

"Oh my God, this is so much fun!" Roxy squeals, "And you have a yummy ass."

"Mmm… Thank you," Candi glances towards Magnum with a twinge of embarrassment, "You're a natural at that."

"I'm learning from Magnum," Roxy giggles while looking at him, "Look, Magnum. I'm licking Candi's butthole," she pauses to do just that, "You looked so fucking hot doing it. I hope I look almost as hot."

"Hotter," he assures her.

"Whatever," she laughs, "I'm still having a blast. Hey, Candi. I'm sticking my tongue in your butthole. Mmm… mmm… mmm!"

"Oh my God, you are, Roxy," Candi moans and giggles while staring at him.

He leans in and kisses her. Getting another taste of Roxy's sweet pussy as their tongues dance. He kisses her mouth with the same passion displayed while kissing her ass moments ago. It doesn't go unnoticed by her. Chills cover her body from head to toe. He's the most dangerous guy she's ever known. And the one who makes her feel safe like no other. Including right now as she breaks new sapphic barriers in his company. Knowing that she's never been jealous of other women he's been with or shown interest in. Rather she revels in the fantasy of being an active participant in his sexual escapades. As she is right now.

"Okay," Roxy breaks up their moment, "I want you two to switch places."

Magnum and Candi look at each other and laugh. For someone who's all tied up, she sure seems to be calling a lot of the shots. He takes Candi's place in the sixty-nine. Lowering his raging cock inside Roxy's mouth. Burying his face in her pussy for deliciously sloppy seconds. Her sweet juices instantly drenching him as his tongue explores her sugar walls. So soft and velvety. Losing himself in playing with her body. Allowing himself to relax for a little while. It's so reassuring. Expressions of sex being how he's always established honest connections with women. Through a sort of naughty innocence that may seem contradictory yet makes all the sense in the world to him.

He moans and sighs into Roxy's pussy. Reacting to the feel of his cock deep in her throat. Her tongue writhing around his head and shaft. Making his juices flow like crazy into her eager mouth. He feels Candi spreading his butt cheeks apart. Her tongue licking along his crack. Tracing his butthole. Sliding inside him. This twin oral stimulation making him shiver and shake. Increasing his hunger for Roxy's pussy. Licking it front to back. Her juices flowing more and more. Devouring every drop he can. But that only makes her even wetter. She's practically sucking the precum straight out of his cock now. Candi's tongue swirling around and inside his asshole.

"This is even better than Batesville," he accidentally says out loud.

"Okay," Candi stops for a second, "You really have to tell me that story later."

"I will," Magnum concedes before returning to Roxy's pussy.

She's on the verge of another orgasm. Him too. Her body is tightening more and more. Just like his. Candi's as well. The three strippers moaning and sighing. Letting go at once. Candi lifts her head. He rolls off Roxy.

"Okay, you can untie me now," she announces.

Magnum unties her ankles while Candi frees her wrists. She jumps off the bed. Walking back and forth. Stretching her arms and legs. Grabbing a Smirnoff Ice, popping the cap, and handing it to her playmates while rejoining them on the bed. They forego the kissing at the pond and simply pass around the bottle this time. Catching their breath. He slides his hand up Candi's thigh to her pussy. Rubbing and fingering her. She's so wet and swollen. He wants to eat her out so badly right now. And she wants it just as badly.

"Ooh, that feels good," she tilts her head back and sighs.

"Lie back," he instructs her.

She does while Roxy goes back to the cooler. He lies to one side of Candi. Roxy joins him on the other with a pair of ice cubes. Placing one in his mouth. The other in hers. They go to work on Candi's tits. Licking and sucking her nipples with cold water in their mouths. Looking up at her. She smiles and grabs their heads. Shaking her titties in their faces as they all laugh.

"You two are so sexy," she giggles.

"So are you, girlfriend," Roxy flirts.

Magnum and Roxy kiss down Candi's stomach. Spreading her legs open. Each taking an inner thigh. Licking from either knee until their tongues converge on her clit.

"Now that's a three-way kiss," Candi coos.

"How about a French kiss?" he thrusts his tongue deep inside her pussy.

Her delicious juices instantly flooding into his wanting mouth. Not noticing that Roxy has left his side.

"Fuck yeah!" Candi grabs his head with both hands and humps his face, "God, I want to fuck your face so hard right now."

"Fuck his face, Candi," Roxy calls from across the cottage.

She returns with two more ice cubes. Once again placing one in his mouth and the other in hers. Pressing their faces together. Kissing and licking Candi's pussy. Each sucking one of her swollen lips with ice in their mouths.

"Oh my God," Candi arches her back and moans. "That's just… Oh wow!"

She grabs their heads while they give her twin tongue action on her clit. Trickling cool water on her delicate button. Fingering her pussy together. Massaging her g-spot. Making her wetter and wetter. She reaches back and grabs the pillow underneath her head. Shivering in ecstasy. Fighting to keep her legs still.

"I kind of see now why you like to be tied up," she laughs, "It's so hard for me to keep still right now."

"Now you're getting it," Roxy nods before turning and kissing Magnum as they savor Candi's sweetness on each other's lips and tongue.

"Aww…" Candi coos, "That's so sweet."

"Sorry," he breaks from the kiss and removes his finger from Candi, "My hand is starting to cramp."

"Mine too a little," Roxy follows suit.

"I'm sorry," Candi apologizes.

"Don't be sorry," Roxy laughs, "It's time for you to fuck my face anyway."

Roxy dives tongue first inside Candi's pussy. Licking her deep and fast. Candi grabs her head with both hands. Thrusting her pussy against the new girl's face.

"Oh, fuck yeah!" Candi shouts, "I am going to fuck your face so fucking hard, Roxy!"

"Do it, Candi!" Roxy demands between thrusts, "Fuck my face, girlfriend!"

"Oh, I'm fucking it!" Candi grinds her pussy on Roxy's face, "I'm fucking it hard!"

"Is this what happened in Hot Springs?" Magnum inquires in shock from never having seen Candi be this aggressive before.

"Not quite, but it's what I wanted to do," Candi answers, "And I'm fucking doing it now."

Magnum has no response other than to move behind Roxy. She's bent over. Her ass bouncing as she gets face fucked. Her pussy swollen. Glistening from being drenched in her sweetness. He feels that animal instinct returning. The same one Candi is displaying right now. He looks up at his longtime partner in crime as she's thinking and feeling the same way. "Never Enough" by L.A. Guns contributing an additional bad influence in the moment.

"Do it," she nods and mouths viciously, "Fuck her now."

He doesn't waste another second. Grabbing Roxy's ass. She spreads her legs wider. Inviting him inside her. He presses the head of his cock against her soaking wet pussy. So unbelievably soaking wet that he instantly slides all the way inside her. Balls deep inside her tight love tunnel. Fucking his sexy new stripper with reckless abandon while she eats Candi's pussy with the same recklessness. It's now officially the second time he's fucked one of his girls. Maybe he'll feel guilty later. But not right now. He couldn't be happier in this moment. Thrusting his cock harder and harder in Roxy's pussy. Her ass cheeks bouncing against his pelvis with each stroke. Making his skin tingle. Intoxicated on alcohol and unbridled lust. Spanking her butt. Fucking her. Deeper. Harder. Shoving her face even further into Candi's aching pussy.

"He's fucking you, Roxy," Candi taunts her, "He's got his massive cock deep inside your pussy."

"I know," Roxy viciously responds as she's possessed by the same aggressive spirit as Magnum and Candi, "I've been wanting his cock inside me ever since we first met."

"Oh, me too," Candi confesses, "During our first meeting, my pussy was so tight and wet the entire time."

"Are you fucking serious?" he slows down and stares at her.

"Fuck yeah I'm fucking serious," she glares at him like he's crazy for asking, "When we did that photoshoot the first time, part of me really wanted you to rip my clothes off and fuck me right there."

"Oh yeah," Roxy agrees, "It was the same way for me. Here I was. Posing for this hot guy who was so kind and polite and in control. Oh my God, I wanted him to take control of me."

"It's true, Magnum." Candi continues, "You have a good idea of how sexy you are to women, but you still don't grasp the full magnitude of the effect you have on us."

"She's right," Roxy adds, "I can't even imagine how many women are in your friendzone."

"Whatever," he scoffs in a combination of flattery and embarrassment, "I don't have a friendzone."

"Bull to the fucking shit you don't," Candi argues, "I've seen you break hearts at every party we've done together. Even tonight."

"Really?" he rolls my eyes, "Who over there wanted me?"

"The bachelorette," Candi responds, "If she'd thought she could get away with it, we'd be having a foursome right now."

"She's right, dude," Roxy interjects, "That girl was hypothetically yours from the second she called you. You think she would've let just any old male stripper spend the night here? Not a chance."

"She's just a really nice person," he laughs off their claims.

"No girl is that nice," Candi retorts, "Not towards just anyone," she looks at Roxy, "That's the thing with him. Despite all his experience, he's still naïve about everything he brings to the table. You know?"

"Oh, I knew that right from the start," Roxy agrees, "He's so wild yet so innocent at the same time. Even when he was forcing his tongue up your ass, he was still innocent. There's not a malicious bone in his body. But he doesn't realize it's this charming innocence that makes girls go wild for him. Because that's what causes him to be naïve like you said. He's truly an enigma."

"I'm an enigma, huh?" he resumes fucking Roxy hard and fast, "You want innocent? I'll show you innocent."

"Oh my God!" Roxy shouts, "You're still innocent, and I can't get enough of it. Fuck me hard!"

"You just keep eating Candi's pussy," he orders her.

"I'm on it," Candi returns to grabbing Roxy's head and fucking her face.

"Get It Right" by Raven pounds their ears as Magnum pounds Roxy's pussy and Candi's pussy pounds her face. A triple fucking machine. Juices gushing more and more. Fucking faster and harder. Deeper and tighter. Furiously. Roxy's pussy squeezing his cock tighter and tighter. Her ever-increasing sweetness making it possible for him to keep penetrating her. Thrust after thrust. Moaning and screaming together in the night. A massive shared climax growing closer and closer. Aching turning to pain as they each fight to hold back for as long as they can. Until they can take no more and Roxy pussy begins squirting.

"Let it go!" he commands.

"Oh God!" Candi squirts on Roxy's face and in her mouth.

"You're squirting, baby!" Roxy drinks up every drop of Candi's girl juice she can, "Me too!"

Roxy ejaculates all over Magnum. Covering him in warm juices. Making him lose control. His cock explodes deep inside her. Filling her pussy with hot cum as they scream together in sweet release.

"Get up here quick," Candi lies back and orders Roxy, "Sit on my face."

Roxy hops on the bed and lowers her pussy on Candi's face.

"I want to lick Magnum's cum out of your pussy." Candi slides her tongue inside Roxy, "Oh my God, you two taste so good together."

Roxy is shocked, but not as shocked as Magnum. He doesn't know what to say. But his cock is immediately hard and throbbing again. Still covered in his and Roxy's combined love potion. Still catching his breath but ready to rock and roll once again. Jumping on the bed. Landing between Candi's legs. Sliding effortlessly inside her soaking wet pussy before she and Roxy know what's happening.

"Oh God! Fuck me, Magnum!" Candi screams, "Fuck me hard!"

"Do it, Magnum," Roxy encourages him, "Fuck her while she eats my pussy."

Candi wraps her legs around his back. Thrusting against him as he fucks the hell out of her. Fast and hard. Balls deep in her pussy with every stroke. Roxy leans forward. Her round booty in his face. Candi's hands grabbing her cheeks. He makes no effort to avoid smacking his face into it with each thrust.

"Hey, Candi," Roxy says, "Spread my cheeks open so Magnum can lick my butthole."

"Oh yeah," Candi opens Roxy's cheeks, "Lick her butthole, naughty boy."

"Naughty innocent boy," Roxy giggles with Candi.

"Whatever," he says to himself.

Magnum eats Roxy's ass while pumping Candi's pussy. Licking the new girl's sweet backdoor. Thrusting his tongue in her asshole with each thrust of his cock deep inside Candi. Burying his face between her cheeks. Bumping his chin against Candi's as she continues licking his cum from Roxy's pussy. They've experienced a lot together but have reached a new level of sexual depravity tonight. He couldn't be happier. And neither could she.

"Ooh… You two are making me cum again," Roxy trembles from the double tongue action.

Candi is trembling too. So is Magnum. Another triple climax on the verge of tearing through them.

"Don't stop fucking me, Magnum," Candi whispers.

"I won't," he whispers back, "Don't stop eating her pussy."

"Never," she whispers, "Don't stop eating her ass."

"I couldn't if I tried," he assures her.

"Are you two whispering about me?" Roxy inquires.

"We're talking about how you're the most delicious playmate we've ever shared," he tells her.

"Mmm-hmm…" Candi moans into Roxy's pussy, "You're cumming."

"Oh God, I am," Roxy moans.

"Me too," Candi agonizes through heavy breaths.

"Let's cum together," he orders the girls.

The three aren't holding back as fiercely this time. Not surprising, considering they all came just moments earlier. Candi's pussy getting wetter and wetter. Growing tighter as Magnum's cock grows even bigger. Roxy shaking as Candi eats her pussy and he licks her butthole. Her juices flowing so much they're reaching her ass. This is all too much for him. Thrashing violently against Candi. Fucking her as deep as he can. To the end of the line. And it's still not deep enough for either of them. Roxy moans and cums all over Candi's face. His cock unleashes a wall of cum in Candi's pussy, which squirts all over him. She squeezes him tightly with her legs while holding on for dear life. All three landing in a shaking and laughing mess on the bed.

"Hold on," Roxy dives between Candi's legs. Licking and sucking Magnum's cum out of her pussy. Then kissing Candi with it in her mouth. Passing it back and forth like Smirnoff Ice until they've swallowed every drop.

"Mmm… Now that's how you do it," Candi sighs.

"Isn't it just?" Roxy agrees.

Magnum grabs the leftover party food and another Smirnoff Ice. The trio has a picnic on the bed. "New Girl Now" by Honeymoon Suite plays as they eat, drink, and converse about their night so far. Laughing and flirting. Reliving everything from the drive down here to their epic three-way fuck fest. The air coming through the windows is still warm, but the girls are getting chilly. Cuddling together for warmth. He gets up and points the box fans away from the bed. The sight of Candi and Roxy. Their naked bodies pressed together. Skin so soft. He can feel the testosterone racing through his body. The adrenaline pumping. The butterflies filling his stomach. His manhood growing erect once again. And despite everything they've just experienced together, he's still a little embarrassed. Quickly lying face down on the bed in front of them.

"Aww… Are you tired?" Roxy strokes his hair.

"No, he's horny again," Candi exposes him, "I saw him getting hard while eyeing us."

"Whatever," he sighs.

"He's getting me horny again," Roxy starts massaging his ass, "I mean, look at this ass. I could just eat it up."

"I don't think he'd stop you from doing that," Candi informs her, "Would you, Magnum?"

"I guess not," he mutters coyly.

"Oh, what the fuck ever," Candi shakes her head and laughs.

"Mmm…" Roxy leans forward. Her tits pressed against his lower back. Spanking and squeezing his butt cheeks. Kissing and licking them. Spreading them open. Licking along his crack. He trembles as she drips saliva on his butthole. Licking it softly. Vigorously thrusting her tongue in and out.

"Oh my God, you taste so sweet," she sighs, "Doesn't he just have the sweetest butthole, Candi."

"He really does," Candi strokes Roxy's hair, "He's the only guy whose ass I've ever wanted to eat."

"So, Magnum's asshole is the only one you've ever licked?" Roxy asks.

"Yeah," Candi leans over and spreads Roxy's cheeks open, "Until now."

"Oh wow!" Roxy gasps as Candi dives tongue first into her tight butthole, "Fuck me."

"Baby, I'll fuck you anytime," Candi giggles while licking Roxy's butthole and pushing her tongue deep inside, "It was Magnum who turned me on to eating ass."

"Well, he's fucking amazing at it," Roxy coos, "I hope we're half as good at it as he is."

"You two are out of this world," he assures them between moans.

"You're the buttlicking master, Magnum," Candi says, "And the buttfucking master too."

"Really?" Roxy is intrigued.

"Oh my God. He truly is," Candi sighs, "Having his cock in my ass makes my pussy squirt like crazy. I cum so fucking hard. Whew!"

"Oh wow," Roxy responds in awe, "You know, I've only done anal with one guy. And it was a horrible experience. Just nothing by pain. I should give it another try with someone else, but I'm hesitant."

"I totally understand that," Candi assures her, "Magnum is extremely gentle. He takes his time working himself in. And he's amazing at getting me loosened up first."

"How's that?" Roxy is curious.

"Get up," Candi rises and slaps Roxy's ass, "Bend over and I'll show you."

"That's what she said," Roxy laughs nervously while following orders.

"Exactly," Candi giggles, "Magnum, I know you have some Astroglide."

"Have I become that predictable?" he gets up.

"As a naughty boy," Candi kisses him, "Yes."

Magnum grabs a bottle of strawberry Astroglide from his stripping bag. Looking up to see Candi on her knees. Holding Roxy's ass cheeks wide open. Face buried between them. The new girl moaning and sighing while his partner in crime devours her delicious butthole.

"First," Candi states, "He licks all around and inside my asshole."

"I love it when he does that," Roxy coos, "And you too, girlfriend."

Candi stands and takes the Astroglide from Magnum. Applying a little to her fingers. Getting it warm. Smearing it all over Roxy's butthole while massaging it.

"Next, he inserts a finger inside my ass," Candi gently slides her middle finger inside Roxy's tight little hole one knuckle at a time.

"Oh my God," Roxy gasps with surprised delight, "That feels so fucking good."

"I'm glad," Candi comforts her, "Just relax, baby."

"Oh, I'm so relaxed right now," Roxy breaths softly, "A hot girl has her finger in my butthole."

"That's right," Candi giggles, "Magnum, you look shocked."

This makes him realize that he's standing there with his jaw dropped. Blown away by the sight of Candi anally penetrating another woman. The sweet and kind all-American girl who is also a dirty sex machine in highly exclusive company. His ultimate sexual fantasy personified right before his eyes.

"You act like you've never seen a girl finger another girl's asshole before," she laughs.

"I haven't," he confesses.

"Bullshit," Roxy's sighs from ass play heaven, "Get up here. I want to suck your cock."

He climbs onto the bed and sits back, facing Roxy. Sliding himself forward as she gets on her elbows. Lowering her mouth onto his once again massive cock. Taking him deep in her throat. Her tongue dancing elegantly around his head and shaft.

"I'm going for two," Candi slowly inserts her index finger along with the middle one in Roxy's ass.

The new girl removing her mouth from Magnum's cock. Tilting her head back. Letting out a long sigh. Looking him in the eyes.

"She has two fingers in my ass, Magnum," Roxy says matter of factly.

"Does he like me sticking two fingers in your ass?" Candi asks her.

"Let me see," Roxy swirls her tongue around his precum-soaked head while maintaining eye contact, "Fuck yeah, he is. His juices are flowing, Candi. And they're so yummy."

"His juices are yummy," Candi confirms, "So, do you like me sticking two fingers in your ass?"

"I love it!" Roxy squeals in delight, "I love your fingers in my asshole, girlfriend."

"I love having my fingers deep in your asshole," Candi flashes a devilish smile, "But just wait until Magnum's big hard throbbing cock is deep inside your tight sexy asshole."

"I can't fucking wait for that," Roxy keeps looking up at him while licking his cock up and down before gently sucking his balls, "I'm getting him all ready for it. Keep getting me ready for it."

"Oh, I am getting you ready," Candi thrusts her fingers in and out of Roxy's butthole. Quickly. Aggressively.

He's still in awe of her in this state. His juices flowing nonstop while Roxy works to consume every last drop.

"Okay, Magnum," Candi removes her fingers from Roxy's ass and licks them while staring at him, "Mmm... She's ready for you."

"Fucking wow," he hops off the bed and races behind Roxy. Shaking with anticipation while Candi rubs his cock with Astroglide and adds more to the new girl's waiting butthole.

"I want to watch you put it in," Candi holds Roxy's cheeks wide open.

He steps forward. Pressing the tip of his cock against Roxy's forbidden love tunnel. Leaning slightly forward. Letting his head push gently inside her as she sighs.

"His head is in," Candi informs her.

"I know," Roxy sighs, "It feels good."

He takes his time. Allowing her to receive him on her own terms. Inch by inch as her asshole relaxes more and more. Until he's finally all the way inside.

"He's all the way in," Candi giggles.

"Yes, he is," Roxy giggles back, "I love it. Your cock feels amazing in my ass, Magnum"

"Your ass feels amazing, Roxy," he returns the compliment.

It's true. So warm and soft. Its tightness making his entire body tingle. Grabbing onto her cheeks while Candi takes his place on the bed. Stroking Roxy's hair as the new girl eats her pussy again.

"How do you like Magnum fucking you in the ass?" Candi asks.

"I fucking love it!" Roxy exclaims, "And, oh my God, he's so gentle. You were right. This is nothing like the other time."

"It just has to be taken easy," he slowly rocks his cock back and forth in her ass, "Even I need to be relaxed too, or it won't feel good for me."

"Are you relaxed enough, baby?" Roxy questions with legitimate concern.

"Oh yeah," he assures her, "You two have me totally relaxed?"

"Roxy has me relaxed too right now," Candi rubs her pussy on Roxy's face, "Girl, your tongue is amazing."

"Oh, your pussy is amazing," Roxy moans, "I could totes get used to this."

"Me too," Candi laughs seductively.

She then gazes at Magnum seductively. As if to say, "Save some of that for me," while watching him fuck Roxy's booty. He starts gradually increasing speed. Relying on her physical and vocal reactions to gauge how hard he can go without hurting her. So far, so good. Her moaning growing louder. Thrusting her ass against him as to take his cock inside her as deeply as possible. And he's going balls deep inside her sexy ass. Fucking her faster and harder. She's keeping up with him every stroke of the way. Her pussy getting wetter and wetter. Girl juices streaming down his balls and thighs. He feels a massive climax building inside each of them.

"Oh God. Fuck my ass, Magnum." Roxy exhales in carnal bliss, "Fuck my ass hard."

"Night Danger" by Pretty Maids cranks forth and he cranks the intensity to eleven. Thrusting his cock in and out of her asshole with reckless abandon. Roxy violently thrusting her butt against him. Her cheeks slapping his pelvis hard with each stroke. He returns the favor by shoving her face-first into Candi's pussy over and over. Candi on the verge of her own climax from Roxy's tongue lashing. Wave after wave of girl juices drenching Roxy's face. Roxy's own pussy drenching his lower body as he buttfucks the hell out of her. Candi pussy fucking the hell out of her face.

"Fuck, I'm cumming!" Roxy screams into the night, "I'm fucking cumming!"

"Me too!" Candi cries in anguish, "Oh, I can't hold back any longer!"

"I'm cumming too!" he shouts, "Just let it fucking go now!"

Screams fill the warm summer air in a three-way fountain of ejaculation. Candi squirting in Roxy's wide-open mouth as she shrieks in ecstasy. Magnum's cock erupting a massive flow of white-hot cum deep inside Roxy's ass. Her pussy gushing and squirting warm juices all over him. Feeling like he's about to shatter into a million shards of glass. Holding onto Roxy's ass while shaking uncontrollably. Candi doing the same with Roxy's head. Roxy arms wrapped around Candi's legs for dear life. All three enduring the beautiful pain of carnal release. Getting through this together as only true friends can.

"Don't move," Candi runs over to him and drops to her knees as he removes his cock from Roxy's ass.

"Stay there, Roxy," Candi places her hand on Roxy's back while taking Magnum's cock in her mouth. Looking into his eyes. Savoring the combined sweetness of strawberry Astroglide, his cum, and Roxy's pussy and ass. Licking it off his cock. Turning to Roxy's ass and thrusting her tongue inside. Licking and sucking his cum from the new girl's butthole. Returning to the bed and sharing with Roxy the dirtiest kiss ever.

"Mmm…" Roxy giggles afterward, "What is all that?"

"Well, let me see," Candi counts off on her fingers, "There's strawberry Astroglide…"

"Yeah," Roxy nods.

"…Magnum's cum…"

"Oh yeah," Roxy gushes.

"…Your pussy…"

"That too," Roxy agrees.

"…And your ass."

"Damn, my ass tastes yummy," Roxy boasts adorably.

"Yes, it does," Candi laughs.

"Fuck yeah it does," he laughs too.

"Okay," Roxy jumps up, "Candi's turn."

"I think Magnum might need a break," Candi protests.

"Don't worry," Roxy winks at him before giving Candi's ass a hard smack, "I'll have up and ready. Now move."

"Damn, girl," Candi laughs in shock from the sting while taking Roxy's place, bending over the bed.

"Get yourself a front-row seat, Magnum," Roxy drops to her knees and spreads Candi's ass cheeks wide open, "Watch me lick Candi's butthole."

Magnum leans over Candi's ass. Looking down while Roxy circles Candi's asshole with her tongue. Licking every delicate ridge. Enjoying the taboo sweetness that he's enjoyed many nights prior. Sliding her tongue inside. Twirling it within Candi's tight booty hole. Keeping her eyes locked on his. Turning herself on as much as him. Clearly loving every second of him watching her eat another woman's ass.

"Is he watching you lick my butthole?" Candi asks softly.

"He is," Roxy smiles, "He's watching me slide my tongue deep insider your delicious butthole. It's making him big and hard."

"Oh my God, Magnum," Candi sighs, "Roxy's tongue feels amazing deep in my ass."

"It's definitely working," he admits with his cock yet again rock hard and ready to rock against all odds, "Take a look at me now."

"Ooh, Candi," Roxy checks him out, "He's getting all big and hard. He's going to fill your ass completely."

"He always does," Candi moans as Roxy resumes licking her, "He fills my asshole completely."

They giggle incessantly. He begins to shake. Roxy looks up at him. Almost lovingly as she continues thrusting her tongue in and out of Candi's butthole. Kissing it before standing and reaching for the Astroglide. He massages Candi's cheeks while Roxy warms lubricant on her fingers. Then spreading them open for the new girl to rub her tight little hole. Gently pressing the tip of her middle finger inside.

"Whew," Candi giggles almost breathlessly.

"Do you like it?" Roxy asks.

"I love it," Candi gushes, "I know Magnum does too."

"Of course he does," Roxy smiles at him sassily, "He's so hard watching me finger your butt."

"Finger it, baby," Candi sighs, "Finger my butthole while Magnum watches."

"Like this?" Roxy slowly inserts the rest of her finger, "How does that feel, girlfriend?"

"Oh God," Candi trembles and exhales deeply, "That feels so fucking good."

"Ooh… Candi," Roxy coos, "Your ass feels so fucking good on my finger."

"Put another one inside," Candi orders, "I want Magnum to see you with two fingers in my asshole."

"Absolutely," Roxy slides her index finger inside Candi's ass and thrusts back and forth.

"Oh, that's it," Candi gushes, "Put your fingers deep in my ass."

Magnum's juices are flowing while watching Roxy explore Candi's butthole Candi trembles and exhales deeply. Candi rocking her ass back and forth on Roxy's fingers. The new girl grabs him by the back of his head. Pulling him in for a passionate kiss. Tongues swirling around their mouths.

"Thank you," she pulls back and looks into his eyes, "Thank you for everything."

"You're welcome," he manages while absolutely floored by her gratitude.

He's still not sure what he did for her. Or Candi. Or anyone else for that matter. Seeing himself as just a guy who loves entertaining women and getting paid for it. Along with helping other talented entertainers make money performing for quality audiences. It's not perfect, but it works more often than not. Never thinking of things like women wanting to fuck him at first sight. Or that he touches people emotionally in some way. He's proud, arrogant really, when it comes to his talents as an entertainer and entrepreneur. But stuff like this? He's humbled to the point of embarrassment. He just wants everyone around him to have a blast. That's all he's ever wanted. Roxy stares at him. Her hand on his cheek. Still fingering Candi's ass. Looking at him as if reading his thoughts.

"Candi," Roxy coos, "Magnum needs his cock sucked."

"I would love to," Candi replies.

Magnum takes the oral sex hot seat before Candi. Getting up on her elbows. Licking him in long wet strokes. From his balls to the tip of his cock. Pressing her tongue in his hole. Knowing he likes that. Something they discovered by chance one night far from home following a party. A night not unlike tonight. Neither had ever heard of it being done. She simply thought it might feel good to him and gave it a shot. And he tingles all over every time she does it. Making his precum gush onto her tongue. Other girls have done it to him since. But no one does it like her.

"Mmm… Baby," she savors his juices, "You taste yummy."

"Thank you," he laughs.

"No," she shakes her head, "Thank you, Magnum."

"For what?" he's so confused right now between these two girls.

"For everything," she laughs, "You always make everything exciting."

"Whatever," he looks away in embarrassment.

"It's true," she smiles before deep throating his cock. All the way to his balls. Running her tongue along his shaft. Licking and sucking every inch of his manhood. Making his juices flow like crazy.

"Oh yeah, Candi," Roxy removes her fingers and licks them while looking straight at him, "Your ass is good and ready for that big juicy cock."

Magnum moves behind Candi. Roxy strokes his cock with a handful of Astroglide. Kissing him while getting his hot throbbing shaft nice and slippery.

"Guess what?" Roxy announces to Candi, "I'm jacking off Magnum."

"Jack him off, girlfriend," Candi giggles.

"Not entirely," Roxy clarifies, "You still have to jack him off with your butt."

"For fuck's sake," he laughs along with Candi and Roxy, "Okay, go for broke."

Roxy opens Candi's butt cheeks. Magnum grips his cock. Massaging her asshole with his head. Teasing her as she and the new girl giggle. Taking a deep breath and pushing inside his longtime friend's ass. There's a familiarity for him about fucking Candi in the ass. One that is comforting and thrilling all at once. He's been here before. Yet each time feels like the first. That first night back in Little Rock. After the party in Sherwood. All those years ago. Savoring every second while sliding his raging cock all the way inside her butthole. One inch at a time. Until he's all the way inside. It's the same for her too. Their anal encounters a physical manifestation of her trust in him. As well as her opportunity to let go completely and be a truly dirty girl without fear of judgment.

"Oh wow. That is so fucking hot!" Roxy exclaims, "Your cock is deep in her ass."

"Balls deep," he adds.

"Fuck yeah it is," Candi sighs, "I love Magnum balls deep in my ass."

"Oh, he is balls deep in your asshole, girlfriend," Roxy sits in front of Candi, "I can't stand it anymore. Please eat my pussy."

"It would be my pleasure," Candi buries her face in Roxy's pussy.

Roxy grabs Candi's head and face fucks her like no tomorrow. Magnum grabs her ass and buttfucks her like no tomorrow. "Everybody Up" by Saxon joins the chorus of moans and sighs. She's loosening up quickly. Rocking her butt against him faster and faster. Thrusting his cock deeper and harder inside her asshole. The velvety inner walls of her forbidden love tunnel caressing his cock. Squeezing him tightly. Sending electrical shocks through every nerve ending in his throbbing, aching cock. Every nerve ending in their bodies. As if the world's eyes are on them right now. Or at least one pair currently burning a hole in his back. He quickly glances towards the window behind him. All he sees is darkness.

"Get ahold of yourself, Magnum," he thinks to himself. Returning to the task at hand. Fucking Candi in the ass. Fast and furiously at an eighties speed metal pace. Banging his head. Thrusting to the relentless new wave of British heavy metal beat. Deeper. Harder. Faster. Throbbing. Aching. Moaning. Screaming. His vicious animalism clashing with the butterflies filling his stomach. The friction of decadence and innocence within him generating endless sparks. The sight of Candi's ass bouncing as he fucks it. The sight of Roxy's tits bouncing while grinding her pussy on Candi's face. The fresh and unspoiled geography all around them. The emotional bond of sharing this carnal experience with good friends. The alcohol in his system. It's all too much.

"Oh God, Magnum!" Candi shouts, "I'm gonna fucking cum!"

"Me too, Candi!" he yells back.

"Me three!" Roxy cries, "I'm gonna cum on your face, Candi!"

"Do it, Roxy!" Candi screams, "Let your pussy cum all over my fucking face!"

"I'm fucking gonna cum in your ass!" he growls, "Deep in your fucking ass!"

"Fucking cum in my ass!" Candi growls back, "My pussy is gonna squirt all over you. Oh God, I'm fucking cumming, Magnum!"

"Fucking cum!" he feels it beginning to flow from his cock, "Both of you!"

"Oh God!" the three of them cry out in near unison into the night.

Roxy holds Candi's head tight. Covering her face with wave after wave of girl juices. Candi's pussy unleashing a tsunami of her own juices all over Magnum. Gushing and squirting nonstop. He throws his hands up in victory. Tilting his head back. Closing his eyes. Allowing the spirits of the night to hold him up. Feeling every nerve in his body shock him all at once. Embracing the sensation of his cock exploding deep inside Candi's butthole. Burning from arousal and exhaustion. Filling her ass full of sticky cum. So much cum that it backflows onto him and down their legs.

"Don't move," Roxy runs over to him and drops to her knees as he removes his cock from Candi's ass.

"Stay there, Candi," Roxy places her hand on Candi's back while taking Magnum's cock in her mouth. Repeating verbatim what Candi did earlier. Sucking the mix of lube and juices from his cock. Then licking them out of Candi's asshole. Returning to the bed and sharing this naughty concoction with Candi, mouth to mouth.

"Mmm…" Candi giggles, "It's like déjà vu all over again."

"That's right," Roxy nods, "But it's your sweet ass this time," she licks her lips and smack Candi's ass.

"Damn, my ass tastes yummy too," Candi laughs along with Magnum and Roxy.

He crawls onto the bed between them with his last ounce of strength. The girls lie down on either side of him. Wrapping their arms around him.

"Aww… You're exhausted, baby," Candi coos softly.

"You two wore me out," he weakly laughs.

"Well, you totally wore us out," Roxy nuzzles his shoulder, "I don't know how you do it."

"I don't know either," Candi muses, "You came four fucking times in a row. How is that even possible?"

"I've never done more than three in a single night, and never that close together," he admits, "I just had excellent motivation tonight."

He leans in and kisses Candi, then turns his head to kiss Roxy. Candi and Roxy lean in above him and kiss. The trio lies in silence. Resting their eyes for a minute...

The morning sun coming through the windows hits Magnum's face. He raises up suddenly. As he always does when spending the night in a strange place. Trying to remember where the fuck he is. It takes a few seconds since he's seeing the cottage in daylight for the first time. Everything is turned off. Something he doesn't remember doing. Must've been one of the girls. The heavy metal of last night replaced with the birds singing outside. The table still strewn with mini quiches, tiny chicken salad sandwiches, and empty Smirnoff Ice bottles. Clothes are fucking everywhere. The windows still open. All he sees outside are trees. He's still naked. And covered by three naked girls.

"What the fuck?!" he wakes Candi, Roxy, and their mystery companion.

"What? What's going on," Candi asks in a half-asleep daze.

"We have company," he announces.

Mystery girl lifts her head. It's Erin.

"Hey," she says with a combination of embarrassment and fear.

"What are you doing here?" he sits up with Candi and Roxy as they stare at her.

"Okay, look," Erin stammers, "Aaron's work called him out late last night on an emergency trip to Dallas."

"I'm sorry," Candi replies with confusion.

"Anyway," Erin continues, "I snuck out here last night. To see if y'all were still up. To, you know, hang out."

"I guess you caught us after we fell asleep," he shrugs.

"Actually, no," she laughs nervously, "I caught you right before you fell asleep."

"I knew I felt eyes on me," he shakes his head, "I figured it was Jason Voorhees."

"No," Erin laughs, "But I've always assumed he lives in the barn."

"So," Roxy looks at her drowsily, "Why didn't you join us?"

"I don't know," Erin looks away.

"But you're here now," Candi is still confused along with Magnum and Roxy.

"And naked," he points out.

"I know," Erin giggles, "I went back to the house and debated what to do. I changed my mind and came back, found you all asleep naked, and decided to join you."

"It's cool," he assures her, "Just an unexpected surprise."

"But a pleasant one," Candi strokes her arm.

"We had so much fun with you last night," Roxy smiles.

"Me too," Erin blushes, "Y'all are out of this world."

"I guess sleeping naked with us is something," he laughs.

"Well," she giggles, "I was hoping we could play for a couple hours before y'all head back to Little Rock. Aaron is gone until tonight."

"Can we?" Candi and Roxy ask Magnum in unison with bright smiling faces.

"Why are you asking me?" he shakes my head.

"Well," Candi replies, "She's mainly here for you."

"Definitely," Roxy concurs.

"Don't mind them," he explains to Erin, "They were trying to tell me last night that you wanted me."

"Well, of course I want you," Erin giggles, "I mean, didn't you girls immediately want to fuck him?"

"We told you," Candi chides Magnum while Roxy smacks his shoulder, "I totally wanted him to fuck me the first time we met."

"Me too," Roxy seconds.

"Oh, I wanted to fuck him the first time I talked to him on the phone," Erin confesses, "He was so confident and authoritative. But there was also an innocence about him. So sweet and kind while being wild and crazy at the same time."

"Whatever," he groans and falls back as three naked girls move in towards his body…

November

"November Rain" by Guns 'N' Roses plays as Candi sits in her car.
A little too fitting. Almost haunting on this cold November night in
downtown Fayetteville, Arkansas. Rain falls. Splattering upon the
blacktop. Tapping the car's roof. Streaking across glass. She's
preparing, umbrella in hand, for the quickest exit possible. Designed to
minimize damage to her meticulously styled hair. Pushing open the
door while simultaneously opening her umbrella outside. Quickly
exiting with her stripping bag and shutting the door. Nearly jogging
across the street in loafers and black leather trench coat. The latter
concealing her sexy schoolgirl outfit from both rain and people in the
hotel lobby.

She's in awe of the lobby itself upon entering through sliding glass
doors. A testament of art deco modernism from top to bottom. Gray
and white with strategic splashes of red throughout. An aesthetic sum
greater than its parts. She struts through the atrium. Entering the

ladies' room. Even the plumbing fixtures are art deco. She commandeers a generous stretch of countertop real estate. Her hair mostly held up, but one side is slightly damp and flat. Teasing it out and holding in place with a healthy dose of hairspray. Touching up her cosmetics. Texting the client before returning to the lobby.

She's here for a fiftieth birthday party. Taking place in a private meeting room. It was his wife's idea to book a stripper, but a friend organized the event. He's visiting from Seattle. Candi finding him friendly and respectful if a little distant. Nothing to raise any red flags. She's chalking it up to shyness. A trait not uncommon amongst clients given factors of uncertainty and intimidation. Are they getting someone great? If so, can they live up to the expectations of a professional exotic entertainer? An entertainer like Candi devotes so much to exceeding audience expectations she forgets that great audiences worry about exceeding hers. When both sides are on that page, that's when the magic happens.

"You must be Candi," Evan greets her.

"That's right. And you must be Evan," Candi shakes his hand, "It's great to finally meet you."

"You too," he smiles nervously, "Um… Yeah… We have Greg ready to go. He's wearing a blindfold and waiting for his big surprise."

"Excellent," she nods, "Lead the way."

"And it's okay if we take photos?" he inquires, "Magnum said it should be fine but to confirm it with you."

"Absolutely," she smiles, "Thank you for asking."

She can't help but notice how good Evan smells as they walk side by side. She usually doesn't go for the conservative appearance, but she's totally digging it on him. The black oxfords and slacks. A white cotton dress shirt with light gray stripes. Not unlike their current location. She can't wait to give him a lap dance and be his splash of red in her plaid skirt of that color. Maybe he'll bend her over his knee and give her a good spanking. She is being a naughty girl, after all. This is going to be a quick performance. They'll want maybe two songs. A common type of booking. Regardless, she can't help but let her imagination run wild.

"Ooh… Spank me," Candi accidentally murmurs out loud.

"Excuse me?" he asks in slight bewilderment.

"Oh... Um… Nothing," she stammers with embarrassment, "I was just talking to myself. Sorry."

"Oh, okay," he laughs, "Here we are."

He gestures her inside. Greeted by thirty or so people ranging in age from twenties to sixties. All trying desperately not to laugh upon her unofficial entrance. Not laughing at her, of course. But excited and giddy for what's about to happen. The birthday boy seated in the center of the room. His wife, Constance, standing behind him. Candi replaces her loafers with clear acrylic platforms. Dropping her trench coat to reveal a skimpy schoolgirl outfit barely covering her tits and ass. Starting the music and making her official entrance.

"Happy birthday, baby!" Constance removes Greg's blindfold, "Don't say we never do anything exciting!"

"What the?!" his jaw drops as Candi walks slowly towards him, "What have you done this time?"

"Calm down and enjoy the show," Constance leans over and kisses him, "Say hi to Candi. She drove a long way to see you."

"Is that so?" he asks as Candi straddles him. She nods. Placing her arms around his neck. Bumping and grinding on him. "Photograph" by Def Leppard energizes the room. Evan circles them with his DSLR camera. Snapping photos from all angles.

"Evan, what are you doing?" Greg demands.

"Never you mind what he's doing," Constance lectures as Candi removes her top, "Look at those pretty titties."

Greg turns back to Candi. She shakes her tits in his face while the audience laughs and cheers.

"Don't act so shy," Constance encourages her husband, "You're always playing with mine. My girls need a break for once."

Everyone laughs. Candi presses her tits against Greg's chest. Sliding down his body onto her knees. Placing her face in his lap. Tossing her hair around as she simulates giving him head. Grabbing either side of the chair and pushing herself up. Turning around and bending over. Pulling down her skirt. Kicking it off her feet and shaking her booty in his face while rocking a red g-string.

"Spank me if you want," Candi looks back at him.

"Oh, I don't know…" he hesitates.

"Stop being a prude," Constance reaches over and smacks Candi's ass, "See? It's all in good fun."

"That's right," Candi stares at Greg until he relents and gives her butt a light smack.

"Now that wasn't so bad," Constance laughs, "She's still wearing a g-string."

Candi pulls down her g-string in the rear and vigorously shakes her booty in Greg's face. Evan quickly moves behind them and gets the shot. The audience howls in delight.

"Oh lord," Greg laughs in embarrassment.

"Woo hoo!" Constance shouts.

Candi pulls up her g-string. Kicking her legs back while falling forward. Landing on her hands. Thrusting back and forth. Her ass in Greg's face. Rubbing her pussy against his cock. Pleased that he's hard. Having fun teasing him. Getting him prepped for fucking the hell out of Constance later. Savoring her current role as professional foreplay specialist. Bringing him out of his shell. Feeling him lightly squeeze her ass when he's not sliding money in her g-string. She feels her pussy getting wet. Growing wetter as she imagines doing this with Evan.

"There you go," Constance enables Greg, "It's not like you ever keep your hands off my ass."

"Quit telling everyone our business," he argues jokingly as everyone laughs again.

"Oh my God," Candi stands and turns to face Greg and Constance, "You two are so adorable."

"So are you," Constance gushes at the compliment, "You are just precious."

Candi straddles Greg once again. Sitting on his lap. Placing his hands on her hips. He holds her in place as she falls back. Thrusting on his lap. Evan taking more photos. The audience cheering them on. Constance holds a hundred-dollar bill in front of Greg.

"Now how do you expect me to take that?" he asks, "Someone has to keep this young lady from falling."

"Fine," Constance laughs, "I'll do it,' sliding the money down the front of Candi's g-string and quickly pulling her hand back.

"For a second there," he antagonizes Constance, "I thought you were going to pull her g-string aside."

"You mean like this?" Candi pulls her g-string to one side and flashes her pussy at Greg and Constance as well as Evan's camera.

"Now it's a party!" Constance shrieks and giggles.

"I don't think I can take anymore," Greg raises a white flag.

Candi pulls herself up. Throwing her arms around her birthday boy's neck. Kissing him on the cheek as the song ends.

"Anyone else want a dance?" she asks the audience, but no one bites, "What about you, Evan?"

"Come on," Constance implores him.

"No thank you," he laughs nervously, "I don't think I can handle that."

"Let's hear it for Candi, everyone!" Constance implores the audience.

Everyone cheers while Candi and Greg help each other stand. Evan runs around snaps one last photo of them posing with Constance. Candi turns down her music and begins dressing. Putting on jeans and a sweater along with her loafers for the long drive home. Packing up while conversing with her audience. They're stunned and greatly appreciative that she drove three hours to be here. And they're packing up too. Candi's performance being the grand finale of tonight's festivities. To hear them say it, she was the best thing about tonight. It melts her heart as she thanks them profusely.

"No. Thank you, Candi," Constance gives her a hug along with a kiss on the cheek, "This was amazing. Better than I ever imagined."

"Aww… You're welcome," Candi kisses her back.

"Thank you so much for coming, Candi," Evan reaches out to shake her hand, "Is there anything else we can do for you?"

"You can give me a hug, silly," Candi pulls him in for a wet kiss on the cheek that's dangerously close to his mouth, "Thank you, too."

She steps back. Smiling at him while he stands there looking slightly embarrassed. Hoping she didn't go too far. But this is her final moment in his company. Wanting to make the most of it.

"You be safe driving back to Little Rock, young lady," Greg instructs her.

"Yes, be safe," Constance and Evan concur along with various audience members.

"Don't worry, I will," Candi grabs her things, "Have a great night, everyone."

Everyone wishes her a great night too as she exits. Back into the art deco atrium. It's still raining. That's when she realizes she's starving. Noticing the hotel restaurant and lounge. "It's probably a little pricy," she thinks. But she did make excellent money tonight. And it beats trying to find someplace cheaper in the rain. The food is probably better, too.

Aside from a few people drinking at the bar, the place is empty. Candi sinks into a red and black leather sofa against a wall. The chairs on the opposite side of her table are gray. Just like the columns rising from the ebony hardwood floor to the rectangular white neon lights suspended from the ceiling. Miles Davis drifting softly through the dining room. A different world under the same roof. She reflects upon her latest performance while enjoying a club sandwich and vodka cranberry. Procrastinating before undertaking her three-hour drive home. She has no complaints about tonight's gig. But doing only one song barely constitutes a warmup for her. Still primed for an hour or two of bumping and grinding but nowhere to do it. And no one to do it with.

"May I join you?" Evan appears to her surprise and delight.

"Absolutely," she sits up straight and quickly wipes her mouth even though it's clean.

"Jack and Coke, please," he responds to the waitress who rushed over to take his order, "And put her bill on my tab. Room 714."

"Oh, you don't have to do that," Candi is both flattered and embarrassed.

"Sure I do," he smiles, "You totally made Greg's night. And everyone else's."

"Thank you so much," she smiles back.

"You're welcome," he looks around nervously as if he's doing something illegal, "So, how long have you been doing this?"

"A few years now," she answers mysteriously.

"Do you enjoy it?" he inquires, "I'm sorry. That's probably a stupid and inappropriate question for me to ask."

"Not at all," she shakes her head and laughs sweetly, "Um… It's fun most of the time. Like tonight."

"That's good," he pauses, "I apologize if I've come across as standoffish at any point during this entire process."

"Not at all," she assures him, "You've been so kind and respectful. I really appreciate it."

"I'm glad you think so," he pauses as the waitress serves him, then takes a sip, "I… Um… Never mind. I'm sorry."

"What is it?" Candi asks with genuine interest, "Don't be shy. I've had lots of men open up to me about all sorts of things over the years. Nothing shared here goes beyond this table."

"Well…" he conjures forth the nerve to open up, "It's just that… My wife passed away a year ago this month."

"Evan, I am so sorry," she places her hand over his, "I won't even pretend to know what you've been through," she pauses, "But I'm an excellent listener."

"Thank you," he nods and pauses for another sip, "It was leukemia. Like, out of nowhere. It was so quick. I had no time to process what was happening until after she was gone."

Candi squeezes his hand while giving him a supportive smile.

"So many things keep going through my mind," he continues, "We never got around to having children. I don't know if that's a blessing or a curse. We were consumed with our careers. I know it's crazy, but that was a big part of our bond."

"It's not crazy at all," she tells him, "You two clearly loved each other deeply, and that's what matters."

"Yeah," he sighs, "We'd been together since junior high."

"Oh wow," she's surprised, "That's impressive."

"I don't know why I'm telling you this," he laughs nervously, "But she's the only woman I've ever been with."

"Hey," she laughs sweetly, "I would've killed to meet the one my first time out. I'm sure most people would."

"I got lucky, I know," he nods, "And now, I'm faced with the prospect of doing it all over. Before you got here, a few of them were telling me that it's time I start dating again."

"I obviously can't speak to someone in your position," she replies, "But, you have to do what's best for you. Move forward at your own pace."

"I think you're right," he agrees, "And I'm so sorry. I didn't mean to make you cry."

"Oh, I didn't even realize I was doing that," she giggles nervously and wipes the tear streaming down her cheek, "Don't be sorry about that. Or anything else."

"Thanks," he smiles as they each pause and take another sip.

"So," she points to his camera, "Can I see the shots you got of me?"

"Sure," he passes it to her.

"Ooh, you got a lot," she looks through her images, "And there's my tits."

He looks around to make sure no one is listening. Covering his mouth to avoid laughing loudly in embarrassment.

"Relax, Evan," she assures him, "We're the only ones in here right now."

"I know," he laughs, "It's just…"

"Aww… You got my naked booty shake," she giggles, "It's a little blurry though."

"Well, you were shaking it really fast," he argues jokingly.

"You bet your ass I was," she nods in mock arrogance, "Hey, you even got my pussy!"

"Oh my God, Candi," he looks around again as she laughs.

"So," she sassily looks him in the eye, "Did you like seeing me naked?"

"Um… yeah," he weakly stammers.

"'Um… yeah,' is not the answer I'm looking for, Evan," she chides, "You're supposed to say, 'Fuck yeah, Candi, I loved seeing you naked. It made my cock throbbing hard.'"

"Okay…" he laughs.

"Ugh!" she sighs.

"I mean… Okay…" he fights to get the words out, "I loved seeing you naked. You're incredibly beautiful and sexy. I found your performance… Um… Very arousing."

"Aww... Evan. That totally melts my heart," she clutches her chest, "I loved having you see me naked,' she pauses and leans in, "It made my pussy wet and tingly."

He's at a loss for words. Shaking his head. Laughing in embarrassment.

"It's true," she coos, "In fact, I'm getting wet and tingly right now just thinking about you jerking off to my photos later."

"What?!" he laughs in denial, "I wasn't… You know… I mean…"

"Um, I'll be insulted if you don't," she lectures him, "You'd better cum hard to my photos, mister."

"Oh God," he drops his head to the table and covers it in shame.

"But you're going to need a sharper naked booty shot," she stands and grabs her bag, "Come on. Let's go."

"Go where?" he looks up in confusion.

"Room 714, silly," she giggles before leaning into his ear and whispering, "Wet and tingly, Evan. Wet and tingly."

Candi is practically skipping towards the elevators. Like a naughty schoolgirl. Her stripping bag in one hand. Evan in the other. Leading him across the spacious atrium.

"Wet and tingly coming through," she announces as they pass a couple before reaching the elevators.

"Are you trying to get us kicked out of here?" he laughs while pushing the up button.

"Oh, believe me," she sasses, "I could get us kicked out of here in a way they'd never forget."

"Please don't," he pleads.

"Don't worry," she laughs, "I want to make sure you get a good photo of my butt."

She turns around, bends over, and smacks her ass as the elevator doors open. He quickly drags her inside the cab. Looking around to make sure no one saw her do that.

"What am I going to do with you?" he shakes his head as they ride up.

Her face lights up as all sorts of naughty ideas fill her head at once. He laughs nervously. Looking all around the elevator. Every inch. Everywhere but her. Until finally glancing her in her direction.

"Wet and tingly," she mouths before making a kissing face.

"You know," he tells her, "There's probably a camera in here."

"Well, if someone is watching, let's give them a show," she lifts her sweater and shakes her bare breasts until stopping suddenly, "I forgot that I'm not wearing a bra right now."

"No, you're not," he laughs while pulling down her sweater.

"I'm just so excited right now," she grabs Evan and kisses him before slowly letting go and backing up at the horror of realizing what she just did, "I'm probably letting myself get carried away. I didn't mean to do anything…"

"Not at all," he breathes a huge sigh of relief as if a massive weight was suddenly lifted from his shoulders, "I like you, Candi."

"I like you too, Evan," she smiles as they reach the seventh floor.

Even the hallways in this hotel are sexy. Dark gray walls, black carpet, and low lighting are complemented by white plastic art deco room numbers in century gothic font. It only takes Candi and Evan a few steps to reach his room. She watches as he gets out his keycard and opens the door.

"Wet and tingly, Evan," she nods and tells him matter of factly, "Wet and tingly."

"Get inside already," he holds the door for her.

"This is great," she observes Evan's room once he turns on the desk lamp. Impressed that a hotel room can be so modernist and cozy at once. Setting her bag on a recliner in the corner before she starts undressing, "Let me just put my schoolgirl outfit back on…"

"Oh, do you need some privacy," he asks.

"Oh my God, you are so adorable," she giggles, "No, Evan. You've already seen me naked. Remember?"

"I guess so," he laughs, "Can I fix you a drink?"

"That would be great," she replies.

He prepares two Jack and Cokes. Slowly at first while watching Candi undress from behind. Removing her sweater and flipping her hair back. Pulling down her jeans and stepping out of them. Wearing nothing but her red g-string as she shakes her booty.

"I can feel you watching me," she reveals, "And you know what that means?"

"Let me guess," he shakes his head, "Wet and tingly."

"Oh yeah," she giggles, "Now you're getting it."

He finishes mixing their drinks while she puts on her schoolgirl costume.

"Here you are," he hands her a plastic cup.

"Thank you," she holds her drink, "What shall we drink to?"

"How about..." he ponders, "New beginnings."

"I like that," she raises her cup, "Cheers, Evan."

"Cheers, Candi," he taps her cup with his before they each take a sip.

"Let me put on some music," she sets down her drink and walks back to her bag, "Get your camera ready."

"How do you want to do this?" he turns on his camera.

"I'll strike some poses of my own, and you can direct me on what you have in mind," she turns on her audio system.

"Time of the Season" by the Zombies sets a seductive mood. Perfectly suited for the décor and dim amber glow of this impromptu glamour shoot. Candi moves around the room. Leaning against walls. Holding onto corners. Effortlessly from pose to pose. As if in one fluid motion. Evan snapping photo after photo. Matching her every step of the way to each British Invasion beat.

"How about a few on the bed?" he suggests.

"Ooh… Yes," she lies on her side and plays with her hair.

"Could you maybe, like, hold your leg up?" he requests shyly.

"Of course," she strikes the pose.

"And maybe on your hands and knees. Facing away," he directs.

"Someone's coming out of his shell," she assumes the position, "Spank me."

"Is that what you said when you first got here?" he asks amusingly.

"Yeah," she giggles, "I kind of forgot to use my inner voice that time."

"You are just something else," he snaps more photos before reaching over and smacking her ass.

"Mmm… That's nice," she wiggles her butt.

"I can't believe I just did that," he shakes his head and laughs nervously.

"I can," she stands and faces him, "Because you're sweet and kind, and you know how to show a girl a fun time."

"I don't know about that," he looks away embarrassed.

"It's true," she nods, "Guess who's wet and tingly right now?"

"Oh my God," he laughs.

"Speaking of which," she continues, "Now, I know I led you up here with promises of getting to photograph my naked booty. And I intend to deliver. But I want something from you in return first."

"What?" he asks nervously.

"That lap dance you turned down earlier," she pushes him onto the ottoman at the foot of the bed, "You owe me, mister."

"About that," he attempts to explain, "I just…"

"You don't have to explain, Evan," she walks over to change the song, "Besides, this is better anyway. I can let myself get as wet and tingly as I like."

"She Rides" by Danzig pumps forth as Candi returns to Evan. Slowly. Each step its own act of seduction. Straddling him. Sitting on his lap. Pushing her tits against his chest. Rubbing her pussy against his cock. He's already hard. Trembling with excitement and anxiety over his new beginning. She can feel it. Doing her best to nurture him while offering forth unbridled titillation. Comforting him. Teaching him. Embracing him tightly within her sexuality. Wrapping her arms around his neck. Feeling her heart racing in time with his. He's growing larger by the second. She's getting wetter by the second. Neither one saying a word yet speaking volumes to each other.

She leans back. Removing her top and tossing it aside. Grabbing his hands. Placing them on her breasts. He's tentative at first, but quickly grows comfortable with massaging her girls. Squeezing and caressing them. Teasing her nipples with his thumbs. She throws her head back and sighs. Wanting so badly to feel his mouth on them. But still careful not to push him too far too fast. Fuck it. She can't wait. Leaning forward and pressing her tits in his face. He looks up. Silently asking for permission. She fights back tears along with the urge to force his cock inside her now while sweetly nodding her head. An electrical shock rushes through her body the instant he places his mouth on her right nipple. The feel of his warm lips and wet tongue making her pussy tighten and throb. She places his hands on her ass. Underneath her skirt. He squeezes her cheeks. Moving to her left nipple. Then back and forth. Making her orgasm for the first time.

Candi stands and turns around. Facing away from Evan. Bending over and removing her skirt. Kicking it across the room. Repeating the process with her g-string. Her pussy growing even wetter knowing he's looking at it while she's bent over. Rising and shaking her booty in his face. Kicking her legs back and falling forward. Landing on her hands. Leaving nothing to the imagination with a closeup view of her ass and pussy. The sensation of his eyes exploring between her legs making her even more turned on. She sits on his lap again. He grabs her hips as she leans back and spreads her legs open. His jaw dropped. Her eyes and pose demanding he fuck her. She can't go easy on him anymore. Still willing to comfort and nurture him, but only with his hard cock deep inside her.

"Time for that naked booty shot," she announces at the end of the song. He helps her up. Grabbing his camera as she turns away and strikes her pose. Letting him snap multiple shots before bending over again. She moves to the bed. Repeating the same poses as earlier. But naked this time. Making sure he gets plenty of clear shot of her entire body. Her tits. Her ass. Her pussy. Getting up and moving to the wall. Facing it as he takes more photos of her bare ass. The experience of being his private dancer and centerfold model has her over the edge. Turning around to face him. Her back to the wall.

"Put down the camera and come here," she invites him in her sweetest, kindest voice.

"Sure. Um…" he agrees anxiously while finishing his drink.

The instant Evan approaches Candi, she grabs him. Shoving his back against the wall. Holding his wrists. Pressing her body against his. Kissing him deeply and passionately. Danzig plays again. "Blood and Tears" this time. Her tongue exploring his mouth. Coaxing his tongue inside hers. He finally gives in to his desire. His temptation. His lust for Candi. Submitting to her demand that he have his way with her. That he takes what he wants from her. Giving in to the new beginning he was finally ready to embrace the instant he first saw Candi. Even in loafers and a trench coat, she dazzled him. Only the second woman in his life he ever wanted to fuck. Overcome with anxiety and guilt that he's fought all night. To emerge victorious in this moment.

"I couldn't believe it when I walked into the restaurant and you were there," he gazes into her eyes.

"Me either," she smiles, "I'm so glad you didn't hesitate to join me."

"Well, about that…" he laughs, "I spotted you just as I was walking in. I sort of went back out and… And I spent the next five minutes working up the nerve to go back in and ask to join you."

"Aww…" she laughs, "I'm not that scary. I swear. Well, maybe a little," she playfully claws at him, "Rowr!"

They laugh even more before she kisses him again. Sliding her body along his. Dropping to her knees. Unfastening his belt. Unzipping his pants. Pulling them down along with his underwear. Freeing his cock. Now incredibly big and hard.

"Oh, that feels much better," he sighs.

"You think that's something?" she sasses, "Watch this."

Evan looks down as Candi takes his cock deep in her throat. All the way in. Swirling her tongue around his head. Along every inch of his shaft. Enjoying the sweetness of his juices. Flowing like crazy in her mouth. Making her pussy tighter and wetter. His hands holding her head. Pressing his back tight against the wall. Knees getting weaker and weaker. She licks and kisses up and down his manhood. Stroking him with her hand while kissing and caressing his balls. Bringing him to the first of what she intends to be multiple orgasms. His trembling now turned to shaking.

"Oh God, Candi," he moans breathlessly.

"Mmm-hmm…" she responds with her mouth full of his cock. Slowly pulling back. A strand of precum stretching from the tip of his manhood to the tip of her tongue. Giggling while looking up at him. Grabbing his hand on her cheek. His other hand strokes and plays with her hair. She leans forwards and takes him deep in her mouth again. So warm and velvety. He can't fucking stand how incredible it feels. Neither can she. But she has other plans for him now.

"Let's get these clothes off," she tells him. Removing his shoes and socks. Helping him take off his pants and underwear. Standing up. Looking into his eyes as she unbuttons his shirt. Pushing it over his shoulders. Pulling it off his arms. Holding it to her face and smelling it. He watches as she puts it on. She helps him remove his undershirt.

"You've been holding out on me," she ogles his naked body, "You sexy motherfucker."

He laughs as she jumps on the bed. Lounging back. His shirt wide open. Framing her otherwise naked body. Sort of a cape in its way. Almost like she's a superhero. A very naughty superhero. He climbs on top. Pressing his lips against hers. His tongue inside her mouth. She instantly follows suit. Running her fingers through his hair while he slides down. Licking and sucking her nipples again. Kissing down her stomach. Her pussy aching for his tongue. Hurting for it. Her juices

flowing like crazy. No more teasing. He needs to taste her sweetness
now.

"Eat my pussy, Evan," she shoves his face between her legs, "I can't
wait any longer. I want you to taste me."

He is more than willing to oblige. Going down on Candi like there's
no tomorrow. Licking her pussy deep. His tongue moving back and
forth between her swollen lips. Thrusting inside her sugar walls.
Dancing on her clit. Her girl juices covering his face as he tries in vain
to consume every drop.

"Oh my God," she trembles while grinding on his face, "Don't stop.
Don't stop licking my pussy."

"Oh wow," he sighs between tongue lashes, "I've missed eating
pussy."

"I miss it too," she looks mischievously into his eyes.

"You mean you miss having your pussy eaten," he corrects her.

"No, I miss eating pussy too," she laughs sassily, "I like girls too,
Evan."

"Really?" he's intrigued by this revelation.

"Oh yeah. Hot is hot, baby," she coos, "I wish I knew a hot girl up
here who likes to party. You could watch us eat each other's pussy.
Then you could punish us for being naughty girls with your big hard
cock."

"Wow," he laughs in shock and awe, "But I think one girl at a time is
a good starting place for me."

"That's right," she agrees, "And I'm glad you chose me."

"Me too," he slides his middle finger inside her and massages her g-
spot while sucking her clit.

"Oh, fuck yes," she moans even louder now, "Finger my fucking
pussy, Evan. Finger it deep."

"You're so fucking tight, Candi," he marvels.

"You've made me that fucking tight," she sighs, "So wet and tingly."

They laugh as he slides a second finger inside her. Then a third. Stroking her pussy back and forth. Making her wetter and wetter. Massaging her sugar walls while moving up her body. Sucking her titties again. Kissing her passionately. She grips his cock tightly and strokes it. Fast and hard. Masturbating each other while sharing another orgasm. She arches her back. Squeezing his fingers with her pussy. They feel incredible, but big strong fingers aren't enough. She needs his big strong cock inside her. Now.

"Fuck me, Evan," she whispers in his ear, "My pussy is so fucking wet and tingly for your massive cock."

Evan slowly removes his fingers from Candi's pussy. Rolling on top of her. She reaches down. Grabbing his hot manhood. Guiding it inside her pussy. So fucking wet that it slides in with ease. Inch by throbbing inch. He closes his eyes. Breathing heavily. Wrapping his arms around her. Shaking as he penetrates someone other than his dearly departed wife for the first time in his life. Candi returns to nurturing him. Stroking his face. Kissing him softly. Wrapping her legs around his back. Pulling him deep inside her in slow, gentle strokes. Letting him have this moment to himself. And yet it's a moment for her as well. Teaching this gorgeous man inside and out how to let himself live again.

"Oh my God," she whispers in his ear, "Fuck me, Evan."

"You feel so amazing," he buries his face in her neck, "So soft. You smell so good."

"Mmm…" she kisses and licks his neck, "So do you, baby."

His speed increases. As does his intensity. His cock growing larger. Her pussy getting tighter and wetter. Aching to get fucked even harder by him. To ride his lengthy shaft like a dirty naked cowgirl. She pushes him off her to his surprise. Then to his delight as she guides him onto his back. Straddling his cock. He grabs her hips. Guiding her pussy down over his shaft. Holding her steady while she bounces up and down on his manhood. Faster and harder. Her pussy beginning to gush and squirt. Lying forward on him. Her tits pressed against his chest. Kissing him aggressively. Pounding his cock with her pussy. He rapidly thrusts his hips upward. Matching her every stroke. Squeezing her ass with both hands. Spanking her.

"Ooh, spank me!" she cries.

"Oh my God," he laughs, "You are something else."

"So are you," she laughs too before moaning, "You are making me cum hard."

"Oh, you are going to make me explode inside you, Candi," he moans.

"Want to try something really hot?" she asks through labored breaths.

"What's that?" he asks with intrigue.

She dismounts from his cock. Getting off the bed. Taking his hand. Leading him back to the wall. She turns around. Pressing her tits against it. Arms wide across its dark gray surface. So cool and smooth against her hot, sweaty skin. Spreading her legs wide. Sticking her butt out. She looks back at him.

"Fuck me against the wall, Evan," she commands him, "Fuck me hard."

He takes a few seconds to find the right stance and reinsert himself inside her. But once he finds his sweet spot, all hell breaks loose. He wraps his arms around her waist. Thrusting his cock viciously inside her hot throbbing pussy. Her ass bouncing relentlessly against him. Warm girl juices streaming down his legs and hers. Moaning and screaming together. Every muscle fiber in their bodies contracting tighter and tighter. Aching for release. Hurting for it. He rests his head on her shoulder. Fucking her as fast and hard as he possibly can.

"Fuck me hard, Evan," she dares him, "Just fucking do it."

"I am fucking you hard, Candi," he growls, "I'm fucking your pussy so fucking hard right now."

"Fuck my pussy hard," she orders, "Make me cum all over you."

"Do it. Cum all over me," he demands, "I'm going to cum so fucking hard inside you."

"Oh God!" she screams, "I want to feel you cum inside me! Do it now!"

"Cum with me, Candi!" he shouts, "Cum with me now!"

"Oh, fuck me!" she cries as her pussy explodes all over him.

Candi squirts like crazy on Evan's cock. All over his balls and thighs. Between his legs. Her entire body shaking uncontrollably. Pushing her fingertips into the wall. Soaking in its coldness to quench the fire raging inside her while his cock erupts deep inside her. Wave after wave of burning cum. Filling her full. Running down her legs. She grips his cock tightly between her sugar walls. Taking in the sensation of his climax with hers. His arms locked around her. Chest pressed against her back. Face buried in her neck. Feeling his heart race. Hers too. Moaning and screaming together for seemingly an eternity.

They remain still for a few moments. Catching their breath. Returning to normal. Whatever normal is. Not a word is spoken. Candi is more than fulfilled, but also a little worried. Hoping that she didn't push Evan too far. Hoping he isn't experiencing guilt and regret after the fact. Finally, he kisses her on the cheeks and removes himself from her. She turns around to find him smiling.

"That was incredible!" he takes her in his arms and kisses her, "You, are incredible."

"Maybe a little," she laughs, "You, though… Oh my God."

"I was just trying to keep up with you," he laughs.

"Oh, you passed me quickly," she argues.

"Whatever," he shakes his head.

She takes his hand and leads him back to the bed. They lie down and hold each other. Stroking each other's hair and face. Staring into each other's eyes. Then resting them for a moment…

Candi awakens at four in the morning. Music still playing. Evan fast asleep. Quietly, she gets up, dresses, and packs her things. Seeing the stationary on the desk, she sits down to write him a goodbye note:

Dear Evan,

Thank you for an unbelievably wonderful night. New beginnings have only just begun for you. I know you'll be just fine moving forward.

Still wet and tingly for you,

Candi

She folds it in half. Placing it on the pillow next to him. Pulling up the covers to keep him warm. Leaning over and kissing him on the cheek. Turning off the light on her way out.

The rain has finally quit, but it's chilly outside. Not even her sweater and trench coat are enough to keep her warm. Shaking from the cold as she drives off. Through the city and back to I-49 on her long homeward trek. Feeling better once warm air begins flowing from the vents. "Don't Cry" by Guns 'N' Roses comes on, but tears fill her eyes regardless. For the sweet man she just met who lost the love of his life. Wondering whether it's a blessing or a curse they never had children. Thinking of the children she wants to have herself someday. And of the man she'd like to have them with. As she travels through the Bobby Hopper Tunnel, she realizes that someday is getting ever closer…

July

Magnum stops for gas in White Hall, Arkansas off I-530. Something he neglected to do earlier in Little Rock. Rushing to get everything else ready for tonight. Including picking up Candi to be his stripping partner for this birthday party in Eudora. A town just shy of the Arkansas-Louisiana border. They still have another two hours on the road ahead of them. He plays out all of this in his mind while standing by his car. Watching the dollar amount on the fuel pump race ever higher. Thankful the client is paying for this and not him. He glances eastward upon the fast-food restaurants and motels typical of freeway exits. The sun low and orange on the western horizon behind him. Its inevitable retirement for the day to soon bring some respite from the crushing humidity of this hot July evening.

They continue forth with southbound I-530 taking them around the western edge of Pine Bluff. More like Crime Bluff. A cesspool of robbery, rape, and murder. And not necessarily in that order. Although the rolled-up windows keep out the mosquitoes, they do nothing for the foul stench of multiple papermills infinitely suspended in the air above town. Magnum occasionally receives calls about parties in Pine Bluff and passes on them every time. Candi is talkative as I-530 terminates on the southern edge of Crime Bluff and segues into U.S. 65. Even more talkative in her own mind. Beside herself with anticipation for tonight. Not just for the party but her entire night with Magnum. Endless wild and crazy thoughts consuming her mind. Serving as motivation for all manner of adventurous things she wants to do with him. Naughty things. One abstraction of debauchery after another. His naked ambition having worn off upon her in more ways than one.

Their journey takes them deep into the Arkansas Delta. Past small towns hosting state correctional facilities. Then through Gould, which recently saw its city council make a failed attempt at a bloody coup against the mayor. The duo is now in one of those areas of Arkansas so rural that all the local radio stations air either church sermons or eighties country. Rather than suffer through brimstone and hellfire or the likes of "Baby's Got Her Blue Jeans On", "A Long Line of Love" and "Fishin' in the Dark" Magnum opts for Mötley Crüe. "Home Sweet Home" carries them through Dumas. A town largely destroyed by a tornado several years ago. They're a long fucking way from home right now. But the drive itself is not without its rewards.

The surrounding farmland is gorgeous. Drenched in shadows growing darker from the sun making its western descent. Lush green fields of rice, corn, and soybean crops fractured by patches of majestic trees. Aesthetics easy to appreciate from within the comfort of an air-conditioned vehicle. Protected from the hot and sticky Arkansas summer air. Safe from the hordes of mosquitoes out for blood in the twilight. It's the epitome of antebellum romanticism. A Hallmark Channel-like façade that ignores the region's economic struggles of recent decades. Struggles that increasingly manifest themselves architecturally the deeper they penetrate. The town of McGehee greeting them with one empty building after another.

Magnum has driven through Chicot County, Arkansas via U.S. 65 on several occasions prior but never stopped. Not in Eudora, Lake Village, Dermott, or the mysteriously named Ross Van Ness. He was traveling to Vicksburg, Mississippi in each instance. A town offering just enough adult recreation to snag him a party now and then. But that doesn't mean Chicot County hasn't caught his attention. He's always been curious about everything he sees along the highway while passing through in the dead of night. In turn, making him curious about the rest of the county. This is partly due to having never received so much as an inquiry about a potential booking in the area until now. It's an exciting first where his interest in physical and cultural geography is concerned.

He's also jazzed about rocking a woman's fortieth birthday party tonight. It's a coed audience, so Candi is along for the guys. And for any women who may be curious. He was immediately sold on Tara. She exuded the sweetness and politeness that always makes him feel positive about a prospective client. Convincing him that she'll take excellent care of them. And he was taken with her aesthetics upon checking out her Facebook profile. So was Candi. Her naughty thoughts racing faster and faster the closer they get to their destination and Tara. Candi wants to fuck her. More specifically, fuck her with Magnum. Her feelings for him growing stronger and scarier. Seeking any chance to bond with him. Including their shared love of seducing women. Loving every minute of their joint sexual conquests of new playmates. She can't get enough of being the alpha female in his life. Frightened by her desire for this status to never end, but even more frightened by the opposite scenario.

They discuss Tara's sexiness while driving through Lake Village. Home to the largest oxbow lake in North America, this once-thriving city is comprised mostly of empty buildings. All that remains of open businesses is a scant smattering of banks, convenience stores, restaurants, and the suggestively named Turn On Inn Hotel. The latter of which Magnum points out while Candi scrolls on her phone through Tara's Facebook photos.

"I'd love to turn on in that ass," she muses without looking up, "Those booty shorts leave nothing to the imagination. She can jog ahead of me anytime."

"Yeah, she's pretty hot," he sighs while keeping his eyes on the road.

"Whatever," she scoffs, "You know you'd fuck that booty. I sure as fuck would."

"Maybe you'll get your shot tonight," he teases.

"No maybes about it," she continues fawning over the client's photos, "We're both going to fuck her tonight. That is our mission."

"Well, our mission is to deliver a naughty birthday performance to end all naughty birthday performances," he reminds her, "Anything else is a bonus."

"I don't think so," she flippantly contradicts him in a way like never before, "I think it's all part of the same package. The performance and the after-party seduction."

"That's kind of moving us into…" he ponders with a reluctance to use any word that describes taking money for sex, "…a gray area."

"No, no, no… We're not meth addicts desperate for a fix," she shakes her head, "I'm just saying that… like… we go above and beyond as entertainers in an unprecedented fashion. Not just here, but anywhere in the world. You know that better than anyone."

"Are you suggesting that we've transcended the limitations of stripping?" he laughs while seriously considering her point, "That our performance style has progressed into something more… elaborate?"

"I'm not telling you anything you don't already know," she looks at him, "This isn't a new point for us. We've been here a while now. And it's perfectly fine, Magnum. We are agents of pleasure."

"Okay. Let's do it. Let's chase after Tara," he nods his head if for no other reason than to avoid upsetting her right before showtime, "And let's use that objective as motivation for the party."

"Well, of course," she turns back to her phone, "And that Hannah girl is rocking some impressive titties as well. We should go after her too."

"Sure, why not?" he laughs.

Candi sighs and shakes her head. She's not disappointed in Magnum's lack of enthusiasm for what she's saying. Rather it worries her. And that's been a thing for her lately. He's clearly running out of steam from operating the agency all these years. She knows it. And she knows he knows it too. Aside from her, he's only representing two other girls right now. And neither comes close to Candi. She remains his girl Friday as he uses the other two sparingly. For little more than parties that Candi isn't available to handle. And that's why she wants him to start focusing on his other talents. The whole agents of pleasure thing intended to inspire him in that direction by using stripping as a metaphor. But the two of them are indeed sex personified to their audiences and have been for some time. In a fashion that goes far beyond taking off their clothes and giving lap dances. She feels it her responsibility to help him experience this revelation himself as not only his professional confidant and partner in crime but also as his girlfriend. And she is his girlfriend whether he realizes it or not.

She wonders how she can be a good girlfriend to her boyfriend as they cruise through Eudora. The self-proclaimed "Catfish Capital of Arkansas" as it were. It's even deader than Lake Village. She decides to liven things up by revisiting Tara's photos. Holding the phone in her left hand. Lifting her short skirt with the right. Spreading her legs as wide as she can in the passenger seat of her boyfriend's sportscar. Pulling her g-string aside. Licking her fingers. Reaching down and gently rubbing her pussy. Massaging her clit. Ogling photos of their client in booty shorts, bikinis, and other revealing attire. Fantasizing about playing naughty games with Tara. Sucking her tits. Eating her pussy. Then having her return the favor. Candi fingers herself while feeling Magnum's eyes upon her. His gaze making her skin tingle. The thought of helping him relax and loosen up making her pussy tighter and wetter.

"You should totally fuck Tara in the ass," she sighs over the booty shorts photo, "I mean… If I had a cock, I'd totally fuck her in the ass."

"If you had a cock," he shakes his head, "You wouldn't be here."

"Just go with it, Magnum," she scoffs, "Besides, I could always get a strap-on."

"There you go," he laughs, "You could line girls up and buttfuck them at parties."

"Yes!" she exclaims, "That's exactly the point I was making before. We need to think bigger. Bolder. Wilder. Crazier."

"Sure," he glances over, "Just don't cum on my seat."

Candi responds to this by placing her fingers in Magnum's mouth. His warm tongue sending an electrical shock through her body. She returns to masturbating, but this time sets down her phone and massages his cock through his pants. Making him throb. So hard in her hand. So hot. Masturbating him along with herself. Head tossed back. Eyes closed. "Fire Woman" by The Cult pulsating in her ears. The purr of the engine in time with the purr of her pussy. She tastes her own sweetness. Loving every drop. It would be a crime if Tara doesn't experience this for herself. She considers that her client may not be into girls but quickly decides to think positively. If that's the case, then she'll be the exception to the rule. After all, she and her partner in crime have made a long and lucrative career out of being just that. Exceptions the rule. Every rule. Even their own.

Magnum turns west onto AR 8. The homestretch towards their destination. A community center located between Eudora and the town of Empire. He's never been to the latter but assumes it's no empire. Candi watches him shift through the gears. Accelerating to a few miles above the speed limit. Once there, she leans over and undoes his pants. He makes no effort to protest. Silently monitoring the situation with a combination of apprehension and curiosity. As well as excitement at odds with his serious professionalism about the task at hand five miles up the road. Part of him wants to stop her, but another part of him is already in deep consideration of what she's been saying during this trip. He also doesn't want to discourage or upset her right before showtime. If this gets her in the mood to bring down the house, then who is he to stop her?

And he's powerless to stop her upon the sensation of her soft, warm mouth sliding over his rock-hard shaft. Inch by inch. Deep in her throat. Her tongue swirling around his head. Gently probing his tiny hole. Making his juices flow. Hers too. Reaching back to pull down her g-string slightly, so it doesn't get soaked. Trying to not let the gearshift press into her ribs. Heart racing as she feels their speed increase. She wants him to relax but worries her actions are having the opposite effect and begins to pull away. He responds by grabbing her head and holding her in place. Her relaxation technique is working in spades. Manifesting itself in unbridled intensity while he races down this lonely state highway. If not for their party, he'd stop right now and fuck her over the hood on the open road. But it'll have to wait. And maybe she's right, and they can get the client to join them. Now he's getting excited over that prospect.

Just as she's bringing them both to orgasm, he spots it. An old feed store building near the Boeuf River. Looking vaguely like an abandoned frame house if not for the words "Rowton's Feed Store" emblazoned across corrugated galvanized steel siding. The lights and music inside combined with the dozen or so vehicles in the gravel parking lot make for a surreal scene. She rises and locks her lips to his. Throwing her arms around his neck as he grabs her waist. Gripping each other tightly. Kissing insatiably. Finally pulling themselves apart. Catching their breath together. Lost in each other's eyes.

"Oh my God," she giggles, "I'm just so happy and horny right now."

"As opposed to being sad and horny?" he quips sarcastically.

"Um… How about those angry, lonely guys who call you and ask for dates with me?" she playfully smacks his chest.

"Good point," he looks down at his erect manhood, "How am I going to get back in my g-string?"

"Just picture some woman who's like totally gross and unfuckable," she instructs him, "Like… Um… Joy Behar."

"That did it," he returns his now flaccid cock to his g-string and buttons his pants, "Thanks."

"Anytime, lover," she kisses him.

They nearly asphyxiate themselves applying insect repellent to every millimeter of bare skin before stepping out of the car. Tara walks towards them. Every bit as sexy as advertised. As are they. Dressed as naughty cops tonight. Ready to make their client, birthday girl, and anyone else who's willing bend over and assume the position.

"Oh wow, you two," Tara greets them, "Hannah is going to love this."

"Yeah. You're all about to get busted, missy," he nods cockily.

"Ooh…" she giggles, "I can't wait."

"Neither can we," Candi eyes her seductively in a not-so-subtle fashion.

"Just give me five," Tara gazes upon them with intrigue before turning to head back inside.

Magnum and Candi watch their client's booty bounce with every step in her long floral skirt. The night has somewhat vanquished the humidity and mosquitoes from earlier. Stars shine brightly, thanks to the absence of light pollution. A symphony of insects comes at them from all directions. The duo put on the remainder of their costumes and touch up their respective fragrances.

"Shall we?" he asks.

She nods in agreement. They grab their gear and strut lockstep towards the entrance. Confidence in full force. He continues paying mind to her musings about them being agents of pleasure. She thinks about it too. Each committed to bringing down the house as always along with giving chase to their client. The birthday girl as well. Both are single, so anything is possible. The entertainers allow this knowledge and ambition to carry them inside. Making their entrance with authority. Prepared to fight or fuck anything that gets in their way. That is how they roll.

Unfortunately, that's not how their latest audience rolls. Although Tara is full of life and Hannah ecstatic to see them, Magnum and Candi know instantly from experience that everyone else here is shit. Amazed to see so many elitist snobs in such a broke ass part of the country. Allowing their collective insecurities to manifest as snark and passive aggression towards professional entertainers devoted to making their night something special to remember. They'd be hard-pressed to find an ultra-sexy male/female stripping duo anywhere in the world. Encountering such a duo in the Arkansas Delta is nothing short of a miracle.

Tara overestimated her friends on this and knows it as per the nervousness in her face. The professionalism and expertise for which she paid allow Magnum and Candi to pay these losers no mind. Zeroing in on their birthday girl instead. Closing in on her across a stained concrete floor under dim industrial lighting delivered by patinated metal fixtures suspended from aged wooden trusses. Any semblance of a functional store long gone. All that's left is an open space for people to utilize in making their own fun. The strippers forego their standard law enforcement introduction. Instead going right into "Bad Boys" to drown out the negative vibes and uncomfortable silence around them. Forming their own inner circle of shameless debauchery with Tara and Hannah. Their birthday girl instantly on the same page as her entertainers.

"Do you need me to assume the position?" she bends over her chair and wiggles her butt, "I'm all yours."

"Someone is being a very naughty girl," he runs his hands up each of her legs before grabbing her hips and humping her ass, "And I think you've been in this position before."

"Hells yeah she's a naughty girl!" Tara is both fired up and overcompensating for the lackluster audience, "And she's been in that position many times. I know because I've put her there myself!"

"Shut up!" Hannah laughs, "Don't be telling everyone our business!"

The audience snootily dismisses Tara and Hannah's pretend sapphic humor as Candi takes Magnum's place behind the birthday girl.

"I can get down with that," Candi inserts herself into the joke and rubs her pussy against Hannah's ass, "With both of you."

Magnum laughs along with Tara and Hannah at Candi's upping of the ante. His longtime stripping partner clearly having picked up on his habits over the years. And he realizes that her earlier musings, at the very least, are apropos in this situation. With a lame audience, the two of them may as well go for broke and set no limits on their potential fun with their client and birthday girl. Especially since they're doing likewise. Causing him to consider that they're intentionally making their friends uncomfortable. It's unusual but a definite possibility. He's witnessed similar instances in the past. So has Candi. But it remains to be seen how far these party girls will go.

"You should feel her tits!" Tara gives him his first clue by grabbing and squeezing Hannah's breasts, "They're fucking huge!"

"Oh my God!" Hannah feigns shock, "Can we ever hang out once without you grabbing my tits?"

"Nope!" Tara beams proudly while the audience members shake their heads and look away.

"Let me check them out," Candi leans forward and grabs Hannah's breasts, "Ooh… Those are nice. You need to feel them, Magnum."

"So… You two drove all the way from Little Rock to play with my titties?" Hannah turns around and sits down.

"Pretty much," he slaps his handcuffs on her.

"Well then," she removes her lowcut black party blouse and frees her girls, "Let me make it easier for you."

"Oh great," a woman mutters snarkily, "Hannah's topless again."

"Hey!" Hannah chastises her, "It's not like you've never played with them."

That shuts her up as "Salt Shaker" shakes the building. Hannah shaking her titties in clear violation of penal code 6969. Given the circumstances, all Magnum can do is go with Candi's idea. He wastes no time stripping down to his g-string. Grinding on his birthday girl's lap. Pressing his muscular chest against her ample breasts. So warm and soft against his skin. His cock growing larger by the second. Barely contained within his g-string. Her enthusiastic massaging of his ass combined with the heat coming from between her legs letting him know she's game for anything he has to offer.

"Mmm…" she buries her face in his neck, "You smell incredible."

"Thank you," he laughs, "So do you."

"He sure does," Tara leans into his neck from behind, "Mmm… You smell delicious."

"Magnum always smells amazing," Candi strips to her bikini as she walks among the audience to their disinterest, "You can count on it."

She joins him in tag-teaming their birthday girl after finding no takers from the audience. Tara spins around the room while Magnum and Candi face away from Hannah. Each straddling a leg and pulling down their g-string in the rear. Double naked booty shaking in her face.

"Hells yeah!" Hannah slaps and squeezes the four bouncing ass cheeks before her, "That's what I'm talking about."

Magnum unties Candi's bikini top. Revealing her perky tits to the approving screams of Tara and Hannah. It's just the four of them in his mind. Their client ups the ante by removing her skirt. Now clad in a thong and belly shirt as she joins the strippers. A bumping and grinding threesome hovering over the birthday girl's lap. The trio faces away from Hannah. Pulling down their unmentionables in the rear and giving her a triple naked booty shake.

"Oh my God!" Hannah laughs, "I don't know which ass to eat first!"

"Get 'em all at once!" Magnum laughs along with Candi and Tara as the trio simultaneously bend over and spread their butt cheeks wide open.

"Oh yeah!" Hannah exclaims, "Show me those booty holes!"

"Gee, that's classy," a shlubby guy mutters sarcastically as the remaining audience voices similar dissatisfaction at this spectacle.

"Hey," Hannah chastises him, "Sometimes, you just gotta eat some booty!"

"That's right," Candi seconds, "Magnum can attest to that!"

"Shut up!" Magnum nearly falls over from embarrassed laughter, "Don't be telling everyone our business!"

"Ooh…" Tara is consumed with intrigue, "Are you two an item?"

"We work hard," Candi runs her hand down Magnum's torso and grabs his cock, "And we play hard."

"Oh, we play harder than that," he slides his hand inside Candi's g-string and fingering her pussy, "And someone is very wet."

"So…" Hannah searches for the words, "Do you two do like, sex shows?"

"Only with sexy birthday girls like you," he walks to his stripping bag and retrieves a can of Reddi-wip.

"And with sexy clients, too," Candi locks eyes with Tara.

"Candi and I discussed you two on the drive here," he reveals to Candi's shocked amusement, "We're here to entertain everyone," he pauses to apply whipped cream to Hannah's nipples, "But we're also here to seduce the two of you."

"Is that so?" Tara asks rhetorically in a seductive tone.

"Well then," Hannah motions the strippers towards her tits, "Seduce us."

Magnum and Candi kneel on either side of Hannah with "Azz &
Tittiez" by Hypnotize Camp Posse thumping forth. Each sucking one
of the birthday girl's large breasts. Kissing and licking her nipples.
Tongues swirling up Reddi-wip into girl-hungry mouths. Tara gently
running her fingernails along each stripper's back.

"Fuck yes!" Hannah grabs their heads and smothers their faces,
"Suck my titties! Everyone does eventually!"

"It's true," Tara explains, "She's so proud of her girls."

"Hey, I'm just spreading the wealth!" Hannah proclaims.

Magnum and Candi break away from their birthday girl as they burst
out laughing along with her and their client. The stripper's g-strings
still down in the rear when they turn around and naked booty shake on
Hannah's tits. Rubbing their butts all over her girls. Wet and sticky
from saliva and whipped cream. Trying in vain to grab her nipples
between their cheeks. The three of them laughing hysterically at these
antics.

"Oh my God! Y'all are a total riot!" Hannah looks at Tara, "Where
on earth did you find these two?"

"Online," Tara shrugs her shoulders, "I'm glad you like them since
theirs is the only agency I found that was legit."

"I guess that explains why they get away with such behavior," a
woman bitchily scoffs.

"Exactly," Tara subtly places a hand on Magnum's chest before he
can lecture this woman, "They're clearly the best in the business."

"Hells yeah they are!" Hannah concurs, "Way better than I ever
could've imagined!"

"Let's kick it up a notch," he sprays Reddi-wip on Candi's nipples,
"Have at it, ladies."

"Come on, Tara," Hannah motions to her friend as Candi straddles
her lap, "Let's do this together."

"Ooh, baby," Tara wastes no time planting her mouth on Candi's
right breast with Hannah doing the same to her left breast. The client

gazes into Candi's eyes while licking and sucking her nipple. Flicking her tongue over it. Candi's pussy growing wetter from the ever-increasing odds that she and Magnum will fuck her tonight.

"Oh wow!" Hannah pulls back and catches her breath, "That was amazing."

"Yes, it was," Tara maintains seductive eye contact with Candi while moving back, "Let's do Magnum now."

"You hear that, Magnum?" Candi teases him, "They want to do you."

"Of course they do," he jokingly retorts while taking Candi's place, "They're women."

"Well, someone's got some attitude," Hannah laughs.

"We'll take care of that," Tara sasses.

"Oh, will you?" he taunts her as Candi gives his nipples the whipped cream treatment, "Let's see what you girls got."

Tara and Hannah waste no time planting their lips around Magnum's nipples. As she did with Candi, the client stares into his eyes while massaging him with her soft, warm tongue. Longingly. Seductively. Magnum's cock growing harder from the ever-increasing odds that he and Candi will fuck her tonight. "Shake That" by Eminem inspires Candi and Tara to shake their asses on either side of Hannah. Magnum grinds his manhood between her titties. Removing it from his g-string. Thrusting between her girls as she presses them together. His juices flowing in her cleavage. Candi glance over her shoulder and smiles at him.

"Are you letting Magnum titty-fuck you?" Tara asks.

"Fuck yeah I am!" Hannah proudly exudes.

"Oh my God!" an obnoxious female voice screeches, "Are you really letting him do that to you?"

"Why not?" Hannah taunts her, "I let your husband titty-fuck me once."

The woman turns her fury upon the man standing next to her as Hannah grabs the Reddi-wip. Drawing a line along the length of

Magnum's shaft. Licking it off. Inch by inch. Her tongue dancing along every nerve ending. Making him tremble when she takes him deep in her throat. Twirling around his head and frenulum. Savoring his warm juices. Squeezing his ass with both hands. Sighing from the combined flavor of whipped cream and precum. Candi and Tara constantly looking over to watch. The audience nearly at its collective breaking point of discomfort. Hannah takes notice.

"You think that's something? Check this out," Hannah motions for Magnum to turn around and guides Candi and Tara to join on either side of him, "Do that thing before where you all three bend over and spread your cheeks. But hold it."

The trio laughingly obliges. One by one feeling the sensation of cold whipped cream sprayed upon butthole. Followed by the sensation of the birthday girl's tongue licking them. Then feeling that same tongue pushed inside. From Candi to Magnum to Tara. Eating three asses in one fell swoop. The participants consumed with arousal, excitement, and laughter. Loving every minute of their unbridled craziness together. Everyone else, however, is not so appreciative of this display. Continuing with their dismissive rhetoric as they drift out the door and into the great humid darkness. Until only the core four is left.

"Oh my God, you guys!" Hannah gushes, "That was totally hot!"

"Are we the only ones left?" Magnum stands and takes stock of his surroundings.

"Yeah," Tara shakes her head, "I think we scared off everyone else."

"Did we go too far?" Candi asks.

"Not at all," Tara assures her, "They've known for many years how the two of us are."

"That's right," Hannah clarifies, "Their no strangers to our craziness. They're just getting old."

"Unlike us," Tara hugs Hannah.

"We're forever young," Hannah kisses Tara, "You two probably think we're crazy for saying that."

"Not at all," he smiles, "It's the story of my life."

"Mine too," Candi seconds.

"I'm so sorry about everyone else," Tara apologizes, "I know they can be reserved at times, but I honestly didn't think they'd be rude. That really isn't like them. But I apologize regardless."

"No, don't apologize from them," he shakes his head, "They're adults. They know how to conduct themselves."

"That's right," Candi adds, "Besides, you two more than made up for them."

"Exactly," he concurs, "We just went ahead despite them and had ourselves a foursome."

"I guess we did," Tara admits sheepishly as everyone laughs.

"Hells yeah we did!" Hannah exclaims while putting on her blouse, "Unfortunately, you'll have to settle for a threesome now. I have to be at work early in the morning. Like six."

"They should cut you some slack," Candi opines, "It's your birthday."

"I know, but you don't want to lose your job down here," Hannah explains, "There's no shortage of unemployed people happy to replace you."

She hugs and kisses Magnum and Candi before doing the same with Tara. The strippers watch the birthday girl and her luscious melons exit the building. Never to be seen or played with again. But the night isn't over yet. They turn their attention to the client. Watching as she pulls her skirt up over her firm round ass. Simultaneously plotting to see it again tonight in all its spankable and edible glory along with the rest of her delectable body. Pondering how to make it happen.

"Thank you so much for coming tonight," she hands each stripper an extra hundred, "Hannah had an absolute blast. Me too."

"You're welcome," he nods, So did we."

"Definitely," Candi agrees, "You two are the best."

"Aww… So, are you two…" Tara gushes before giggling nervously, "You two don't have to leave right away, do you? I can feed you first. Back at my place. It's right on this road. On the way back to U.S. 65. It's the least I can do."

"That would be great," he looks at Candi as she nods enthusiastically, "I'm starting to get hungry."

"Me too," Candi seconds, "And I don't know where we'd find a place to eat around here this late."

"Outside of the McDonald's drive-thru, probably nowhere," Tara smiles mischievously, "Let me pack up everything while you two get dressed, and then we'll head out."

The trio does just that before heading out into the night. Tara leads the way. Magnum and Candi follow her back towards Eudora. He cranks the air conditioning and "She Wants Money" by Ratt. His heart racing in time with the engine along with his stripping partner's. Her grand scheme unfolding more and more with the passing of each mile marker. Now he's genuinely contemplating that she may be onto something tonight.

"She doesn't want money," she grabs his crotch, "She wants us.:

"Then let's give her what she wants," he rubs her pussy through her yoga pants.

Tara leads them down a long gravel driveway to a renovated old farmhouse on the western edge of town. Camouflaged from the highway by towering bald cypresses and shortleaf pines. A vast farmland of rice crop stretched into infinity behind the house. The trio enters the appropriately rustic interior and head for the kitchen. Magnum and Candi are hungrier than they realized. Chowing down on snack food from the party as soon as their client sets it on the counter. She serves them each a cold beer as they thank her between bites of cheese, crackers, and pepperoni.

"I know it's not much," Tara downplays their appreciation.

"No, this is great," Candi assures her.

"Totally," he agrees, "After all the parties I've done, I'm at home eating with eating this kind of stuff."

"Me too," Candi concurs.

"You two are so sweet," Tara laughs, "What are you even doing in Arkansas?"

"I get that a lot," he shakes his head, "Honestly, I make as much money stripping here than I would anywhere else. In fact, more so than in some places."

"It's true," Candi adds, "We have our own monopoly on this region."

"Yeah, I kind of got that impression," Tara admits, "Of course, I'm glad you do. I mean… If all I could find around here was trash, I would've done something else entirely."

"Well, we put 100% into every performance," he explains, "The last thing we'd ever want to do is ruin someone's party."

"Oh, you two definitely made Hannah's night," she smiles, "And mine too."

"The night's not over yet," Candi flirts.

"Ooh…" Tara heads into the living room to put on music, "I can't wait."

Magnum and Candi can't wait either as they follow. With blood sugar levels replenished, they join her for a threesome bump and grind to "Pour Some Sugar on Me". Bodies writhing seductively. Enveloped by a dim amber glow. The insect symphony outside so loud that it's faintly audible amidst the pounding rock and roll. The strippers may have struck out on their birthday girl but are now officially in the foreplay stage with Tara. Candi not deviating from her convictions expressed earlier. Magnum totally on board. Throwing caution into the night. Letting himself go within the company of two wild and crazy girls instead of stressing about business as he does so often these days. If anything, he's earned a night of pure decadence and then some.

"I'm so sorry about tonight," Tara reiterates, "About everyone else."

"Just stop already," he shakes his head, "You've made the experience more than worth our while."

"I still feel like I owe you two something more," Tara laments coyly.

"Well…" Candi muses seductively, "Why don't you show us your bedroom?"

Tara wastes no time practically dragging her strippers down the hallway. The master bedroom illuminated by a full moon. Its rays invading via the large bay window. Onto the king-size bed centered in the room. The strippers show her their gratitude for all she's done for them tonight. Pushing her onto the bed before crawling on it themselves. Removing her top and sucking her tits together. She grabs their heads. Holding them against her breasts. Throwing her head back and moaning while the agents of pleasure lick their tongues over her nipples.

"Ooh… Yes!" Tara exclaims with delight, "I've been wanting this all night!"

"So have we," Candi looks into her eyes, "We were talking about it on the drive here."

"Okay, ladies," he orders his playmates, "Time to strip."

"Really?" Tara removes her skirts and thong, "What all were you talking about doing with me?"

"Candi was rubbing her pussy while looking at your photos on Facebook," he informs her while undressing, "Weren't you?"

"That's right," Candi shamelessly confesses after removing her t-shirt and bikini top, "You make my pussy so fucking wet."

"Well, you've both been making my pussy wet ever since I saw your photos online," Tara lies back and masturbates, "I've been rubbing my pussy to them this whole time."

"We talked about Hannah as well," he strokes his rock-hard cock while watching Tara play with herself, "But that was probably us being too ambitious."

"Oh, she's going crazy right now about having to work in the morning," Tara watches Magnum and aches to feel him deep inside her, "She'd love to be part of this."

"I noticed you two seem very… familiar with each other," Candi removes her yoga pants and g-string, "I'm sorry. That's none of my business."

"No, it's fine. I'm sure it was obvious to you two from your experiences," Tara laughs, "Hannah and I have been friends for a long time. And playing together has always been a part of our friendship. It's just… I don't know… Fun and comforting."

"I totally get that," Candi looks affectionally at Magnum, "Having a close friend you can experience all sorts of pleasure with."

He slaps her ass. Directing her towards the bed. Upon which they return butt-ass naked. Spreading Tara's legs open even wider and eating her pussy together. Circling their tongues on her clit. Sucking her swollen lips. Licking up her girl juices as she arches her back. Gripping the comforter with both hands. Crying out on ecstasy. Her pussy getting wetter and wetter. Warm sweetness gushing into their wanting mouths. "Rock 'n' Roll" by The Plasmatics thundering from the living room down the hallway and all around the naughty trio. Rocking and rolling one another's world on this hot and sticky night.

"Don't stop," Tara whispers in anguish, "Don't stop licking my pussy."

She once again grabs their heads. Pushing their faces together and tighter against her hot, throbbing pussy. Magnum and Candi take turns licking deep inside her. Consuming wave after wave of juices flowing from within her velvety sugar walls.

"Your pussy tastes yummy," Candi giggles.

"Thank you," Tara strokes her face, "I can't wait to taste yours."

Oh, I'm not done with yours yet," Candi offers a compromise and lies on her back with Tara getting on top in a sixty-nine.

"Mmm…" Tara half giggles and half moans while teasing Candi's clit. Tracing it with the tip of her tongue. Licking her pussy back and forth. Tongue fucking her as Candi continues exploring her pussy. Tara's girl juices glistening on Candi's face in the moonlight. Making each other wetter and wetter. Magnum spreads Tara's firm round ass wide open and reveals her sexy butthole. Kissing and caressing her soft cheeks. Licking the length of her crack. Touching her tight booty hole with the tip of his tongue. Pushing it inside her. She's sweet like candy. Like Candi. Tara moans louder now. One stripper eating her ass while another consumes her pussy. Candi getting even more excited from her up-close view of him licking deep inside Tara's asshole.

"Save some of that action for my booty, Magnum," Candi sasses.

"He's amazing at that," Tara sighs.

The girls swap places while Magnum rushes to his stripping bag near the front door. Retrieving the strawberry Astroglide he keeps handy for these situations. His playmates continue eating each other's pussy as he spreads Candi's cheeks wide open. Licking her yummy butthole. Pushing his tongue inside as he warms lubricant between his fingers. Inserting his middle finger inside Candi's ass. Sliding deeper. Moving it in and out. She trembles from the combined sensation of having her pussy eaten and asshole fingered at once. Her booty loosening up to take his raging cock. "Animal (Fuck Like a Beast)" by W.A.S.P. perfectly narrating the moment.

Tara stops licking Candi to take Magnum's cock deep in her throat. Swirling her tongue around his head and shaft. Making his juices flow like crazy. So out of this world. He can't wait a second longer. Removing his manhood from Tara's mouth and pushing it gently against Candi's butthole. Slowly working it deep inside her tight ass. Inch by inch. Until he's balls deep. Thrusting back and forth. Once again experiencing the magical ecstasy of buttfucking his partner in crime. Candi screaming and moaning. Unable to get enough of Magnum fucking her ass or Tara eating her drenched pussy. Juices finally squirting all over Tara's face and into her mouth.

"Oh God!" Candi shakes, "I want you to fuck my pussy!"

"Fuck yeah!" he pulls out of her ass, "I'm going to fill you up."

She rolls onto her back. Magnum and Tara ensure Candi's pussy is fully prepped for fucking by licking her together. So ridiculously wet as they drink up her sweet girl juices. He positions himself between her legs, puts her feet on his shoulders, and slides his cock deep inside her hot throbbing love tunnel. Slowly at first while Tara gets behind him, spreads his cheeks, and licks his butthole. A beautiful girl eating his ass as he fucks his beautiful partner in crime. He and Candi are truly agents of pleasure. Not only for Tara but themselves as well. Maybe they should get paid for this. And, to a certain degree, this is exactly what their client paid for. He further ponders Candi's suggestion while they stop momentarily. She gets on her hands and knees. He fucks her doggy style. Deep and hard. Tara squeezes Candi's bubble butt before spreading it open and eating her ass. She cries in ecstasy as he fucks her harder and harder while their client tongues her butthole deeper and deeper. It's all too much for Candi.

"Oh God! I'm cumming!" Candi screams in the night.

"Me too!" he shouts with vicious authority.

"Let it go, you two!" Tara encourages them, "Fucking cum on my face!"

Candi's pussy explodes all over Magnum's cock and Tara's face. Electricity pulsates through her body in a seemingly endless climax. He can't hold back any longer either. His massive aching cock erupts inside his partner in crime. Filling her with waves of hot sticky cum. His body tingling and shaking uncontrollably. Ejaculating so much love potion that it overflows into Tara's eager mouth. Experiencing her own major orgasm from the sensation of playing with two unbelievably naughty strippers and tasting their combined sweetness. Savoring and swallowing every drop. Candi can't help but feel somewhat vindicated right now. Knowing she's made her point to him and that he's contemplating it. Even if she's not entirely sure where she was going with that argument herself.

Candi and Tara cuddle while giggling uncontrollably. Magnum needs a few moments to recuperate and heads for the kitchen. Consuming a few more snacks and another beer. Enjoying the solitude for a few moments while "Hysteria" plays. Taking in everything this hot and humid summer night deep in the Arkansas Delta has given him tonight. Enjoying his conquest in progress. Still thinking about Candi's ideas. Is this the evolution of his business? The evolution of them? Is there a them now? Has there always been a them? He's never considered that before. At least not in a serious way. Maybe it's just the endorphins. Whatever. He struts back down the hallway. Carrying his manhood with both hands as he lets go and embraces the moment for what it is. Even after all that's happened so far, he can't believe his eyes. Tara is lying on her stomach. Candi's face buried in her sexy ass. Tongue deep in her tight butthole.

"Oh my God," Tara moans softly, "You're so fucking incredible at that."

"Thank you," Candi smiles naughtily at Magnum, "I learned from the best."

"Well…" Tara glances towards him and his once-again hard cock, "The best needs to come up here and see me.

"Yes, get him ready," Candi licks her ass again before looking at him, "I'm getting her ready for you."

"I can't wait," he sits before the client.

She takes him deep inside her throat. Her tongue dancing and twirling along every inch of his shaft. Around his head and frenulum. Licking up his rapidly flowing precum. Candi lubricates her middle finger and penetrates Tara's tight butthole. Smacking her cheeks. Making them bounce. Tara moans and giggles at this. Candi motions him to her. She licks and sucks him while now fingering Tara's ass with two fingers. Magnum's juices filling his stripping partner's mouth. She removes her fingers from their client and her mouth from him. He positions himself behind Tara. Slowly pressing his cock against her waiting asshole. Pushing his head inside. Then his shaft.

Slowly. Gently. Until he's balls deep inside her butt. Both moaning and tingling with delight as he pumps her man-hungry rump.

"Oh yeah. Fuck my booty," she sighs between heavy breaths, "Fuck my asshole with your big hard cock."

"Oh fuck, Tara," he sighs, "Your ass is out of this world."

"That's right," Candi coos, "Fuck her booty for me."

"Fuck That Booty" by Wendy O. Williams appropriately crushes through the night. Their bodies trembling in near unison as they explore anal pleasure together. It's not every night he gets to buttfuck a client. Candi gets behind him. Licking his butthole just as Tara did earlier. Getting his ass eaten by one girl as he fucks another in her ass. It's beyond his wildest dreams. He keeps fucking Tara's tight asshole as Candi continues licking his. But now he wants to feel his cock squeezed between Tara's sugar walls. He pulls out of her ass and slides deep insider her tight wet pussy. They fuck hard from the start. Thrusting violently against each other with every stroke. Candi watches him pound their client's love tunnel with excitement and a degree of envy.

"Oh my God," she encourages him, "That's so fucking hot."

"Your cock is amazing in my ass and my pussy," Tara moans aggressively.

"Oh, I know exactly what you mean," Candi sticks her tongue out at him and laughs.

"Yeah… Candi was talking about how she wanted to fuck you in the ass," he reveals while thrusting even harder, "I told her she needs to get a strap-on."

"If she gets one," Tara sighs heavily, "She can come back and fuck me in the ass anytime."

"Maybe we'll do that," Candi sits before her and spreads her legs wide open.

"We should," Tara dives tongue first into her wet pussy, "The three of us… and Hannah."

"I'm down," he fucks her with even more reckless abandon.

Magnum repeatedly slams Tara face-first into Candi's pussy with every thrust. Their client squeezing him tighter and tighter. Licking his partner in crime deeper and deeper. A triple climax of epic proportions. Building and building. Moaning and shaking themselves into sexual oblivion. Until none of them can hold back any longer. Candi unleashing a tidal wave of girl juices on Tara's face while pussy ejaculates all over him. His cock erupts like an erotic volcano deep inside her throbbing love tunnel. The trio screaming in the night as they share an earth-shattering triple climax the entire Arkansas Delta is likely hearing right now. Finally collapsing into a trembling heap. Gasping for air. Comforting one another for what feels like an eternity.

"So, did I make it up to you two?" Tara breaks the silence with a charming sincerity that's adorably innocent, considering the debauchery that just occurred.

"You'd already made our night with the birthday party," Candi assures her.

"But…" he interjects, "This made it a night we'll never forget."

After a moment, Magnum and Candi get dressed. Saying their goodnights to Tara with passionate kisses before disappearing into the night as she wishes them a safe trip home. Just like with any party, regardless of how wild things may get during or after. Some things never change. Candi is quiet as he crawls back down the long driveway to the road. He knows she's worn out and won't be any company on the drive. Some things never change.

She's fast asleep by the time they return to U.S. 65 in Eudora. He's lucky enough to locate a classic rock station just as "Screaming in the Night" by Krokus comes over the airwaves. The mosquitoes have mostly turned in for the night. He rolls down his window. Taking in the fresh night air while cruising back to Little Rock after midnight. His thoughts keeping him company because, indeed, some things never change. But plenty of other things are changing. The very being of his agency. His relationship with audiences. His relationship with

Candi. That scary r-word. Wondering if she's serious about what she said earlier. Does she want to settle down with him? And if so, what exactly would that entail? Kids by day and threesomes by night? Fuck if he knows.

January

A blonde woman sits naked on the edge of a hot tub. Her naked brunette companion kneeling between her legs. Licking her pussy in deliberate strokes. Back to front. Sucking her clit and lips while she grabs the edge for stability. Shaking uncontrollably as she's brought to orgasm. The brunette stands. The blonde drops to her knees underneath the water. Enthusiastically returning the favor to her sapphic playmate. Devouring her sweetness. Gazing into her eyes. The water's heat and turbulence matched by the brunette's approaching climax. Grabbing the blonde's head. Squirting girl juices into her wanting mouth. Coating her smiling face. They kiss. Giggling uncontrollably from their naughty playtime. Followed by girl talk.

Magnum has no idea what they're saying. The video on mute this entire time in favor of music. "On and On" by Raven playing at the conclusion of another pornographic masterpiece. Both going on at once to get him in the mindset while he prepares for his performance tonight. Sure, he's been in this moment countless times over the years but still makes the most of it. Perhaps more so now than ever. Knowing his stripping career is in its golden years as he once again dons his police uniform. There's no definite end in sight. Yet he's aware it's coming one of these days. Not because he's slipping as an entertainer. He's currently at the top of his game. If anything, it's prospective clients and audiences who aren't getting it done anymore.

He thinks about making the most of tonight while cruising east on I-630 through Little Rock. Towards downtown. Avoiding reckless drivers and the concrete barriers of an auxiliary freeway seemingly forever under construction. He receives a text from Candi. Her birthday party performance tonight was a quick one. Which they knew it would be. He hopes his own birthday gig tonight is more elaborate. She voiced the opinion that it would be after he told her about the client and girls. He was instantly struck with high hopes for them too during a winter of largely mundane audiences. Nothing bad, but nothing to write home about either.

Even worse are the calls that went nowhere and for no good reason. Like the one courtesy of a woman who bitched at him because she wanted a male stripper who is at least 6'7" tall. Smacking of self-sabotage for whatever reason in her deranged mind. Tonight's gig is his second this year. The first, also a birthday party, was a mediocre affair. Somewhat his fault for doing business with a woman who called to book while driving. That's just rude. He knows better than to take on such a client but still feels a little too eager to please at times. Despite knowing better than anyone that he'll inevitably end up wishing he'd said no. The type of booking Candi has long warned him against taking.

Tonight's client, a vibrant and dynamic woman named Vicki, wasn't driving when she called Magnum in late December. She's been sugar and spice and everything nice in each conversation they've had. Expectations are great for this group visiting from Tennessee. He finds her attractive too. In fact, all four women to be in attendance tonight impressed him on Facebook with their respective fun and glamorous dispositions. Candi was also impressed. Wishing him luck over the phone with a figurative wink and a nudge. Part of him wishes she were coming along, but she'd already been booked for her show out of town. She's always made things more exciting, and he's always known that. More and more, however, he can't help but think about it. Especially now as he makes a concentrated effort to savor every second of every party as if it's his last.

The drive improves upon exiting I-630 and driving north through downtown. "Running for Cover" by Girlschool fills the space around his thoughts. He'd normally park in a deck three blocks from this grouping of hotels on River Market Ave. Tonight, however, he's lucky enough to score a space on the street. A half-block away from his destination. The sidewalk lined with bare trees. Streetlamps just bright enough to let him see what he's doing. Wrought-iron fencing encloses a landscaped walking trail belonging to the adjacent bank building. A man sits on a bench about fifty feet away, looking surly. Magnum grabs his gear and crosses the street to avoid him.

It's a frigid January night but not unbearable. His three-quarter length leopard print fur coat keeping him warm and concealing his party cop identity. Strutting towards the hotel and his awaiting party girls with high hopes. A brick and glass structure towers above him upon turning the corner. Somewhere within it awaits epic debauchery incarnate in the making. Directly across the street stands another hotel of equal imposition. Something about the idea of so many people being within shouting distance of his performance fires him up even more. If only they knew…

Magnum enters through sliding glass doors as if he owns the fucking place. Not that there's much to own. It looks like any other chain hotel lobby. Indistinguishable in its faux pretentiousness. The front desk clerk greets him with nary a hint of suspicion. She either doesn't know or doesn't care why he's here. Nor should she. He's truly in his element now. Within his own world of pure decadence. Growing increasingly hedonistic with each step towards the elevators. The shiny cab interior barely containing his energy as he rides to the sixth floor. The hallway drenched in more overwrought garishness. He passes an empty luggage cart and commandeers a table several rooms down from the party suite.

"Hey there, foxy buns," he texts Vicki, "This is Magnum. I'm in the hallway."

Something about addressing his client with a complimentary euphemism for her butt gets him raging even harder. It's aggressive in a playful manner. Something so simple yet so beautifully deep and complex in his world. And she's not at all put off by this verbal show of affection. All smiles while eagerly striding in his direction. Shaking those foxy buns every step of the way. Even sexier than advertised in her photos. He decides right there on the spot to seduce her and the others tonight. All of them. To go for broke and turn this birthday party into a sex orgy for the ages. If for no other than to see if he can do it. No, it wouldn't be the first time he's fucked a girl during his show. But he's never fucked all of them.

"Jamie can be shy, but we've got her pretty buzzed right now," she can hardly contain her excitement to his delight, "She's into bondage, so I can't wait to see how she reacts when you place her in handcuffs."

"Me either," he laughs while fighting to maintain his cool over this information that he can use as a way in, so to speak.

She returns to the suite as he touches up his cologne and pops a Tic-Tac.

"Police! Open up!" he pounds on the door with just enough volume to shock his party girls inside without alarming the neighboring guests.

Magnum is greeted by a nervous yet excited woman opening the door for him. There are four women total, including Vicki and Jamie along with Abby and Breanna. Like everything else here, the suite is nothing special. But it's spacious. Warm and cozy. Dimly lit. Stocked with alcohol. Perfect for stripping. Even better for a sex orgy.

"Alright, which one of you naughty girls is Jamie?" he asks despite knowing which one she is.

She gives herself away as they always do. Pointing in a random direction while her friends point her out in unison. After frisking her to discover "a little crack" between her butt cheeks, he slaps the cuffs on her. Placing her under arrest for violation of penal code 6969 like so many bachelorettes and birthday girls before her. The suite's living room window faces the hotel across the street. Specifically, the windows at the end of its hallways. Vicki notices him making this observation.

"Oh, should I close the curtains?" she asks.

"Leave them open," he responds with authority, "I'm feeling adventurous tonight."

"Us too!" Jamie shrieks in intoxicated delight, "Nothing is off-limits in here!"

"That's right," Vicki sasses, "We've been waiting on this moment for weeks."

"Oh my God," Jamie smells his neck, "You smell incredible."

"Thank you," he laughs.

Abby and Breanna giggle in agreement as "Bad Boys" invades the suite before shifting into "Salt Shaker". Proving that some things never change. Magnum straddles Jamie. Tearing off his shirt. Grinding on her lap. She half dances and half fidgets in her chair. He steps back out of his tear-away pants while she holds onto the waistband. Turning around and kicking his legs back. Landing crotch to crotch on his birthday girl. The heat coming from between her legs confirming to him just how excited she is. The other girls cheering them on. Encouraging their friend's naughty habits.

"That's right!" Vicki excitedly informs Jamie, "He's got you handcuffed, you sexy bitch!"

"Ooh..." Abby taunts her, "Get it girl!"

"Hells yeah!" Breanna chimes in, "Take it all in, you dirty girl!"

"All the way down your throat," he wraps his right leg around Jamie's shoulders, shielding her face from view of her friends, and thrusts his hips rapidly in her face. The other girls continue losing their minds. It's all in good fun. Yet he's entertaining the idea of Jamie licking and sucking his cock. Making him hard. She takes notice and rubs her face on his g-string before pulling back in embarrassment. He looks down into her eyes with a smile that is devilishly approving. She giggles nervously before displaying a hint of disappointment when he removes his handcuffs from her wrists.

"Oh, look!" Vicki points at the window, "We have company!"

Magnum looks to his left and sees three older women watching from the adjacent hotel. Visually shocked yet unable to look away from this racy spectacle. What else can he do but wave at them? Amused, they wave back.

"I'll give them a wave," Vicki pulls down her black cocktail dress and shakes her titties at them, "Check out these girls!"

The women respond by pressing their chests against the glass. Magnum decides to up the ante. Turning away from the window, pulling down his g-string in the rear, and shaking his naked booty at them. Vicki puts her arms around his neck, and they turn to the side. He decides to get this orgy underway. Going for broke by leaning forward into her breasts. She's immediately receptive to his oral affections upon her nipples. Shooting come hither glances towards the audience across the street. Drake's "Hold On, We're Going Home" adding an extra layer of seductive sheen to the preceding.

"Oh yeah!" Jamie laughs, "You know, Vicki's been joking all week about getting you to suck her tits."

"Is that so?" he looks up at Vicki.

"Well…" she giggles with embarrassment, "I thought I'd give it a try."

"It doesn't look like you had to try very hard," Abby playfully snarks.

"I know," Vicki drops to her knees and places his cock between her tits, "Ooh… Yeah. Let them see you fuck my titties," she glances back to the pleasantly shocked women across the street.

"Fuck 'em good," Breanna chimes in, "She paid a lot of money for those fun bags."

"And it was money well spent," he thrusts his raging manhood rapidly between her girls, "I'm glad I'm not the only one who showed up here tonight with ultra-naughty intentions."

"You mean intentions like this?" Vicki takes his throbbing cock deep in her throat.

"We have ultra-naughty intentions too," Jamie massages his ass, "All four of us are single and ready to mingle."

"That's right," Breanna adds, "We were hoping we'd be up to your standard."

"Yeah…" he sarcastically shrugs his shoulders, "You'll do, I guess."

"Oh gee, thanks," Abby laughingly scoffs while Jamie smacks his butt, "You hear that, Vicki? He says we'll do. He guesses."

"Well…" Vicki stops briefly and looks at Abby, "The juices flowing from his cock say he's more into us than he wants to admit."

"I'm sure he fucks hot girls all the time," Jamie laments, "We're just another party to him."

"Not even close," he assures her.

"So," Jamie laughs, "You fuck a bunch of ugly girls all the time?"

"You're just asking to be tied up and punished," he informs her.

"Ooh…" she licks his neck and whispers in his ear, "I wish you would."

"Jamie loved being in your handcuffs," Vicki stands and kisses him, "You know. If you put them back on, you could probably do anything you want to her," pausing before adding, "And so could I."

"Then it really would be a party," he nods, "I'm down."

"Me too," Jamie shakes with excitement.

"Does this mean you're finally going to let me go down on you?" Vicki tosses her arms around Jamie's neck.

"You know what? Fuck it. It's my birthday," Jamie enthusiastically concedes, "You can eat my pussy, you dirty bitch."

"Oh, I'll gladly eat your pussy," Vicki kisses her as they giggle uncontrollably.

"Well, before we go all Caligula on each other…" Abby returns from the kitchenette with Breanna and five shots of Patrón Silver, "Let's do a shot first."

"Who do we toast to?" Jamie wonders.

"How about our audience across the street?" he suggests.

"Perfect," Vicki holds her shot up towards the women along with Magnum and the other party girls.

"Damn, that's good," Jamie exudes, "A nice change of pace from vodka."

"Oh my God, Magnum. I'm so sorry," Abby apologizes, "I haven't offered to fix you a drink yet."

"Don't worry about it," he assures her, "What do you have?"

"Oh, we've got it all," Brenna boasts, "Grey Goose, Malibu, Jack…"

"Jack and Coke?" he interjects.

"Absolutely," Abby returns to the kitchenette with Breanna.

Magnum returns Jamie to her hot seat. Placing her once again in handcuffs to her kinky satisfaction. He sets Vicki upon an ottoman situated opposite his birthday girl. "Low" by Flo-Rida issues the challenge to how low he and his party girls can go tonight. He goes back and forth between his birthday girl and client. Grinding and thrusting against their bodies. Trembling with hedonistic enthusiasm. The women across the way still watching. Now joined by a half dozen young women on the floor above. He trades waves with them before kicking his legs back. Landing crotch to crotch with Jamie. Face first between Vicki's legs. She spreads them open and reveals that she's going commando tonight. He immediately explores her pussy with his tongue. She's soaking wet. Juices so sweet. She grabs his head. Pulling him in closer.

"Oh, Vicki," Abby returns, carrying drinks along with Breanna, "You're always starting something."

"Thank you," he stands and takes his drink from Abby, "Maybe I'm the one starting something."

"That's true," she concedes, "You are paid to do this."

"But I don't think he's paid to lick pussy," Breanna chimes in.

"No," he laughs, "That's something for me."

"It's for me too," Vicki argues, "I could never put a price on your technique."

"You have no idea how much that means to me for you to say that," he is visibly flattered, "And I can say the same thing about your technique."

"Aww…" she coos.

"So…" Jamie wonders aloud, "Whose technique is better?"

"Take off your clothes and find out," he replies so quickly and authoritatively that even he's surprised by it.

"That's right, missy," Vicki concurs, "It's your birthday. You need to be in your

birthday suit."

"Okay!" Jamie begins undressing without hesitation.

Magnum retrieves the can of Reddi-wip from his stripping bag while Vicki helps Jamie strip. He returns to his birthday girl, now seated naked in her hot seat, and applies whipped cream to her nipples. She giggles as he and his client each take a breast. Kissing and licking them clean. Sucking and flicking their tongues over her. She grabs their heads. Shaking her titties against their faces. Making everyone laugh uncontrollably.

"So…" Abby inquires, "Whose technique is winning so far?"

"Um… It's a tie," Jamie answers, "I don't know. They're both amazing."

"Okay, Jamie," Vicki orders, "Your turn to lick some off him."

"You do it with me," she counters.

Magnum sprays Reddi-wip on his nipples. Jamie and Vicki each take one and lick it clean. The sensation of two soft, warm female tongues swirling on his nipples at once is positively electric. He doesn't have to glance over to know that their audience across the street is going crazy right now. But this is nothing compared to Vicki pulling down his g-string and applying a line of whipped cream to the length of his rock-hard cock. Still handcuffed, Jamie leans forward and licks him clean. Then places her mouth over his shaft. Her tongue dancing elegantly all over his manhood. He throws back his head in ecstasy and glances out the window. A thirtysomething couple has joined the older women. Every jaw is on the floor. But it doesn't look like anyone is calling the cops. Meanwhile, "Hot in Herre" persuades Vicki to lose her dress.

"Come on, you two," Vicki chides Abby and Breanna while helping Magnum out of his g-string, "Get out of those clothes."

"Ooh… Are you going to eat our pussies too?" Breanna laughs sassily.

"Yes, she is," he responds matter of factly.

"I see you're making decisions for me now," Vicki playfully smacks his arm, "But that's not a bad idea."

"Oh my God, Vicki," Jamie giggles, "You're just fascinated with the idea of eating pussy."

"I am. It's just hot, I think," Vicki shrugs with a combination of naughtiness and embarrassment, "It's no different than your fascination with being tied up."

"True," Jamie agrees, "What's your kinky fascination, Magnum?"

"I guess eating ass," he confesses as sheepishly about it as ever.

"Ooh, that sounds sexy," Vicki is instantly intrigued, "I mean… Of course, I'm aware of that. But I never thought about doing it myself. Until now."

"Maybe I'll have to show you sometime," he feels more confident about it now.

"How about you show me now," she bends over and spreads her cheeks open.

Magnum immediately drops to his knees and buries his face in Vicki's ass. She moans as he circles her delicate butthole with his tongue. Then she squeals with excited disbelief when he thrusts inside her tight backdoor.

"Oh wow!" she gushes, "Magnum's tongue is literally inside my asshole."

"Really?" Jamie is beside herself with burning curiosity, "What does it feel like?"

"Like nothing else," Vicki sighs, "It's so fucking amazing. He'll have to show you."

"That's right," he agrees.

"Oh, I'm totes down," Jamie enthuses, "But I think I need to be tied up for something like that."

"Hmm…" Vicki glances around, "How do we do that in here?"

"There's a luggage cart in the hallway," he suggests, "We could do something with that."

"Well, since these two are still dressed," Vicki playfully snarks at Abby and Breanna, "Maybe they can go fetch it."

"Fine," Abby sets down her drink and heads for the door.

"Make sure things don't get out of hand while we're gone," Breanna remarks sarcastically.

"Whatever," Vicki stands and laughs before turning to Magnum, "Your turn. Now I have to know what it's like to eat booty."

"I'll get the front," Jamie drops to her knees and resumes sucking his cock. Deep in her throat. Making his juices flow. Making him tremble. Vicki makes him tremble too. On her knees behind him. Holding his cheeks wide open. Her eager tongue licking the length of his crack. Tracing around his butthole. Pushing inside. Twirling within him. In and out. Everyone across the street on their phones. Attempting in vain to capture this spectacle on video. But the dim amber glow within this den of iniquity provides only enough illumination for the voyeurs to watch with their eyes. Protecting him and his party girls from mass exposure via the internet.

"Oh my God, this is so fucking hot," Vicki gushes, "Jamie, I may need to eat your ass too."

"Tie me up tonight and you can do anything you want to me," she responds while stroking Magnum's shaft and licking his balls, "Both of you."

The trio is interrupted by Abby and Breanna making a huge racket of giggling and banging into things as they return with the cart.

"Jesus Christ!" Vicki shakes her head, "Are you two trying to get us kicked out of here?"

"Oh, eat my ass," Abby scoffs.

"Don't tempt her," Jamie warns, "She has a taste for it now."

"That's right," Vicki stares seductively at Abby and Breanna while swirling her tongue all over Magnum's butthole.

"Oh my God," Brenna's jaw drops along with Abby's, "That's kind of hot."

"What can we use to tie up Jamie?" Vicki glances around.

"Let me see," Abby wonders into one of the bedrooms and then its bathroom, "There's some bath towels in here!"

"Will that work?" Brenna wonders aloud.

"Maybe if you tear one into strips," he suggests, "If you want to destroy hotel property."

"Meh, it's just one towel," Vicki shrugs, "I doubt they'll notice it's missing."

"Okay," Abby returns with a white bath towel, "How do we do this?"

"I've got it," he goes to his bag and retrieves a switchblade.

"Um…" Jamie giggles, "I'm not sure I'm ready for knife-play."

"Oh, come on," Breanna snarks while she and Abby roll the cart into the living room, "Where's your sense of adventure?"

"I have this just because," he cuts into the hem on either short side of the towel before tearing it into strips, "I mean... You never know."

"Good point," Vicki nods in amusement, "Not everyone is as cool as we are."

"Fucking A they're not," Jamie stands on the luggage cart, "I'd cut a rude bitch in a heartbeat."

"Maybe you should be my security detail at parties," Magnum laughs while he and Vicki tie their birthday girl's wrists and ankles to the brass frame.

"Don't encourage her," Vicki shakes her head, "She'll do it."

"It's true," Jamie nods, "I will."

"Why are you two still dressed?" Vicki glares at Abby and Breanna.

"Oh, I'm sorry," Abby reacts sarcastically, "Did you want us to go out into the hallway naked?"

"I think you should've," he offers suggestively.

"I'm game," Breanna starts getting undressed.

"Maybe later," Vicki interjects, "Priorities, people."

"You know what, Jamie?" he returns to his bag and produces his bullwhip to excited gasps and shrieks, "You've been an extremely naughty girl tonight."

"Oh, I've been unbelievably naughty," she sighs insatiably between heavy breaths.

"Well, naughty girls have to be spanked," he stands behind her and swats her bare ass with his coiled whip.

"Come on," she taunts him, "You can spank my ass harder than that."

"How hard can you take it?" he makes her round cheeks jiggle with each smack.

"Harder! Make it red!" she cries.

"It's your birthday, sweet cheeks," he goes even harder. The other girls giggle and cheer nonstop. Jamie's sweet cheeks jiggling even more as they grow red from hit after hit. Chills cover her body while she laughs and moans in ecstasy.

"Oh, fuck yes!" she screams, "Spank my ass like you're fucking it!"

"Or he could just fuck your ass," Vicki faces Jamie and kisses her.

"Hey," Jamie laughs, "The night is still young."

"Hells yeah it is," Abby is now naked and raising her drink.

"Get that birthday booty," Breanna cheers while fully nude.

Magnum continues whipping Jamie's butt. Vicki begins sucking her tits. Kissing and licking her nipples. Applying more Reddi-wip to her breasts. Enthusiastically consuming every drop in decadently sapphic fashion. Abby and Breanna serve the trio and themselves more tequila shots. The audience across the street hanging on their every move. For everyone's sake, including his, it's time to up the ante. Now nice and red, Jamie's rear is inviting as he loses the whip and drops to his knees. Spreading her cheeks wide open, he dives tongue first into her tight asshole.

"Fuck yes! Eat my ass!" Jamie screams with enthusiasm, "You were right, Vicki. This feels like nothing else!"

"Neither will this," Vicki drops to her knees and eats her friend's pussy, "Mmm… You're even sweeter than I've fantasized all these years."

"You've been fantasizing about me?" Jamie asks sassily, "Ooh, you dirty bitch."

"Oh yeah," Vicki licks deep between her lips, "I'm your dirty bitch. And you like it."

"I do," Jamie admits sheepishly, 'And I love Magnum's tongue in my asshole."

"He's amazing," Vicki circles her tongue around the birthday girl's clit.

Magnum feels pandemonium breaking out across the street. And he hears it coming from Abby and Breanna. Expressing shock and awe as they drink some more. Jamie's butthole tastes so sweet. Thrusting his tongue further and further into its soft, warm confines. He can't lick her ass deep enough. Nor can he get enough of eating delicious girl booty before an enthusiastic audience. This is what it means to feel alive. Perhaps the business of pleasing is taking on a new meaning for him. Or are the two diverging? Maybe it's both in some abstract fashion he's yet to decipher. He wishes Candi were here to partake in these festivities. And he instantly takes notice of that wish.

Jamie moans and screams from the dual tongue lashing she's receiving. Vicki making the most of her opportunity to play with her friend. Licking and sucking her clit. Fingering her pussy and massaging her g-spot. Making Jamie wetter and wetter. Tidal waves of sweetness rushing into Vicki's girl hungry mouth. Devouring every drop as if truly the nectar of the gods. Teasing Jamie's lips before sliding her tongue deep inside her friend's sugar walls. Thrusting in and out. Her face becoming coated with warm girl juices.

"What are you two waiting for?" Vicki admonishes Abby and Breanna, "Get over here and suck her tits. That won't kill you."

Abby and Breanna look at each other and shrug their shoulders. Having apparently consumed enough alcohol to render their collective sexuality sufficiently fluid. Taking position on either side of Jamie. They opt for the whipped cream treatment. Repeatedly licking and sucking it from her nipples while giggling incessantly. "Freek-a-Leek" serving as an apropos soundtrack in the moment. Does she want it in her pussy? Does she want it in her ass? She has a tongue in either right now.

"You know," Abby muses, "Part of me always knew we'd all wind up having a lesbian orgy someday."

"It's not a lesbian orgy," Jamie counters, "There's a guy here."

"Yeah," Breanna laughs, "So, that makes it okay."

Magnum can feel the unbridled excitement of the crowd across the street. Flowing from their windows, across the street in the cold January night air, and into their libertine haven. Filling all five with electric impulses. Making them go all out in unison. Jamie is in bad girl heaven. All tied up. Two girls sucking her titties. Another girl lapping up her pussy. A male stripper eating her ass. Her shaking grows increasingly uncontrollable as she moves closer to climaxing. Struggling against her restraints. Needing to hold onto something. Anything. But she must instead bear the full force of sexual overstimulation.

"Oh, baby. You're squirting," Vicki coos as the birthday girl ejaculates into her friend's mouth.

Jamie screams out in carnal anguish. Overcome with orgasmic bliss. Her pussy so drenched that her sweet juices have made their way to Magnum's tongue deep inside her tight asshole. He and Vicki hold hands as they orgasm themselves while orally sharing their birthday girl. Abby and Breanna cheering on the three of them. The voyeurs across beside themselves with ever-growing intrigue. Every muscle fiber in their bodies contracting tighter and tighter. The stripper and the client sharing a white-knuckle grip upon the birthday girl's skin. Until the trio's shared tension releases all at once into a relaxing high like no drug could ever possibly deliver.

"I want you to fuck me, Magnum," Jamie pleads with all the anguish of carnal desire, "I want you to fuck me deep and hard."

"Me too," Vicki coos, "I think we all want that."

"Sure," Abby shrugs, "Why not?"

"Don't sound so enthusiastic," he chides her.

"I didn't mean it like that," she laughs, "What about you, Breanna?"

"I'm in," Breanna responds, "Honestly, it feels like forever since I've had a cock inside me."

"I don't know," Jamie ponders, "Is Magnum up to the challenge of four girls at once?"

"Bend over," he unties her from the luggage cart, "And I'll show you."

"Do it, you sexy bitch," Vicki smacks Jamie's butt as she steps off the cart and he rolls it against a wall.

"Abby, you're first," Vicki points to the floor, "Get on all fours."

"God, someone's feeling high and mighty," Abby laughs while assuming the position.

"Don't sass me, missy," Vicki smacks her ass, "You're just asking for some licks."

"Are you gonna eat my pussy too," Abby laughs.

"Yep," Vicki drops to her hands and knees behind Abby and licks her pussy.

"Whoa!" Abby trembles in shock, "That's… Um… Okay… That's not bad, actually."

"Not bad," Vicki spanks her again, "Whatever."

"Fine, you're really good at that," Abby giggles, "I think you've had some practice before tonight."

"Not really," Vicki confesses while licking and sucking Abby's clit, "Mostly just this one time on a boat."

"Well, I have to admit," Abby laughs with a twinge of embarrassment, "You're a really good pussy eater, Vicki."

"Thank you," Vicki looks at him, "She's ready for your cock."

"Oh yeah," Abby wiggles her butt, "Give it to me, Magnum."

"It's my pleasure," he drops to his knees behind Abby. She reaches back and helps guide his cock inside her pussy. Arching her back as he slides inside her. He grabs her ass and thrusts back and forth. Fucking her fast and furiously. Working to bring her to an orgasm before moving onto the next girl. Pacing himself while still ensuring that each one gets something from the experience along with the experience itself. He looks towards his audience across the street, watching in disbelief before watching Vicki repeat the process with Breanna. Eating her pussy while both are on all fours beside him and his current lover. "I Don't Mind" by Usher giving the scene a romantic feel that feels surprisingly right to all of them.

"You know what? I'm not going to be shy about it," Breanna reaches back and pushes Vicki's face deeper between her legs, "Eat my pussy, you dirty bitch."

"That's the spirit," he reaches over and smacks her ass.

"Hells yeah," Breanna trembles from the sensation of Vicki's tongue thrusting in and out of her, "It was bound to happen at some point."

"Hey, what are friends for?" Jamie laughs.

"That's right," Vicki licks Breanna back and forth, "You know… We can stop being friends. But we can never undo me eating your pussy."

"I don't want to," Breanna moans.

"Oh fuck!" Abby claws at the carpet while orgasming.

"Save some of that for me," Breanna reaches over and strokes her hair.

"It's a lot to take in," Abby laughs.

"Flattery will get you everywhere with me," he slaps her ass before moving behind Breanna as Vicki heads for Jamie.

"Oh wow!" Breanna exhales while taking in every inch of his rock-hard manhood, "You weren't kidding."

"Nope," Abby lounges on the carpet next to them with another drink.

"You should go next, Vicki," Jamie guides her to the floor, on all fours.

"So, who's going to eat Vicki's pussy?" he challenges his party girls.

"I am," Jamie drops behind Vicki and enthusiastically devours her friend, "Mmm…"

"Ooh… Jamie," Vicki laughingly sighs, "What's gotten into you?"

"Everything," Jamie excitedly licks up her friend's rapidly flowing sweetness, "This is so much fun! Why didn't we do this sooner?"

"Um… I've been trying to get you to do it for a few years now," Vicki playfully admonishes her, "But I love that we're doing it now."

"Me too," Jamie coos.

All this sapphic action and adorable girl talk have Magnum pumping the absolute fuck out of Breanna's pussy. His body tingling from head to toe. Her ass smacking against his pelvis relentlessly. She lays her face on the carpet. Gasping for breath as he goes deep and hard within her tight love tunnel. Her moaning gets louder as she nears orgasm.

"Whew! I needed that." she giggles with the pleasure of sweet release, "Your turn, Vicki."

"Get you some of that," Jamie moves to the side.

"Oh, I've been wanting Magnum's cock inside me since I first laid eyes on his photos," Vicki confesses.

"And I've been wanting to fuck you since I first laid eyes on your photos," he gets behind his client and rubs the head of his cock along her pussy and butthole.

"Aww… Were you stalking me on Facebook?" she laughs, "You should've asked me for nudes. I have lots on my phone."

"It's true," Jamie explains, "She texts us nude selfies all the time."

"Well, I've got the real thing right now," he slides his massive shaft deep within Vicki's throbbing sugar walls.

"Oh my God, you really do!" Vicki moans in decadent ecstasy, "Sit in front of me, Jamie."

Abby and Breanna lying alongside him. Drinking and giggling away. The audience one hotel over live texting the pornographic exploits unfolding before their eyes to God knows who. As much as Magnum is into Vicki, she's now become a proxy for Candi as he fucks his client from behind. Shoving her face-first into Jamie's pussy. He finds himself thinking about his longtime partner in crime. Imagining himself fucking her right now. Pushing her face between another woman's legs. Just as he's done multiple times in the past. She'd be having a blast with these girls right now. Especially Vicki and Jamie. Right alongside him. And not in an Abby and Breanna sort of way.

Wondering why he can't shake these notions. Yet embracing them with a strange enthusiasm.

"Oh fuck, Magnum!" Vicki snaps him back to reality with her trembling orgasm.

"I can't wait any longer," Jamie switches places with Vicki.

"It's all yours, lover," Vicki kisses her, "This is your birthday, after all."

"That's right," Jamie assumes the position before Magnum, "Have a seat, lover."

Magnum rubs the head of his throbbing cock all over Jamie's soaking wet pussy. Lubricating his manhood with her warm juices and Vicki's saliva before sliding it deep inside her tight pussy. Vicki spreads her legs. Jamie eats her newfound lover's pussy while getting fucked from behind. He grabs her ass with both hands and penetrates her love tunnel with reckless abandon. Deeper. Faster. Harder. Shoving his birthday girl face-first into Vicki's pussy with each vicious, primal thrust. His client making flirtatious expressions at him He's totally in his element. His mind back in the game. "Yeah" fills the space around them. Yeah? Fuck yeah.

"That's right. Take that big cock while you eat my pussy," Vicki encourages Jamie between moans, "I want Magnum to watch you lick me."

"It's totally hot," he moans while keeping the rhythmic pace with his birthday girl. Jamie moans as well. The overstimulation of being fucked while consuming her friend's pussy is too much for her. Too much for all of them. Her sweetness gushing incessantly all over his aching cock and body. So much for him to take in. Every muscle fiber contracting tighter and tighter. Now fucking the fourth of four girls right down the line. Yet another first for him at a point in his life when he can't imagine things getting any wilder or crazier. How long can he hold back from exploding in animalistic ecstasy?

"Oh my God, you taste so sweet," Jamie sighs while licking and sucking Vicki's swollen clit before pushing her tongue inside, "Mmm…"

"God yes, Jamie. Tongue fuck my pussy," Vicki grabs Jamie's head with both hands and grinds her throbbing pussy on her friend's face, "You look so sexy getting fucked by that hot stripper."

"Fuck me hard, Magnum," Jamie demands as he strokes viciously within her love tunnel. She squeezes him tighter and tighter. Wave and wave of girl juices gushing upon him. Now beginning to squirt all over his cock, balls, and pelvis. Running down his thighs. Making him tingle all over. One electrical shock after another consumes his body. Abby and Breanna squealing with excitement. The voyeurs hanging on their every thrust. They're all about to climax in one way or another. No one can hold back any longer. Especially not Jamie and Vicki as they cum together. Vicki squirting hot juices on Jamie's face. Jamie ejaculating all over his body.

"Ooh, cum on her ass!" Vicki requests.

Magnum pulls out and shoots wave and wave of white-hot cum all over Jamie's firm round cheeks and in her crack. Holding her hand on Jamie's back, Vicki makes her way to him on her knees. Taking him in her mouth. Licking him clean of Jamie's sweetness and his. Spreading her friend's cheeks wide open, she devours his remaining love potion off Jamie's asshole. Shoving her eager tongue deep inside to ensure she has consumed every drop. Jamie gets on her knees. She and Vicki kiss passionately before taking turns kissing Magnum. The trio crashes to the floor. Catching their breath while Abby and Breanna marvel at the naughty spectacle they just witnessed.

And then… Back to normal. Their audience next door disperses while Magnum and his party girls get dressed. Resuming the lighthearted conversing that began when he arrived. Not one beat skipped. No one is ashamed. There's simply nothing to say. Their shared experience speaks for itself. It is what it is. Experimentation for each in letting go within the company of kindred spirits. Another special memory from his long and extensive career as an exotic entertainer. Even their goodnights are as simple as they are with any other group of girls.

"Thank you so much," Jamie hugs him, "Be safe driving home."

"Thank you," he replies as he has on seemingly a million nights, "I will."

"Thank you so much," Vicki takes her turn hugging him goodbye, "You totally made our night."

"I'm glad," he grabs his gear and heads out the door, "Have a good night everyone."

"You too," Abby responds.

"Be safe," Breanna chimes in.

Magnum half expects the cops to be waiting outside the room when he departs. They aren't there. Not in the lobby while passing the desk clerk who bids him goodnight without a hint of suspicion. Nor are they waiting for him on the street. The technically public sex orgy between him and his party girls was ultimately a private affair between them and their audience. An intimate affair at that. They were all in it together. He has no regrets. Only the inkling that something was missing. Someone.

The night has grown colder. The streets emptier. Walking back to his car around the corner. His leopard fur coat keeping him warm. The dim amber glow of streetlamps above illuminating his path. Eliminating shadows from endless trees in an area known for crime. But he's an unstoppable force of nature right now. Stalking through the night like a wild animal. Ready for the thrill of his next chase. His next conquest. Whenever and wherever it may come. They seem to be getting fewer and farther between these days. Glad in hindsight that he went for broke with tonight's audience. For all he knows, this was his final shot at an encounter with strangers this explosive.

"Devil Rides Out" by Saxon tears from his speakers on the drive home. There may have been no love in what happened tonight, but it wasn't without nonsexual merit. He and his party girls enjoyed a special bond across a relationship that lasted only two hours. It was what it was. And it was out of this world. Part of him is now consumed with an overwhelming urge to call Candi. To drop by her place. An urge he's never felt before. But he resists. Are these sudden thoughts about her rooted in something honorable? Or is he being needy like the obnoxious loser protagonist of that shitty Lady Antebellum song? While he's never been one to use a girl, he plays it safe and drives home to sleep alone tonight.

March

AR 25 begins.

Candi veers right off U.S. 65 onto the final third of her trip to Heber Springs. Twenty-five miles to drive as fast as she wants. Save for passing through the speed trap communities of Guy and Quitman. A slightly crisp mid-March night with hints of spring in the air. The vegetation already green along the highway. Every winding curve ultimately guiding her northeast towards her destination on Greers Ferry Lake. A forty-fifth birthday party organized by the guest of honor's wife. Two other fortysomething couples will be in attendance. All the hallmarks of a quickie performance. But she's happy to make some money while enjoying one of those magical nighttime Arkansas country drives. This time as "Love Like Blood" by Killing Joke pounds from the speakers.

She's intrigued by her client. Having looked her up on Facebook to discover a striking beauty appearing younger than a woman in her mid-forties. Coming across as friendly and full of life. Full-blown sexy. The sort of woman Candi hopes she grows up to be someday. One who took on marriage and motherhood while retaining her youth and identity. Living proof that such balance can be maintained. Candi also can't help but find her attractive. Everything about her makes Candi's imagination run wild and her motor run.

"Hey there, I'm Sandra," she greets Candi in the driveway in a skimpy leopard print cocktail dress that leaves nothing to the imagination, "It's so nice to finally meet you."

"Same here," Candi shakes her hand, "Is everyone ready?"

"Pretty much," Sandra looks back towards the house, "Tell you what. Give me five minutes to get Jeff and everyone else in place. I'll turn off the outside light to signal when you can come inside."

"Sounds great," Candi agrees, "I need a few minutes to get ready anyway."

"Oh my God, I can't wait!" Sandra gushes excitedly while turning to walk back inside, "This is so exciting!"

Candi ogles Sandra's round ass as it returns inside along with her client. Back to the task at hand. Getting her music ready. Popping a breath mint. Touching up her perfume. Swapping out her loafers for red platforms. Taking off her black leather trench coat to reveal a sexy firefighter costume. So what if real firefighters never wear skirts? Much less, skirts that are booty length? "It's fucking hot," she thinks. Hot like Sandra. She zips up her bag and puts on her helmet. Waiting for the signal to strut inside and start more fires than she puts out.

There it is. Instant darkness across the front lawn. The cover of night so conducive to acts of naked naughtiness. Candi feeling so purely decadent. Striding confidently down the concrete walkway towards the front door. Something she's done countless times over the years, but the sensation never gets old. Each time still feels like the first. Because it is. Every audience is different. And some clients make her wetter than others with every step closer to erotic entertainment heaven. A heaven that erupts with astonished hysteria upon her entrance.

"Oh no, Sandy!" Jeff exclaims with intoxicated laughter, "What have you gotten me into now?"

"Happy birthday, sweetie!" Sandra kisses him, "Candi, meet Jeff. Jeff, this is Candi. She drove a long way to come see you tonight."

"Is that so?" he tries to mask his embarrassment.

"That's right," Candi informs him coyly while setting up her music.

She takes him by the hand. Seating him on a dining room chair in the center of the living room. Def Leppard's "Rock of Ages" fills the area. Illuminated by multicolored disco lights. Sandra takes photos from all angles. Everyone else piled on the sofa. Watching from the side while Candi goes to work on Jeff. Straddling him and placing her helmet upon his head. Dropping to her knees between his legs. Tossing her hair around in his lap. Feigning oral sex on him. Rising slowly. Rubbing her tits along his torso until they're face to face. Everyone cheering them on.

"Don't be shy, Jeff!" Sandra yells, "She's fucking hot!"

"Aww…" Candi can barely contain her excitement over that compliment.

"Of course she is," he argues, "I'm not being shy."

"If you don't have fun with her." Sandra declares with a hint of liquid courage, "I will," everyone laughs in shock and awe as she thinks twice and looks at Candi, "I apologize if I'm crossing the line."

"Not at all," Candi smiles devilishly, "I'll be coming for you soon enough."

She turns her attention back to Jeff. Reaching down and pulling off her sexy firefighter dress. Unleashing her girls upon this intimate new world and its inhabitants. Down to nothing but platforms and a red g-string. Shaking her tits in Jeff's face while Sandra captures the moment. Loving every minute of everyone's eyes on her. Especially Sandra's. Shaking her ass in his face to the same effect. Reaching down, grabbing his wrist, and leading him to spank her. He lightly slaps her butt repeatedly with the encouragement of everyone around him.

"Ooh… Look at that sexy ass!" Sandra enthuses as she reaches over and smacks it before rethinking again, "Oh my God, I'm so sorry."

"Stop apologizing already," Candi struggles to downplay her excitement, "Or else I'll have to spank you."

"In that case," Sandra moves in front of Candi and bends over, "Spank me, baby."

Candi feels her pussy growing wetter at the sight of Sandra's ass in a red g-string of her own. Wasting no time spanking both cheeks before squeezing them. Sandra giggles and stands. Candi kicks her legs back and falls forward. Landing on her hands to everyone's delight. Thrusting her pussy against Jeff's cock. Getting herself worked up about humping her birthday boy in front of his wife and friends. Imagining doing this to Sandra with everyone watching. Or alone. It doesn't matter. She just wants to fuck her client every way she can. And she can't believe she's thinking that to herself right now. But she can't help it. Nor does she want to. The song ends, and it's all Jeff can handle.

"Can I fix you a drink?" he offers.

"Oh my God, I'm so sorry," Sandra apologizes to Candi, "I should've offered you a drink before. I'm being a terrible hostess."

"Will you stop already?" Candi laughs, "You're the hostess with the mostess."

"You're so sweet," Sandra gushes bashfully, "Let me fix you something. Jeff, this is your night to have fun and nothing else. Or I'll have Candi here spank you."

"Way ahead of you," Candi slaps Jeff on the ass.

Both girls giggle as Sandra heads for the kitchen. Jeff sinks into his recliner and continues drinking. Watching Candi take her turn with the other husbands in attendance. Their wives cheering them on with playful antagonism. Candi quickly getting a buzz from the incredibly stout vodka cranberry Sandra made her. Embracing the moment and letting herself fall into pure decadence. Excited that she's exciting these sweet and kind men. Excited by Sandra's undeniable sexiness. Wanting to know her better. Wanting to get as close to her as she can in the short time they have together. This is already running longer than the usual in and out coed birthday party, but tonight won't last forever.

"Your turn," she looks seductively at Sandra, "I told you I'd be coming for you."

"Candi, you can come for me anytime," Sandra giggles while moving to the hot seat, "Hold on," she pulls off her dress and is left in nothing but heels and her red g-string, "Look, we're twins!"

"Oh Lord. There she goes again," Jeff laughs in a highly intoxicated stupor along with everyone else.

"I have something special for this naughty girl," Candi retrieves a can of Reddi-wip from her stripping bag as "Looks That Kill" by Mötley Crüe tears through the living room.

"Oh yeah," Sandra nods sassily, "I'll be your dessert. Lay it on me, sweet cheeks."

Candi giggles as she straddles Sandra. Shaking her titties in her client's face. Sitting on her lap. Pressing her girls against her client's. Grinding on her lap. Candi's pussy tingling from the sensation of Sandra's nipples rubbing against hers. From the heat of Sandra's pussy radiating onto hers. Gazing into each other's eyes. Excitedly. Nervously. Butterflies filling Candi's stomach. She can see the same thing happening with Sandra. The tension mounting. Until it's broken by uncontrollable giggling.

"What are you doing?" Sandra glances towards Jeff while he records this display of sapphic affection with his phone.

"Collecting incriminating evidence," he answers nonchalantly, "You know? For future considerations."

"Whatever," she laughs and turns back to Candi, "He likes to record me with other girls and watch it later," she pauses, "I'm into girls."

"Yeah, I kind of got that," Candi laughs facetiously.

"Of course you did," Sandra laughs with a tinge of embarrassment, "Don't mind me. I can be a little ditzy sometimes."

"Relax," Candi assures her, "You're so much fun."

"Aww… So are you," Sandra gushes before inquiring, "Forgive me for asking. Are you into girls? I mean, I really don't want you to feel obligated to…"

Candi interrupts her with a forceful kiss. Pushing her lips against Sandra's open mouth. Their tongues wasting no time twirling around each other. Bodies trembling. Hearts racing. Pussies getting wetter. After what feels like an eternity, Candi pulls back.

"There's your answer," she laughs naughtily.

"I guess so," Sandra giggles, "Wow!"

"Wow is right!" Jeff watches through his viewfinder, "I need another drink."

"Take mine. It's nearly full," Sandra nods towards the glass near his recliner, "You don't want to miss this."

"That's right," Candi seconds, "You ain't seen nothing yet."

Sandra spreads her legs and Candi drops to her knees between them. Applying Reddi-wip to Sandra's nipples. Leaning in and placing her mouth over her client's right breast. Sucking as she swirls her tongue. Looking into Sandra's eyes the entire time. Then licking and sucking her left breast. Sandra moaning softly while stroking Candi's hair. Lifting her up to share a whipped cream kiss. Candi stands and turns away from Sandra. Pulling down her g-string in the rear and shaking her naked booty.

"Oh yeah!" Sandra exclaims, "Take it all off!"

That's all the encouragement Candi needs to bend over and pull off her g-string. Kicking it onto her bag. Sandra stands and removes hers as well. Tossing it behind the chair.

"You're not twins anymore," Jeff laments jokingly.

"Sure we are," Sandra places her arm around Candi, "We're butt-ass naked twins now."

Everyone laughs hysterically as Candi motions Sandra back to the hot seat. Straddling her client's legs while facing away. Once again kicking her legs back and falling forward on her hands. Shaking her booty in Sandra's lap. Rubbing her wet pussy along her client's thighs. Feeling her client spanking and squeezing her cheeks. Spreading them open ever so slightly. The thought of Sandra sneaking a peek at her butthole make Candi's pussy even wetter. Gliding effortlessly along her naked twin's thighs. Feeling delicate fingers rubbing her clit. Making her juices flow even more.

"Your turn," Sandra stands and guides Candi to the hot seat.

Sandra sits on her lap. Bumping and grinding her pussy on Candi's stomach. Shaking her tits in her face. She spreads her stripper's legs, drops to her knees, and reaches for the Reddi-wip. Topping each of Candi's nipples. Circling them with her tongue. Sucking them long after the whipped cream is gone. Sandra's mouth on her breasts sending electric shocks through her body. Her pussy tingling and drenched. Wondering if Sandra is planning to eat her out. Wanting badly for Sandra to eat her out. The suspense is killing her.

Sandra pulls Candi's head down and kisses her passionately before dropping down between her legs. Applying a line of Reddi-wip on either side of Candi's pussy. Leaning forward and slowly licking it off. Looking into Candi's eyes. Smiling as she gives her pussy a long lick from back to front. Candi sighs and slides her butt forward to the edge. Spreading her legs wide open. Raising one hand in the air. Grabbing the back of Sandra's head with the other as her client eats her pussy. Sandra's tongue expertly teasing her clit. Licking deep inside her. Her juices gushing uncontrollably. Reveling in her own hedonism while Jeff and the other guys encourage them. Even the other two women, while apparently not into girls themselves, remark how sexy the two of them look.

"Oh, and don't worry," Jeff suddenly and thoughtfully informs Candi, "No one else is ever going to see this video."

"That's right," Sandra removes her mouth from Candi's pussy, "I'd lose my job for this."

"Oh, I'm not worried," Candi assures them, "I trust you two."

Sandra rises. Candi leans in and kisses her. Turned on even more by the taste of her own sweetness on her client's lips.

"Okay," Candi orders her, "Your turn again."

They giggle as Sandra takes the hot seat again. "Dance" by Ratt comes on. Candi now a woman possessed. Wasting no time hopping onto Sandra's lap. Grinding her pussy on her client's pelvis. Their tits pushed together. She no longer attempts to hide her lust for this unbelievably fun and sexy woman. Sandra slides forward. Allowing Candi's pussy to rub against her clit. Both girls moaning between their incessant giggling and the encouragement of their audience. Candi stands and turns around. Grabbing Sandra's legs and spreading them wide. Dropping down and grinding her ass on her client's throbbing wet pussy. Shaking from the sensation of warm girl juices covering her cheeks. Smiling back at the expressions of shock and awe on the faces before her.

"What?" Candi asks them, "You act like you've never seen a girl rub her butt on another girl's pussy before."

"I've never seen it before," Sandra admits, "But I like it!"

"Girl, you are so fucking crazy," Candi touches her ass, "You've got my booty all wet."

"That's all you, honey buns," Sandra laughs.

"Mmm…" Candi licks her fingers while looking into Sandra's eyes.

"I'm glad you like the way I taste," Sandra smiles.

"I really do," Candi lunges aggressively between Sandra's legs. Tongue first inside her client's soaking wet pussy. She can't wait a second longer to finally taste Sandra. Wanting to taste her the instant she saw her on Facebook. And it's better than she imagined. Girl juices so fucking sweet and delicious. Candi so consumed with excitement. Trying to explore Sandra's pussy in every way at once. Kissing and licking her clit. Sucking her swollen lips. Licking between them. Deep inside her velvety sugar walls. Sandra holding her head. Grinding her pussy on Candi's face. Drenched in Sandra's warm sweetness. It's almost too much for them to handle.

"This is too much for me to handle," Jeff sets down his phone and retreats to his recliner.

"Not so fast, mister," Candi tells him, "I'm not done with you yet."

"Come on," Sandra agrees, "Let's get him."

Candi grabs the Reddi-wip as she and Sandra head for Jeff. Facing away from him. Shaking their butts in his face while he spanks them. Piling their naked bodies on his lap. Applying whipped cream to each other's nipples. Having him lick and suck their titties clean. Giggling nonstop. He laughs with a mixture of intoxication and embarrassment.

"Uh oh," Jeff pushed them off his lap, "I need to get up."

"Oh no," Sandra watches him run down the hallway, "I'll be right back."

She races after her husband. Candi turns down the music and grabs her drink. Sitting naked in the hot seat. Conversing with the other guests. Learning that Jeff often gets sick if he drinks even slightly too much. And like that, the party is over. But Candi is far from disappointed. She made excellent money tonight and got to have sex with an incredible girl. Even this relaxed conversation with the guests while sipping her vodka cranberry is a blast. Regaling them with sexy and hilarious tales of parties past. Reveling in their hanging onto her every word.

"Sorry, everyone," Jeff announces as he and Sandra return, "I think the whipped cream did me in."

The other couples express their sympathies and prepare to leave. Candi heads to her bag. Turning off her music and preparing to get dressed.

"Hey, Sandy," Jeff calls out, "Why don't you see if Candi wants something to eat."

"Oh yeah," Sandra looks at Candi, "We still have a whole bunch of food left. Pizza. Chips and queso. Veggies and ranch dressing."

"That sounds great," Candi replies, "But I don't want to be a burden."

"Nonsense," Sandra tells her, "I wouldn't be the hostess with the mostess if I sent you home on an empty stomach."

They're interrupted by the other couples saying their goodbyes. Telling Jeff to feel better. Giving hugs to naked Sandra and naked Candi before leaving.

"Come in here and help yourself," Sandra motions Candi towards the dining area.

"I should probably get dressed first," Candi laughs.

"If you want," Sandra says coyly, "But I'm not."

"Okay then," Candi giggles and joins Sandra at the dinner table to snack on a little bit of everything while chatting.

"Thank you for coming all the way up here," Sandra smiles, "You totally made Jeff's night."

"You're welcome," Candi replies, "I'm sorry he's not feeling well."

"Don't worry about it," Sandra shakes her head, "His stomach is a little sensitive at times."

"Sorry about that," Jeff shouts from his recliner, "I guess I overdid it on the booze tonight."

"It's okay, Jeff," Sandra calls back, "Just take it easy. It's your birthday, after all," turning back to Candi, "He's just the best. Always has been. To the kids and me. I'd do anything to make him happy."

"I can totally see that," Candi agrees, then pauses to lose herself in thought for a moment, "I hope he had fun tonight."

"Believe me. He really did," Sandra assures her, "Especially watching us together."

"That was so much fun," Candi giggles.

"It really was," Sandra agrees, "He loved watching me with the girl who used to live down the road. Before she moved to Florida."

"Oh wow," Candi muses, "I'll bet that was hot."

"She was hot," Sandra sighs, "But not as hot as you."

"Aww… You're so sweet to say that," Candi laughs, "And you are just rockin' hot."

"Thanks," Sandra is consumed with flattery, "I'm glad you think so."

"I know so," Candi doubles down as they share a moment of silence, lost in each other's eyes.

"Hey. Would you like to join me in the hot tub?" Sandra offers, "I mean, I know you have a long drive home. But… Um… It's still kind of early…"

"That sounds like fun," Candi stands and grabs her drink, "Let's do it."

"Okay, great," Sandra leads her outside.

The crisp night air results in chills upon their bare skin. They walk across the spacious rear deck to the hot tub. Each grabbing one side of the cover and pulling it back. Gently stepping inside. Sandra turns on the pumps and fiber optic lighting before taking a seat next to Candi. Sipping their vodka cranberries. Relaxing as hot water jets forth. Massaging them. Any shred of a care in the world remaining on their shoulders now completely gone. The coolness upon their faces a perfect contrast to the heat enveloping their naked bodies.

"Oh," Sandra says abruptly, "Let me put on some music."

She grabs a remote off a nearby bench and presses a few buttons. Four speakers rise from each corner of the tub. "Avalon" by Roxy Music floats upon the dimly lit space surrounding the girls. The water endlessly changing color across the spectrum. From blue to purple as Sandra leans in and kisses Candi. Feeling even more relaxed. Losing themselves in each other's mouth. Tongues dancing in pure decadence while hot water caresses their skin. Passionately making out. Getting wetter in more ways than one. Their hair increasingly damp. Strands sticking to their faces. One finally intruding on their oral embrace. They giggle and pull apart.

"I think that was mine," Candi pushes her hair back, "Sorry about that."

"Don't be," Sandra grabs a strand of Candi's wet hair. Sliding it across her lips. Then holding it under her nose like a makeshift mustache as they giggle some more.

"Oh my God," Candi muses, "You are so much fun."

"Aww… Thank you," Sandra pushes Candi's hair back and leans into her, "And so are you."

They resume their make-out session. Each girl losing herself in the moment of sitting in a hot tub and enjoying the erotic company of another woman. Candi's arousal heightened further by Sandra's overall state of being. A devoted wife and mother who retains her youth and identity. Still making time for herself. Time to explore her sexual desires. Living proof that it can be done. That a shrewd enough woman can indeed have her cake and eat it too. Or pie, in this case. Candi's thoughts suddenly interrupted by Sandra's hand on her pussy. Rubbing it gently.

"You like that, Candi?" Sandra whispers in her ear before kissing and licking it.

"Mmm-hmm…" Candi tosses her head back. Eyes closed. Taking it all in. The sensation of the hot tub. The sensation of Sandra playing with her pussy. Massaging her clit. Then her g-spot as she feels a finger slide inside her.

"We used to do this," Sandra confesses, "The girl who lived down the road I told you about before."

"She's a lucky girl," Candi smiles breathlessly while being fingered.

"I was the lucky one to get to play with her," Sandra continues, "And now I'm lucky to get to play with you."

"Oh God, I'm the lucky one right now," Candi looks into Sandra's eyes and begins playing with her client's pussy in return. Rubbing her clit and lips. Inserting a finger within her tight sugar walls. Candi's own pussy tightening around Sandra's finger as they masturbate each other.

"She was the first girl I was ever attracted to. The first time I ever thought about having sex with another girl. And the first one I ever did have sex with," Sandra recollects, "I'm sorry. You probably don't want to hear all of this."

"No, I love hearing about it," Candi assures her, "It's not something you can talk about with many people and they'll understand."

"Exactly," Sandra agrees, "I just like girls. Certain girls, of course."

"Oh, I know what you mean," Candi moans softly before continuing, "My first was a girl I worked with at a strip club back East. We became friends and used to team up for dances on men in the backroom. God, she was so sexy. It was easy for me to play with her as part of our act," she pauses and laughs, "Then we started playing together occasionally on our own time."

"I'm sure you have a lot more experience than me," Sandra smiles, "I've only played with like three girls beside you."

"You know, I've met girls here and there thanks to stripping," Candi laughs coyly, "I've shared a few with Magnum as well. He and I play together too sometimes. I probably shouldn't be telling you that."

"Don't worry," Sandra shakes her head, "I got that vibe talking to both of you. I think that's totally hot."

She fingers Candi's pussy faster. Thrusting her finger in and out. Rubbing her stripper's clit with her thumb. Candi works her client's pussy vigorously. Manipulating her g-spot. Breathing heavily. Their moans getting louder. Kissing aggressively. Bringing each other to mutual orgasm. Feeling their bodies overheating as the water changes from purple to pink. Then red as they each breathe a sigh of release.

"You're just… Oh wow!" Candi giggles as she reaches for her drink.

"No, you're the one who's oh wow," Sandra argues playfully before raising her glass, "To playing with hot, sexy girls."

"Absolutely," Candi agrees as they clink their glasses and take a sip in silence before Candi breaks the spell, "So, what else did you and the neighbor girl do in here?"

"Sit your butt up here," Sandra slaps the outside edge of the tub, "And I'll show you."

Sandra guides Candi as she stands. Purposely touching Candi's ass while she turns and sits on the edge.

"Are you okay up there?" she asks while spreading Candi's legs open, "You may want to hold onto my shoulders."

Candi follows the suggestion. Placing her hands upon Sandra's shoulders. Watching her lean forward. Feeling her client's tongue lick along each side of her pussy.

"I liked teasing her first," Sandra explains.

"You're such a tease," Candi giggles.

"That's right," Sandra agrees sassily before kissing Candi's clit. Exposing it with her thumbs and flicking it with the tip of her tongue. Circling. Sucking. Candi shudders with delight, watching her new girl crush eat her pussy.

"I think you like that," Sandra looks up at her.

"Oh my God, I love it," Candi answers breathlessly.

"That makes me feel incredible," Sandra licks Candi's pussy from back to front, "Someone's getting wet."

"Someone's making me wet," Candi coos.

"Mmm…" Sandra buries her face in Candi's pussy. Sucking her lips. Licking deep inside her. Making her juices flowing rapidly, "I see why they call you Candi. Your juices are so fucking sweet."

"I'm glad you like them," Candi moans softly from Sandra's tongue lashing.

"I really do," Sandra licks Candi's pussy more vigorously and brings her to the verge of cumming.

"Oh my God," Candi moans, "You're making me cum."

"Cum for me, Candi," Sandra encourages, "Cum on my face."

Candi braces herself. Digging her fingertips into Sandra's shoulders. Choking up. Heart racing. Her client's tongue expertly teasing and pleasing her pussy. Inside and out. Making her tighter and wetter. Lips swelling. Throbbing. Aching for release. Closing her eyes. Opening them to the dark wilderness before her. Looking down at Sandra's enthusiastic face devouring her sweetness. She can no longer hold back. Crying softly into the night while releasing a flood of girl juices on Sandra's face.

"Mmm… Baby!" Sandra exclaims, "That was amazing."

The chill of the air finally hits Candi's skin. She immediately gets back in the water to warm up. Helped by Sandra's embrace as they kiss and giggle.

"Okay," Candi slaps the edge of the hot tub where she just sat, "Your turn on the hot seat. Park your butt, missy."

"Yes, ma'am," Sandra laughs as Candi helps her to position and dives tongue first into her client's pussy.

"Oh wow!" Sandra marvels, "You're not wasting any time."

"Mmm-mmm…" Candi shakes her face in Sandra's pussy. Sliding her tongue deep inside her client's sugar walls. Devouring her sweet juices as they flow forth. Licking up to her clit and back. Sucking her swollen lips one at a time.

"Oh my God," Candi looks up at Sandra, "You taste delicious."

"Thank you," Sandra whispers breathlessly.

"Your pussy is sweet like candy too," Candi giggles. Licking and sucking Sandra's clit. Sliding her middle finger inside. Rubbing her g-spot. Her client's juices flowing like crazy.

"You're so incredible at that," Sandra muses.

"Did the neighbor girl ever do this to you?" Candi inquires.

"Mmm-hmm…" Sandra sighs, "But not quite as good as you."

"Aww…" Candi responds, "You're so sweet to say that."

"It's true," Sandra confirms, "I'm learning so much from you tonight."

"That's so sweet," Candi coos between licks, "Well, I'm learning a lot from you too."

"Whatever," Sandra laughs while moaning, "I just want to do so much with you."

"Ooh," Candi's curiosity is peaked, "Like what?"

"Oh, I don't know…" Sandra drifts off in embarrassment.

"You know what I liked?" Candi confesses, "When I was giving you that lap dance. And I felt you spreading my butt cheeks open."

"Oh my God," Sandra covers her face in shame, "I'm so sorry."

"Don't apologize, silly. I said I liked it," Candi assures her, "The thought of you sneaking a peek at my butthole made my pussy even wetter."

"Really?" Sandra asks, "I… Um… It's just something I've been curious about."

"Eating ass?" Candi clarifies for her, "It's totally hot. I love it with the right person."

"Oh, I know that. It's something my husband and I have always enjoyed doing to each other," Sandra explains, "But I just… you know… meant with a girl."

"Ooh… You want to eat my ass, Sandra?" Candi starts rapidly thrusting her finger in and out of her client's pussy, "I'd love for you to eat my ass."

"Oh my God. Yes!" Sandra cries out as Candi licks and fingers her pussy, "I want to eat your ass, Candi."

"I want you too, baby," Candi encourages, "I want to feel your tongue in my asshole."

"I want that so bad," Sandra moans loudly while Candi licks and sucks her clit, "I want to taste your sexy asshole."

"It's making me wet thinking about it," Candi admits, "It's making you wet too."

"You're making me wet," Sandra shakes with anticipation as Candi brings her to orgasm, "You're making me cum."

"Ooh… Cum for me, Sandra," Candi orders sassily, "Cum on my face, and then you can lick my ass."

"Oh God, I'm going to lick your ass!" Sandra unleashes a tidal wave of sweetness upon Candi's face, "Oh God, I'm cumming!"

"You are cumming, baby!" Candi squeals with delight, "You are cumming all over my face."

Candi rubs her face all over Sandra's gushing pussy. Helping her to stand as "Eyes Without a Face" by Billy Idol fills their ears. Sandra turns around to get back in the water. Her ass right in Candi's face.

"Hold up," Candi seizes the opportunity before her, "Bend over."

"What?" Sandra is puzzled yet complies.

"Just do it, sexy butt," Candi grabs her client's cheeks and spreads them wide open, "Ooh… That's nice."

Sandra's laughing turns to moaning when Candi thrusts her warm wet tongue deep inside her client's tight butthole. Sliding in and out. Her face buried between Sandra's firm round cheeks. Her pussy growing tighter and wetter. Beside herself with excitement that she's eating Sandra's ass. Tracing every delicate ridge with the tip of her tongue. Licking within her. Sandra sighing incessantly. Shaking as much as Candi is. Not only from the physical sensation of having her asshole expertly pleased but from the knowledge that it's courtesy of a hot girl. A stripper no less. It's the same for Candi as she continues exploring and bonding with her new role model in the most intimate fashion possible.

"Oh wow!" Sandra moans in delighted astonishment, "You are fucking incredible at that."

"Thank you," Candi replies, "I've had a little practice eating girl booty."

"Oh, I can tell," Sandra coos, "I can't wait to eat yours."

Candi removes her tongue from Sandra's butthole and smacks her cheeks. They help each other switch places. Candi bending over the edge of the hot tub. Fully basking in the sensation of Sandra squeezing her cheeks and spreading them apart.

"You have such a pretty butthole, Candi," Sandra enthuses.

"Thank you,' Candi revels in this flattery, "And so do you."

Anticipation grips her body as she awaits Sandra's tongue. Followed by chills of forbidden pleasure when she feels her client's gentle warmth swirl around her asshole. Tentatively at first. But enough to make Candi's juices flow. The sheer excitement of this sweet, kind, wonderful, and sexy as all fuck woman eating her ass right now. Her new idol exploring the joys of orally pleasuring another woman's booty for the first time. Candi beyond enthusiastic to be her first. Her moans and sighs filling Sandra with confidence. Licking Candi's tight hole with authority now. Pushing her tongue inside. Thrusting it back and forth. Candi rocking her ass in unison. The rest of her body tightening as she feels another orgasm coming on. Until a wave of release overcomes her. She gets back underneath the water with Sandra. They kiss and laugh insatiably.

"Oh wow!" Sandra exclaims, "That was fucking amazing."

"It really was," Candi seconds, "You were fucking amazing."

"Oh, I don't know," Sandra laughs, "But you are totally out of this world."

"Aww…" Candi giggles, "So are you."

"I think it's time to get out," Sandra looks at her wrinkly fingertips then towards a nearby bench, "Yeah, I've got some towels out here already. Come on, let's go back inside."

Sandra turns off everything before she and Candi help each other get out. Drying each other off. Grabbing their drinks and running back inside. Escaping the night air growing colder by the minute. Retreating to the warmth of inside the house where Jeff has dozed off in his recliner.

"Oh, he'll be out until morning," Sandra fixes she and Candi another drink, "I guess he'll have to fuck me tomorrow. But it's okay," Sandra puts her arms around Candi's waist, "You can fuck me right now. Come on."

Butterflies fill Candi's stomach as she and Sandra take their drinks and cross through the living room. Sandra grabbing Jeff's phone along the way. Leading Candi down the hallway to the master bedroom at the end. Sandra turns on the nightstand lamp. Filling their sapphic love nest with a dim amber glow. Revealing zebra print bedding and large wall mirror. She grabs a tripod leaning in the corner, mounts Jeff's phone to it, and frames her shot of the king-size bed. Then turns on the stereo. "Touch Too Much" by AC/DC struts across the night.

"Want to star in a porno with me?" Sandra asks seductively, "It'll be for Jeff's eyes only. And mine too when I want to relive some good times."

"Ooh… That sounds totally hot," Candi wraps her arms around Sandra's waist and kisses her while made even wetter from the naked reflection of she and her client in the mirror, "I've always fantasized about doing porn, and I've had offers, but I didn't want to be expected to work with anyone I didn't like."

"Yeah, I've wondered about that myself when I watch porn," Sandra ponders, "Well, I hope you don't mind costarring with me."

"Maybe we should just produce our own porn videos," Candi laughs sassily, "Performing together exclusively."

"Well then," Sandra presses play on the phone and lies down, "Let's get started on our first naughty cinematic masterpiece."

Candi climbs upon Sandra in a sixty-nine. They waste no time devouring each other's pussy. Floodgates of sweetness instantly opened. Candi sucking and pulling on Sandra's swollen lips. Licking her clit and deep insider her sugar walls. Her client doing the same to her. Shock waves consume Candi's body as Sandra's tongue dirty dances all over her pussy. Feeling herself getting tighter and wetter. Her client thrusting rapidly in and out of velvety love tunnel. Then feeling Sandra doing the same thing to her ass.

"Oh my God!" Candi laughs, "That's fucking amazing."

"Hey, Jeff," Sandra narrates for the camera, "I'm licking Candi's butthole. And it's sweet as fucking candy."

"Roll your hips up a little," Candi instructs Sandra.

She obliges and Candi moves her tongue further south. Licking her client's asshole. Pushing her tongue deep inside. She can't contain her swelling enthusiasm.

"This is so fucking exciting!" Candi inadvertently exclaims.

"I know, right?!" Sandra agrees, "Hey, Jeff. Candi and I are eating each other's butthole at the same time. What do you think of that?"

The girls keep this up until the position gets uncomfortable. Returning to eating each other's pussy. Drenched in girl juices. Candi basking in the delight of savoring Sandra's incredible sweetness. Sandra doing the same with Candi. Moaning and sighing together. Each girl's face buried between the other's legs. Drowning in unbridled ecstasy. Embracing the heat of the moment for every ounce it's worth. This wild night won't last forever, but they're making it last for as long as they can.

"Oh wow," Candi feels Sandra's wet finger penetrate her asshole.

"Do you like that?" Sandra asks nervously.

"I love it!" Candi exclaims, "Hey, Jeff. Sandra is fingering my butthole."

"That right, baby," Sandra narrates, "I'm working her ass just like you work mine before you fuck it."

"Ooh," Candi giggles, "Are you going to fuck me in the ass?"

"I hadn't thought of that," Sandra laughs with embarrassment, "Do you like it in the ass?"

"I really do, actually," Candi admits, "I guess you do too."

"Oh yeah," Sandra confides, "Jeff is awesome at fucking me in the ass. Aren't you, Jeff?"

They laugh and continue eating each other out. Candi fingering Sandra's pussy. Massaging her g-spot while licking and sucking her clit. Sandra's tongue buried deep in Candi's pussy. Her finger all the way inside her stripper's ass. Both girls aching and throbbing for deep penetration as they near another shared orgasm. Trembling from the impending release and the hunger for something more. Candi imagines Magnum being here to give them both a good hard fucking. It pushes her over the edge. Gushing and squirting warm girl juices in Sandra's mouth. Her client following suit. Candi catches and swallows every drop.

"You know, I should've booked Magnum too," Sandra muses as Candi rolls off her, "I'd planned to if more couples wanted to come, but everyone acts like they're too good to have fun."

"Yeah," Candi laughs, "He and I would've done some wild stuff together."

"That's what I'm saying," Sandra nods, "Oh well. Maybe next time," she reaches over to remove a double-headed dildo and bottle of Astroglide from the nightstand, "I suppose this will have to do for now," Sandra holds them up to the camera, "Huh, Jeff?"

"Oh wow," Candi confesses, "I've never done this before."

"You haven't?" Sandra lubes up the dildo, "Well… It's time for you to learn, young lady."

The girls giggle as they sit facing each other. Legs spread. Candi watches Sandra rub Astroglide all over her pussy. Her breath taken away by watching her client play with herself.

"So, is that what it looks like when you play with yourself?" Candi giggles.

"Oh yeah," Sandra smiles sassily, "This is how it will look every time I'm reliving tonight in my mind."

Candi gets choked up by the suggestion. And even wetter as Sandra reaches forward and lubes up her pussy. "Thrills in the Night" by Kiss setting the tone for what's to come next.

"Scoot your butt closer to me," Sandra instructs her.

Sandra presses one end of the dildo against Candi's pussy and inserts it. Candi exhales and lies back while holding her end in place. Sandra

lies back and slides her pussy over the other end. Lifting on their
elbows. Rocking their pussies back and forth. Each girl taking as much
of this giant purple toy deep inside her as she can. Smiling and
giggling. Gazing into each other's eyes. Candi lifts her leg in the air so
they can both go deeper. Sandra holds onto her calf for leverage. Their
butts slapping together with each mutual thrust. Nearly pussy to pussy
as each girl takes her end all the way inside. Candi sets her leg down
and rubs her clit. Sandra follows suit. Each getting wetter watching the
other play with herself. And from the other watching her play with her
own pussy. Driving them faster and faster.

"Wanna do it doggy style?" Sandra offers breathlessly.

"Hells yeah I do!" Candi reacts enthusiastically.

The girls sit up as Sandra removes the dildo from their pussies.
Leaning in and kissing Candi passionately. They roll over onto their
hands and knees. Ass to ass. Each girl inserting her end of the dildo
insider her pussy. Riding it deep together. Butts slamming with each
thrust. Candi lies on her face. Grabbing her ass with one hand.
Rubbing her clit with the other. Sandra doing the same. Each moaning
and crying out in sweet anguish. Fucking each other's pussy at the
same time. Their toy cock rubbing g-spots relentlessly in this position.
Shaking uncontrollably. Cumming together. Candi's pussy gushing
and squirting all over her client's pussy, ass, and legs. Sandra ups the
ante by hitting her stripper's tits and face with a stream of warm girl
juices.

"Oh my God!" Candi exclaims with impressed delight, "You just
came on my face. And my tits."

"Did I really?" Sandra is stunned, "I mean… You just made me cum
really hard. But damn. Did you see that, Jeff? I hope you did."

Sandra removes the dildo from her and Candi. Setting it on the
nightstand. The girls face each other on their knees. Sandra licks her
own juices off Candi's tits and face. Giggling and kissing insatiably.
Candi falls forward on her elbows and knees. Resting her head on the
pillow after experiencing such an explosive climax. Sandra rubs her

shoulders and back, then moves down to her ass. Squeezing and massaging her cheeks.

"Mmm… That feels so good," Candi sighs.

"I'm glad you like it," Sandra muses, "You have such a sexy ass."

"Thank you," Candi gushes, "So do you."

"Aww… Thanks," Sandra laughs nervously, "I… Um… I don't know how to…"

"What?" Candi asks sweetly.

"Okay," Sandra takes a breath, "Can I fuck you in the ass? I mean, I totally understand if you don't want to. I probably shouldn't have even asked."

"No, that sounds totally hot," Candi assures her as she's instantly turned on by the idea and doesn't want her client to back out, "Do it, Sandra. Fuck me in the ass."

"Oh wow! Um… Okay," Sandra laughs as she goes for the nightstand again and produces a strap-on harness with three dildo attachments of varying sizes, "I got this a while back. The neighbor girl moved before I had a chance to try it with her. So, it's just been sitting in here."

"How about that one?" Candi points to the thinnest of the dildos, "I've never had a strap-on in my ass before, so I don't know how big I can handle."

"Whatever you're comfortable with," Sandra smiles, "Hey, Jeff. I'm going to fuck Candi in the ass."

"You've done that before," Candi observes Sandra attaching the dildo to the harness and strapping it upon herself.

"Yeah," Sandra giggles, "I've modeled it in the mirror a few times."

"You wear it well," Candi giggles back.

Sandra smacks Candi's ass and kneels before it. Spreading her cheeks wide open. Licking her crack. Then her butthole.

"Oh my God," Candi sighs, "You are getting incredible at that."

"I'm making the most of it," Sandra admits between licks, "I don't know when I'll get to eat girl booty again."

"You will," Candi assures her, "You just have to be patient when it comes to finding the right playmate."

"Oh, I know," Sandra pushes her tongue deep inside Candi's asshole. Thrusting it back and forth with reckless abandon. Candi moans while reaching back and rubbing her pussy.

"You're so sexy when you do that," Sandra coos, "Keep playing with your pussy, Candi."

Sandra goes back to the nightstand and grabs the Astroglide. Working it between her fingers. Returning to Candi's ass and rubbing it around her butthole. Slowly working her middle finger inside. Candi gasps in delight. Massaging her own pussy while Sandra slides that finger in and out of her butt. Then two fingers as Candi relaxes even more.

"Look, Jeff," Sandra announces to the camera, "I'm doing the same thing to Candi you do to me before you fuck me in the ass."

"And she does it so fucking well, Jeff," Candi moans from the wicked sensation of ass fingering and pussy rubbing.

"I think she's ready, Jeff," Sandra gets more Astroglide and thoroughly lubricates her strap-on dildo, "Are you ready, Candi?"

"Fuck yeah, Sandra," Candi wiggles her butt in the air, "Fuck my ass."

Van Halen's "Unchained" pounds forth as neither girl can contain her excitement. Both trembling in anticipation. Candi lies on her face. Reaching back and spreading her cheeks wide open with both hands. Sandra gets on her knees behind Candi. Slowly lining up her toy cock with Candi's asshole. Holding her breath. Pushing the head inside. Candi shivers and exhales a long sigh.

"Does that feel okay, Candi?" Sandra asks.

"It feels fucking amazing, Sandra," Candi coos.

"I'm going to go slow," Sandra assures her, "Let me know if you need me to stop."

"I will," Candi promises.

Sandra leans forward. Slowly. Gradually pushing her strap-on dildo inside Candi's ass. Until she takes it all the way. Sandra grabs her stripper's ass. Thrusting gently inside her. Candi rubbing her pussy. Her butt cheeks slapping against her client's pelvis.

"Whew!" Sandra exclaims, "I'm doing it, Jeff. I'm fucking Candi in the ass."

"It's true," Candi seconds, "She's balls deep in my asshole."

The girls laugh at that. Candi slides a finger insider her pussy. Massaging her g-spot. Rocking her ass against Sandra while her client buttfucks her. It's a strange feeling. Wonderful. Liberating. Sandra's silicone toy is no match for the explosive sensation of rock-hard man-flesh expertly fucking her asshole. But the sheer fact that her sexy new gal pal is penetrating her anally right now excites her beyond belief. So thrilling and deliciously naughty all at once. Definitely the sort of female bonding she can get behind. Sliding two fingers in her pussy now. Even wetter as Sandra fucks her a little faster and harder. Reveling in the moment of being totally submissive to her client.

"Do you like that, Candi?" Sandra makes sure everything is okay.

"I love it, Sandra," Candi moans, "I love you fucking me in the ass."

"I love fucking you in the ass," Sandra coos, "Do you want it faster?"

"Faster and harder," Candi rocks her butt faster against Sandra, "Fuck my ass fast and hard."

"Ooh, baby," Sandra slaps Candi's ass and thrusts aggressively, "I'm fucking your ass fast and hard."

"Oh my God!" Candi cries, "You're so deep in my asshole, Sandra."

"Mmm-hmm…" Sandra moans, "I'm fucking deep in your tight little asshole, Candi."

"Oh fuck!" Candi screams in anguish while shaking profusely and unable to hold back any longer, "I'm cumming, Sandra!"

"Cum for me, Candi," Sandra orders, "Cum as I fuck you in the ass."

"Fuck me!" Candi shrieks as a massive climax washes over her body. Her pussy squirting all over Sandra's thighs. Her client leans forward and embraces her body. Sandra holding her silicone cock all the way inside Candi's ass.

"Oh wow, Candi!" Sandra exclaims, "That was fucking amazing!"

"It really fucking was," Candi catches her breath, "Hey, Jeff. Sandra fucked me in the ass until my pussy squirted all over her."

"She sure did," Sandra rises back on her knees. Slowly pulling out of Candi's ass. Candi turns around on her knees to face Sandra. Taking her in her arms. Kissing her deeply.

"Okay," Candi announces, "Your turn."

"Ooh…" Sandra giggles, "Are you going to fuck me in the ass?"

"Mmm-hmm…" Candi licks Sandra's neck and slaps her ass before pressing her finger against her butthole and whispering in her ear, "I'm going balls deep in your asshole, Sandra."

The girls laugh as Sandra removes her strap-on harness. Helping Candi into it before getting on her knees. Bending over. Lying on her face. Reaching back with both hands. Grabbing her butt cheeks. Spreading them wide open.

"Come and get it, Candi," Sandra flashes her tight butthole at Candi.

Candi immediately dives tongue first into Sandra's ass. Thrusting and licking deep inside her butt. Spanking her cheeks. Squeezing them tight. Ramming her face between them. Shoving her tongue as far into her client's asshole as she can. Savoring her taboo sweetness. Making every second count since there's not many left tonight. Aggressively sliding her tongue in and out of her girl crush's deliciously tight booty hole. As if she truly can't get enough. Because she truly can't get enough.

"Oh wow! You are so fucking unbelievable at that!" Sandra exclaims, "Hey, Jeff. Candi has her tongue all the way inside my butthole right now. And it feels so fucking incredible. Oh my God!"

Candi continues thrusting her tongue recklessly within Sandra's ass until her mouth finally needs a break. She grabs the Astroglide, warms it on her fingers, and slathers it along Sandra's entire crack. Rubbing circles on her butthole. Then sliding her middle finger inside. Slowly. Gently. One knuckle at a time. Until she's all the way in, and Sandra lets out a long sigh. Deep inside the soft velvety walls of her client's forbidden love tunnel. So tight and warm. Trembling from the sheer excitement of feeling the inside of Sandra's ass. From the sheer excitement of Sandra enthusiastically accepting her inside. Rocking her butt back and forth on Candi's finger.

"You can go faster, baby," Sandra lets her know.

"My pleasure, foxy buns," Candi thrusts her finger rapidly in and out of Sandra's asshole. Feeling her grow looser. Relaxing more and more. Moaning softly as Candi continues fingering her butt. Stopping briefly to invite her index finger to the party. Sandra's tight hole eagerly accommodating the added digit. "She truly is the hostess with the mostess," Candi muses to herself. Wondering if her role model is feeling the same excitement she is. Of course she is. Her body language makes it so fucking clear. Candi wants so badly for Sandra to feel the same excitement she's feeling that she can't help but doubt herself slightly. She has to know.

"Are you as excited as I am right now?" Candi inquires despite her embarrassment.

"Oh fuck yes, Candi," Sandra assures her between moans, "I am loving every second of tonight. Are you?"

"Absolutely, Sandra," Candi answers without hesitation, "I'm so glad you booked me."

"Me too," Sandra sighs in delight, "You have no fucking idea."

Sandra's raspy moaning gives Candi chills. So does looking at the toy cock between her legs while still fingering her client's ass. Looking at Sandra's naked body. Ass in the air. Trembling with excitement over everything right now. In anticipation of what's soon to come. When Candi fucks her in the ass. She's as enthusiastically submissive to Candi right now as Candi was to her just moments prior in the same position. And now the tables have turned in more ways than one. Candi is now not only the aggressor but the mentor. The nurturer. The hostess with the mostess of all things fun and naughty. Teacher of all things forbidden and taboo. With Sandra as her obedient disciple.

"I want to fuck you, Sandra," Candi whispers while removing her fingers and lubing up her strap-on dildo, "I want to fuck you in the ass."

"Do it, Candi. Fuck me in my ass," Sandra whispers back submissively while spreading her cheeks wide open, "Fuck me deep in my asshole."

"Oh, I'm going balls deep in your asshole," Candi presses the head of her virtual manhood inside Sandra's butt.

She grabs her client's cheeks and squeezes them tightly. Sandra rubbing and fingering her pussy. Shaking as Candi slides deeper inside her ass. Taking her in every inch of the way. Relaxing more with every drawn-out exhale. Embracing the moment. The willful submission. The unbridled excitement of it all that she and her stripper have shared on this exciting and unforgettable night. Candi penetrating Sandra's butthole with long, slow strokes. Sandra rocking her ass back and forth. Matching Candi every step of the way. Wanting her more and more.

"Fuck me faster, Candi," Sandra requests breathlessly.

"Like this," Candi thrusts her silicone cock faster and harder insider Sandra's ass.

"Oh, fuck yeah!" Sandra squeals with delight, "Just like that."

Candi glances over and catches the reflection of her fucking Sandra in the ass. The sight of their naked bodies, of Sandra in her submissive position, of her thrusting relentlessly, is all too much for Candi.

"You like that, huh?" Candi taunts her aggressively, "You like me fucking you in the ass?"

"I do, you naughty girl," Sandra concedes breathlessly, "I love you fucking me in the ass."

"I love it too, Sandra!" Candi exclaims between clenched teeth, "I love fucking you deep inside your tight sexy asshole!"

"Oh, fuck my asshole, Candi!" Sandra moans loudly, "Fuck it deep! Don't stop!"

Sandra fingers her pussy with reckless abandon. It's already squirting. Her warm juices streaming down both their legs. Moaning in anguish as Candi buttfucks her fast and deep. Candi's pelvis smashing against Sandra's cheeks with each thrust. Bouncing off them when she pulls back. She leans forward. Pressing her tits on Sandra's back. Grabbing her client's titties. Fucking her even deeper in her asshole. Faster. Harder. Sandra screaming and moaning in ecstasy. Her pussy explodes all over Candi. Drenching her in hot girl juices that just won't stop.

"Oh God, you're making me squirt!" Sandra cries out, "You're making me cum so fucking hard!"

"Oh yeah!" Candi encourages her, "Cum for me, baby!"

Candi experiences her own orgasm while comforting Sandra through her massive eruption and aftermath. Shaking uncontrollably together. Candi's arms wrapped tight around her client. The dildo held deep insider her ass. Their screams turning back to moans. Then sighs while catching their breath. And then laughter as they bask in the afterglow of taking turns fucking each other in the ass. Neither can believe what she's just done, but she's so glad she did it. Candi rises and pulls out of Sandra. She removes the harness as Sandra falls onto her back. Candi pounces on top of her. Embracing and making out. Giggling nonstop.

Sandra rolls Candi onto her back and lies on top of her. Exploring each other's mouth with their tongues. Sandra slides down and sucks Candi's titties. Going back and forth between each breast. Licking and sucking her nipples while reaching down and rubbing her stripper's soaking wet pussy. Candi turns the tables. Rolling them both over and sucking Sandra's tits. Swirling her tongue all over her nipples while rubbing and fingering her client's pussy. Making her wet and ready to go again. Candi spreads Sandra's legs open and presses her pussy against her client's. Rubbing back and forth. Holding onto her leg. Sandra wrapping her arms around Candi's back. Kiss returns with "Heaven's on Fire" as the girl set their own heaven on fire.

"Oh wow!" Sandra exclaims, "I've always wanted to do this."

"Me too," Candi giggles.

"You haven't?" Sandra asks surprised.

"Nope," Candi admits, "We're losing our scissoring virginity together."

Sandra laughs and Candi kisses her passionately. Romantically. Losing themselves in each other. Tongues dancing. Breasts heaving. Hearts racing. Pussies grinding. Tighter and wetter. Swollen and aching. Tingling and throbbing. All at once. Candi feeling dominant again as she girl fucks Sandra. Gazing upon her from the top of this missionary position as men have gazed upon her. Allowing herself to entertain the thought of knowing how they feel during lovemaking. She knows that male sexuality isn't as simple as the media makes it out to be. That it's just as deep and complicated in its own way as female sexuality. The years working and playing with Magnum have taught her that. But she can at least pretend to understand while making love to Sandra in this highly elaborate kiss goodnight.

"Oh my God, Candi," Sandra sighs, "You are just totally out of this world."

"Thank you," Candi whispers before kissing her, "So are you."

"Candi," Sandra whispers, "Are we making love?"

"Mmm-hmm…" Candi nuzzles her face in Sandra's neck. Shocked by her instant and nonchalant response. Yet unable, or unwilling, to stop herself. Never has a term so innocuous as "making love" ever seemed so dangerous. So exciting. Candi kisses and licks Sandra's neck, "We are making love, Sandra."

"It feels amazing," Sandra sighs, "Making love to you."

"I know," Candi swallows nervously, "Friends can make love to each other."

"Yes, they can," Sandra grabs the back of Candi's head and pulls her in for a deep and romantic kiss.

Butterflies filling Candi's stomach now more than ever. Losing herself in the throes of intense passion with her new friend. Will they remain friends? And lovers? The odds are highly stacked against this based on experience. But Candi is willing to keep her fingers crossed on this one. Her girl juices mingling with Sandra's as they slide back and forth on each other's sweetness.

"I have to confess something," Sandra giggles nervously, "I was attracted to you the instant I saw your photo," she pauses for more nervous giggling, "And… I may have looked at it while playing with myself a time or two before tonight."

"Oh wow!" Candi's heart skips a beat, "I was totally attracted to you when I looked you up on Facebook. And I was so excited to meet you. I couldn't wait for this night to come."

"Aww…" Sandra pulls Candi in for another kiss, "You have no idea how that makes me feel."

"It's true," Candi assures her, "As soon as I saw you, I totally wanted to fuck you."

"You did, huh?" Sandra laughs sassily, "Well then. Fuck me, Candi."

Candi feels her aggressive side returning. Feeling her body instinctively thrust faster and harder against Sandra's. Grinding their pussies together even tighter. Warm juices flowing like crazy. Running down their thighs. On their butt cheeks. The electric sensations of their clits and lips rubbing together sending nonstop shockwaves through Candi's body. Sandra's too as she grabs Candi tightly. Kissing her insatiably.

"Ooh…" Candi giggles, "We are totally girl fucking right now."

"That is so adorable," Sandra laughs in agreement, "I love it. We are girl fucking right now," she pauses, "Hey, Jeff. Candi and I are girl fucking right now."

"And making love," Candi adds sassily.

"That's right, Jeff," Sandra smiles at Candi, "We are making sweet, passionate girl love right now. You're just going to have to share me with Candi from now on."

They giggle and kiss some more. Then bump and grind even faster. Tighter. Harder. Their moans growing louder. Pussies wetter than ever. Gushing upon each other. Squirting slightly. The sheet underneath them now soaking wet from their combined girl juices. Candi can't hold back her emotions. Kissing Sandra all over her face and neck. Sandra does the same to Candi. Smiling seductively at each other. Moving closer to a shared climax of epic proportions. Both physical and emotional. Shaking uncontrollably. Each thrust sending a bolt of lightning through their bodies. Holding back for as long as they can. But time is running out.

"Oh God!" Candi screams, "I'm fucking cumming!"

"Me too, baby!" Sandra cries, "Cum with me!"

"Oh fuck!" Candi and Sandra shout in near unison as their pussies explode on each other. Squirting hot juices all over their bodies. Embracing tightly. Riding out the beautiful anguish of their climax together. Seemingly never-ending. Never wanting it to end. Trying in vain to make tonight last forever while it reaches an unforgettable end. Candi's face buried in Sandra's neck as her crush turned lover rubs her back in comfort. Both girls shivering from the tension flowing out of them. From every muscle fiber outward into infinity. Across the night. Lips locked. Riding out the orgasmic storm as closely as possible.

"Whew, Candi," Sandra exhales, "I think you finally wore me out tonight."

"I think you wore me out too, Sandra," Candi catches her breath.

"You can stay the night if you want," Sandra offers, "There's a spare bedroom down the hall. And a bathroom right across from it."

"I really appreciate that. Thank you," Candi smiles, "But I have things to do tomorrow in Little Rock that I need to get up early for."

"Are you sure you're okay to drive?" Sandra catches herself and laughs, "I'm sorry. You know what you're doing."

"No, that's sweet," Candi assures her, "I'll be fine. I think the alcohol has worn off. And I have a Red Bull in the car."

"Okay," Sandra kisses her before they get up.

Candi runs to the bathroom to clean up while Sandra stops recording on Jeff's phone. She makes sure Candi has all her money and things as her stripper throws on a sweatshirt and yoga pants. Sandra walks her to the front door. Still butt-ass naked.

"Thanks again for coming," Sandra hugs Candi, "In more ways than one."

"Well," Candi laughs, "Thank you for making me come."

"I… Um… Don't know if like… I'm being out of line," Sandra stammers nervously, "But can I text you sometime? You know, to chat…"

"I'd love that," Candi smiles, "I don't make a lot of friends being in this business."

"Great," Sandra breathes a sigh of relief, "Well, I won't keep you a second longer. Be safe driving back to Little Rock."

"I will,' Candi assures her before leaning in for one last kiss. One last chance tonight for their tongues to play. She pulls back and smiles, "Have a good night, Sandra."

"You too, Candi," Sandra touches Candi's cheek before her stripper turns and walks out the door.

Other than being cooler out, the drive back to U.S. 65 is no different than the drive from it to Heber Springs. "Lack of Communication" by Ratt feels oddly appropriate right now. Candi cruising along at any speed she wants. Taking it easy passing through Quitman and Guy. But her mind is totally lost in tonight's events. Having made a new girlfriend. Perhaps. Still not getting her hopes up entirely. Knowing all too well how fickle some people can be. Especially in Arkansas. But she's willing to hold out a little hope. Particularly for a sweet, kind, and sexy as hell woman who proved to her that she can have it all in life. Not only the gal pal she's long desired, but the confirmation for all her dreams and ambitions as well. If only the man upon whom she has set her sights could finally see it all too.

AR 25 ends.

December

"Oh, thank God you're here!" Emma exclaims upon Magnum and Candi entering as sexy cops, "I've been such a naughty girl tonight!"

"That's what we were told," Magnum responds to the bachelorette in the living room of a Hot Springs lakefront condo rental on a cold late December Saturday night. Its open floor plan illuminated by an assortment of party lights with an emphasis on red like a makeshift sex club, "So, just how naughty have you been, Emma?"

"Naughty enough to warrant a strip search!" Emma declares enthusiastically before removing her black cocktail dress. Now totally naked as she bends over a dining room chair in the center of the room and wiggles her butt, "And a cavity search!"

Magnum and Candi can't believe their eyes. Not even after all these years. Not even while sort of expecting it. Emma knew they were coming. Because this was her idea. Tonight isn't her last night of freedom. It's the beginning of a new double life as she enters a marriage for appearance's sake. Tapping the dynamic stripping duo to catalyze this secret rebellion. Magnum and Candi are here to play with Emma and fellow high society gal pal Allison. Money for sex is something the two entertainers have always steadfastly refused. But the kind and persuasive Allison, acting as the client, instantly sold the strippers on the two of them via phone conversations, photos, and an obscene amount of money.

But there's more to tonight than meets the eye for these longtime collaborators. Magnum's agency has clearly reached the end of the line. The talent pool for Arkansas exotic entertainers having dried up completely. Leaving he and Candi as the last two strippers standing. For her, tonight is about proving to Magnum that she'll always be a wild child. Even in marriage and motherhood. But for him, tonight feels like the last hurrah. Nothing is definite, yet his gut instinct tells him this will be their swan song as a duo. He knows Candi is ready to hang up her g-string. Professionally, at least. It's not so easy for Magnum. Agency or not, he'll have to keep stripping in the foreseeable future due to financial reasons alone. And he can't imagine spending his Friday and Saturday nights any other way.

"Oh, I'll give you a cavity search," Candi licks her middle finger and slides it inside Emma's pussy, "All clear."

"Not so fast," he licks his middle finger and presses it gently inside his bachelorette's asshole, "Okay, now we're good."

"We are good!" Emma squeals with Allison capturing the moment on her phone.

"So, Magnum," Allison asks sassily, "Is this how you greet all your bachelorettes?"

"Of course," he doesn't miss a beat.

Magnum and Candi remove their fingers from Emma and have her take a seat. Tonight may be a whole new ballgame, but some things never change. "Bad Boys" properly introduces the strippers to their bachelorette. Slapping handcuffs on her. Red beacon spinning. Strobe flashing. Quickly shifting to "Salt Shaker" as the entertainers each straddle one of Emma's legs. Both turned on by the naked bachelorette underneath them. Impatient to join her. Impatient to encourage Allison in doing the same. Magnum and Candi waste no time undressing each other. Down to their g-strings in a matter of seconds.

"No, don't stop there," Emma chides them, "I'm here for some cock and pussy, damn it!"

Magnum drops to his knees on the large oriental rug covering a white tile floor. Removing Candi's g-string. Grabbing her ass. Licking her pussy. Teasing and sucking her clit before a cheering audience of two. He stands and Candi drops to her knees. Removing his g-string. Stroking and sucking his shaft. Swirling her tongue around his head. Both strippers feasting on the ecstatic eyes upon them. Something they've experienced together countless times but soaking in the moment like never before.

"I can tell you two have done this before," Allison playfully antagonizes them.

"Well…" he throws back coyly at her, "Maybe a time or two."

"Yeah, okay," Allison laughs.

"Hey, that's what you said about you and Emma," he comes back.

"Really?" Emma asks with surprise, "Allison has eaten my pussy more times than I can count."

"Yeah," Allison laughs, "And that's how many times you've eaten my pussy."

"We're really close friends," Emma informs the strippers.

"You two are so adorable," Candi straddles Emma.

She smothers the bachelorette with her titties while Magnum retrieves a can of Reddi-wip from his stripping bag. Taking a moment to observe Candi giving a lap dance to a girl. A sight he's always enjoyed personally, but there's a lump in his throat this time. Which he immediately swallows and rejoins the fun.

"Oh my God," Emma sighs from her pussy being bumped and grinded upon by Candi's.

They kiss passionately. Allison cheering them on. Magnum sets down the whipped cream. Coming up behind Candi. Grabbing her hips. Pressing his big hard cock between her firm round butt cheeks. Humping her ass while she continues humping their bachelorette. His juices beginning to flow down his stripping partner's crack. She squeezes his cock tightly. Stroking him with her ass while tribbing their bachelorette. A three-way lap dance machine of the naughtiest proportions. Make that four-way when he feels a suddenly naked Allison rubbing her warm wet pussy on his ass.

"Oh wow!" he's pleasantly caught off guard.

"You know you like it," Allison sasses, "And I was feeling left out."

"I was coming for you," he assures her.

"Well," Allison sassily makes a double entendre, "Maybe I'll just come for you right now."

"Ooh… Do it, Allison," Emma instructs, "Cum on Magnum's ass."

"Then you should eat his ass," Candi suggests, "He loves that."

"Do you just tell that to everyone now?" he still harbors a touch of embarrassment despite his experiences.

"I think it's hot. I love having my ass eaten too," Allison announces before leaning forward and whispering in his ear, "Maybe we can each other's ass later."

"Yeah, Allison is the one who got me into eating ass," Emma confesses, "She was always curious about butt stuff."

"You know you like it," Allison sasses.

"I do," Emma admits, "I'm all about the girl booty."

"Me too!" Candi exclaims.

"Wow!" he breaks up the party once the song concludes as he's overwhelmed by all the dirty talk coming from three sexy girls at once.

"Okay everyone," Allision motions the naked and naughty gang of four to the kitchen, "Time for a drink."

"What does everyone want?" Emma reaches for bottles of booze on the counter.

"Get back," Allison slaps her hand away, "This is your bachelorette party."

"I'm just trying to help…" Emma protests.

"Your job right now is to get comfy with Magnum and Candi," Allison smacks Emma's ass, "You can mix drinks for them when they come back for my bachelorette party someday. Now, what does everyone want? We've got like fucking everything."

Allison mixes four drinks while Magnum and Candi dance with Emma. All three lightly fondling each other. Each pleasantly burdened with their individual anticipation for what's to come. Candi smiles at Magnum. Keeping the faith that she can sell him on having it all. Magnum smiles back, but only in maintaining a façade of strength in a time of tremendous uncertainty in his life. They both know she's not long for the profession at this point. The fact that tonight is such a different gig for them is probably why she was instantly gung-ho on the idea. As if she's ready to eschew entertaining others and embrace a lifestyle of angel by day, demon by night. Which is what she's always been. But now the duality of her nature is more pronounced than ever. Magnum, however, is still every bit the entertainer he was born to be. And that's the first void he'll have to fill upon hanging up his g-string someday.

"But first," Allison brings everyone back into the moment, "Let's do a hairy navel together."

"God, I hope you're talking about a shot," he jokes as the girls laugh and go, "Eww…" to the thought of body hair.

"I'm so glad that none of us is rocking any body hair," Emma toasts, "Let's drink to that."

"Oh, I know," Candi laments, "Girls now are letting their pussies get all hairy and shit. That's just fucking nasty."

"Yes, it is," Allison seconds, "And let's also drink to Magnum being circumcised."

"Oh God, yes," Emma agrees before looking at him, "Wait. You're not one of those anti-circumcision people, are you?"

"Do I look like I can't get pussy?" he asks rhetorically with a cocksure tone.

"I think you can get pussy on your scent alone," she presses her nose against his neck, "Oh my God, you smell incredible. What are you wearing?"

"Preferred Stock," he answers, "It's always been my go-to cologne for parties. Girls really seem to dig it."

"It's true," Candi affirms, "Every party I've been at with him, the girls always remark about how amazing he smells."

"Well…" Emma continues sniffing his neck, "I'll smell you anytime."

Everyone laughs and does their shot. Allison serves drinks before they head back to the living room. "Hold On, We're Going Home" by Drake slinks through the air.

"Ooh," Emma expresses, "This is a sexy song."

"I'll show you how sexy it can be," Magnum motions her back to the hot seat and grabs the Reddi-wip.

He decorates her nipples before he and Candi kneel on either side of her. Each taking a breast. Sucking and caressing it free of whipped cream. Continuing after it's gone. Emma enjoying every second. Holding her stripper's heads. Pressing their faces tight against her girls. Allison capturing all the action.

"Damn, Emma," Allison narrates, "You got two hot ass strippers sucking your titties right now."

"I know," Emma sighs from the sensation of Magnum and Candi flicking their tongues over her nipples and sucking them even harder, "I'm in heaven right now."

"Maybe Ira will learn a thing or two from watching this video," Allison muses sarcastically.

"Whatever," Emma scoffs, "I'm not sure he was even capable of sucking his mom's tits as a baby."

"Hold up," Candi removes her mouth from Emma's breast, "I'm sorry. You're marrying a guy named Ira? Who the fuck names their kid Ira in the past hundred years?"

"Candi?!" Magnum looks at her in shock before turning to apologize to Emma.

"It's cool," Emma stops him, "I totally agree."

"I've asked that same question countless fucking times," Allison assures the strippers, "What was his mom thinking?"

"She's a stupid fucking bitch," Emma laughs, "She wasn't thinking."

"So," he jokingly asks, "If you have a son, you won't be naming him Ira?"

"Fuck no!" Emma laughs, "I'm gonna name him Magnum."

Everyone laughs. Magnum stands and straddles Emma. Pressing his cock upwards between her titties. Thrusting rapidly as she pushes them together. Candi spreads Emma's legs. Kissing along her inner thighs before licking her pussy back to front. Sucking her clit and lips. Emma shaking from all this attention.

"Candi is eating your pussy," Allison informs Emma facetiously.

"Oh, I know," Emma moans, "Her mouth is magic."

"Magnum knows all about that, huh?" Allison sasses, "And he's totally fucking your titties right now."

"Fuck yeah he is," Emma enthuses.

"Emma's got the best tits of the two of us," Allison opines while turning around and bending over, "But I've got the booty."

"Yes, you do," he gives her butt a loud slap.

"Damn right she does," Emma smacks it too.

Magnum continues pumping Emma's tits. Cock tingling from the sensation of stroking between her soft breasts. Precum dripping on her chest. Smearing it across her skin. She watches and grows even more excited by this as well as from Candi's sensual tongue lashing. An animal is about to emerge. He recognizes is all too well.

"Oh my God, give me your cock," Emma demands breathlessly.

She grabs his manhood. Leading him upward and down her throat. Squeezing his butt. Devouring his throbbing shaft. Running her tongue along every inch. Pressing the tip into his tiny hole. Making his juices flow even more. His knees getting weaker. He hangs onto her shoulders. Trembling while wondering if he should be getting paid for this. Then he remembers that she's about to marry a guy named fucking Ira. And Emma's constant moaning on his cock confirms the epic cunnilingus she's receiving from Candi right now.

"Oh, Emma. You are so fucking wet," Candi giggles, "And so fucking sweet."

"She really is a sweet girl," Allison moves behind Candi, "In every single way."

"Oh wow!" Candi is pleasantly caught off guard by Allison's pussy rubbing on her ass.

"That's what Magnum said when I did this to him," Allison laughs.

"Well yeah," Candi sighs, "It feels amazing."

"Hells yeah it does," Allison brags.

"Is that like your thing you do?" Candi laughs sarcastically.

"Oh, honey," Allison laughs devilishly, "We haven't scratched the surface of what I can do."

Emma shakes from Candi exploring deep inside her pussy. Licking her soft velvety walls up and down. Thrusting her tongue in and out. The bachelorette's juices flowing relentlessly all over Candi's face. She slides her middle finger inside Emma. Massaging her g-spot while licking and sucking her clit. Making her shake uncontrollably. Moaning louder and louder with Magnum's cock in her mouth. The bachelorette finally comes up for air. Stroking her male stripper. Licking his balls. Swirling her tongue around his head. Consuming every drop of his juices.

"Oh fuck!" Emma orgasms.

"Fuck to the yeah!" Allison stands and shouts.

Magnum and Candi smile at each other. Hiding their silent argument from tonight's party girls. Each attempting to sway the other to their way of thinking. He's not upset that she wants to retire from stripping. And he could totally see himself making a personal commitment to her. But he refuses to subject himself to socializing with the Ira's of the world. Or their moms, for that matter. The bullshit expectations that come with living a "normal" life. What exactly does that intellectual self-flagellation accomplish in the long run anyway? Rounds of golf that lead to getting involved in skeevy business ventures? Fuck all that. He sips his Jack and Coke. Watching Allison's booty bounce as she runs to the kitchen.

"Time for another shot!" she goes for the vodka and peach schnapps while everyone else gathers around her, "To new beginnings!"

"Naughty new beginnings!" Emma seconds as they drink.

"What's up?" Magnum whispers to Candi upon noticing what looks like tears in her eyes.

"Oh, nothing," she smiles while quickly composing herself. Wishing he would get over his anxieties about settling down, "He's trusted me all these years. Why can't he trust me on this?" she ponders.

"Alright, ladies! Back to it!" he orders Candi and their party girls as "My Humps" by The Black-Eyed Peas" pumps forth while taking Allison by the hand, "Your turn, missy."

"Ooh," Allison sasses, "Have I been a naughty girl?"

"You bet your sweet ass you have," he smacks her butt, "Now sit."

Magnum stands before her in his black cowboy boots and nothing else. Dropping forward and catching himself on the edge of the chair. Pulling himself closer. Running his face along her silky thighs. Pleasantly surprised when she spreads her legs wide open. His cheeks brushing against her inner thighs. Immediately raising the stakes when his lips meet her pussy. Kissing her clit. Flicking it with his tongue. Dropping to his knees. She places her legs upon his shoulders. Grabbing his head and moaning softly. He sucks her swollen lips.

Pulling on them. Letting them go. Licking from back to front, then deep inside, as her delicious girl juices flow rapidly.

"Oh my God, Magnum," Allison whispers in all seriousness for the first time tonight, "You're even better than I imagined."

"You've been imagining this moment?" he inquires seductively.

"Mmm-hmm…" she bites her lip, "Ever since we first talked."

"Me too," he admits, "And this."

Magnum drops down and lifts Allison legs higher. Rolling her hips back. Exposing her tight butthole. Licking it softly before pushing his tongue inside.

"Oh fuck," she grabs his head tighter, "You're fucking amazing at that."

"Well, you've got the ass," he smiles before thrusting his tongue in and out.

"And you've totally got the tongue," she coos, "Hey, you two! Magnum is licking my butthole, and… Oh my God!"

Magnum instantly turns his head to see Candi facing away from them. Standing before the black leather sofa. One bare foot on a cushion. Emma kneeling between her legs. Enthusiastically eating her pussy. Licking and sucking her like there's no tomorrow. Candi looks back at Magnum and gives him a cocky head nod.

"Oh yeah?" Emma challenges, "Well, he's not the only one here who knows how to lick a butthole."

Emma rapidly slides her tongue in and out of Candi's ass. Twirling deep inside her.

"Oh wow!" Candi laughs with aroused astonishment, "Lick my asshole, you naughty girl!"

"Well, two can play that game," Allison guides Magnum to his feet and has him turn away from her before spreading his cheeks wide open. "I taught her how to do this."

Magnum trembles from the sensation of Allison's tongue circling his butthole. Tracing every ridge with the tip. Gently pressing inside him.

Then sliding deep inside him. Thrusting in and out of his ass. He breathes heavily. Knees growing weak. Struggling to stand. Electric shocks throughout his body. He and Candi looking into each other's eyes. Experiencing together the joy of being rimmed by a woman. Candi wanting him to believe that tonight could be the start of a new beginning. One even more exciting and depraved than all their wild nights to date. But Magnum still believes that the wild nights of Arkansas strippers are reaching their climax in this moment.

"I want to taste your cock," Allison confesses breathlessly.

She turns Magnum around and takes him down her throat. He grabs her shoulders as she massages his manhood with her lips and tongue. Inflicting his head and shaft with intense pleasure. Making his entire body tingle. His juices flowing like crazy into her soft warm mouth. He watches Candi and Emma switch places. His stripping partner licking back and forth between their bachelorette's pussy and asshole. Exploring inside both with her tongue. Emma moaning and sighing from all this intimate treatment. He imagines she's feeling the same way he is while her best friend sucks his cock with no mercy.

It's all too much for Magnum. He pulls out of Allison's mouth. Pushing her legs up to her chest. Grabbing the edges of her chair. She holds her ankles. Spreading her legs wide open. Smiling as he slides his massive cock deep inside her soaking wet pussy. So fucking tight. Both throbbing and aching as he fucks her relentlessly. Shockwaves through their bodies with each vicious thrust.

"Fuck me, Magnum," she demands, "Fuck me hard."

"Take it, Allison," he admonishes her, "Take it fucking deep."

They grind and grunt with reckless abandon. Allison arches her back. Looking to the ceiling. Moaning and sighing. Magnum pushes balls deep inside her and sucks her right breast. Then her left. Sucking each nipple while swirling his tongue over it.

"You're killing me," she giggles in anguish.

"What better way to go, though?" he laughs.

"Need some help?" Candi asks as she and Emma drop to their knees on either side of Allison. Candi applies Reddi-wip to her nipples. She and Emma lick and suck Allison's titties clean. Making her shake profusely.

"Now all three of you are killing me," Allison laughs between moans.

Magnum fucks Allison even harder. Not noticing as Candi and Emma move behind him.

"Whoa!" he exclaims from the shock of cold whipped cream being sprayed in his butt crack.

"Go for it, Emma!" Candi orders.

Magnum feels his bachelorette's tongue sliding between his cheeks. Shoving his cock all the way inside Allison's tight, velvety sugar walls. Holding it there while Emma spreads his cheeks and licks his asshole. Thrusting her tongue in and out. Candi and Allison watching with delight. Encouraging her every step of the way. Cheering as she emerges all smiles from her taboo sexual triumph.

"My first time eating man ass!" Emma proudly declares.

"What about Ira?" Allison asks sarcastically.

"Oh please," Emma scoffs, "He freaks out when I slip my tongue in his mouth."

Everyone laughs before Candi announces, "My turn," and buries her face in Magnum's ass. She's done this to him countless times, but it's always as exciting as the first. If only she didn't want kids and a normal façade. He'd rather be happily monogamous with her, if that's what she wanted, than deal with the other nonsense. They could leave stripping behind. Embark on new entrepreneurial ventures as business partners. Enjoy all sorts of fun and exciting adventures together. He's not afraid of a new beginning, but he doesn't want the one she has in mind.

Magnum starts pumping Allison's pussy again while Candi explores his butthole with her tongue. Emma moves around and kisses Allison as she nears climactic ecstasy. Her girl juices drenching Magnum's cock. Sliding in and out of her love tunnel. Harder. Faster. Candi grabbing his ass tightly. Still pleasing him orally. Magnum and Allison moaning louder and louder. The strobe light keeping pace with their racing hearts. Every muscle fiber in their bodies contracting tighter and tighter. Until…

"Fuck!" he shouts, "I'm cumming!"

"Me too!" Allison cries, "Cum inside me!"

Candi and Emma cheer them on as Magnum's cock explodes in Allison's pussy. She responds by unleashing a tidal wave of hot juices all over him. Leaning forward and kisses him passionately. Forcing her tongue inside his mouth. He gladly reciprocates.

"Oh wow, you two!" Emma exclaims, "That was so fucking hot!"

"It really was," Candi agrees.

Magnum pulls out of Allison. Candi immediately dives between her legs. Licking and sucking all of Magnum's cum from her pussy. She jumps up and kisses Allison. Swallowing every drop between them.

"Oh my God!'" Emma squeals with excited disbelief, "You two are nasty girls!"

"That's right," Candi nods confidently.

"Ooh…" Allison giggles, "Magnum tastes yummy!"

"So do you," Candi strokes her hair.

"I'm glad you think so," Allison flirts, "Because my pussy could use a little tongue therapy after Magnum fucked the hell out of it."

"It would be my pleasure," Candi takes Allison by the hand and leads her to the sofa where she lies down.

"Why don't you get on top?" Allison suggests.

"Ooh… Even better," Candi engages her in a sixty-nine.

With those two eating each other's pussy and Emma having disappeared, Magnum rests on the hot seat. Taking in the action on the sofa. It's not the first time they've shared a girl between them. But there's a lump in his throat this time while watching Candi achieve another sapphic conquest. Her girl on girl exploits suddenly filling him with sentimentality. Something he rarely feels about anything. Although sharing girls isn't the reason why he'd commit to her, sans kids and bullshit, perhaps it's a necessary component of their relationship. One they'd be required to maintain for the sake of staying together. It truly is kind of their thing.

"Here you go," Emma returns with a bath towel and cleans Magnum with it.

"Thank you," he responds with embarrassment to her gesture, "You don't have to do that."

"Of course I do," she argues sweetly, "You've totally made our night," she pauses to hand him another Jack and Coke, "Here. I made you another."

"I appreciate that," he takes a sip, "You've made our night too."

"I'm so glad we could," she sits on the floor and rests her head on his thigh, "You don't mind me putting my head here, do you?"

"Not at all," he strokes her hair while they watch Candi and Allison eat each other out. Candi sucking on their client's clit and lips. Licking deep inside her pussy. Girl juices covering her face. Allison doing the same to Candi. Her face buried in her female stripper's pussy. Savoring every drop of sweetness. Stopping briefly to lick her middle finger. Inserting it into Candi's ass while still eating her.

"Oh my God," Candi giggles and sighs, "That feels incredible."

"Yeah," Emma informs her, "Allison is all about the butt stuff."

"You know you like it," Allison jokingly scoffs at Emma.

"I do," Emma concedes before turning her attention back to Magnum, "She really is good at it."

"So are you," he continues stroking her hair.

"I guess," she laughs, "I'm glad you liked it."

"I really did," he assures her, "You two are a total fucking blast."

"Aww…" she melts, "Allison and I have been friends since junior high. We were each other's first sexual experience. She stayed over one night and… It just happened. And it felt so right. Like just a natural component of our friendship. If that makes any sense."

"It totally makes sense," he nods, "Candi and I are the same way."

"No," she shakes her head, "She's in love with you. Big time."

"I don't know about that…" he trails off in denial.

"Yes, you do. I know you're not dense," she gently lectures him, "I noticed it the instant you two walked in," she pauses, "You know… Your relationship may have an… openness to it, but the two of you are peas in a pod."

"In some ways," he explains, "But we're heading in two different directions."

"Are you sure?" she laughs, "Of course, I'm not one to be giving long term relationship advice since I'm about to marry a man I don't love. I mean, he'll be a good father and provider. I'll live a comfortable life. But he and I really have no deep connection. You and Candi though… You two were made for each other. I truly hope you two work through whatever differences you have, because I'm sure I'll need to party with you both again in the future. Allison too."

"Thanks," he rubs her shoulder as they watch Candi and Allison now eat each other's ass in their sixty-nine. Allison holding Candi's cheeks wide open. Thrusting her tongue in and out of her female stripper's tight sexy butthole. Her hips rolled up while Candi has her asshole spread open. Licking deep inside. Giggling and moaning nonstop.

"What did I say?" Emma laughs and cheers them on, "Eat that booty! Both of you!"

"Candi's all about the butt stuff too," he discloses.

"You're the one who got me into it," Candi playfully protests.

"No, I got you into eating ass," he clarifies, "You got me into buttfucking."

"You two do anal?" Allison's curiosity is piqued, "I'd pay extra to see that."

"That could be arranged, and then some," Candi suggests, "Huh, Magnum?"

"First thing's first, though," Magnum is now recovered and motions for Emma to stand. Having her bend over the chair. Legs spread wide. Getting on his knees behind his bachelorette. Hands firmly on her cheeks. Leaning in and licking her pussy back and forth. She's already soaking wet. Her juices so fucking sweet. The two of them trembling as he teases her clit. Sucking it. Flicking it with his tongue. Then licking within her soft velvety love tunnel. Rocking his tongue in and out. Her sweetness flowing forth more and more. Burying his face in her pussy is so comforting. As it's always been with Candi. But he's now preparing to find that comfort elsewhere.

"Oh my God," Emma cries out, "What are you doing to me?"

"Isn't he just fucking amazing?" Allison asks.

"Fuck yeah he is," Candi backs her up.

"That's right," he nods cockily, "I've eaten every pussy in this room," pausing as he eyes Emma's tight butthole, "And now every girl booty in this room too."

The room fills with enthusiastic shrieks as Magnum presses his face between Emma's cheeks. Kissing and licking her ass. Pushing his tongue inside. His bachelorette rocking her butt on his face while he basks in her taboo sweetness. Staying as long as he can before he must come up for air. Her pussy juices streaming down his chin. Both moaning louder and louder. He can't maintain it any longer, but not for lack of oxygen. Rather, for the desire to fuck his bachelorette fast and hard.

"Whew!" he jumps up and guides his throbbing cock to Emma's swollen pussy, which takes him easily thanks to being absolutely drenched.

"Oh God. Magnum is fucking me," Emma happily informs Candi and Allison, "His cock is in my pussy."

"And I have now fucked every girl in this room," he proudly announces to enthusiastic cheers and laughter.

"Two can play that game," Candi sasses while dismounting from Allison. Lying down opposite her. Pressing her soaking wet pussy against the client's, "Allison and I are going to girl fuck."

"Ooh…" Allison giggles, "Girl fuck me, Candi."

She and her female stripper bump and grind their pussies together. Bodies tingling. Trembling. Candi holding onto Allison's leg. Her ass sliding along the client's other thigh while thrusting against her pussy. Kissing each other's lips in the naughtiest way imaginable. Giggling. Sighing. Moaning. The temperature rising with each stroke of clit on clit. Lips on lips. Juices mingling. Making everything all kinds of slippery fun. Shaking from the delicious intensity of pussy rubbing on pussy. Each girl purring with delight. Each girl insatiable in her thirst for mutual stimulation. Each girl enthralled with the sheer thrill of committing such an act.

Each girl also enthralled with having a front-row view of Magnum fucking Emma. Gripping her chair. Thrashing her hair around. Tits bouncing back and forth while he dominates her from behind. Spanking and squeezing her ass. His body tingling from the sensation of her sweet cheeks constantly bouncing against him. And, of course, he's tingling and trembling from the heaven that is her pussy. Growing tighter as he grows larger insider her. Clamping down on his cock. Gushing wave after wave of warm juices that keep him thrusting insider her. Deeper. Faster. Harder. He and Candi look at each other knowingly. Each impressed with the other's girl fucking prowess. Truly performing partners in more ways than one. Such different life aspirations yet so alike in many respects.

"Oh fuck!" Emma cries, "You're making me cum!"

"Candi's making me cum too!" Allison moans loudly, "Let's cum all over them together!"

"We're cumming too!" he shouts.

"Oh my God, we are!" Candi screams.

A four-part climax erupts. Screams and cries of sweet release fill the room. Juices gushing and squirting. Magnum filling Emma's pussy with hot cum. Shaking uncontrollably. Holding tightly onto her hips. Riding out the orgasmic storm. Her pussy squirting warm juices. Streaming down his legs. Rocking her chair violently back and forth. Enduring this gloriously intense release. Candi and Allison driving their pussies together. Moaning in anguish. Flooding each other with wave after wave of girl juices. Each girl gripping the leather cushion underneath her for dear life. Everyone together experiencing the most beautiful suffering in the world. Never wanting it to end.

"Now it's a bachelorette party!" he breaks the silence.

"Hells yeah it is!" Allison concurs.

Candi runs over to Magnum and Emma as he removes his cock from their bachelorette. Dropping to her knees. Licking and sucking his cum from her pussy. Emma stands and Candi kisses her. Savoring and consuming Magnum's climactic juice together. Allison then locks lips on Emma. Sharing a passionate oral embrace.

"Thank you for throwing me the best party ever!" Emma exclaims.

"Hey, I just put it together," Allison shrugs before motioning to Magnum and Candi, "These two are the ones making all the magic happen."

"You know what?" he explains, "It doesn't matter how tame or wild a party is. Its success depends on the efforts of both entertainer and audience."

"That's right," Candi concurs, "We couldn't do it without you too."

"Well, this calls for another shot," Allison runs for the kitchen and fixes another round, while the others casually walk over, "To group sex!" she distributes shots before everyone laughs and toasts.

"Ooh…" Emma suggests, "We should get in the hot tub."

"You're just now telling us there's a hot tub?" Candi asks.

"I could certainly use the relaxation," he laughs.

"I'm sure you could,' Allison shakes her head in astonishment, "And I'm highly impressed with your performance, by the way."

"Well, I have excellent motivation," he replies cockily.

"What are we waiting for?" Emma demands to know.

"Let's fix some cocktails first," Allison suggests.

Magnum and Candi take a moment to gather up their belongings. Grabbing the audio system and Reddi-wip before heading onto the rear deck with Emma and Allison carrying drinks and towels. Magnum and Allison remove the hot tub cover while Candi looks at his phone, which has stopped playing music.

"I think we ran through all the hip-hop stuff," Candi surmises.

"Then go with rock," Magnum suggests.

"Fuck yeah!" Emma exclaims, "Let's rock out with our cocks out!"

"What are you talking about?" Allison laughs, "Magnum is the only one here with a cock."

"Okay… Well, he can rock out with his cock out," Emma compromises, "And the rest of us can jam out with our clams out."

"Have you been drinking?" Allison asks facetiously.

"Maybe a little," Emma giggles.

Everyone laughs while entering the hot tub. Getting settled with "Rocket" by Def Leppard kicking in. Drinking and conversing. The heat of the bubbling water consuming their naked bodies. The light show inside carried over as fiber optics rotates through the color spectrum. Seamlessly. Endlessly. Instigating Magnum's thoughts. Does Candi have any idea how fucking expensive kids are? Meanwhile, Candi is imagining she and Magnum doing this regularly thanks to her large family clamoring for more grandkids, nephews, nieces, and cousins for sleepovers and such.

"What are we doing with that?" Allison nods toward the can of Reddi-wip setting on the tub's black fiberglass edge.

"It's for this," he applies whipped cream to Allison's nipples before sucking them clean with Candi.

"My turn," Emma takes the can and sprays it all over Allison's tits.

"Jesus Christ, Emma!" Allison exclaims, "You know you have to lick this all off."

"Piece of cake," Emma starts lapping up whipped cream from Allison's chest. Having clearly bitten off more than she can chew.

"It's getting in the water," Allison chides her.

"We've got it," Candi laughs as she and Magnum help Emma lick and caress Allison's titties free of whipped topping.

"Emma, you have a little on your face," Allison laughs.

Magnum licks it from her face, and they kiss.

"That was totally worth it," Emma sighs.

"Okay," Allison seizes the can and sprays it on Emma's tits, "Your turn."

"Ooh... I feel like royalty," Emma muses while Magnum, Candi, and Allison take turns licking and sucking her nipples while trying not to choke on whipped cream at her silliness.

"Now you two do Candi," he applies Reddi-wip to his stripping partner's nipples.

"Oh, we'll do Candi anytime," Allison sasses.

"Do me, girlfriends," Candi flirts while Allison and Emma each take one of her breasts and suck her nipples free of dessert topping.

"What about Magnum?" Emma wonders out loud.

"Set her up for me," he orders.

His party girls comply. He leans in. Gazing into her eyes. Taking her right breast in his mouth. Swirling his tongue around her nipple while sucking it. Reaching down and rubbing her clit. Repeating the process with her left breast. Sliding his middle finger insider her pussy. Massaging her g-spot. She tosses her head back and sighs. So many times, he's sucked her titties before an audience. And this may be the last.

"Oh wow," Emma enthuses as Magnum and Candi giving each other a knowing look, "That was totally fucking hot."

"Yes, it was," Allison agrees, "Now it's Magnum's turn," snatching the Reddi-wip before Emma does, "No, you'll just make a mess."

"Whatever," Emma scoffs.

Allison sprays whipped cream on his nipples. Pectorals twitching as each party girl takes one in her warm mouth. Tongues dancing on his nipples. Sucking them clean. Giggling incessantly.

"Set him up for me," Candi glances seductively at Magnum.

Allison obliges and Candi moves in. His muscular chest now trembling as she massages his right nipple with her tongue. Looking up at him with that sexy and sassy expression he knows by heart. Reaching down and gripping his once-again hard cock. Moving to the left while stroking his throbbing manhood. Not only to pleasure him and wow their audience. But to seduce him into her wants and desires for the future. There's no fucking way she's giving up this lifestyle. She wants them to continue partying with the Emmas and Allisons of the world. The Sandras, Taras, Erins, and Aprils too. Hell, tonight could be the start of a new entrepreneurial venture where they get paid for this. No one in Arkansas has the balls to admit knowing either one of them. Much less admit to playing with them.

Magnum is too far gone into the ecstasy of ultimate relaxation to ponder the future in this moment. Instead embracing the physical pleasures of Candi expertly licking and sucking his nipples. Expertly stroking his cock the way he likes. He closes his eyes. Arching his back. Breathing heavily. Chills covering his entire body despite much of it being submerged in hot water. Every sense of touch reacting all at once. Emma and Allison cheering wildly.

"Oh my God, you two," Allison marvels at the sexual and emotional intensity of this spectacle.

Candi sits back and takes a sip of her drink. Emma nods knowingly at Magnum per their conversation earlier.

"What about you two?" he throws back at them.

Though he's witnessed and been in the middle of it many times, his enthusiasm for girl on girl is as fresh as the first time he witnessed the phenomenon courtesy of the Playboy Channel at age five.

"What about us?" Allison sasses, "You wanna see me and Emma in action?"

"Of course they do," Emma embraces Allison.

They kiss each other passionately while gigging. "Rock Me Shock Me" by Girlschool thumping forth. Magnum and Candi settle in side by side. Water jets providing their muscles some much-appreciated therapy. Drinking and enjoying the show. Emma lets go of Allison. Reaching for a towel. Spreading it out on the deck. Lying back with her butt on the edge of the tub. Allison holds Emma's legs open. Diving tongue first into her best friend's pussy. Emma moaning instantly from Allison's tongue lashing.

"Oh my God," Emma sighs, "Are you watching Allison eat my pussy?"

"Oh, they're watching," Allison smiles at Magnum and Candi while running her tongue back and forth between Emma's swollen lips. Kissing and sucking her clit. Licking deep inside her. Magnum fingers Candi's pussy. She strokes his cock. Allison rolls Emma's hips forward and licks her butthole. Thrusting her tongue in and out. Both girls giggling from the excitement of doing this before an audience. Allison licks her middle finger and slides it inside Emma's ass. Rocking it back and forth. Once again eating her pussy. Emma shaking as her best friend brings her to orgasm.

"Ooh... you dirty bitch," Emma gets back in the water.

She kisses Allison before having her bend over the edge of the tub onto the blanket. Emma sucks and caresses her best friend's clit and lips. Spreading her pussy wide open. Tongue fucking her tight wet love tunnel. Allison moaning and shaking from Emma's aggressive sex attack. Inserting her middle finger inside Allison. Massaging her g-spot while licking her asshole. Lapping it rapidly. Pushing her tongue in and out. Allison crying out in delight from this sapphic double penetration. Finally letting go with a primal scream. Magnum and Candi applaud with genuine enthusiasm. Emma pulls Allison back into the water. They kiss each other like there's no tomorrow. Giggling as they stand and take a bow.

"That was totally fucking hot," he nods in approval.

"Oh my God. You two are just so sexy and adorable," Candi gushes, "If only I had a best friend like either of you."

"What are you talking about?" Emma laughs, "You've got Magnum. He can do all of this. And he brings the D."

"Fuck yeah he does," Allison agrees, "So, what about you two? How do you do it?"

Challenge accepted as Magnum and Candi instinctively fall into a passionate kiss. The dance of their tongues long second nature but electrifying as ever. Everything about their physical intimacy is exciting and comforting at once. She motions for him to sit on the edge of the tub. Taking the head of his cock in her mouth. Swirling her tongue all around while stroking his shaft. Making his juices flow uncontrollably in her mouth as she coos approvingly. Still jacking him while sucking his balls. Then licking his asshole before taking every inch of his throbbing cock down her throat. Emma and Allison watch intently. Rubbing each other's pussy underneath the water.

Magnum turns Candi around and bends her over onto the towel. Spanking and squeezing her butt cheeks as she giggles. Holding on and touching the tip of his tongue to her clit. Making her sigh immediately. Drawing circles upon her delicate love button. Sucking her. Flicking her rapidly. Kissing and sucking her swollen lips. Thrusting his tongue deep within her throbbing sugar walls. Consuming her warm sweetness gushing forth upon his lips. Burying his face in her pussy. So soft and wet. So safe. Part of him never wants to pull away. Even as she's on the verge of pulling away from him forever.

"Fuck it," he thinks while sliding his middle finger inside her love tunnel. Growing ever tighter as he teases and pleases her g-spot. She reaches back and spreads her cheeks wide open. He licks the length of her crack. All around her butthole. Along each delicate ridge. Pressing his lips tight against her while pushing his tongue inside. Rocking back and forth. Still massaging her g-spot. Making her moan louder and louder. The silence from Emma and Allison is deafening. Even as

"Wild Side" by Mötley Crüe fills the brisk winter night air. Candi was the first girl to encourage his kinks. The first to make him feel confident in them as he returned the favor with her. And this may be the final time he experiences them with her.

He moves his finger from her pussy to her ass and resumes eating her pussy. Sliding back and forth in her soft, velvety asshole. Licking deep inside her. Wave after wave of girl juices covering his face. Her entire body shaking as he brings her to orgasm. But also shaking at the thought of this being the last time they do this. She knows full well his resistance to where she wants to go. Wishing he could see that her desires aren't just for her sake but his as well. Tired of seeing him beat his head against the wall for his agency day after day. Seemingly every good party now offset by some douchebag calling apparently for the sole purpose of disrespecting him. She's cool with him still doing parties for nice clients if he wants. But she wants to see him finally capitalize upon his other talents.

"Ooh…" Candi orgasms on his face. "Fuck me."

"Let's do it," he slaps her ass, "Roll over for me."

Candi lies on her back and Magnum crawls on top. Her pussy so drenched that he instantly thrusts all the way inside her. Wrapping his arms around her. Pressing his chest against her tits. She wraps her legs around his back. Kissing insatiably as they fuck hard. Fast and furious. Each stroke more viciously affectionate than the last. All their admiration for and frustration with each other exploding in one rhythmic motion repeating faster and harder with every violent thrust. His cock growing even larger as her pussy grows ever tighter. She holds out hope that he'll come around to her way of seeing things. He loses himself in the joys of fucking his friend and collaborator, as well as carnally punishing her for betraying him. Maybe it's not fair, but not much of anything has been fair to him recently. Burned out on it all. Disappointed in watching his longtime business die yet secretly relieved in a way. A way that causes him guilt. Taking this admittedly illegal booking wasn't about getting them some needed cash or simply playing with other girls. He and his partner in crime needed fun and excitement in their lives again. Perhaps him most of all.

And here they are. Moaning and screaming incoherently. Attempting in vain to make the moment last forever. Holding back a massive shared climax until it aches. Then until it hurts. Kissing each other's mouth, face, and neck while fucking at the speed of light. Thrusting with reckless abandon. He can barely keep from slipping out of her soaking wet pussy. Her incessant gushing turning to squirting as they get closer and closer. Tightly embracing each other while racing towards that wall together. Falling together in this sexual kamikaze mission. There's nowhere to go from here but down into the depths of an uncertain future after tonight.

"Oh fuck!" Magnum feels his cock erupt deep inside Candi. The sheer volume of cum. The sheer intensity behind it. Like white-hot lava that seemingly refuses to stop flowing. Pleasantly scalding her as she digs her fingernails in his back. Holding him tight with her legs.

"Oh my God!" Candi ejaculates with epic force against Magnum. Hot girl juices covering them both. Her body shaking uncontrollably. Comforted by his arms wrapped her. His body pressed against hers as they endure this deliciously painful release together. Feeling his heart racing in time with hers. Pushing her lips hard against his. Taking him in every way she possibly can. They hold each other in silence for a moment after. Until finally remembering their audience. Both getting up to be greeted by dropped jaws.

"I'm sorry," he laughs, "Did we traumatize you?"

"I… I think… maybe you did," Allison stammers before quickly composing herself, "And I fucking loved it!"

"Oh wow!" Emma stares in wide-eyed disbelief, "That was like the hottest fucking sex I've ever seen. And I watch a lot of porn. I mean, like, a lot."

"Well," Candi licks her lips, "How was that for live porn?"

"I'm fucking speechless," Emma shakes her head and laughs.

"I said I'd pay extra to see you two do anal," Allison states, "But consider it done because that works too. Oh my God."

"We can still do anal," Candi taunts her.

"We can?" Magnum is doubting he has anything left after cumming hard in three girls tonight.

"You've cum four times in a night before," Candi assures him, "I know because I was there."

"Really?" Allison looks at him with intrigue, "I mean, don't overdo it. You both have shown us more excitement than we ever imagined."

"Yeah," Emma concurs, "I don't even know if I could handle anymore."

"Oh, you will, "Candi challenges, "I said we could arrange anal. And then some. You two aren't done yet. Besides, is it midnight yet?"

"Um…" Allison reaches for her phone, "It's five after."

"Happy birthday, Magnum," Candi kisses him.

"Is it really your birthday?" Emma asks with a hint of skepticism.

"Yeah," he shakes his head at Candi, "I didn't realize someone was going to bring it up."

"Well, fuck," Allison's face lights up, "We have to celebrate this."

"That's okay…" he gently protests.

"Bullshit," Emma interrupts, "We're celebrating your birthday. And that's all there is to it, mister."

"Shall we go back inside?" Allison asks everyone.

"Yeah," Candi explains, "That works best for what I have in store."

"Ooh… I can't wait," Emma giggles as everyone helps one another exit the hot tub.

Magnum wraps a towel around his waist and takes the music back inside.

"I'll fix more drinks," Allison collects everyone's glass and leaves Candi and Emma outside together.

"I heard a little of what you and Magnum were talking about before," Candi admits while drying off.

"Oh, I hope I didn't sound like I was prying into your business," Emma clarifies, "I really wasn't."

"Not at all. It's totally fine," Candi assures her, "If anything, I'd kind of like to get your input as well."

"Look. It's like I told Magnum," Emma laughs, "I'm not exactly in a place to give relationship advice to anyone. But even Ira represents a comprise within my life overall. You know… To, like… get most of what I want. I don't know if that makes any sense."

"It does," Candi nods.

"Anyway," Emma continues, "I guess all I can suggest is that you both may need to make compromises for each other. If you two are going to be together, my guess is that you'll each have to let go of something significant. Something you each want or whatever. You know?"

"Thanks, Emma," Candi smiles as she and the bachelorette head inside.

"No, birthday boy," Allison informs Magnum while he waits in the kitchen while she fixes more drinks, "You go park your butt on the sofa and I'll bring you your drink."

"This isn't my party…" he protests.

"It is now," she interrupts him, "Just do it, mister."

"That's right," Emma chimes in as she and Candi grab and escort him to the living room.

"Just go with it," Candi laughs as he looks at her for help.

"Fine," he relents and sinks into the sofa. Its soft leather upholstery embracing him. So relaxing. Perhaps too relaxing as fatigue begins consuming his body. Fighting to stay energetic, but it seems a futile effort. And he still has to drive him and Candi back to Little Rock tonight. Although he's sure that Allison and Emma would be happy to let them crash here until morning. He hears them and Candi in the kitchen. Whispering and giggling up a storm. There's every reason for him to feel exhausted right now, but he beats himself up for it nonetheless.

"Here you are, birthday boy," Allison serves him another Jack and Coke.

"You just like calling me that," he takes a sip.

"Yes, I do," she playfully taunts him.

"Okay," Candi walks over to the audio system, "We've planned something special for you."

"A three-girl lap dance!" Emma exclaims.

"It was supposed to be a surprise, Emma," Allison admonishes her.

"Don't worry," he laughs, "I sort of figured that. And I can't wait to see it."

"Oh, you'll do more than see it," Candi sasses as she changes the song to "Girls Girls Girls".

All three girls line up naked before Magnum. Facing away. Candi in the middle. Allison to her left. Emma to her right. Gyrating their hips. Shaking their butts. Wiggling them in his face. Bending over and touching their toes. Candi straddles him on her knees. Rubbing her ass on his chest as they laugh. A second wind begins to form within his core. Emma repeats the process. Followed by Allison before she turns and sits on his lap. Pressing her tits against him. Shaking them on his face while the other two grind their asses on hers. She presses each breast against his lips for him to lick and suck.

"My turn," Emma declares as they switch places, "Time for Magnum to get him some big ol' birthday titties."

"For fuck's sake," he laughs while Emma smothers him with her breasts. Pushing each nipple in his mouth. He sucks her girls with unbridled enthusiasm. Teasing them with his tongue.

"Whew, that's nice," Emma sighs, "Okay, Candi."

It's Candi's turn. Looking in each other's eyes. She strokes his face and hair while he massages her nipples with his tongue. Sucking each one. Flicking rapidly. Reaching between her legs and rubbing her pussy. Fingering her. Making her wet. Completely losing himself in the moment with his longtime stripping partner. After all these years. Everything they've been through together. And only now can he truly allow himself to freefall backward into the ether. Because he finally realizes she's always been there to catch him. And she always will be if he lets her.

"Okay, girls," Candi orders while standing, "Assume the position."

Emma and Allison drop to all fours. Facing away from Magnum. Candi spanks them both. Then spreads Allison's cheeks open. Gazing into his eyes as she licks their client's butthole. Making her tremble and sigh. Smiling devilishly while thrusting her tongue in and out. Repeating the act with Emma. Sliding her tongue deep inside their bachelorette's asshole and causing her to giggle and squirm. He feels his cock growing larger underneath his towel. Building forth one last ejaculatory assault before the night is over. Candi knowing all too well by this point how to squeeze every last drop of love potion from his body at any given time.

"Stay there," Candi instructs her playmates. Running to her stripping bag and returning with Astroglide. Rubbing an ample amount between the fingers of both hands. Simultaneously inserting either middle finger into each girl's ass. Looking at Magnum the entire time. If this doesn't prove how devoted she is to maintain their naughty after-hours lifestyle, then nothing will. Allison and Emma moaning even louder when Candi slides an index finger inside each of them as well. Massaging the soft interior of each girl's butthole. Getting them loosened up for something bigger. To be followed by something even bigger than that.

Magnum undoes his towel and strokes his cock. As hot as Candi finds watching him masturbate, she's having none of that right now. Leaning forward and taking him down her throat. Gazing into his eyes while licking and sucking his manhood and fingering two girl booties. Aside from herself, she wouldn't do this for anyone else. Only

Magnum. The one man who has always had her back like no other. Looked out for her. Protected her from all manner of potential danger. Who's given her the freedom to be herself and encouraged her every step of the way. And viewed her as an equal partner in crime during their sexual adventures together. He's not only appreciated her intellect from day one, but he's always expected it of her. Never allowing her to make excuses or sell herself short in any fashion. She knows he'd die for her in a heartbeat. And she'd gladly do the same for him.

"Okay," Candi removes her mouth from his cock, "Who wants to go first?

"I do," Allison beats Emma to the punch. Getting up and straddling Magnum's cock. Wasting no time in sliding her wet pussy over him. Holding onto his shoulders. Riding him like a naughty cowgirl while he grabs her hips. Thrusting up inside her tight love tunnel. "Never Enough" pounds through the dim red glow. Watching Candi approaching her from behind. Placing her hands on their client's butt cheeks. Allison stops and tilts her head back. Closing her eyes. Exhaling deeply. She resumes pumping Magnum's cock as he observes Candi thrusting behind her.

"Oh my God, Magnum," Allison sighs, "Candi is fucking me in the ass with a strap-on."

"That's right," Candi nods arrogantly at a shocked Magnum, "We're fucking her together."

Magnum's second wind shifts into overdrive. Feeling his cock grow even larger inside Allison's ever-tightening pussy. Especially as he sees Emma standing behind Candi.

"Emma's fingering my ass," Candi informs him seductively, "She's getting me ready for your massive cock."

"Oh yeah," Emma blows a kiss at Magnum.

Allison moans softly while Magnum and Candi fuck her tight holes. Both excited about their first experience double-penetrating a woman together. Candi wanting it to be the first of many over the years to come. Magnum seizing the moment as if it's their last time doing this together. And anything else.

"Ooh… I need a break already," Allison laughs, "Your turn, Emma."

The party girls change positions. Emma riding Magnum's cock with unbridled enthusiasm while Candi pumps her rump. Allison moves behind them.

"I've got two fingers in her Magnum," Allison fingers Candi's ass, "Two fingers deep inside her tight asshole."

"She really does, baby," Candi sighs, "It feels fucking amazing."

"You are fucking amazing fucking my ass," Emma giggles, "And you, Magnum. Your cock is heaven in my pussy. I can't wait to feel it in my ass."

"Why wait?" Candi suggests, "Let's switch."

Before Magnum can even figure out what's happening, he and Candi have switched positions. She sits on the sofa. Emma riding her strap-on. Allison lubes up his cock before he spreads his bachelorette's cheeks and slides every inch deep inside her butthole.

"Oh, fuck yes!" Emma exclaims, "This really is the best bachelorette party ever!"

"I told you I'd take care of you," Allison replies.

"I never doubted you for a second," Emma assures her, "You know what? You can put together every event from now on."

"I'm down with that," Allison agrees as Magnum feels her once against grinding her pussy on his ass.

He and Candi establishing a rhythm to fuck their bachelorette at once. Their naughty partnership and tag-teaming of women reaching a new high. He ponders Emma's advice from earlier as he thrusts in and out of her tight asshole. His cock tingling madly from the sensation of rubbing along her velvety rear entrance. At the very least, he and Candi should have an honest talk about the future and their respective wants. After all, she's been just as much an indispensable part of his agency as he has. The one entertainer he could always depend upon to deliver phenomenal eroticism to audiences anytime he needed. He guesses he can at least hear her out on the whole kids thing.

Allison takes Emma's place. Riding Candi's toy cock and making out with her. Magnum fucking her ass. Emma rubbing her pussy on his. Candi's never been the slightest bit jealous of other women showing Magnum attention. And this time is no exception. Sharing girls has always been a cornerstone of their relationship. Besides, it seems like without her involvement in Magnum's sex life, he winds up wasting time with girls who aren't at all right for him. Like that idiot Janice some years ago. The way Candi sees it, and not in a self-serving way, Magnum needs her. Just as she needs him. And maybe he's right about kids, she thinks. Right now, she's certainly having thoughts about keeping up appearances. About socializing with losers like Ira. And even worse, Ira's mom. But Allison and Emma? Fuck yeah.

Candi starts considering the pros of a childfree lifestyle as she and Magnum double fuck their client. She also starts thinking about feeling him fuck her in the ass. The pure magic of it. His touch and technique. The comforting familiarity and exciting taboo of his cock deep inside her asshole. Relentlessly thrusting in and out. Filling her full of cum. And the deliciously filthy aftermath of feeling his thick juices ooze out of her. That's something she's never expressed to him. Maybe it's time. And that's when inspiration strikes.

"Fuck me in the ass, Magnum," Candi requests with breathless anticipation, "I want you to cum in my asshole."

"Oh, fuck yeah!" Emma exclaims, "Get out of the way, Allison."

"I'm about to fuck you in the ass, Emma," Allison laughs.

"Don't let us stop you," Magnum encourages them.

"Hold up," Candi stops everyone, "I have an idea. Emma, sit down. It's your party, so I want you to have an excellent view."

"Ooh… I love watching," Emma takes the sofa hot seat, "Have I mentioned that I watch lots of porn?"

"I think you might've," Candi laughs, "Maybe Allison will eat your pussy."

Allison responds by diving face first between Emma's legs. On her knees. Butt in the air. Licking her best friend's pussy back and forth. Candi gets behind Allison and penetrates her ass again. Holding in place while the client shudders in delight from Candi once again buttfucking her. Candi leans forward onto Allison's back. Providing the angle for Magnum to grab her butt cheeks, spread them wide open, and slide his hard, throbbing cock deep inside her asshole. She's easily loosened up. Not only from Allison and Emma fingering her before but from being totally relaxed by the mere thought of her longtime stripping partner fucking her in the ass. Knowing he'll strike the perfect balance of being simultaneously gentle and aggressive. As he always has since their first time.

Feeling even more like Magnum and Candi's first time as "Hysteria" floats through the air. Providing a haunting eroticism that sends chills down their spines. Along with the sensation and knowledge of his raging massive cock deep in her ass. The secret thrill she confessed to him that first night. A thrill they took to unprecedented heights together from there. Heights she never could've achieved without him. Nor he without her. Their shared passion for naughty adventures not only emboldening him sexually but serving as a calming influence in his life as he carried the weight of the world on his shoulders. And now. Watching Emma fuck Allison's face with her pussy. As Candi fucks Allison's ass. While he buttfucks Candi. Where could he and Candi possibly go from here? All he knows is that he's dying to find out.

"I never want this to end, Candi," Magnum whispers about more than their foursome.

"Me neither, Magnum," Candi's heart swooning as she knows what he means.

"Oh fuck!" Emma screams while gushing warm girl juices all over Allison's face, "I'm cumming!"

"Me too!" Allison rubs her own pussy while devouring her best friend's sweetness as her own juices squirt upon Candi's legs.

"Oh God, Magnum! Cum in my fucking ass!" Candi cries.

Her pussy erupting an endless stream of warm juices all over Magnum. Streaming down both their thighs as she wraps her arms around Allison. Burying her silicone cock deep in their client's asshole. He yells out incoherently. It's all too much for words. Too much for him. The physical and emotional sensations. Pleasure and pain all at once. Throwing his head back. Holding his breath. His throbbing and aching cock exploding deep inside Candi's butthole. Making her squirt even more. Endless waves of hot sticky cum flowing from his cock and filling her ass. Gripping her cheeks. Holding himself inside her while shaking uncontrollably. Once again, she's brought an epic performance out of him. One he's not sure would be possible without her. And she feels the same way about him.

"I need to get up," Candi wastes no time announcing once Magnum has finished cumming in her ass.

He removes himself from her as she does the same from Allison. The other three watch with concern that quickly turns to curiosity when Candi races to the glass coffee table. Facing away from everyone and squatting over it. They watch in shock and awe as she holds open her butt cheeks. Letting Magnum's cum drip from her asshole. Every drop onto the glass below. Candi's heart racing as she tears a page from Magnum's playbook. The page about always upping the ante with audiences. She turns and stares at him while leaning over and licking his ejaculate off the glass. Every trace. Then lifting her head to face him. Maintaining her gaze as she swallows his love potion. Opening her mouth to prove it. Smiling at him.

"Emma's right, Magnum," Allison whispers in his ear, "Candi is totally in love with you," she pauses, "What are you gonna do?"

About the Author

"I didn't pretend to lick a girl's butthole at a bachelorette party once. I fucking did it."

As the real-life Magnum, Stefan Diamante was a professional exotic entertainer and talent agent for eighteen years. Fourteen as owner of Hardbodies Entertainment of Arkansas. He specialized in delivering private parties and is arguably the greatest bachelorette party entertainer of all time. Combining aesthetics with charm, intellect, humor, and outrageousness to put forth a dangerous rock star sex appeal that goes above and beyond anything the vapid gym bros infesting this industry can muster. Stefan is also the author of *Naked Ambition: A Male Stripper's True Account of Making Girls Behave Badly*. A bare-all memoir that provides raw insight into the ups and downs of the business and documents everything he gave to be the best against all odds. All things stripping aside, he is an award-winning creative writer and accomplished photographer with interest in music and filmmaking.

Stefan currently resides in Little Rock, Arkansas and ponders his personal and professional future after stripping. He still enjoys dancing and runs through his basic performance daily as his preferred fitness regimen.